Cursed Desire

Nightfallen Duet Book One

T.R. Ortego

Book Cover by Christley Creations with The Author Buddy.
Scene Break Illustration by Morgan Teal
Map Illustration by T.R. Ortego
First Edition 2026

Trigger Warnings

I want to give a brief and broad overview of the potential
triggers in my book for anyone who wants that.
Please take care of yourselves and read at your discretion.

Past Mentions of:
Physical Assault and Torture of Main Characters
Dubious Consent
Psychological Torture of Main Characters
Grief
Suicidal Ideation
Self Harm
Kidnapping
Abuse
Rape and Sexual Assault of Side/ Unnamed Characters

On Page:
Murder
Torture
Blood
Significant Suffering of Main Character
Scars
Brainwashing
Psychological Abuse
Attempted Murder
Prejudices
Allusions to People Trafficking (Humans, Elves, etc.)

Dedication

To the person reading this book who needs the reminder: sometimes, those around us seem to suggest that we are somehow both too much And not enough. They're wrong. We can, and should, be loved for exactly who we are.

To my beloved husband, David, who has supported me throughout all of these years, who has been my biggest cheerleader and best friend, and who was a major inspiration for Dorian's behavior:
I love you.

The Known World
Jharena
Cobanath
Keatarax
Varnal
Mealis
Death's Forest
Vlideron
Sertalina
Plarishak
Shorevethia
Thleesa
Tri-Nation's City
Valeena
Kantio
Beletha
Mentra
Sonel
Polcah
Hjarlan
Corosa
Morta
Huvil
0 100 200
Miles

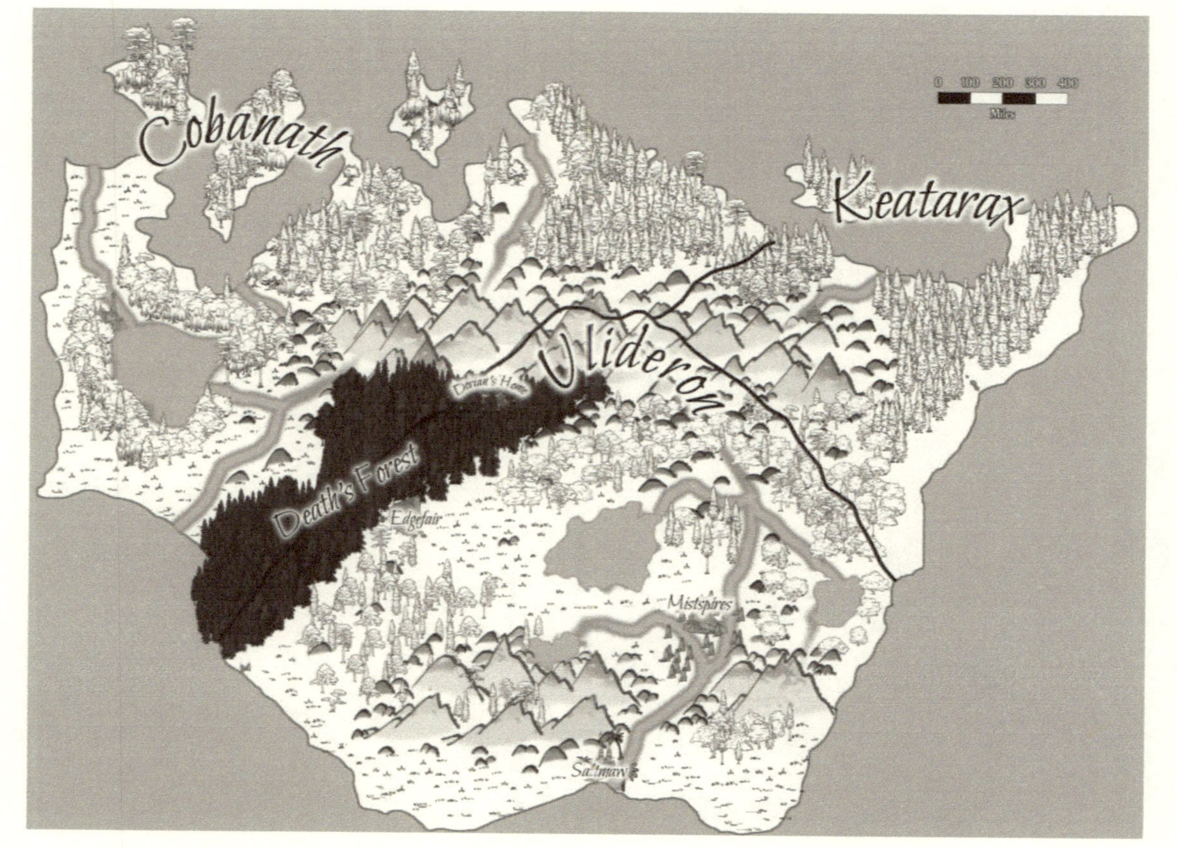

Cobanath
Keatarax
Ulideron
Death's Forest
Dorian's Home
Edgefair
Mistspires
Saltmar
0 100 200 300 400
Miles

CHAPTER ONE

Ruby

"Sir, please, I'm begging you," Ruby squinted through the clouds of dirt kicked up by early morning workers for the other members of her patrol group, "Just go inside your home and sleep it off. If any of the others see you like this..."

"Yeah, what?" The man's speech slightly slurred, "You'll arrest me for not having the time to clean up before I start laboring away my life for nothing? By M'lvia's revenge, you witches always ruin what little joy we get!" Spittle flew from his mouth with the vitriol he spewed.

"I won't! But the others will... Please!" Ruby's eyes darted up and down the busy street, spotting the colorful hair of her fellow witches already turning in their direction.

No... No... They'll see him soon... Then he'll go to jail and I'll be in trouble for not already arresting him...

"You all come around here and bully us common folk. And for what? You know what?! Fuck you! And FUCK YOUR PATROLS!"

The man reared back. Ruby saw a glint of metal in the split second before his fist connected with her face. Everything went dark. Her training kicked in, though only enough for her to land on her hands and knees on the packed dirt road. It was better than landing flat on her back or having a second impact to her head.

Blood. The moment Ruby opened her eyes, she became transfixed. Captivated by the golden rays of the dawning sun glinting off the quickly growing pool of muddied red beneath her. With each fresh drop that kissed the ground, melding into the rest, Ruby drifted away, the stinging of her scraped hands fading. She stared at her life pooling beneath her.

Her cheek throbbed in tune to the rhythm of her pounding head. Muffled, jumbled sounds filtered in. Shouting. Ruby shook off the concern attempting to worm its way in. Each splattering drop of blood that fell from her face created a new ripple beneath her that drew her in more, shielding her from the chaos unfolding around her.

No, I need to be there for the others... I can't hold them back by being useless again...

With a gargantuan effort, Ruby yanked her eyes up to study the scene playing out in the street. With the throbbing of her cheek and the pounding of her head worsening, Ruby gingerly sat back onto her feet, her knees remaining firmly planted in the dirt. Ruby's vision blurred with unshed tears, her body finally registering what happened. Blinking rapidly to dismiss the unwelcome pooling of salt water, Ruby inhaled sharply.

Enraged faces surrounded her. The others had rushed over when she hit the ground. Juniper and Vanella enforced a circle around their group to keep the commoners at bay while Violetta lectured the man who'd punched her. Silently, Ruby thanked her inability to hear the condemnations commoners would be throwing at her. Seeing their aggressive demeanor, Ruby sank inside herself once more, her eyes drifting back to the blood on the ground.

The violent jostling of her shoulder sent another bolt of pain shooting through her skull. Looking to the source, Juniper's frozen glare sent her scrambling to her feet. Her head spun, stomach dangerously heaving. Lightheadedness threatened to bring her back to her knees. Juniper's intervention to her immobile state came without the kindness he'd once shown her, but she was grateful for the reminder he'd delivered with just a look, even as she held her head against the swimming of her mind. Ruby's hand became slick, the warmth registering a moment later.

Ruby pulled her hand away, shaking at the sight of so much blood coating her hand from just a moment's touch. The normally cool brown skin disappeared beneath deep crimson the same shade as her hair. Ruby's name exemplified the truth of her particular unnatural-to-humans coloring, a trait which marked all witches from birth.

Turning her attention to the man who hit her, who was being held immobile by Violetta's gleaming gold magic, Ruby spotted her blood dripping from the glinting metal that wrapped around his two middle fingers. The sheer loss of blood astounded her, despite the knowledge that she had been struck with a vampire's ring. A human commoner never should have gotten their hands on such an instrument.

He must have stolen it somehow.

The odd ring limited the dexterity of the wearer's hand but provided a steady base for the sharpened point to puncture mortal skin. Those rings were known to hold a vampiric enchantment that increased bleeding. A part of Ruby's brain stuttered over the sight, a whirlwind of emotions gripping her tightly, squeezing the strength from her bones and weakening her knees, though it was not fear or anxiety, or even the loss of blood clouding her mind. Ruby struggled violently against her own body's fury. Rage flooded her veins and she could do nothing about it. Her fingers tightened into a fist, face twisting into a snarl as she glared at the man who dared strike her. Being assaulted so viciously when she had only been trying to help dug into the shadowed wound within her soul and screamed in her mind.

Unwanted!

Vanella, pacing along the edge of the circle their patrol group now occupied, glared at Ruby with unnaturally golden eyes that stopped all thoughts as Ruby belatedly realized what she had done. Dread curled up from deep within. Her fellow witch gave her a long look as Ruby hurriedly fixed her face, settling into the neutral expression that she should have maintained throughout the whole ordeal. Ruby knew that the sooner she rectified her behavior, the less reeducation she might be subjected to. She couldn't completely avoid it anymore, but maybe she could avoid another solitary retreat, or worse.

What will they do with me if I keep failing? Will I still have a place in the coven? Will I lose my meager powers if I cannot become a better witch?

Ruby's legs grew increasingly unsteady. In all her nearly 30 years, Ruby had never known Vanella to take it easy on her. Beyond that anxiety, Ruby continued bleeding at an alarming pace, and she knew that no one would help her until they had dealt with the man unless she fully lost consciousness. Strength drained from her muscles with each moment. Her sight took on multi-colored spots. Vaguely, she saw Violetta's signal to move, apparently ready to take the man to jail for his assault on Ruby. Thumping heartbeat in her ears, Ruby trudged along behind the others as they forced their way through the blurry crowd, unwilling to give in to her worsening physical condition.

I can't let myself become more of a burden.

Internally shrinking in on herself, Ruby saw the metallic golden hair of Vanella approach the purple of Violetta, surely reporting her transgression. The two of them would, undoubtedly, inform Elder Moss. It was her own fault. Her rage was inappropriate for a witch. The others never struggled with their emotions. Ruby owned that failure alone, and she must answer for it. Her steps slowed, fury with her own pathetic self-control taking over, blurry vision turning to her surroundings.

Why aren't the commoners attacking me?

The thought startled her as she realized just how far behind the others she had fallen. The commoners that surrounded the group appeared furious, but so far back, and so injured and weakened, Ruby would have been an easy target. She scanned the crowd, unable to discern the faces of the people clearly. Surely, they were simply too disgusted. She reasoned that they probably didn't want to sully themselves by getting witch blood on them. Even besides the fact that it was a heinous crime to hurt a witch, they would probably not want to touch her tainted blood, no matter how much they might like to finish the job their fellow started. That settled in her soul as the only thing that made sense to her; the sensation of pity caressing her senses could only be wishful thinking. Regular humans did not pity witches.

Ruby hurried to catch up to their others, though her weakened state from blood loss kept slowing her down. The dilapidated houses of Death's Edge Quarter, where the commoners lived, and the poorer shops of Edgefair Center, the merchant district, passed in a blur while the people followed them. The road beneath their feet transitioned from packed dirt to intricate cobblestone. The people of Edgefair stared as the crowd of commoners dispersed behind the group, but none dared to get in their way. Consciousness threatened to flee her.

The steps of the jail house seemingly sprung out of thin air before her as she continued to trudge along, each step an exercise in will power, in forcing herself to remain standing and moving. She could hardly lift her legs enough to climb them, each step up an agonizingly slow experience, teetering on the precipice of total collapse. The whispers of her mind insisted that she hurry.

I can't keep being useless to the others... It's bad enough that my magic is so weak... I'm just more and more of a burden... I have to hurry. I have to keep up. I can't be falling behind like this... Hurry up! HURRY UP!

Her calm ran as thin as the blood in her veins. She felt her tongue tingle with the urge to scream for someone to help her, to save her life, the panic welling up inside. Entering the jail house at last, Ruby waited for the song and dance of getting the man booked into holding to complete their patrol. Only once that was done would she be allowed healing. They had to do it soon. Her vision started fading to black. Her heart beat slowed to an inexplicable crawl, ignoring her desperation to live, and she felt her mind drifting into the void. The peace that beckoned her battled with the promise she'd made to herself; to keep going. That promise kept her conscious. Kept her alive.

Golden-white light enveloped her with stinging warmth for a mere moment, someone in her patrol group finally taking pity on her. Ruby squinted, then blinked rapidly as her vision cleared and some of her strength returned. Her ears popped and the crystalline sounds of the world once more swirled around her. Her senses restored, she realized that Juniper had been the one to heal her, but he scoffed and turned away as soon as she was stabilized, her cheek healed and just enough strength returned to keep her alive. The moment stung more than the healing, hitting at the heart of the disconnect that had formed between them. Ruby caged in her own pain, turning to her restored hearing and sight.

"This was obviously premeditated, so it should be added to the man's charges. That is all," Violetta's neutral voice dictated to the staff of the jail house, concluding their business there, and she turned to leave.

Vanella and Juniper smoothly followed Violetta out the door, leaving Ruby scrambling after them. She forced her body forward, her feet tangling and sending her slamming against the door on the way out. The others swiftly continued on. She tried to keep up as Violetta led them back to the compound on the outskirts of Edgefair, but her body remained mostly bloodless.

She silently thanked her witch blood for healing her faster and keeping her moving in such dire circumstances. The nature of her blood couldn't completely fix her, but it would keep her going in situations where regular humans would have died, and allow her to recover faster once healed. Nevertheless, as a result of her blood loss, Ruby now struggled with a pounding heart, shaking legs, and the way her body so desperately wanted her to lay down and stop. She watched the ground cautiously as she walked, afraid that she would miss some obstacle and send herself sprawling.

Her once nearly-white-beige robes transformed into a dark, wet red. Only upon seeing it did Ruby notice the feeling of the heavy fabric sticking to her skin, her blood soaking it beyond all hope of recovery. The robes would be laundered, but if the stains remained as noticeable as she suspected, they would need to be burned promptly. The coven wouldn't accept such sullied attire from a witch in their compound, let alone a patrolling witch who needed to maintain the public image of the coven. With a sigh, Ruby realized that she likely wouldn't be on a patrol for a while anyways. Reeducation would come first.

The other three walked ahead of her, the buildings of Edgefair disappearing as they traversed to the park that acted as the boundary between the witches' compound and the districts of the commoners, the minor nobility, and the merchants. The cobblestone disappeared, the path of grass and dirt leading to the compound keeping Ruby's feet moving forward.

As they approached the towering gates of the compound, Ruby tried not to listen to the whispers of Violetta and Vanella as they discussed what Elder Moss should do with her, but not listening in felt impossible. Each woman expressed different ideas about what should happen to Ruby, and they weren't quiet enough on the matter to escape her attention, no matter how hard she tried. Juniper, for his part, remained silent. Ruby glanced up and caught the glint of his muted, curly green hair in the growing golden light, briefly reminding her of times long past. Pain accompanied flashes of fumbling, lackluster, stolen moments that represented a connection she'd never before experienced and could never touch again.

Her attention shifted to the glistening of Violetta's vibrant purple tresses and Vanella's metallic golden waves—whose unnatural coloring made the "golden" blond of regular humans seem lacking—swinging with their fervent discussion and rushed steps.

"She is a disgrace to us all! Elder Moss should have tossed her out years ago!" Vanella spat out.

"Those decisions are not up to us. They belong in the hands of the elders. Elder Moss will handle her as she sees fit," Violetta breezily replied.

"Please, Ruby's too much of a failure, even for our elders to handle. What hasn't Elder Moss tried with her yet?"

"It is not my place to keep track of the education efforts of our fellow witch. And she technically is a fellow witch."

Ruby's heart soared at the defense Violetta offered her, gratefully clinging to the hint that she mattered in the coven. She turned her head back down to the grassy path beneath her feet as she walked behind the others. Privately, Ruby considered Violetta to be something of a sister to her; they were given to the compound around the same time, gaining the same birth estimations. Being abandoned by humans on the same day made Ruby feel more connected to Violetta than the others, though she knew her fellow witch did not share the sentiment. None of them did.

Putting the coven in terms of regular families, Elder Moss felt like Ruby's mother. She could never say such a thing aloud, being obviously inappropriate, but Elder Moss practically raised her and the others in her patrol group. For that reason, Ruby imagined that disappointing Elder Moss felt like disappointing her mother. It seemed that way as someone who never had a mother, at least.

Since Ruby continued to fail and fail and fail, someone would have to be charged with handling her reeducation efforts. Elder Moss decided to do it herself. She professed it her failure that resulted in Ruby's shortcomings, though Ruby would never agree with the elder on that. The youngest elder to ascend to leader of the coven in history could never be the failure; Ruby obviously held that role. Ruby's shame at making Elder Moss feel responsible for her failures pounded into her chest once more.

The gates of the compound loomed ahead, brightly imposing in the morning light. As the group approached, they opened just enough to file in one at a time. Ruby ensured that she entered last, feeling her face heat as the witches tasked to watch the gate that morning gave her robes a long, meaningful look. Their faces did not shift from their usual, neutral expressions, but Ruby could still feel the judgment at her disheveled state. She watched as Violetta and Vanella walked away in unison to inform on her to Elder Moss, while Juniper stomped away, his silence all too familiar for so long now. The gates slammed closed, locking her in with the other witches, as alone as she always had been.

Ruby sped back to her personal quarters, ignoring the lingering looks of the other witches as she traversed the winding garden paths of the compound. There, she quickly peeled the sticky, blood-soaked clothes from her body, piling them in a heap in the corner of her barren bedroom to deal with after she bathed. Covering herself in a spare towel and rushing to the communal baths in her building, Ruby tried to quiet the racing of her mind, to no avail. Thoughts relentlessly pounded against the confines of her skull.

What if they give me another solitary retreat? They will give up on me... I am worthless... I cannot do this... I am such an unspeakable failure... What will I do when they throw me out..? Will I be killed for being a witch without a coven and the Great King's legal protection..? What will happen to me?

The buckets of prepared water for bathing were as icy as always. Ruby gritted her teeth as she doused herself, scrubbing her skin vigorously as she hurried to finish her frozen washing. Tears pricked at her eyes as the cold speared her with the clarity that her response to the attack was too much. She was always too much.

If only I didn't react to him...

Her only source of relief as she rushed through cleaning herself came from the fact that her hair remained unsullied by her blood; having to wash her hair would be extra exhaustion. She had tied the numerous braids at the back of her head in a bun that morning, allowing them to escape the clinging, sticky blood that soaked through her robes to color the skin beneath. Still, Ruby grimaced as brown skin revealed itself when she washed away more blood, the pebbling from the cold causing her skin to bring to mind the boring rocks that Vanella had always said her skin resembled. Admittedly, the rocks held more gray than her skin actually did, but it wasn't an inaccurate comparison, especially when juxtaposed against Vanella's own glimmering golden coloring.

Back in her room, Ruby dried and redressed in another set of robes identical to the ones that lay in a heap on her floor. She really needed to do something about those, but she debated if she should go send them to the laundry immediately or if she should wait for Elder Moss to show up or summon her.

What would she want me to do?

Ruby looked around the sparse furnishings, seeing the beige expanse of her room, identical to all the others' rooms. Garishly, her blood-soaked clothes contrasted with the uniformly bland room, standing out painfully. She imagined her hair stood out much the same way against the beige room that matched her robes.

Once finished dressing, Ruby opened her door in accordance with the daytime rules, and heard approaching footsteps. Listening carefully, the sound wasn't familiar enough for her to recognize them, but when they stopped in front of another room, she knew they were not there to summon her for Elder Moss. A combination of relief and dread swirled against Ruby's ribcage. Indecisiveness plagued her. What would Elder Moss want of her? If she rushed to get the laundry cared for, perhaps Elder Moss would be upset at having to wait to speak with her. On the other hand, Elder Moss had never taken kindly to mess in the bedrooms of her witches, encouraging perfect order. The back and forth left her immobile as she heard a new set of footsteps approaching.

Steady, purposeful steps, Ruby recognized the cadence and force immediately, each footfall pounding the nails in her coffin. The choice had been made for her. There would be no rushing off to get the laundry taken care of.

As the elder turned and entered Ruby's room, Ruby watched as hazel eyes landed on the pile of bloody clothes and lingered. The serene smile plastered on Elder Moss's face tightened minutely.

Elder Moss's smile didn't approach her narrowed eyes, giving Ruby the haunting stare that told her she would pay for her loathsome indiscretions. She scrambled to find the right words to fix the situation. The words wouldn't come. They never came. Ruby tried to turn her attention away from the elder's gaze, but the image of Elder Moss's displeasure burned itself into her retinas. Even as she took in the lines forming around Elder Moss's beige face, Ruby couldn't shake the shame that settled over her like the suffocating heat of a summer's day. Blanketed in the familiar sensation of her failure and ineptitude, Ruby waited for Elder Moss to finish her perusal and speak. The seconds ticked by, dragging, as Ruby's fingers twitched, her feet tingling with the desire to squirm where she stood, though she forced herself to remain still.

Finally, Elder Moss spoke, her voice subtly tinged with

discontent, "I heard what transpired in Edgefair. The results, I see, have not been properly managed either."

The air rushed from Ruby's lungs as if struck. Clearly, she'd compounded her failures. In an instant, Ruby imagined herself cast out from the coven, barred from any other, banging her fists bloody to be allowed back in before something horrible befell her. She narrowly managed to save herself the additional failure of another emotional display as she took a deep breath, quelling the desperate panic that threatened to break her carefully controlled expression.

"I failed in my management of my emotions, Elder Moss. I could blame the blood loss or the injury, but it was my failure and I apologize to you and the coven at large for my transgressions. I am ready to do whatever you deem necessary to improve myself, though it is past clear that I am unworthy of the calling I have been given as a witch. I miscalculated on the matter of the robes, as I thought it would be most important to discuss what I needed to do with you first, before I put any action to other concerns. I am sorry you had to see this failure as well. You are such an exemplary witch and I aspire to your skills, though I know that I will never measure up."

Ruby hid her surprise that her voice remained so steady while answering for her behavior. Watching Elder Moss carefully, Ruby waited to see if she said the right thing. Her heart pounded in her chest. Her palms grew slick, a trickle of frozen sweat dragging down the back of her neck. The elder's eyes remained coldly trained on Ruby, seemingly evaluating her utterance. Ruby watched as the elder's expression softened finally. The tightness around her perfected, closed-mouth smile dissipated as she nodded, and Ruby breathed again.

"It is good that you see the errors you have made. Surely, we know that it is my failure as your teacher to guide you. I will have to endeavor to rectify this situation."

"No, Elder Moss! The failure is with me, entirely," Ruby hurried to supply, certain that the elder needed reassurance.

She was wrong.

How does she make such a warm hazel look that cold?

CHAPTER TWO

Dorian

"PLEASE!!!!" The nasally cry bounced from the stone walls, piercing Dorian's ear drums.

Dorian rolled his eyes, sneering down at the pathetic heap of a man attempting to curl in on himself, despite the bindings holding him upright. His vampiric ability to observe the emotional field of others allowed him to see the man's disgustingly yellow-green desperation. He watched until his hunger and the excessive noise started to trigger a pounding headache. Shadows of pure magic seeped forth from Dorian, curling around the man's mouth at his mental command. At the same time, Dorian banished his emotional field view, uninterested in seeing any more of the man's feelings in such vivid color.

Basking in the silence, Dorian located an enchanted dagger, sending some of his shadows to pick it up and deliver it to him. Dorian fiddled with it as he approached the squirming man locked against the back wall. He reveled in the way that the man's eyes overflowed into waterfalls. The scent of his terror filled the air as he sobbed. Briefly, Dorian imagined what the worthless man's victims felt before he descended on them. It likely resembled what the man now suffered. A small-name nobleman who no one would really miss, his enemies too eager to gain access to his lands to care who finally acted.

A bitter taste filled Dorian's mouth.

If only I hadn't been seen collecting him.

Dorian slid the tip of the dagger into the man's neck, holding his glass up to the wound. A short stream of blood poured into the glass, slowing to a trickle as the enchantment in the dagger healed the nobleman's neck within seconds. Dorian took a few steps back, locking eyes with the man once more as he savored his first sip. The man's eyes widened with horror as he watched Dorian.

"This is quite the unique dagger. It heals its victims but without any change in sensation. Cuts you can't see continue to hurt and give the impression of bleeding, making you weaker and colder over time. I wouldn't waste blood, though. You're perfectly healed."

Finding, and secretly purchasing, the particularly cruel enchanted item for his purposes took decades, but it proved worth it in the centuries since. The people he used it on deserved it. Dorian had been looking forward to this well-deserved slaughter. Being seen, though not totally unexpected, infuriated him. The news of his actions would reach the vampiric council in a matter of hours. He would only have a couple of days before he was called to meet with them.

"So many preparations I have to make now, because of you. Such a shame." Dorian tsked as he sipped more blood.

The man whimpered, his stifled sounds carrying despite the silencing of Dorian's shadows holding his mouth shut. Dorian suppressed a mirthless laugh, waiting for the man's eyes to calm enough for him to make the fall that much harder. When they thought they had a chance, only for him to dash those hopes, Dorian experienced euphoria. Tilting his head in contemplation, he debated how best to facilitate the calm cliff he could push the man from.

"Yes, such a shame. The vampiric council always takes these sorts of things so seriously with you nobles."

Suddenly, the man's eyes grew sharper, less afraid, and he squirmed for the ability to speak, his muffled sounds pounding against the shadows covering his mouth. Dorian mentally directed his shadows to slowly pull away from the man's mouth, affecting a surprised and intrigued expression.

"Yes, I am a nobleman! A Lord! You have to know that you will be caught, and if anything should happen to me, there will be a hefty price! I am sure we can work something out. Please!"

Desperation clung to the very breath that pushed forth the man's words, polluting the scent of the air in the room, despite the haughty tone and conspiratorial end. He grasped desperately for anything to save his skin. Dorian had long ago decided the man's fate, and nothing the despicable backstabber could say would alter that decision.

"I am not totally familiar with the Vampiric Council, but I know that they do follow certain guidelines for us nobles as set out by the Great King! Surely, you know that you would not be able to get away with harming a noble!" His eyes lit with triumph, sure that he had just cinched his survival with the pale, pathetic threat of the king's rules.

Got him.

"Well, then how do you explain that I already have?" Dorian smiled, embracing the feral energy behind it.

His smile only deepened as he watched a deathly pallor fall over the man. There, in the man's eyes, Dorian watched the shattering of hope he so relished. He covered the man's mouth with some of his shadows before he could protest anymore, or resume begging for his worthless life.

"Now, I can see that you understand the gravity of your situation. The fact I've already murdered more nobles than I can count over the centuries is irrelevant right now. Instead, would you like me to explain why I'm going to kill you no matter what?" Dorian paused for another sip, sending some of his shadows to caress the man's face, "It's quite simple. You deserve to die."

Dorian noted the man's dawning horror at being found out; people who tried to hide their cruelty knew how wrong they were, and the man before Dorian was no exception. Secrets never stayed in the dark forever. They festered and spread like disease, passed along through whispers in dark alleys. Commoners to the more respected servants of the nobility to nobility themselves and back again. Few kept their dirty dealings secret for long. It took both money and influence. Money kept them free. Influence kept them clear. The man before Dorian never gained the influence half.

"Using the young women—some of them still just girls—of your small village is hardly a new activity among your ilk. It's a dismal inevitability when talentless, tasteless, and tactless fools ascend into power, knowing that they will never convince someone to willingly love them. Your desire for feeling powerful, when you know deep down that you are not worthy of such power, leads you to the most predictable behavior. Exploitation, coercion, control. You used all of it to harm and punish the women under your thumb for, what? Existing? Despising you?"

The man's stare flashed with confusion, anguish, then rage as he listened to Dorian speak. He fought against his bonds, not wanting to hear what a weakling he was in Dorian's eyes. Too bad. Conjuring more of his shadows into a flurry of whips, Dorian started listing the names of the young women from that small village that disappeared or died. Then the ones who returned broken, physically or emotionally. He listed every single one, lashing the man with thick shadows, bruising him, punishing him for each detestable crime. Originally, the village consisted of a few hundred people. They couldn't afford to leave or escape their lord, so they suffered the indignities, the atrocities, the losses. 65 names. 65 women and girls that man defiled, harmed, destroyed. Not a woman between the ages of 15 and 35 escaped his cruel attention. Time passed slowly as Dorian listed each one, watching with perverse delight as the man realized just how much Dorian knew about him, realized how futile his efforts to escape his fate were, and suffered.

"The only regret I will ever have for what I am going to do to you, is that I did not find out about you sooner, so I could have put you down like the rabid beast you are earlier, to save them from ever suffering the grotesque contamination of your presence."

Broken eyes, devoid of hope, looked back at Dorian. The nobleman was finally brought to the same low that he'd inflicted on so many innocent people. He would never harm anyone else. The tendrils of shadow Dorian had left covering his mouth during the torture remained firmly in place, and if they'd held a more corporeal form, would surely have been covered in the man's tears and snot.

Reminded of the last moments of the man who shattered his mother, Dorian imposed that face over the one before him. They weren't similar in appearance, but they displayed the same void in their eyes where kindness should reside.

Others might have the same icy blue eyes as the man physically before him, but theirs would seem positively molten compared to his. Others might have the same straight blond hair slicked back from their faces, but theirs would not give the impression of slime, despite being clean. Where his face may have been handsome to some, Dorian could see nothing but a monster, sniveling like a child caught doing something wrong, begging for mercy. But this man was not a child who'd snuck a sweet in the middle of the night. He was a grown man who harmed people because he felt too inadequate to exist with his own mediocrity.

"But, for now," Dorian sighed heavily, "I would like to rant," turning away, savoring the blood in his glass, Dorian continued, "You see, I do have a problem with having captured you. I *will* still kill you, but I'm upset. I'll have to do it sooner than I would have liked to. Normally, I keep pieces of human refuse like you for a few days or weeks, collecting your blood, letting you replenish it, and collecting more, before I finally kill you. I won't have that option with you, sadly. You'll have to die by morning. Such a pity," Dorian said with mock sympathy.

Dorian reveled in the man's free-flowing tears.

"Unfortunately, it will only take the vampiric council a few days to decide to bring me before them. I will have to plan my response carefully. You see, I have no intention of letting them mete out some punishment on behalf of something so righteous as me turning you into dust. My method of managing them will have to be careful, however. There are a lot of them, after all. They have that pesky little barrier enchantment on the whole country, too. If I were to try to flee, they would know exactly where I exited the borders of Vlideron. That leaves far too much to chance for my liking."

Dorian hummed, as if mocking the thought. In truth, his mind rushed downriver at a break-neck pace. While considering what he knew of the council and what he could use against them, Dorian knew his top priority remained evading capture. Dozens of previously plotted plans flashed through his mind until he landed on one he thought would work.

With that firmly in mind, Dorian continued his monologue, "I suppose I could always blackmail them. That might work. I know an awful lot about the larger picture, though I must admit that I've never paid attention to the individuals. I just avoid them as much as I can. I've evaded notice for far longer than I truly thought I would, always playing at being an average, weak vampire. It's allowed me to notice their oddities, however."

The man's gaze grew more distant with each word. Dorian looked down at the nearly empty glass in his hands, sighing.

With a few long strides, he stood before the man again, startling him into fear once more. Repeating his earlier maneuver to secure a full glass of blood, Dorian smiled sadistically at the man's pain. At his suffering.

He'd never show it, but Dorian exhausted himself emotionally by listing each woman. He hadn't gone over the details, since he didn't want to give the man the pleasure of reliving his crimes, but he knew everything done to those young ladies.

At least I made this monster suffer for what he did.

"Something interesting about the vampiric council is how they pay for the living allowances of all the vampires in Vlideron. Astonishing that they should have so much wealth and influence when the witches, who enforce the law of the 'Great' King," Dorian's voice dripped with venom as he mentioned the title the king gave himself, "so despise vampires. Do not even get me started on the myriad of disappointments I have with the witches. How is it that this king allows vampires to run amok with many of the laws of this land that he has laid down? Of course, the wealthy nobility can do as they please. I am sure you know that all too well. I still wonder what it is that the vampiric council offers the king and his cronies, and what all they get in return."

Dorian drank deeply before continuing, "Now I know what you'll say, 'Well they get the money to pay the livelihoods of all the vampires in Vlideron!' But I have to say, that just doesn't fit. You see, I also know that they are far stronger than they ought to be. They claim that vampires have natural gifts that affect their natural strength levels, and most vampires just aren't that strong naturally. There's just one problem with that. I know the truth. Thus, I know what I need to do—and it isn't running."

With the nagging pull of his internal clock, an innate trait of becoming a vampire, Dorian knew the sun would rise in a few short hours, but he needed to prepare for his inevitable confrontation with the council in a few days' time, so he could hardly dilly dally. Looking at the man bound to the stone wall, Dorian felt a pang of regret that he could not spend more time tormenting him.

Alas, I have work to do.

"I wish I could brainstorm with you more. It's been so nice to speak aloud of the things I need to consider. Ah well. Are you ready?"

His feral grin returned as he watched the man's eyebrows

furrow, eyes squinting, before they widened and grew wet with new tears as he realized what Dorian's words meant for him. Dorian's shadows muffled renewed screaming and begging. The sniveling little creature tried anything and everything to save his worthless life. Dorian almost felt as though he should commend his insistence and desire for survival, no matter how futile. He took his time, enjoying the frantic energy. Dorian had his shadows undo the man's physical restraints, but hold him firmly in place. Dorian stood before him, tilting his head side to side as he examined the worm.

Without giving the noble warning, Dorian had his shadows turn the man upside down, a startled shout just barely audible behind the writhing mass of magic made manifest. Dorian took a few steps back, grabbing a new dagger with a very different enchantment. Sending a few tendrils of shadow out, Dorian had them retrieve his blood collection and storage supplies, then settle them in place beneath the floating upside-down man. The apparatus featured a magical collection bowl which held any volume of blood in stasis. A funnel exited the bottom of it to a spout from which Dorian could refill his pouches of blood. The whole thing was enchanted so that not a drop of blood would go to waste, either by dripping accident or becoming stuck to any side.

Dorian waited for the man's eyes to reopen before he sliced his throat, watching as the light drained from the monster's horrified stare with the draining of his blood. As he moved through the motions of properly collecting and storing the blood for future enjoyment, Dorian felt a familiar bubble of unease settle in his stomach.

Dorian tried to disregard the odd feeling, knowing he had a lot to get ready for, but he couldn't help but ruminate on the idea. He considered that man a monster, but was Dorian a monster too? Did it matter if he existed as a totally different kind? Without the loved ones who once grounded him, should he even care?

CHAPTER THREE

Ruby

Through the permeable but invisible barrier that created the library's windows, Ruby heard birds chirping from outside. Sounds, smells, and light entered freely but did not exit. The magic also prevented any critters from entering and safeguarded the journals within. Ruby breathed deeply, delighting in the smell of the garden-laden compound, delightfully warmed by the morning sun. From her spot in the center of the bottom floor, she could see outside through the many one-way windows. Golden light filtered in, where a few hours earlier there had been rain and darkness. The early autumn sun remained warm, though, and Ruby relished the feeling as she sat alone.

This is the best reeducation I have ever experienced.

Cataloging and reorganizing the past 200 years-worth of witches' journals was a large task. While encouraged to not take too long to complete her work, Ruby lacked a formal deadline. She was required to read through them all first, of course. Knowing it could take months to complete, Ruby settled in with her stack of pages for notes and started slowly. There would be no point rushing a job requiring regular reports.

She wouldn't be allowed to socialize with the other witches, attend any gatherings that they regularly held, go on patrols, or otherwise do anything not strictly necessary until it was completed. Despite this, relief washed her nerves free of jitters. Time spent with the coven highlighted her status as a failure, since she was the only one who seemed to struggle with her emotions, she had weak powers, and always needed more reeducation. After absorbing everything from the last 200 years of witches, Ruby hoped to be able to rejoin their ranks better than before.

Most of all, Ruby savored relief that, despite being practically shunned and alone, she avoided enduring another solitary retreat. While she would have accepted and attempted to survive another retreat, she was gratified to know that wasn't her fate yet. If she succeeded at this, it would redefine the rest of her life.

If I continue to be a failure after this...

Ruby couldn't finish that thought, shaking away the bone-deep chill that spread through her body. Returning to her reading, Ruby felt another unwelcome but familiar sensation.

"The Great King has fully ascended to the monarchy, at long last. It is only right, after the trials and persecution he has faced in his climb. I am honored to support his direction for Vlideron. That we might whip the populace into shape is a great responsibility, but us witches have been called to it since birth. I feel that call now. The Great King has decreed that we need not examine the nobles in the same way that we patrol the peasantry. Naturally, I am not surprised. It is only right, as the nobility have proven themselves worthy in the eyes of the Great King. He would never be wrong on such a matter. So we shall focus our efforts on the rabble that make up the majority. If we can effect the proper changes in their behavior, Vlideron shall surely flourish."

The words of her ancestor by coven-lineage rattled around her brain, unable to find comfortable purchase. Something always seemed strange about considering the nobility above reproach, to the point that they didn't even patrol the estates. How could the Great King be so certain about so many he never really interacted with?

She scrunched down in her seat, looking around the empty library, fear trickling down her spine at the treasonous thoughts. She was not to think negatively of the Great King. That doctrine held the greatest importance of any they followed. Why Ruby failed at even that most basic task, she never knew. Thankfully, she knew never to express those thoughts aloud, lest she surely be tossed out to the beasts of Death's Forest, or the cruel mercies of the streets. The elders, especially Elder Moss, tolerated much from her over the years, but she always knew how intolerable doubting the Great King's wisdom would prove.

Ruby's attempts to shake the pervading sense that the Great King was wrong were in vain. She overhead just enough from the commoners to give her pause. Snippets of alleged cruelty and blatant law-breaking by nobility merged with moments of apparent bribery to conceal their dirty dealings. As a result of being unable to patrol the residences of the nobility, Ruby never glimpsed any evidence of such nefarious activities, and she wondered how much of it could be attributed to the nobles as opposed to the vampires.

According to the elders, the vampires would be at fault for all such nefarious actions. Ruby privately didn't know how she felt about vampires, since everything she heard about them from her elders and fellow witches was that they were cruel and despicable, corrupted creatures. She found it difficult to believe that everyone of a particular group could be so similar, since she herself was different from the other witches.

I'm worse than all of them...

Refocusing on reading through the journals, Ruby tried to force herself to accept the words of the witch who came before her. They must know the heart and mind of the Great King better than she ever would, since the entries implied that this witch had met the Great King in decades past. His longevity was legendary, apparently owing to his divine right to the throne, despite being a normal human.

Ruby read on, her eyes darting around whenever a doubt crept into her thoughts. She chastised herself for her inability to accept the words of her superiors. If only she were a better witch, she could accept everything. Accepting the doctrines of her elders and the decrees of the Great King would make her a worthy witch. If only she could drill the material directly into her thick skull.

The sun transformed the world outside, shadows shortening as it approached its zenith. Finally taking a break to stretch, Ruby's stiff body protested the hours of study with aching agony. Looking out one of the windows, Ruby spied the muted green hair of Juniper, bobbing through the tall plants of the compound.

"You are nothing but a vile temptress."

Ruby heard Juniper's voice seething in her ear as if those events were happening all over again. He'd scrutinized her with the same contempt Elder Moss held for her when she failed again. That he'd been amiable only hours earlier left her lost. Juniper was never particularly gentle with her. She wouldn't have called him her lover, either, despite the intimacy they shared. Experiencing his sudden, unexplained hatred slashed through the heart of her, tearing out what small piece of connection she thought they shared and burning it before her eyes.

Before she could drown in the memory any further, Ruby tore herself away from the window, walking deeper into the library. The light wood shelves had been swept clean of journals by the other witches, since Ruby would need to reorganize the journals upon finishing reading them all, leaving them all barren and, admittedly, boring to look at. Throughout the majority of the library, no decoration or embellishment disrupted the endless beige, just like the rest of the compound. Although she'd never seen inside the private rooms of the elders in their central manor, Ruby assumed they were much the same: bare, beige, boring.

Ruby looked over her shoulder, relieved to see no one there, just in case her thoughts showed on her face for a moment. Private musings needed to be kept private. While Juniper had reinforced that lesson, Violetta taught her that first.

When Elder Moss demanded Ruby kneel down on a bed of small, hard grains to recite the entirety of their code of conduct 100 times, she knew that Violetta had told the elder of Ruby's doubts. Further confirmation arrived when Elder Moss told her to reflect on her foolishness to doubt their codes as she healed. It took weeks for the aching in her knees and the harsh bruises to go away. In all of that reflection, Ruby learned to keep her thoughts silent.

Her face betrayed her often, though. Elder Moss often corrected her attitude, noting times when Ruby failed to notice herself making any kind of face, and ensuring she experienced swift reeducation in that event. Sometimes, despite knowing she must be wrong, Ruby found herself furious with Elder Moss for these adjustments, so often certain she had not been making any face or giving the elders any attitude. She tried exceedingly hard to ensure that she maintained a neutral expression at all times and a neutral tone of voice, but her body kept betraying her, conveying emotions that she wasn't even aware of having.

Sighing her relief, Ruby wandered the library, grateful to have the freedom of movement. Towards the back of the library, Ruby noted a shift in the old building. Though rarely discussed, she recalled the story of the library burning down 200 years prior. Only this single room survived the blaze. The least read journals had been kept there, being in an inconveniently out-of-the-way room, one Ruby couldn't remember ever visiting, since it took a few odd hallways to reach. Curiosity drove her forward, noting the shift to dark, rich brown wood of the empty door frame.

Ruby's eyes went wide as she looked around at the wholly unique room. If one didn't go looking for it, or wasn't wandering aimlessly, they may never locate it. The detail struck her as curious, since the history of the old library would surely have been of importance. Some thought wriggled around in her subconscious, desperate to pierce through, leaving Ruby feeling inexplicably uneasy.

The grandeur of the old library room captivated her. Stately bookcases covered the walls, interrupted only by slices of windows on the back of the building. More proud bookcases dotted the open floor. Each had been intricately carved with the same dark brown wood that graced the floors and lined the doorway. More shocking was the sapphire ceiling. Color in their surroundings only came from the flowers in the gardens and the witches themselves, whose inhuman, inborn color in their hair, eyes, or even skin marked them as witches.

The carvings on the empty bookcases caught her attention as she turned away from the vibrant ceiling. Delicate flowers and celestial markings lined the front and sides of the shelves. A rainbow twinkle caught her eye from a shelf on the front wall, decorated exclusively with roses and thorns, carved so intricately into the thick wood that Ruby swore she saw movement.

Ruby ventured closer, gaze fixating on the roses as she spied magic twinkling, apparently embedded in the shelf. Curiosity got the better of her, despite knowing she ought to go inform Elder Moss of the confusing phenomenon. She only hesitated long enough to blink before reaching out a finger to trace the lines of magic as they snaked through the carved roses and thorns.

A blue-tinged line of iridescent magic lit up the path Ruby's finger traced as she followed the enchantment. Slithering vines and plush roses danced at her touch until the rainbow disappeared. Silence stretched out as she lifted her hand from the glowing line of magic she had unintentionally drawn, leaving Ruby wondering if the enchantment served any purpose at all.

She couldn't imagine such a frivolous gift being accepted by the witches, and it must have been a gift since they could only use light magic. Healing and defense against the darkness. Destruction of the shadows and, by extension, vampires.

A strange grinding filled the room as the bookcase slowly moved towards her, sending her stumbling backwards. Ruby froze, waiting for Elder Moss to come admonish her. She peered at the edge of the bookcase curiously, noticing a gap. Gingerly widening the opening, Ruby gazed in wonder and terror at the darkness beyond what she belatedly recognized as a door. Glancing at the entrance to the room, Ruby knew what she should do: go inform the elders.

How has no one discovered this secret door before? Did I do something differently? Did the shelves need to be empty to trigger the enchantment? Wait, no, that doesn't make sense. What good would a secret door fashioned as a bookcase be if it couldn't have books on it? And a better witch would have noticed this, for sure!

Something must have changed, however, to allow her to open it.

Ruby summoned a weak orb of light, grimacing at the dim, poorly formed magic, and sent it into the darkness beyond. It lit up a staircase leading down into unknown depths. Ruby plunged forth, hurrying down the stairs before she could change her mind. Sending the orb in front of her, Ruby gasped, and the question that had been begging for acknowledgment finally sprang free.

If this section of the library remained perfectly intact, how did all of the old texts burn to ash?

At the bottom of the stairs, Ruby twirled, gawking at the massive circular room. The curved walls were made exclusively of shelves, housing thousands of books. It took her only a second to realize that these must have been the old texts that survived the fire. Why the texts that survived the fire were locked away, hidden underground, Ruby couldn't say, but she desperately wanted to find out.

Unlike the journals of modern witches, which used exclusively light brown leather, the tomes lining every shelf of the secret library were bound in a rainbow of dark and vibrant shades. She had never spied such variety in the tomes of other witches. Ruby's fingers tingled with excitement at discovering their words, hoping for guidance to be a better witch.

Picking up a random book from the shelves, Ruby opened and began to read. Her stomach plummeted. Her heart rate skyrocketed. She dropped the book, not caring how it landed as she grabbed wildly for another book. Then another. Then another. Over and over again, Ruby grabbed books off the shelves at random, devouring the words found within as she questioned everything she had ever been taught, and began to understand what she might learn from the forbidden texts. With every new book, she grew more convinced that these would be forbidden by the elders. With every new book, she knew she had to find out more.

The books told an entirely different tale of witches than she knew. These witches held powers and skills she'd never imagined, beyond the light magic she'd always been told was the only magic witches could use. Most importantly, the paths of the witches who authored those texts were not emotionless or consistent. They were, each of them, unique individuals.

Starting to accept what the books were showing her, Ruby returned to the first book she'd dropped. The grimoire started 205 years ago, a full 5 years before the oldest journal Ruby had ever read. Both spell book and private journal, Ruby flipped to the last entry. Dated the same year as the fire that destroyed the library and killed many witches..

"We have again been approached by the man who calls himself 'the Great King.' Such a crock of horse shit. The man has been removed from the crown before. He hasn't the moral character to lead Vlideron. That any of my fellow witches stand by his side astounds me. He only wants to use us to serve his own power-hungry means. I dread the results he might have if no one puts a stop to him. I have contemplated leaving Vlideron in recent days. I fear that if I do not escape soon, I will be unable to. I have also considered hexing the man, though I worry that the witches and vampires who have allied themselves with him will be prepared for such things and strike back. But how could I not seek to end his reign of terror before it has a chance to truly blossom?"

Ruby nearly fell to the floor, sitting down hard as the air rushed from her lungs in shock. What did this mean for the witches that had been teaching her her whole life? Had they truly all been wrong? What really happened during the fire 200 years earlier? Was the Great King truly as power-hungry as these witches thought? How had their ideology changed so much in such a short time?

The questions grew as she flipped through the grimoire, noting the variety of spells and types of magic used. How had they switched to only utilizing light magic when they were capable of so much more? Ruby desperately wanted to know. She wanted to know the fate of the author of the grimoire. Had they escaped before the fire? Before Vlideron began blocking citizens from leaving? Had they truly been capable of hexing? Ruby knew vampires could cause curses, and some commoners referred to them as hexes. Were those the same thing?

Ruby's control over her orb of light magic wavered, leaving her in the dark for a moment. Grabbing as many journals as her arms could carry, Ruby thanked her past self for bringing her bag to the library. Expecting she would need to carry journals back to her room that night for study, she'd been prepared. Rushing back up the stairs, Ruby paused only long enough to encourage the secret door to close, grateful when she saw that she only needed to push it a little to re-engage its locking enchantment.

Before she did anything else, Ruby stuffed the forbidden texts in her enchanted bag, covering them with loose notes and one of the known, approved journals. Guilt gnawed at her insides for going far beyond simply breaking the rules. Maybe the texts were hidden away for a good reason. Maybe the elders didn't know about them, and she would be able to redirect witches going forward more towards their roots. Or maybe she failed her coven again by even investigating the dark recesses of magic she spotted in the pages.

Ruby couldn't focus on anything else for the rest of the day. A pit formed in her stomach as she debated if her choices to not tell the elders and taking the books to read herself were justifiable. Her mind remained stuck on the secrets that might be found within. Her eyes drifted to the bag at her side more times than she could count as she tried to continue the studies assigned to her.

By the end of the day, Ruby could feel her skin buzzing with the need to explore the pages further, to discover more of the magic and history that could be found within. She shoved her mostly-blank notes into her bag, rushing towards the main doors. Elder Moss breezed in, stopping Ruby in her tracks, her face falling into familiar neutrality.

"Ah, just heading out I see?" Elder Moss asked, her glare sharp.

"Yes, Elder Moss. I wanted to ensure I spent the most time here that I could, so I have yet to go eat dinner or bathe. I thought to hurry through those tasks and get some more work done in my room before sleeping." Ruby gestured to her bag, hoping her explanation proved sufficient to avoid further inquiry.

"I see. And did you find anything interesting here today?"

Ruby imagined she heard an edge to Elder Moss's voice, casting her head down as she tried to avoid looking at her bag or back towards the old room of the library. "The words of our elders are of such vital importance. I could hardly say it was not interesting to discover the depths of their devotion to our way of life."

Elder Moss remained silent. The seconds ticked by, prompting her to look up. Her heart stopped for a second the moment Moss's eyes narrowed as she stared Ruby down. Ruby remained silent, praying the elder would just let her go to her room without further questions. She didn't want to disappoint her elder with the deception, but she needed to learn more. Maybe, just maybe, she might be able to help her esteemed elder fly even higher if she could find evidence that witches could be more. She just needed the time to research first.

"Enjoy your evening studies," Elder Moss finally responded, her serene smile returning.

Ruby tried not to sprint away as she left the library, ignoring the sensation of scrutiny boring into her back.

CHAPTER FOUR

Dorian

Dorian swaggered into the council building, sending the gawking vampires who worked as servants there scrambling to get out of his way. The opulent building, draped in all shades of gray and black, was designed to show off the might and wealth of the council. Dorian couldn't help but smirk at the absurdity of the monotonous surroundings, even as he admired the surprisingly delicate crystal chandeliers. While Dorian enjoyed black in his decor, the council brought it to lifeless proportions. As immortal beings of the night, surviving on mortal blood, some thought vampires among the dead. Some vampires leaned into that foolish view, removing the life from structure and decor.

I wonder why they lean into such absurdity.

The large lobby took up what easily could have been a full block of market homes, where the shopkeepers would live above their stores, renting from the local lord at exorbitant prices. In Edgefair, that rent was as likely to go to the highest ranking visiting noble as to be managed by the vampiric council, since nearly half of the shops in the city were run by vampires. The oddity that such greedy beings as the nobility would allow vampires to live in the shop homes for no rent paid to them stuck out to Dorian enough to bolster his suspicions.

Further, that a vampire could keep both a shop and an estate when the nobility forcibly shuffled and traded lodgings during their mandatory stays seemed odd. Why did the council have the ability to reward certain vampires in such a way when the nobles surely desired to keep permanent estates in Edgefair? Sure, some of the higher ranks held permanent estates in Edgefair that sat empty when they were not in residence, but the lower ranks were required to trade around, buying a new home every time they were stationed in the out-of-the-way locale, and selling upon the end of their term. It sounded tedious. That vampires could maintain permanent residences in such valued homes for the performance of their shops proved more noticeable to Dorian than he thought the vampiric council had ever banked on.

Most vampires in Vlideron were too weak to achieve such status. The standard vampires in Vlideron would exchange services for their daily blood, since most vampires in Vlideron were younger than 200 years old and didn't know the truth. They needed three pints of blood a day. Whatever services they could offer, they would charge a pint of blood for their work. Stronger vampires could charge gold for their services as well. Dorian had avoided drawing that much attention to himself, since the older vampires who did that, and didn't join the council, tended to disappear. It was those stronger vampires who earned permanent residences.

Of course, being a noble as well changes the rules.

His strides did not slow as he passed through the lobby, each employee of the council turning to stare at him with open-mouthed astonishment. Whispers buzzed in the air like a simmering pot of oil on the precipice of explosion. Dorian caught a few phrases as he glided past various groups, each expressing the same sentiments—that he marched to his doom. Was he a fool? A madman? Did he not know he approached his own execution? Or did he think he could escape it somehow? They all wanted to know what in the many mountains and rivers of Vlideron he could be thinking.

Smirking, Dorian cracked his neck in front of the council doors, the blackened metal strangely absorbing all light, and threw them open. A long, dark hallway stretched ahead as Dorian proceeded, claustrophobic walls to either side of him. He strode forward, noting the silence accompanying the echoes of his heavy footfalls. At the end of the obnoxiously cramped and long hallway stood a circular dais, lit up with silver spotlights, stationed more than a full orc's height below the lowest seating of the council.

The stone walls, floor, and auditorium tables absorbed the light as thoroughly as its doors had. Subtle, false starlight from luminescent crystals in the cavernous ceiling lit the rest of the chamber. The effect, with the spotlights on him, would have blinded a vampire as weak as he should have been. Dorian no longer felt a need to pretend ignorance or weakness.

No need to hide anymore.

Emerging into the light, Dorian looked around in mock surprise, "What, no chair for me?"

"Dorian Seagrave?" a youthful human voice questioned from behind him.

Dorian tensed as he turned to look over his shoulder at the speaker, noting from their position at the lowest level in the back of the chamber that they were likely low-ranking. From the paper and quill in their hand, Dorian guessed that they were the record keeper. He forcibly relaxed his jaw, as he confirmed his accursed last name.

"It is good of you to join us, Mister Seagrave. Or is it Lord Seagrave?" A deep, jovial voice pierced the air.

Dorian looked up at the speaker, noting the way that he occupied a seat above all the others in the center of the chamber, directly opposite the hallway Dorian came in through. This was the leader of the vampiric council of Vlideron. Oh, they might say they were all equal voices in those seats, but Dorian knew the truth. The design of the council chambers showed it. The strongest vampires occupied the higher, central seats. The sides and lower seats were all taken up by those showing sufficient strength while possessing the desire to gain the notice of the council.

The leader in the center was cut from a different cloth than the squirrelly note-taker behind Dorian. He could see the power emanating off of the old vampire, unrestrained, left to flow wildly around him in an obvious act of intimidation. Dorian considered the ghostly white skin, wrinkled from the man's time as a human, pure white hair blending into his skin, with a beard cropped just a few inches below his jaw. Despite the excessive lighting attempting to blind him, Dorian could see the leader's vermilion eyes clearly, as if those red irises were glowing with power.

He just wants to get under my skin.

"Did I have another choice? And just Dorian is good."

"No, you did not have another choice," someone answered

venomously.

Dorian kept his examination trained on the leader as he asked, "So what should I call you?"

Surprise colored the energy of the 40 or so vampires in the chamber, but Dorian kept his focus on the leader. The leader's eyes widened with surprise, momentarily narrowed in annoyance, and returned to the affectation of jovial curiosity under Dorian's scrutiny. Dorian measured that against what he already knew of the council's overall actions, observations and suspicions aligning. Despite never bothering to learn their names, Dorian knew enough about the council's dealings from Sigrid.

"You have always portrayed yourself to be so casual in your connection to authority," the leader shook his head, "I am Elmer Nossvel. I am the designated arbiter of the council. It is, of course, such a great honor. I will be directing most of the questions today."

"You could just say you're the leader of the council, you know." Dorian laughed.

"Well, that is not how we would describe it. The council is a voting entity that collectively leads the vampires of Vlideron. We do not have a leader, as such."

Dorian couldn't help but note the monotone Elmer took on as he rattled off the canned response. Not even he could pretend to believe his own words enough to make them the least bit convincing.

Dorian dragged out the syllable as he responded, "Right," before rolling his eyes.

While most of the vampires in the chambers began to grumble about his sarcasm, calling it inappropriate and uncalled for, Elmer and those in the seats nearest him lit up with amusement. While most of the vampires in the chamber—and Vlideron at large—had once been human, the six vampires seated just below Elmer were more diverse. Two elven vampires, two orcish vampires, a dwarven vampire, and a vampire who used to be a human made up what Dorian guessed were Elmer's real colleagues. Each of them showed some sign of enjoyment at his response, whether through a bemused smile, the way they leaned over the stone table that curved along each row of the chamber, or the raised eyebrows that spoke to amused astonishment.

"Well, you are a bold one, aren't you?" purred the elven woman near Elmer, her full lips curved into a predatory smile.

Dorian could admire the way her nearly-obsidian skin glowed in contrast with her scarlet dress, her curly hair caressing her bare shoulders, and her long ears adorned with copious amounts of gold. He could see how she would leverage that boundless beauty to convince foes and victims alike to underestimate her. He admired that tactic, but wouldn't fall for it himself. He didn't say anything, watching as her gaze narrowed and brow slightly furrowed.

"Yes, Dorian," Elmer drew out the sound of his name for a hair longer than necessary, "is quite bold."

Noting the edge to Elmer's voice, Dorian struggled not to outright laugh. The meeting with the council kept proceeding better than he could have hoped for. He riled up the majority with exceptional and shocking ease.

"So, what did you call me down here for?"

"Surely, you know the answer to that," the orcish man's grinding gravel voice seemed at odds with his refined demeanor.

Dorian barked out a laugh, then feigned embarrassment for the outburst, rubbing the side of his face, "Well, yeah, I suppose I do. So, you going to kill me now or something?"

"You know the truth, don't you?" Elmer asked.

"What truth would that be?" Dorian exaggerated the innocence in his voice despite rolling his eyes.

"You've been consuming the blood of those you've killed. You know the act of killing strengthens the blood and increases our powers."

"Well, you have me all figured out. I'm curious, though, why did you start hiding that from Vlideronian vampires?"

"Please, can you imagine the carnage in the streets if those reckless masses learned the truth of our powers?" Elmer scoffed.

The lesser council members all murmured their agreement, while the six direct underlings to the leader all maintained their silent mirth.

"So why should there be so many vampires? If they cannot be trusted to control themselves, why should they be allowed to continue?" Dorian tapped his fingers on his chin in mock contemplation, "Oh! It must be to provide something for you lot!"

Elmer's eyes narrowed. The vampires who directly served him all stiffened, some of their amusement bleeding from their expressions and postures. The rest of the council hissed their disapproval of his statement. Seeing the reality of the situation,

Dorian realized that only the leading seven knew the full extent of why power was so hoarded at the top. Most of the council thought the bullshit explanation to be the truth. He almost didn't have the heart to push the issue and shatter their illusions.

Before he could, however, Elmer spoke again, "So you have the truth of our powers in your hands, and have for some time now, I surmise. Tell me, would you like to grow more powerful?"

"I will grow more powerful."

"If you join us on the council, we will help you grow more powerful." Elmer sat back, satisfied with his pitch.

Dorian met the gaze of the old vampire. He'd seen Elmer around at vampire events for centuries, but never paid the man much mind. All he'd known was that the man had been a vampire for many centuries by the time Dorian turned. With such a long time of consuming his murdered victims' blood, Elmer would be staggeringly powerful, and despite his fervent efforts, Dorian would lose in a one-on-one fight with him.

"Why should I join the council when what I've been doing has been working so well for me?"

"Because you won't leave this room alive if you don't," One of the lesser vampires replied flatly.

Dorian raised his eyebrows at Elmer.

"We can offer a regular supply of fresh blood to empower you, without the hassle of hunting and sneaking around," Elmer stated.

"How?" Dorian felt relieved at the direction the conversation had taken, playing curious.

"It's quite simple. Surely, you've realized that we enjoy an elevated position in the kingdom. We offer certain services to the Great King and the nobility. In exchange, they maintain our coffers and offer us fresh meat."

"Fresh meat?" Dorian questioned when Elmer did not continue.

"Yes. Anything we want, except nobility of course. But anything the rabble has to offer. Talented young upstarts to join the Great King's armies, would-be priestesses for the goddess M'lvia. Truly, anything you can think of, we can get for you. And you can toy with your food if you wish, however you wish. The space you want to experience their death is provided, no questions asked."

Seeing the movement of the beard, Dorian perceived Elmer's smile, his leer boring into Dorian with a ferocious hunger of his own. With a sinking feeling in his stomach, Dorian realized the full extent of the man's meaning. No one blinked an eye at the implications of cruelty he made. Elmer's silver tongue could not blind Dorian into believing this would ever be a good deal for him either. It would mean the forfeiture of his own control over his growth. To combine that with needless, senseless cruelty would leave him feeling as slimy as his biological father had been.

"Such a tempting offer surely hides thorns."

Elmer's head tilted to the side, curiosity coloring his gaze at first before starting to harden. As the leader of the vampiric council spoke again, his voice crept into every slithering shadow, snaking its way into Dorian's ears, a lower and tighter sound than it had been before, "We are the thorns, Dorian. Some of us, more than others. We come together for the betterment of our kind. We control the masses so that our kind might go on. And yes, we do it all for our personal gain. But what is life as a vampire if not for our own purposes? I assure you that the Great King will not take kindly to a rogue vampire, killing those he has not deemed worthless."

Dorian imagined he could feel the cold caress of the shadows slithering down his spine as he listened to the old vampire's thrown voice which had unnaturally whispered in his ear. Maintaining his smirk, Dorian faintly listened as one of the younger vampires piped up to rattle off the specifics of the deal they were offering him. How they would upgrade his shop, how they dealt with deciding who got to kill and when, and other specifics about the nobility that were most directly involved in their clandestine operations to take the poor citizenry and use them for their personal gain. He kept his attention locked on Elmer, ignoring the prattling.

Eventually, the talkative vampire trailed off, silence falling as they processed Dorian's failure to respond. Elmer, especially, had clearly expected Dorian to jump on this "opportunity." Instead, Dorian let the council sit in disquieting emptiness.

"What do you think, just Dorian?" Elmer choked out after a minute or two passed, and Dorian could see his beard shifting, seemingly grinding his teeth.

Dorian started, his voice light, "Well, you are making quite the offer," dropping the smile and darkening his tone, he continued, "for just another bullshit cage. No."

They exploited commoners just like the nobles he slaughtered did, while keeping all of the real power for themselves. Dorian rankled at the idea of acquiescing to such blatant corruption, so reminiscent of the man who forced his existence. The council, as it pertained to Dorian, were afraid of what he could do if he wasn't under their boots. Offering a way to keep him in check so that he might not feel their grip on his throat probably seemed like a perfect solution. It might have worked if he were more of a fool, or just less concerned with the lives of the commoners he came from. They were suggesting he could move from his easily escapable wire cage to an iron one they'd painted gold.

Palpable tension and anger radiated through the chamber, thickening the atmosphere as they processed his rejection. Nearly all of the council members sat back as if he had managed to slap them all in the face at once. Only Elmer leaned forward. Dorian couldn't help the smile that spread across his face again as he saw the contrasting movements in his audience.

"That's too bad." Venom filled Elmer's words.

The spotlights over Dorian dimmed and the pinpricks of light in the ceilings became instantly swallowed by coalescing shadows, writhing above the congregation of furious vampires. Some of the vampires who had not directly addressed him leapt from their seats, smoothly surrounding him. Looking around, Dorian felt the bubbling laughter well up in his chest, incapable of preventing it from escaping his lips. His whole body shook as he devolved into snorting laughter.

The vampires surrounding him exchanged confused glances. The true councilors varied in their responses, some stiffening with fury, others leaning forward with amusement. Dorian heard the orcish vampires humming with interest. Elmer's face colored with disgust as he looked down at Dorian.

"I fail to see why you are laughing. You are going to die here." Elmer spoke slowly, condescension oozing from each word.

Dorian shook his head, waiting. The vampires on the dais with Dorian hesitated a moment, looking to Elmer, though for guidance or confidence, he couldn't tell. Their precision disintegrated as an explosion of shadow tendrils burst from Dorian's position, blotting out every light in the grand room. Screams of confusion and rage echoed through the cavernous chamber.

They never suspected a thing.

Dorian's senses began to fade from the council chambers, noting with satisfaction as Elmer shot to his feet, eyes wide, mouth already stringing commands laced with copious cursing, the seething rage riling up the shadows that leaked from the leader's body. As he blinked away the experiences from the chamber, Dorian reoriented himself, sitting in the front hall of his main Edgefair manor. The shadow-puppetry that allowed him to attend the meeting from the relative safety of his estate took a lot out of him. He retrieved his bag and grabbed a blood pack from it, drinking as he stood. Finishing the pack, Dorian put it back in his bag, where he had all of his blood collection tools, clothes, daggers, and other needs for his journey home, and strode to the front door.

His gaze passed over the details of the place he used as his base of operations for so many years, wistful nostalgia overtaking him for a moment as he recalled the faces of the lovers who had once shared the space with him, their faces far stronger in his real home but nevertheless present. Leaving this Edgefair home for the last time, sadness battled with joy. True freedom, beyond the constraints of countless secrets, was in his grasp. But it represented the start of being hunted down by other vampires, and the end of his comfortable cowardice the moment he stepped outside.

With a steadying breath, Dorian turned and rushed out the door into the chilled night air, bursting with the scent of autumn's promised rain. Tossing one last glance at the outside of the manor over his shoulder, Dorian let the smirk he wore as armor finally slide into nothingness. Dorian allowed the solemnity of the moment, his transition from one life to the next, wash over him, feeling the fates tugging him deeper into Death's Forest. The time arrived for part two of his plan.

CHAPTER FIVE

Ruby

Strange, slithering sensations stirred Ruby from her slumber. Something crawled in her bed with her, but a blanket lay over her mind. She tried to recall what she did before bed and why she would be so incapable of opening her eyes. For the last few days, her life had been utterly predictable. She woke early in the mornings, gathering the secret grimoires, walking to the library, giving a little bit of time to studying the material she was supposed to be looking through, then spending the rest of the day looking through the forbidden texts. She would return the ones she finished, grabbing new ones to devour. In the evenings, Elder Moss would check on her, stirring Ruby's anxiety, but every day she left without incident. The consistency of her life, including staying up late reviewing grimoires, meant that she couldn't understand why she wasn't waking.

Ruby fought against the darkness sealing her eyes shut. A nagging sensation of wrongness pressed upon her, squeezing her ribs, crushing her throat. The moving, slithering tendrils of something she couldn't place dipped beneath her clothes, stilling her breath as terror welled up within her. She stopped feeling the pillow against her head, stopped feeling the blanket on her body. She stopped feeling much of anything at all. Whatever moved along her body stilled for just a second, like a rider going out for the first time taking a deep breath before they guided their winged mount to dive off a cliff and finally fly.

Choking back a scream, Ruby's mind went blank as dozens of different spots along her body lit up with excruciating pain. Her eyes finally shot open, only to see a different darkness undulating unnaturally. The slithering wrongness that disturbed her sleep pierced her skin, wriggling into her flesh, drawing a ragged, raw scream from her lips at last. And she kept screaming. The moving shadows revealed flashes of her bedroom. Ruby couldn't keep a coherent line of thought.

Her own screams echoed in her ears and a part of her wondered if she really screamed at all. Maybe she just thought she was screaming. Maybe her screams were a hallucination brought on by the pain. Or maybe whatever attacked her dampened them to all but her own ears. Ruby didn't know, couldn't know. Writhing in agony, she knew only one thing.

I am going to die.

Ruby couldn't hear anything above her own screams. Her eyes darted around, noting the thinning tendrils. The tendrils drilling into her skin began to coil around her internal organs, squeezing and moving and stabbing. Raw throat giving out, her relentless screams lost volume. Others' shouts became audible.

Golden-white light surrounded her, the sight briefly welcome before the sensation settled in. Burning. Ruby crashed to her bed and bounced onto the floor as the tendrils attaching themselves to her reacted to the light. Frantically, they sought purchase in her body, the light magic enveloping her like cleansing fire. Only she wasn't cleansed. Her broken skin knitting back together could not stop the agony. The light burned too much. Voicelessly, she begged the unknown caster to stop.

When they stopped at last, Ruby lay in a heap on her floor, screams subsiding into broken sobs, the pain lingering despite being healed. The shadows hiding within her body stilled. Ruby fought to catch her breath, unable to focus on the voices in her room. She felt brittle, down to her bones, as she shook. Her lungs were still burning.

Eventually looking up, Ruby saw Violetta and Elder Moss standing over her. The doorway filled with the faces of the others who lived in her building, all of them bearing the same serious, measured expressions. Violetta and Elder Moss were discussing the events, neither sparing her a glance.

"Yes, as I said, I heard the screams and came rushing. When I opened the door, one of those tendrils ended up catching me a little, but it was nothing to heal. I left to retrieve one of the elders and of course ran into you." Violetta explained, her voice so calm that Ruby might have mistaken it for bored.

"Yes, my insomnia seems to have helped matters here tonight. Wandering the grounds, I heard the screams and came rushing to render aid as necessary. It is good I did so. I will need to wake the elders and we will convene an emergency meeting of the entire coven. Ensure she is there in half an hour. Don't bother getting her changed or cleaned up. We ought to show the coven the full extent of what has occurred here." Elder Moss swept from the room, her steps smooth, showing little urgency despite the tight schedule she had set for the coven meeting.

Elder Moss didn't even look at me once before she left...

Violetta looked down at her, face unchanging as she helped Ruby to sit against her bed. As Violetta cocked her head to the side, the dim light in the room emphasized a rosiness to her coppery brown skin, complimenting the purple eyes and hair she'd been named for. Ruby imagined her fellow witch's portrait, painted in the style of the regular humans, if taken that very moment. Chastising herself for her constant need to observe beauty in the world, Ruby turned her efforts to standing.

After commanding the observers to go ahead, Violetta helped Ruby stand, offering her an arm to lean on. Ruby hobbled along beside Violetta, who showed no indication of the concern, or even annoyance, one might expect at Ruby's slow pace. Glancing at Violetta from the corner of her eye, Ruby noted that she presented herself as neutrally as always, unmoved by suffering or waiting.

Violetta is the perfect modern witch...

The coven meeting hall filled quickly, a seat prepared for Ruby directly before the elders, who waited behind their long table on the raised dais. Sitting in the center as head of the Edgefair elders, Elder Moss maintained perfect serenity despite the grim circumstances. Each second waiting for the meeting to begin put Ruby more on edge. Something would have to be done with her, but what?

They were all there to decide exactly that, but Ruby couldn't take her attention off the elders. Only Elder Moss would meet her gaze. A familiar unease told Ruby that, somehow, she'd disappointed her elder once again. Worry lanced her as she considered why. Maybe whatever happened to her was because of those forbidden texts. Maybe Elder Moss did know of them and Ruby disappointed her by failing a test. Maybe she ruined her life when she'd discovered that secret door.

Gods... what is happening to me? Why is it happening? What will they do with me? Oh gods... Am I keeping my face neutral enough?

The meeting convened after an eternity, with a brief explanation of events by Elder Moss and Violetta. Requested to stand, Ruby showed the assembled witches her bloodied night clothes. Her night clothes were a tattered mess of scratchy, beige material with whole sections missing. The coven-assigned pajamas were so nightmarishly miserable that Ruby felt relieved to have even less of it on her skin, even in the cold meeting hall.

"Clearly and without reservation, I tell you: Ruby has been cursed by a vampire," Elder Moss announced.

Ruby's brain stuttered over the statement, confusion and shock warring for supremacy over her mind. Questions flooded the room as nearly everyone clambered to understand. Elder Moss's scanning perusal of the meeting hall emphasized a strange light in her eyes, fully in her element. Elder Moss had always thrived in her role as leader of the coven. What greater expression of that leadership could there be?

Silencing the congregation, Elder Moss held up a hand and spoke, "I understand you all have many questions. I will endeavor to answer them all in a concise fashion, though please forgive me if I ramble on. I observed this attack on young Ruby here carefully as I worked to contain the issue and heal her. The attack was one of shadows."

Ruby waited with baited breath, the crowd around her doing the same, when Elder Moss paused to let it sink in. Taking her time to scan the room, Elder Moss's inspection locked on Ruby.

"The shadows, as we know, are the realm of the vampires. Their insidious powers can take time to assault a victim. I believe we all know that a human assaulted Ruby several days ago. What you may not have heard is that this human wore a vampire's enchanted ring. The jail took charge of the ring, but I would not be surprised to find it has conveniently gone missing."

Murmurs of aggression towards the bloodsuckers began to cycle through the coven behind her. Ruby tried to ignore them, failing to see how Elder Moss figured it out so quickly.

"Furthermore, Ruby lost a great deal of blood throughout the town as she accompanied the rest of her patrol group to lead the man to jail. Vampires often need their victim's blood to enact their disgusting curses. It is, therefore, my belief that Ruby was the target of a vampire, who has cursed her to suffer their shadows within her body. As I healed her and sought to dispel this most vile curse, I noticed that it did not flee. It burrowed, hiding within the confines of her flesh. Even now, you can feel the corruption of the shadows, can you not, Ruby?"

"Yes," Ruby croaked painfully.

"What will we do?" one of the elders asked with alarm.

It took Ruby a moment to place her as Elder Marigold. She had never sounded so concerned, but almost none of the elders were acting with their usual calm detachment. Only Elder Moss seemed unaffected. A chorus of the other elders chimed in with their own takes on the situation.

"We cannot allow this to spread to the rest of the coven."

"What if the vampires decide to do this to more of us? What will we do?"

"How do we discourage future attempts? We must ensure something happens to prevent the vampires from deciding this is a good tactic to use against us!"

"We must prevent future witches from suffering this same fate by any means necessary."

On and on, they spoke over each other, posing unanswered questions, volleying concerns over Elder Moss's head, ignoring Ruby sitting right before them. None of them offered solutions. None of them suggested calming down or considering things more rationally. Their panic, counter to the teachings she'd grown up with, infected the rest of the crowd. Most stood from their chairs, pacing or forming smaller discussion groups. Ruby felt their scrutiny boring into her back as she sat, listening to everyone discuss her fate without her.

Ruby's heart squeezed with more than the anxiety the discussion produced. That darkness, the shadows, stirred within her, her terror rising with their increasing activity. They squeezed her heart, twisted her guts, compressed her lungs. She sought Elder Moss's gaze for comfort, only to feel lanced by the inexplicable impression of glee in the elder's eyes.

No! No, that can't be right. Elder Moss cares about me. At least a little. Why else would she spend so much time trying to fix a failure like me? She must want to see me push through the pain and suffering to greater heights as a witch.

Spikes of shadow suddenly burst from Ruby's torso in all

directions, sending nearby witches scrambling to get away. Alarmed shrieks filled the chamber, the shadow spikes shooting into the ground beneath her and tossing her into the air. She tried to scream, her voice still broken, as tears streamed from her eyes. Her body, like a puppet dangling from a single string, jostled about as spikes exited and re-entered her body. The shadows healed the broken skin upon reentry, only to break her anew. The seconds dragged on in agony.

More golden-white light surrounded her, sending the shadows retreating with the same burning pain as before. Falling into a heap on the slick floor, Ruby looked around. The wood floors, normally pale beige like everything else in their compound, were coated in slippery red. She'd been turned around, somehow, to face the rest of the coven. Horror, disgust, and even anger looked back at her. It was the most emotion she'd ever seen other witches show. Only Violetta remained as neutral as they were supposed to be. Vanella looked angry. Juniper wore his revulsion plainly. Ruby didn't know what to think of it all as she turned to face the elders again.

All of them were on their feet, looking down at her. Most showed concern or some other strange sadness on their faces, as if looking at a dead woman walking. Elder Moss, however, held the same expression as before, her eyes appearing lit from within. Ruby looked around for the chair she'd been in, only to discover its scattered remains. As a result, she remained sitting in the pool of her own blood.

"Thank you, esteemed Elders, for your aid." Ruby hoped she chose her words wisely.

Her statement broke the astonished crowd's silence, bringing an onslaught of praise for the swift, masterful response of the elders. They left a wide berth around Ruby as they profusely complimented the elders on their ability to contain such danger. Her last vestiges of hope were drained by the others moving around her like her curse might be contagious and infect them.

As she teetered on the brink of despair in her loneliness, Ruby felt the shadows within her stirring again. A bolt of unwelcome clarity shot through her: her emotions might play some role in the curse. With practiced ease, Ruby stuffed the rejection and her sadness down further, choosing to ignore it. It would come out, eventually, she knew, but control should be maintained as much as possible. That kept her safe. That was how she always kept herself safe.

All she'd secretly read on the witches that came before ate at her resolve. Ruby only half-listened to the lobbied suggestions on her future, trying to recall what she'd read and what might be relevant to her curse. Some witches of old dabbled in curses. Perhaps she had accidentally cursed herself, though that didn't quite make sense. A vampire must be involved to get the shadows to act upon her in such a way. None of the witches of old used the shadows. They certainly could dabble in darkness magic, but the shadows were the purview of the vampires exclusively. The schools of magic were similar, but fundamentally different for one major reason. Vampiric shadows were alive.

The shadows within her behaved with enough autonomy that Ruby could be sure that Elder Moss must have been correct in her assertion that the curse could only be vampiric in origin. Shadows listened only to the commands of vampires, with each possessing their own, living within their bodies. Ruby didn't know how vampires came to have the shadows within them, but she knew that they were a means of magic used by the bloodsuckers. They did little but benefit the immortal beings they inhabited.

Vanella's voice rose above the rest, addressing the room and snatching Ruby's attention, "This is all well and good to discuss until our heads turn purple, but we must remember who and what we are dealing with! Ruby may have been born a witch, but let us all acknowledge that she has always struggled with the tenets of our calling! Now, she is afflicted with this curse. Perhaps it is the divine's way of punishing her for failing in her calling! This would be bad enough, but to consider the danger this curse poses to the rest of us?! I saw what it did, and we can see the evidence in the gouges taken from the wood of this most sacred place for our order. It was the power of the vampires. That should tell us enough about what we must do! We cannot risk her endangering us all!"

"What are you suggesting?" Elder Moss asked, her voice perfectly neutral, her face still unchanged, unmoved.

"She must be killed, to protect the coven!" Vanella proclaimed.

Her proclamation split the room. The elders all remained silent, though Ruby could not tell if it was because they were contemplating the situation, or if they had already made up their minds. The rest of the coven erupted into shouts on either side of the issue. Some vehemently agreed with Vanella, who stood with gleaming, metallic golden skin in the soft light of the meeting hall, not looking around at the chaos her statement made, but glaring at the elders. The other half of the coven screamed back that Ruby may have been a failure of a witch, but she was still a witch and member of their coven. It wasn't her fault she had been cursed by a vile leech, and they needed to consider how to manage future curses through managing her.

Violetta raised her voice as she walked to the front of the room, standing before the elders but facing the coven as she spoke, "Please, everyone, let us remember ourselves and not give in to fear at this time. We must think of this rationally. Obviously, this curse afflicting Ruby is a danger to us all. I would never ignore or argue against that. But, as others have said, she is still technically one of us. This curse might become a regular tactic by vampires, should they have the chance. In that case, I believe it would be prudent for us to keep Ruby locked safely away from us while we experiment to discover ways to rid her of this affliction. That way, we might prevent unnecessary loss of witch life."

Her words were perfectly measured, each calm syllable borne of rationality and logic. It broke Ruby's heart more. Violetta, proving what she'd known deep down, exemplified how little Ruby mattered. She would not be kept alive for mercy or sentimentality, but as a means to an end. Violetta would keep Ruby alive and in the compound so that she could be the object of investigation, and her suffering could protect the actually important members of the coven. Violetta's solution would be a special sort of solitary retreat. Ruby hurried past the thought, knowing better than to dwell on it, despite each statement being a gut punch.

I cannot feel this pain right now or the curse will act out again.

The hits kept coming as Juniper's voice cut through the air, "I agree with Vanella. We cannot allow this curse to fester in our coven. We would risk it consuming us all."

Ruby's gaping attention shot to him. She saw his clenched fist, the sepia-brown skin becoming startlingly pale at the knuckles. Instantly, she knew that, to him, she was the curse that should be eradicated. All because they had enjoyed a lustful time together when they were younger. He didn't even know about all of her lustful indulgences over the years, but the fact that he gave into temptation by pursuing her in the first place damned her in his view. Ruby hadn't even initially wanted him. She knew that her urges weren't right in the eyes of their doctrines, which forbade romance and intimacy, so she tried to avoid infecting him as well. He relentlessly insisted that it would be okay.

Now, he blamed her entirely. It became her fault that he ever strayed from the correct path of a witch. It was her fault that he dealt with the shame of that knowledge. Her fault. Always her fault. For him to be absolved, she couldn't live. If she lived, she'd be kept in confinement for the coven to poke and prod as they saw fit, attempting to cure her in any number of ways, with no regard for her mental state or happiness. But Ruby didn't want to die, either. No matter how bad it was, she lived through the solitary retreat once. She promised herself then that nothing would be able to force her into that horrible place again. She would never accept death.

Death or life in captivity.

According to the coven, either option held merit and bore consideration. The discussion went around in circles, the same points reiterated over and over. Ruby retreated into herself, knowing that if she left the meeting hall alive, she couldn't hesitate to take matters into her own hands.

Calling for calm, Elder Moss announced that no decision could be reached at that time, since the coven would need to be in agreement on either course of action. She emphasized that either way would be a deviation from the ways the coven treated each other, leading to a new precedent. The time wouldn't be that night, as they would all need rest to think clearly and come to a consensus. The elder implied that they would reconvene the following afternoon. Witches filed out of the meeting hall dissatisfied while Ruby held back.

"Am I free to go bathe and return to my room?" Ruby asked when only the elders remained.

"Yes, Ruby. I apologize to leave you in this limbo, but know that we will do what is right for the coven." Elder Moss nodded as she spoke.

Inclining her head in respect, Ruby slowly left the meeting hall alone.

I'm sorry, Elder Moss... I've made my own decision.

The others essentially disappeared from the grounds. She assumed they rushed back to their rooms promptly.

Hurrying through washing herself off, Ruby winced at the icy water, scrubbing away the drying blood. The disgusting process completed, Ruby returned to her destroyed room. As quietly as she could, Ruby picked through the remains of her furniture, finding the hidden outfit she used to blend in with humans, with the cloak and hair covering she used to use to avoid detection. She dressed in a fresh set of winter robes to keep warm. Grabbing the bag with the forbidden grimoires, Ruby stuffed her soap, some towels, her spare nightclothes and human outfit, and other miscellaneous needs in, thankful for its spatial enchantment. Before leaving, Ruby put her silver dagger in her bag with its thigh sheath. Though unseemly for a witch to need a physical weapon, when her light magic never grew strong enough to fight a vampire, physical combat became her only choice.

Ruby scurried through the night to the communal provisions building, stocking up on travel provisions and water. Creeping to the back fence of the compound, which protected the coven from Death's Forest and the beasts within, Ruby made a beeline for the small gate she knew would lock behind her. Terror threatened her composure at what she would find in the unnatural woods which blocked all sunlight from entering. The forest bred unspeakable beasts that would relish in tearing her limb from limb. It always intimidated and intrigued her. She never wanted to enter it alone, but she didn't see a better choice when the humans would not accept her either. She hesitated, her hand on the gate, when she heard a shout behind her.

Light magic extended out in orbs around the group that yelled at her, revealing Vanella, Juniper, and several others who touted the benefits of killing her. Ruby felt her stomach plummet as they focused on her, the light from their magic extending just enough to illuminate her. Without another word, they fired their light magic at her, missing by mere inches in all directions, as if boxing her in.

Violetta came up behind the group, shouting to be heard over the barked orders of Vanella and the enthusiasm of the others. Ruby didn't have the time to listen. She ran through the gate, avoiding another lobbed bolt of light magic that held such power, it seared the wood behind her. She heard them pursuing her. Looking back just before she entered the eternal darkness of Death's Forest, Ruby saw that she only had a few hours before sunrise.

That won't matter in Death's Forest, even if I live that long.

CHAPTER SIX

Dorian

Despite the hours left until sunrise, Dorian settled into one of his many prepared hiding spots in Death's Forest. The low branch offered a wide view of the surrounding wood, but the remarkable discomfort couldn't be ignored.

I should figure out how to rest anyways.

Sunlight didn't penetrate the canopy in that part of Death's Forest, allowing vampiric hunters to pursue him day and night. Having laid false tracks through the forest near Edgefair, Dorian thought it wise to rest and give the council hunters time to follow his wild-goose chase.

Discovery remained a risk as a result of the enchantments on his hiding spot. No simple survey could penetrate the illusion of empty space where his body sat against the trunk. No sound escaped his hiding spot. The danger came from attempts to pierce the protective bubble, where an unnatural rebuffing or dispersing would give him away. Thus, Dorian needed to remain alert.

Flashes of light caught Dorian's eye from the direction of the witch's compound. He angled his head to get a better look. The witches were not known to send out patrols into the forest, but he always took more cautions near their compound. Witches had become murderous with vampires in the last 200 years. Dorian knew it must have something to do with that damned king's ascent to power. It annoyed the M'lvia's revenge out of him whenever he recalled what witches once were in Vlideron, what they could still be. But no, they'd become absurd, disappointing monsters in their own right.

Regardless of his opinions on their newfound way of life, Dorian knew that they were a danger to him now. Their adherence to light magic proved a decent counter to his shadows, leaving him vulnerable to their attacks if they caught him off guard. They were, in that moment, more dangerous to him than the hunters pursuing him. Dorian zeroed in on the light, curiosity warring with a desire to run and keep as far away from the hassle as possible. The witches were shooting off orbs of light magic at something, but he couldn't quite yet make out what he saw.

Seconds ticked by, the lights growing closer as Dorian began to make out details. Figures were running towards him, one far ahead of the others, who were the ones firing off their spells. The figure in front began to come into focus, leaving him more confused and shocked than he thought possible after over 500 years alive.

She's a witch?

Unnatural, deep crimson hair arranged in long, thin braids flew around her head as she repeatedly looked back at her pursuers. Her skin reminded him of the polished smoky quartz he bought for Leandra; the glowing shade of cool-toned brown captivated him as Leandra had. The drab, beige robes she wore did her no favors, from the way they were getting caught up in her legs to the way the color drained some of the glow from her skin.

Without his permission, Dorian's body leaned forward to look more intently at the approaching witch. He couldn't quite tell from his elevated position, but he would guess she only stood a few inches shorter than him, her body invisible beneath the loose, heavy clothes. From the speed and power with which she ran, Dorian surmised that her body would show impressive physical strength. Her frame, though smaller than his own, was not dainty. Her frantic movements slowed her, but he guessed that if she were calmer, she would be faster. Most reacted to being hunted down the way a rabbit reacted to the sudden appearance of a panther. Sheer panic.

The pursuers of the red-haired witch became visible, shouts tossed between them as they scrambled to keep up. None showed quite the same athleticism as the witch they targeted. Dorian wondered why such a disparity existed. Though sloppy in her rush to get away, the red-haired witch gained distance on her pursuers as she made a beeline for his tree.

Concerns stacked as orbs of light flew wildly off their mark. One of those errant orbs might hit his hidden barrier, revealing his location and turning their full attention on him. He slowly eased himself up to a crouch on the branch, preparing to either attack or run. He didn't know if the red-haired one would join in on an attack if they inadvertently revealed him, but he knew the others would turn their focus on a vampire so near to their compound if they found him out.

Dorian looked at the emotional energy of each approaching witch. The crimson witch, running for her life, glowed with a mass of emotions, barely kept contained within her body, but he spied a strange swirling darkness there that looked like vampiric shadows. That couldn't be possible; she was still as much a human as any witch could be considered.

His ears perked up as snippets of the pursuers' arguments became clear. Dorian felt taken aback by what he heard.

"She is still one of us and we should be waiting for the decision of the elders, made based on reason with our entire coven."

Despite her volume, Dorian could not view the purple-haired one as shouting. She was too empty. The hairs on the back of his neck stood up as he took in the details of her. She formed no emotions. Not the common, muted suppression that witches adorned in recent years; she represented a true absence. She was not emotionless the way some people were accused of it, their expressions subdued and straightforward to the point of discomfort for some less direct others. No, this witch with purple hair produced no emotions at all. Dorian only glimpsed such an absence once before, when he encountered a truly heartless assassin, who told him they had never experienced any emotions. They were, therefore, adept at their job because they felt no qualms about it in any way. They felt no fear to stop them or make them hesitate. They felt no anger at obvious provocations attempting to goad them into mistakes. They felt no love to force attachments that would only hinder them. Nothing. That was the void Dorian saw in the witch advocating to stop the chase.

"Don't be a fool, Violetta! We must get her now! She is too dangerous to us all to be left alive! What if this damned curse corrupts her and she returns to the coven and slaughters us all?!"

The golden-haired witch with matching golden skin screamed her response, rage and indignation swirling around her, let loose more than most witches allowed. Taking a quick count, Dorian counted seven witches actively hunting the apparently cursed woman, and one extra trying to talk the rest of them out of it. She was doing a piss-poor job, in Dorian's opinion. If she really wanted the crimson witch to be allowed to live, why just weakly raise her monotone voice rather than actually do something to stop them?

That doesn't make sense.

A male witch with dull green curls shouted his agreement, "She isn't even a good enough witch to be among us anyways! If she had any decency, she would stop running and accept what needs to be done for the good of the rest of us!"

Dorian rankled at the words the man shouted. It had little to do with the ever-more intriguing red witch and everything to do with the man's choice of words as he advocated for murdering someone. While Dorian had murdered countless people in his centuries, he knew what it looked like when a man just wanted to kill a woman he resented. He knew the words they used and the tone they took. He knew the justifications such men made. Further, Dorian found it ridiculous that the man could fault the woman for simply wanting to survive. What was so wrong with wanting to live?

Having chosen the extended life of vampirism, Dorian knew he may be biased. Regardless, mercy danced beyond his reach for anyone faulting someone for the natural desire to live. Dorian began to actively root for the crimson witch to make a clean escape from fools like the green-haired one who actually just hated her.

The fury, lust, and resentment swirling around the green-haired man were nearly palpable from a hundred yards away. The combination felt somehow both surprising and expected. Dorian was surprised to find that a witch would experience such lust and depth of emotion, but it made sense that their doctrine would lead a man experiencing lust to decide he hated the woman who inspired that feeling. The last Dorian had heard about the witches, they lived celibate lives and demanded the entirety of their kind be walled off in their covens except during their excessive surveillance of commoners. People raised with such repression surely suffered greatly when wayward thoughts intruded upon them.

None of that excused the man in Dorian's view. It was pathetic to take one's own feelings and repressed difficulties out on someone else. He couldn't blame the man for lusting after the red-haired witch, but that didn't give him the right to demonize her. Parsing out what he could, that seemed to be the reality playing out among the witches drawing precariously close. Dorian pulled his shadows free, positioning them to cushion his fall if he needed to jump from his tree swiftly.

For a moment, it looked like they might pass right under his tree. Crimson witch was making good ground on the arguing and frustrated pursuers, and she would have been able to flee past his tree easily. But one of the orbs of light glanced her shoulder, sending her tumbling to the forest floor with a high-pitched cry. Dorian's eyes narrowed as she hit the ground a few feet away. Light magic healed mortals; it never should have hurt a witch. Burning away disease and injury, light magic left stinging in its wake, working quickly.

For vampires, the light magic burned without healing. Vampiric shadows sat between light and dark magic, but were more closely aligned with dark magic. The light would cast shadows, but also disperse them. As a result, the shadows within vampires ensured that the healing burn of light magic didn't heal them at all. It just burned. As Dorian watched the witch below, writhing in pain as she struggled to crawl away from the others, he realized she simply burned too.

Those nebulous shadows in the weaving emotions and magic of her body were not a simple curse. They were vampiric shadows. Dorian's mind raced, wondering how that could have happened, and how in the names of the gods she still lived. It seemed impossible. While no one really knew how the shadows came to the bodies of new vampires, all knew that they did not simply wander the world on their own. Some magical process occurred during the transformations that drew the shadows, made them alive, and bound them to the body of a vampire.

Yet there they were, in a non-vampiric witch's body.

Impossible.

Her face tipped up as she crawled along the ground, her will to survive pulsing through the air around her in equal measure to her pain and terror. Her face was gently rounded, though her full lips added a touch of sharpness, the cupid's bow sharply defined. The round softness returned with her short, wide nose, and disappeared with the sharp furrow of her brows, concentration billowing from her very pores. As she got closer, Dorian thanked the way his vampiric senses enhanced his vision as he looked into her eyes. Black eyes the depth of a starless, moonless night glared at the world around her from behind deep red lashes. The juxtaposition of emotions playing through her gaze told him that she was suffering and still prepared to fight. He respected and understood that combination immediately.

The hunting witches fanned out as they caught up to her. Dorian worried about their horrible aim. If any of those attacks hit his protective bubble, he would be given away. They would notice that it dispersed against empty air. He needed to act and it had nothing to do with wanting the witch below him to survive. Nothing at all to do with the way she turned around and wobbled back to her feet, preparing to fight for her life, knowing she couldn't match the odds before her, but preparing to do it anyway. Respecting a drive to survive bore no significance in his decision.

Eight versus one. I like those odds for me, though it doesn't look like those are good odds for her.

Dorian sent thin shadow tendrils to the ground, making his descent slow, measured, silent. The witches shouted back and forth at each other, but Dorian found their chatter annoying and irrelevant. None of them addressed the woman they clearly sought to slaughter, so Dorian decided not to draw extra attention to himself by demanding they shut up. He just moved, slowly, calmly, carefully. Nearly having reached the ground, they finally began to notice him. Silence overcame the witches, their gazes morphing from murderous ecstasy to confusion, from confusion to shock, and from shock to murderous rage.

Landing directly behind the red-haired witch, Dorian noticed how long her thin braids were, landing at the top of her hips. Her body stilled as she sensed him behind her. His shadows reached out in all directions on the ground, blending in with the nearly black forest floor. Everything was dark in that portion of the forest, with the brown of the bark on the massive, wide trees nearly as blackened as the ground beneath their feet. It served perfectly to hide the moving shadows.

The witches, having turned their vicious attention on Dorian, summoned orbs of light, preparing to attack him. The purple one joined in for the first time. Dorian pulled his lips up into a vicious smile, his glee dampening as that crimson hair shifted, looking over her shoulder at him with wide, frightened eyes. He didn't drop the smile, but felt a tinge of guilt that she feared him. While he didn't know all the details, she appeared to be the victim of a wrongful pursuit. Even though he didn't care about her survival, he didn't want the witches hunting her to have the satisfaction of finishing her off.

In a flash of blinding motion, Dorian sent the crimson-haired witch off to the side, his shadows cushioning her fall only enough to ensure she didn't die, and sent the rest of the witches flying in all directions around the forest. Their fanned out positions made it easy to separate them from each other. He moved, their spells flying at random as they crashed to the forest floor and into the indestructible trees all around them.

None of their attacks landed near him, leaving him free to glide through the forest floor and reach the first of the witches he decided to kill. The man with the dull-green hair lay crumpled on the ground, having smashed against a tree before falling to the ground. He looked to be built well enough, Dorian supposed, but he was weak. As Dorian reached him, the man began to stir, groaning and wheezing. Dorian lifted him up by his throat. He tried to smack at Dorian, summoning some of the weakest offensive light magic Dorian had ever encountered. Instead of responding to the ridiculous attacks, Dorian tilted his head as he examined the man. A part of him wondered at the extent of his connection to the cursed one, but it didn't matter. A blandness suffused the repressed and angry man's brown eyes, showing no inner light even before Dorian turned him around, forced him to his knees, and snapped his neck, casually tossing his body aside.

It didn't matter how any of these witches were connected to the woman laying in a heap, surrounded by those braids of beautiful, blood-red. They endangered him.

They have to die.

CHAPTER SEVEN

Ruby

Ruby's head swam, the sensation becoming far too familiar in recent days. She winced as she opened her eyes. The darkness around her pulsed with bursts of light and swirling shadows, the movement impossible to follow. Fuzziness clouded her mind, muffling sounds. She'd been hit and knocked out entirely too much lately, it was becoming absurd. Trying to push herself up, Ruby's view adjusted to the darkness. There were some details becoming clear, but she couldn't quite tell what she was seeing.

Her eyes were not that adept in the dark, thus Ruby spent most of her journey tripping. Any details were lost to the depths around her, leaving her staring at a formless mass on the forest floor several paces away from her. She could tell it wasn't just another root, even if she struggled to identify what gave her that impression. Something stuck in her mind about that mass.

She heard shouting as she sat up. A fight had broken out. The flashes of light magic were attacks, but weren't aimed at her. Someone or something else battled her fellow coven members. Or would they be considered former coven members now? Ruby couldn't be sure. She kept staring at the heap on the ground, the color lighter than anything else around.

Except my robes... They look the same in this light...

Ruby's body stilled as her eyes rapidly glanced between her

robes and the heap on the forest floor near her. A wayward orb of light shot past her, impacting a nearby tree, giving her a brief flash of sight, revealing the truth. Juniper's body lay there, head at a strange, broken angle, and haphazardly discarded. The realization came crashing through her as the sounds became clearer and her memories sharpened from the moments before she had lost consciousness again.

That man appearing from the darkness behind me...

He was a bit taller than her and built with obvious strength, based on the way he moved, as well as the toned and compact muscles she saw from his bared arms. Black, straight hair that reached down to his sharp cheekbones and gently grazed his even sharper jawline, visible in the light of the others' readied magic. Through that light, she spotted the gleam of his red eyes. While his skin was almost the same brown as hers, his was more golden, where hers looked gray. It seemed ironic that his should look so much more full of life than hers, when the bloodsuckers only survived by the life force of others. His fangs, glinting in the limited glow, spoke perfectly to his blood-sucking nature while the taunting grin that revealed them emphasized the malice of his kind.

Then, she flew. The ground beneath her was solid stone upon waking, but she wasn't any more hurt than she'd been before. Ruby lost consciousness more from the exhaustion of exertion and the burning pain from the light Vanella flung at her than being tossed through the air, which struck her as odd since such hard ground should have injured her a great deal more. Instead, she felt as if she'd merely fallen asleep, rather than been tossed aside violently. She awoke so swiftly because her brain knew she remained in grave danger, insisting that she get up and move as quickly as possible. Witch instincts, Ruby once read, were famous for getting witches up and moving at times they shouldn't have been alive.

Those instincts might have woken her, but they couldn't get her moving as she tried to process the death of the first person she had ever been intimate with. The split second image of his features granted by the wildly flying light became instantly seared into her mind, the afterimage as clear as if she could still see him in the darkness of the forest. His eyes, sightless, gazed out in frozen horror. His crumpled body lay in a strange array of limbs set in odd directions.

A shrill cry of agony echoed through the woods, ripping Ruby's attention from the image burned into her retinas. Movement and lights rippled through the forest, the strobing lights creating the distinct impression that the man cloaked in shadows was dancing. Ruby tried to shake her head free of the image, but his graceful movements in the irregular light made the notion persistent. He moved smoothly through the ranks of the other witches, his vampiric shadows blending in with the natural shadows of the forest. Shock immobilized Ruby as she watched him strike with those fluid shadows solidifying in an instant, standing out against the natural shadows of the forest, impaling one of the others. Flashes of light revealed more bodies, the vampire having killed at least four of them already.

When the impaling shadow retreated, she watched as the 5th witch dropped dead. Ruby looked around, finding herself oddly numb at the sight of the dead witches littering the forest floor. The sight should horrify her, but she couldn't bring herself to feel much of anything for most of their deaths, standing out against her history of excessive emotions. A small, wretched part of her brain that was always whispering grew louder as she gazed at the bodies littering the forest floor. Try as she might, Ruby couldn't ignore it.

They were going to kill me. Now they're dead... and I have a chance to live.

Ruby watched as the vampire mowed down the remaining witches until just Vanella and Violetta remained. Tripping on a root, Ruby glanced down at herself, surprised to find that she'd unconsciously begun walking through the forest toward the trio. Looking back into the depths of the forest, Ruby debated running off, escaping while she had the chance. Curiosity kept her feet moving toward the vampire and her fellow witches. Stumbling around to avoid running into the body of a fallen witch, Ruby tried to summon some real care for them.

Nothing came.

Part of her wondered if the curse dampened her ability to feel empathy or compassion. Maybe it would corrupt her the way that becoming a vampire corrupted regular humans. She didn't know. Looking towards the body of Juniper, Ruby suspected that not to be the case. She was horrified to see his corpse, but she wasn't sad to see him dead. Not anymore. A few hours earlier, Ruby knew she would have been sad. As they chased her out of the compound, which she had fled to save them as much as to save herself, Ruby felt the last of her care for Juniper die. He decided she deserved to die. He was willing to murder her himself. A part of her suspected that he felt eager to do so. And why?

She represented his greatest temptation and shame. Ruby knew that was what fostered such hate in him. That she went on to sleep with humans in secret for a while after things ended with him would have driven him mad. She had seen the glares he threw her and the humans of Edgefair when any expressed physical attraction to her. Some nobles they encountered would get bold and assert their sadness over her being a witch when they wished she could join them one on one. Juniper would become furious at these interactions, blaming her as much as the humans who said such things.

That he was so quick to proclaim she needed to die because of the curse initially shocked her, but the betrayal of it all sank in while running from them. Condemning her to die because of the curse, something completely out of her control, was unforgivable. She had never been a good enough witch, but she didn't deserve death for being a nuisance-level problem. She tried her best her whole life. She did everything ever asked of her to the best of her ability. She never hurt anyone or complained when she suffered the consequences of those actions, only hurting herself in the end. The second they could discard her, though, they were ready to do so. She was a troublemaker because she was curious and struggled to suppress her feelings.

Guilt crushed her even as she felt fury for the way she was being tossed aside and treated as though she were nothing. She was still wrong. Still being a bad witch. She had always been a poor excuse for a witch. Ruby didn't know why the witches changed and dedicated themselves to light magic. That lack of knowledge left her unsure of how much of a failure she proved to be for never embracing the light as she should have. The idea that she would never succeed as a light witch slammed into her just as another bolt of light slammed into a tree, missing the vampire it had been aimed at. None of it changed how she viewed herself for her failures and incapability of doing what she should do. In the face of their betrayal, it left her all the more confused, guilty, and furious.

She bathed in confusion as to how they could ignore her status as a witch, just like them. How could they so quickly discard her as one of their coven? Guilt plagued Ruby as she stared at the bodies and couldn't summon grief for them. If she had the strength or knowledge, she might have killed them herself just to get away and survive. That surely made her a monster, just like their actual killer. How could she blame them for discarding her when she showed herself to be so capable of disregarding the weight of their lives? But she remained furious. Ruby could feel the rage stirring the shadows in her body, leaving her uncomfortable and even angrier. They put her in this position emotionally. She would be alone and suffering in the woods enough without the posse of witches hunting her straight to their doom.

The vampire might have just satisfied himself with killing her, had they not chosen to slaughter her themselves. They would still be alive, safe in the compound, sleeping in their beds or rising to greet the sun in a little while. They wouldn't be crumpled, broken, bloody corpses on the forest floor. The fact that they wanted to kill her is what got them killed. No way existed around it. So Ruby found that she just couldn't summon genuine care for the fact that they were just corpses.

Inspecting the combatants ahead, Ruby watched the fighting slow. Vanella and Violetta stood nearer to her, lights prepared over their heads, illuminating the forest around them, sending dancing shadows all around as they faced the bloodsucker. He stood opposite the duo of capable witches and Ruby got a better look at him. Walking forward to stand behind the others, still able to see between them, Ruby's gaze zeroed in on every detail of the murderer she had unwittingly led the others to. His skin glistened with unexpected sweat and the blood of her fellows. Streaks of dirt marred his bare arms. Ruby's mouth went dry as she noted the powerful musculature of those arms, their strength evident. His broad shoulders heaved with every breath as his gaze flicked between the two witches he fought.

That feral gaze intensified the instant it landed on Ruby. His taunting grin, still present from when she first saw him, widened slightly. Confusion flooded Ruby as she tried to tear her attention away from him, to look anywhere else. Instead, she thought of the blood she had shed days before in town, of how she couldn't tear her eyes away. He was like that blood she couldn't look away from. Revulsion warred with an instinctual sensation that welled up within her. She should hate vampires. She had to hate that he'd killed her fellow witches. What kind of irredeemable monster would she be if she didn't?

Ruby latched on to her obligatory hatred as she tried to look away. A flicker of fear passed through her, worrying he may be placing her in a trance. Despite how much she wanted to believe that explained why she couldn't look away, she suspected other feelings were involved that would prove her a hopeless wretch.

"What are you doing near the witch's compound, leech?" Vanella boldly broke the silence that had fallen over the paused battle.

"Nothing to do with your lot."

Ruby wondered how true that could be. What other reason could a vampire have for hiding out in the woods near their coven besides assaulting the witches? Either they were missing a great deal of information, or he could be lying. Something in his demeanor said he wasn't lying, but she couldn't be sure. Vampires were known to be slippery and devious.

"HA! As if we could believe that!"

"Believe what you want. It's the truth. I wouldn't have even bothered with you if you hadn't chased that poor lady right to me."

Poor lady... Me? Is this vampire... pitying me?

"POOR LADY?! She is a vile excuse for a witch and needs to be put down!" Vanella's voice came out hoarse with her rage.

"Vanella, let us remember that she is one of ours and we have greater concerns than her curse right now."

Ruby listened to Violetta's way of rebuking Vanella's outburst numbly.

"Oh please, don't start in with that again," Vanella scoffed, and Ruby could practically hear the other witch's golden eyes rolling, "I don't see how you don't understand the importance of dealing with her now! This leech be damned! We need to deal with her!"

"I just think we could study her curse. What if someone else is cursed like this in our coven? We should test her to see how we might help others."

"Testing, dealing, testing, dealing. Neither of you seem to give a damn what *she* needs. Neither of you are talking about curing her or helping her or fucking caring about her at all. Is the famed compassion of the witches just for show then?"

Ruby's mind stuttered as she processed the bloodsucker's words. Was he advocating for her? Expressing confusion at their lack of care for her?

No, that couldn't be. Surely, he merely took the opportunity to poke at witches and throw us off.

"What would you know?! You're just some leech who drains people to keep up your pathetic survival, serving no purposes but your own!" Vanella screamed back at him.

Violetta nodded her agreement with Vanella on that matter.

The vampire looked between the two of them for a moment, laughing as his gaze settled back on Ruby, "They care absolutely nothing for you. Do you care about them?"

Ruby couldn't speak. He perceived things accurately, no matter how much she wished he hadn't. In mere seconds, he had realized that the others didn't care about her at all. What would he do if he found out that she felt so conflicted about them? Would he taunt her with their deaths? Would he lay the blame for it all at her feet? Would he agree that she should have died if he found out the truth about her?

"Ruby is a witch. She knows that we are not to form personal bonds amongst ourselves, and despite her many failings, I trust that she has succeeded in this regard. This is why my companions have struggled with remembering that she is to be treated as the elders command. Not as our whims might have it," Violetta dutifully responded.

Each word drove another knife in Ruby's heart. She had actually failed in that regard. She used to care about everyone else. Sadly, no one cared for her in return. On that front, Violetta was completely correct. She didn't personally care about Ruby either.

"Please, that's not why no one cares that she is supposed to be a witch too. It's because she is a failure. I doubt she would even be cursed right now if she hadn't been such a worthless excuse for a witch."

"Ruby," the vampire drug out, tasting the sound of her name as if tasting a delicacy. "Those are some strong words to describe someone. Worthless. Failure. Saying no one cares about her. My, that just seems so cruel. I suppose I knew that your famed compassion was nothing more than a facade," the vampire shook his head slightly, stare still trained on Ruby.

Ruby felt stuck considering how this bloodsucker seemed more interested in how they treated her than about what was wrong with her. Surely he simply sought the chance to undermine the others, mess with their heads, but it messed with hers more. He professed so much more concern about her, even in his flippant manner, than anyone else ever had. Glancing in the direction of Juniper's body, Ruby remembered how much of herself she gave to connect with him, and how little her desire for connection meant to him in the end. None of them had ever cared about her, except probably Elder Moss.

The teachings they had all grown up with never stuck with her the way they should have. If they had, she wouldn't have cared so much for them. She wouldn't be feeling a pit in her stomach at the way Vanella itched to kill her. She wouldn't be drowning from Violetta's callous disregard. She wouldn't have considered what the void of death might have been like when Juniper cast her aside. Most of all, she wouldn't be contemplating how much nicer a vampire might be to her, despite his horrific nature. That must make her a beast as well. A beast and a fool. She would still die when the battle concluded. By Vanella, the vampire, or the curse.

The curse assaulted her in an instant. Shadows burst forth all around her, shredding the new set of robes and sending her blood flying all around. In the blink of an eye, Ruby managed a single scream before Vanella tossed her light at Ruby instead of the vampire. The impact sent her flying back, twisting through the air before the ground greeted her again. Ruby barely escaped injury to her face as she landed, still conscious and facing the ongoing conflict. The pain bordered on overwhelming, but she desperately needed to remain conscious, if only to know her killer.

Choosing to focus on Ruby's curse cost Vanella. Ruby didn't see the movement, but she saw the vampire suddenly appear behind Vanella. His hand captured the witch, holding her in the air by her throat before any of them could process what happened. Shock enveloped Ruby as she watched while Vanella began to beat on the vampire's arm. She didn't even summon her magic in attempts to counter him. Ruby wondered if Vanella panicked and forgot that she could.

Ruby couldn't bring herself to feel too bad about Vanella's predicament. The light she had tossed at Ruby could have been lethal if the shadows of the curse had not absorbed so much of it outside of her body. No healing intent suffused it, despite the inherent properties of light magic. Deadly purpose suffused the light that struck her, chilling her to the bone even as her flesh cooked from the burned shadows returning to hide within her body. The lack of concern Ruby felt for her fellow witch had her stomach churning, however. Shame flooded her system once again as Ruby reminded herself that, according to her upbringing, she should care about Vanella in that moment. A good witch would. A good witch wouldn't have so much emotional connection to the others, but would be ready to fight to the death to protect her fellow witch.

Knowledge that she remained a colossal failure of a witch in the eyes of her coven crashed in on Ruby as she watched, knowing that if she really wanted to save Vanella, she could stand and fight. She would surely die, but she could do it. She just didn't want to, deep down. She didn't want to die for the woman who attempted to kill her.

Does that really make me so bad?

"It's astounding to me how little you respond." The vampire directed his statement at Violetta, though his disdainful smirk didn't leave Vanella's darkening face.

He choked Vanella, just enough to keep her off the ground and struggling, but not quite enough to kill her quickly. Ruby didn't know how she could tell the difference in her weakened state, the area now only lit by Violetta's suspended magic.

"I am a witch. We do not dally with emotional outbursts," Violetta responded coolly.

"Ahh but that's not totally true, now is it? This one," he gestured with Vanella's body, the motion drawing Ruby's attention to his flexed arm muscles, a gleam of blood streaked across the bicep, "has a lot of emotional outbursts. And Ruby," he paused on the sound of her name again, "looks quite emotional as well. No, I have seen hundreds of witches over the years. I've seen plenty in the last few centuries since you all became a little weird. You are a unique case. Tell me, have you ever felt anything? At all?"

Violetta remained silent. Ruby looked to her, noting the way she reacted, or rather, didn't react. Her face remained completely still, in the same expression she always wore. Ruby wondered if she was calculating what to say in response, since it didn't seem as though she had any emotional response to the statement.

"Tell you what, if you can honestly tell me that you have ever cared about anything or anyone, I will let you all go free. Tell me you have cared about something. Someone. Anything. You cared about an animal or some clothing or a book. M'lvia's revenge, give me something you disliked. Give me anything you had a genuine emotional response to, and I'll let you live."

Ruby looked at the vampire, perplexed at the low bar for survival. Violetta never violated the tenants of their order, but surely she had felt something. Everyone had emotional responses to things they liked or disliked. Maybe she could even say she would get annoyed at Ruby. There had to be something there.

Silence.

Violetta looked deep in thought when Ruby turned to examine her. Time kept ticking. Violetta kept silent. Seeing the gears turning in Violetta's head, Ruby was stunned into silence. Violetta was truly the perfect witch of modern Vlideron. She couldn't think of anything she honestly felt something about. That idea sounded so foreign and strange to Ruby.

How has she never cared about anything? Never liked anything? How could she not point to anything in nearly 30 years of life and express a true response to it? It makes no sense. How could anyone exist like that?

Without warning, the vampire turned Vanella around and snapped her neck, letting her body fall to the forest floor. Vanella lacked even the opportunity to cry out in surprise before she became another crumpled corpse littering the ground.

"Once again, you felt nothing."

It wasn't a question, but a statement. The vampire scrutinized Violetta, his head cocked to the side. Was that disapproval on his face? Ruby didn't know, but her odds of dying by the vampire's hand had just gone up. Violetta blankly observed the falling of Vanella's body, her own head turning to the side in what might have been mild acknowledgment.

"I don't know what to tell you, leech," Violetta responded in her usual monotone, sending her own light magic at the vampire.

The light dispersed as it hit the tree behind him. The last thing Ruby saw before the light faded was the vampire appearing behind Violetta in the same moment, ripping her throat out with a shadow-cloaked hand. Her fate sealed, Ruby allowed herself to be enveloped by the darkness of the forest, then the darkness of unconsciousness. She would be killed by the vampire, but she didn't have to be awake for that.

CHAPTER EIGHT

Dorian

Stopping at each of the bodies, Dorian took care to cover all traces of his involvement in their deaths, ripping greater wounds to hide bite marks in one victim and tearing more at the flesh of others to distract from the clean punctures his shadows caused. Finishing with that, he considered Ruby.

Dorian sighed as he looked at the unconscious woman.

I can't in good conscience leave her here with these bodies.

While certain she wouldn't want to come with him, the smell of the carcasses would draw beasts and vampires alike, and the missing witches would be noticed soon too. Any of the three groups would be trouble for Ruby.

Annoyance flooded him as he carefully lifted her into his arms and took off running to the north. Dorian tried to avoid placing his hands directly on her body as he lifted her into his arms, but his fingers grazed some of that silken skin. She wasn't difficult to carry in the least, but she was an unexpected addition to his concerns.

I'm just bringing her along so that she can't blab about me. That's it. I'm just curious about her; that's all that makes me care about her outcome.

Curiosity did exist there, absolutely. But Dorian couldn't ignore the empathy there too. Currently hunted by his own kind, he understood her predicament. His connection to her emotions went deeper than that. Dorian knew what it felt like to be betrayed by those he cared for, only to find they never cared for him at all.

That strange witch named Ruby lit up with far more untamed emotions than he saw out of witches in centuries. While never personally close with a witch in his life, he saw them often in his earlier years. He admired their strengths, passions, and prowess. Witches had once inspired him to enjoy his vampiric life. Ironic in light of the state of modern Vlideron. The witches of his childhood were fearsome and incredible. The red witch, timid though she appeared, screamed of a quality he sorely missed glimpsing. Authenticity seemingly warred with her for purchase against suppression.

Dorian could understand that war too. Hiding for most of his existence allowed Dorian only snippets of authenticity.

Moments when he murdered deserving nobles.

Moments in centuries past spent with lovers and friends.

Those moments had become fewer and farther between as he lost friends and lovers, refusing to make more.

Arriving at his cave a few hours later, Dorian carefully settled Ruby into his bed in an alcove of the cave he'd transformed into a bedroom. He would need to wash the bedding at some point. Her robes had been horribly tattered by her curse, leaving streaks of blood visible on the remains of the fabric, bathing her skin in glistening red, which was visible in disturbingly large swathes. In any case, he gently pulled the blankets up over her body, trying to arrange her in a comfortable position without touching her too much. He moved some of her braids out of her face.

A part of Dorian wondered if he made a mistake, bringing her there, as he exited the alcove and took a seat on the far side of the main cave chamber, contemplating his choices. His curiosity and the way he felt himself projecting qualities on her was a dangerous combination. If he actually started to care for her, to befriend her, what would he feel when she inevitably left him as well? He'd been left behind enough to last an eternity.

No, Dorian decided. He would sate his curiosity about her. He would make his offer and move along regardless of what she decided. He wouldn't get attached because he couldn't. Not anymore. That part of him had died such a slow death, and even still it was around 200 years dead.

Interestingly enough, Dorian thought, half of all Vlideronian witches either died off or had suddenly changed at the same time. Funny how such events coincided. The witches ceased being an inspiration to Dorian, allying themselves with that joke of a king and neutering their power, and Dorian had let go of all attempts at personal connection with others. He'd been alone since then. Dimly, he considered that the connection may be more than coincidence. Maybe he had given up then because the witches had, as a whole, disappointed him.

It didn't really matter. Dorian had moved on with his life and the witches of Vlideron had continued down their strange path. The vampires had become stranger as well in that time. Many died off along with the witches. The council instituted new rules to align with what the king wanted, leaving Vlideronian vampires incapable of leaving the country. Few entered the borders either. Those of other races who visited their lands were confined to places like Mistspires and Saltmaw. Dorian hadn't seen the glimmering waters of the ocean from Saltmaw in centuries, and he likely wouldn't for centuries more. It would take the king dying and his ideals dying off to allow Vlideronian vampires to enter the port town again.

Mistspires, on the other hand, Dorian had seen a few times in the last few centuries, recalling his most recent visit. The once glittering city rising from the mists made by the confluence of the rivers dulled when the king took over. He had cleared most of the gardens that once brightened the interior of the city walls to make space for his own outdoor sporting fun, barring anyone from enjoying the same activities unless he participated with them. Dorian recalled inspecting the bland details that had taken over the city, noting the horrifyingly inadequate huts of the gaunt-faced and sleep-deprived servants, and found himself cursing that he could not personally slit the king's throat.

The man who called himself the 'Great King' was a monster in his own right. Dorian heard only rumors, since there was no one in the kingdom with more influence than the king. He could keep much of his activity hidden effectively. But that didn't mean Dorian knew nothing of it. There was a reason the worst of the worst flocked around him. Cruelty, exclusion, the camps for political enemies and those he deemed lesser. It all added up in Dorian's mind.

Alas, Dorian needed to keep his head down and continue on like none of it bothered him. He had been stalking a different victim, needing to gather information so that he could properly decide how to handle the bastard. While the kill had ultimately been worth his efforts, he'd dealt with a sour taste in his mouth ever since that he couldn't do the same to the worthless man sitting on a throne of oppression. The king had too much protection and too many allies, ensuring Dorian wouldn't even be granted the satisfaction of taking the piece of shit down with him.

Among those allies included the witches, amplifying the bitterness that rotted within his throat whenever he considered the king. Dorian never bought into the new narratives that the witches were now true enemies of vampires, since he knew that these notions were limited to the borders of Vlideron. According to the early days of letters from acquaintances outside of Vlideron, it was the only kingdom where this strange change had taken place. But he couldn't deny the witches' complicity with the cruelty of the king and their clear blood lust for the deaths of vampires. Sometimes he wondered how that vicious hatred worked in the confines of their relationship with the king, who clearly got along well with the vampires in private. Publicly, the king behaved as if vampires might as well be myths. He didn't speak of them at all in his addresses to the public, and rarely added them to his decrees.

The whole thing reeked of something suspicious, but Dorian wasn't sure the depths of it all. What he did know was that the majority of witches he encountered were under the same mandates as it pertained to vampires. They avoided them in the cities, but sought to kill on sight anywhere that the laws of the king might be blind to. The forests, mountains, abandoned ruins, and even private residences, if they could gain access, were all areas deemed fair game for witches to attempt slaughtering vampires.

Vampires were allowed to return blow-for-blow if they were attacked first, but were barred from taking further vengeance under penalty of the council. Dorian found the rules governing the witches and vampires in this apparent feud that sprang up out of nowhere to be needlessly restrictive and silly. If someone sought to kill him, why should he hesitate to kill them in return? Just to make sure they employed a sanctioned degree of retaliation?

Silliness.

It was pure silliness that witches attacked vampires at all. That behavior, however, left Dorian uneasy about the witch in the alcove. Perhaps he had made a bigger mistake than he previously feared. What if she tried to kill him on sight? He didn't want to leave another body closer to his home, creating a more defined trail with which his hunters could follow him. He would have to do some serious cleaning up if that proved to be the case. It would delay his trip and leave him vulnerable.

That wouldn't be ideal.

He would prefer to help her get to a safe place, rather than going off on her own, but maybe it would be for the best if she refused his aid. He would certainly be able to make it to his home faster without needing to go at her pace. Vampires were so much faster than humans. She might have been a bit faster than the average human, but she would never be able to keep up with him. If she decided to accept his offer, she would be setting their pace for the rest of their travels.

Unless, of course, he could carry her again. That would solve his problem of time smoothly, but he suspected she would be as uncomfortable with the knowledge that he had carried her as he felt doing it. One could look at the incident as a kidnapping, Dorian realized. Hanging his head low, he softly groaned. He hadn't intended on kidnapping the woman. But he had picked up an unconscious woman, carried her hundreds of miles away in a matter of a few short hours, and deposited her in a magically hidden cave. It was so far away, she'd have no hope of navigating her way back on her own.

Putting his newly emptied blood pack back in his bag, Dorian shook his head, trying to dispel thoughts of how she felt in his arms, her perfect form that he'd tried desperately to ignore as he ran to the cave. She was hardly smaller than he was, but he noticed enough of a difference to be surprised by how densely packed her muscles were, giving her form a firmness he had always enjoyed in partners. Dorian had nearly dropped her to smack himself at that thought. Even recalling it left him furious with his own brain. The connection was entirely inappropriate and unwelcome. Ruby had no business being in his mind like that at all. None whatsoever. She was a witch he absconded with so that he could sate his curiosity about the curse afflicting her and why they labeled her a bad witch.

The labels around her intrigued him. She wasn't a good witch. She wasn't good enough. She wasn't doing things correctly as a witch. An utter failure. They referred to Ruby as a failure so many times that he'd begun flashing back to memories of Lord Leonarch. Shaking away those thoughts, Dorian had decided he required more information about her.

That curse of hers fascinated him. The vampiric shadows occupying her body had been healing her when he approached her after dealing with the corpses. He wondered what she knew of the curse infecting her. Perhaps she could tell him how someone had gotten those shadows in her in the first place. If not, maybe he could convince her to come with him to his home. Maybe he could even help cure her of the curse. Wouldn't that be a hilarious twist of fate? Cursed by one vampire, cured by another.

Gods, he would probably enjoy thwarting another vampire's goals even more after he got confirmation of what the council had been up to all these years. No doubt, any vampire capable of creating such a curse must be a council member. They deserved to have their plans fucked with, and Dorian doubted that Ruby deserved the devastation that curse caused her.

Beyond the cruelty witches are raised to commit in Vlideron now, maybe she could have a hope of becoming better, since she was chased out of the coven so thoroughly. Maybe she could be better. Maybe she could even become like a witch of old.

No, that took things a step too far. Too much hope for a woman he didn't know. Dorian had to remind himself that he couldn't assume so much about her without actually speaking to her one on one. Getting ahead of himself would only get him hurt. Plus, it wouldn't be fair to her to go into meeting her properly with such random expectations of her borne of his own hopes and projections.

Dorian doubted she even knew enough of the world she participated in to judge her accurately. Would she even care how much harm she'd caused the people by participating in the present-day roles and duties of witches? Though he felt unsure, something in his gut told him that she would care. His intuition rarely steered him wrong. He would lead with the assumption she might be a good person underneath the cruelty of her history and participation in a broken kingdom's management.

Ruby would hardly be the first person duped into participation in the cruelty of the world she lived in. Considering the background she came from, Dorian could guess at the numerous thoughts rattling around in her mind as it pertained to the people she helped subjugate. He wondered how many excuses she would make for that, excuses he knew would come. Most people found it difficult to disregard years of programming to participate in oppressing others in order to grow into half-decent people. Maybe she would disappoint him and cling to those ideals more as a result of her ostracization from the group she had been a part of her whole life. Some took being cast out as further proof of the correctness of the in-group.

No matter what the case turned out to be, if she didn't go straight for killing him or prove herself to be a bull-headed fool, maybe he could work with that. While it would be funny to destroy the machinations of the vampiric council with this random witch, it would be hilarious to take a present-day witch and destroy her preconceived notions about Vlideron, to free her from being a tool of tyranny. Presented with the opportunity to do both, Dorian could hardly sit still. Excitement and nerves danced along his veins.

But things could go the other way. She could be a terrible person, who relished the harm she knew herself to be causing the commoners. In which case, Dorian would just have to kill her himself. It would be a shame if that turned out to be the case. He'd never enjoyed killing average citizens, preferring to focus his attention on the wealthy ruling class who pitted everyone against each other in the first place. For all her participation in policing the commoners, she was essentially a commoner herself. If she saw that, she could be an excellent ally of the people, able to do things they could never dream of. But if she enjoyed hurting the people for the benefit of the rich, as the fools who worked as security for the nobles sometimes did, then he'd have no option. His own morals would not let an empowered individual with that sort of mentality walk free forever. He had plans to eventually handle the vampiric council himself.

I just need time. I need to get home, safe behind my barrier and regroup. Grow stronger. I don't want to have to kill a witch before I get the chance to handle the council.

Witches in Vlideron struck him as a largely brainwashed group in the modern day. They, by and large, seemed to truly believe the absurdity that spilled from their lips. To Dorian, that made them more forgivable. Most didn't know or understand the harm they caused. That didn't make them any less responsible for it, but that was something that could be worked with. He could send Ruby on her way to Sigrid once they got the curse resolved, if that proved to be possible. Then, Sigrid could use her in her crusade against the king and the nobles. Witches could have a hope of becoming worthy of admiration in Vlideron again.

Dorian heard Ruby stirring in the alcove, and sat up straighter. The moment of truth. Would she cling to the brainwashing that made witches attack vampires on sight in such circumstances? Or would she lead with curiosity? Despite how hard he tried not to hold hope or interest, he couldn't help the way his pulse quickened.

CHAPTER NINE

Ruby

Ruby felt consciousness pulling at her, forcing her awake. She stubbornly kept her eyes closed, refusing to face the day just yet. Exhaustion suffused her bones in a way it hadn't since her solitary retreat.

I miss that first night of sleep after my retreat... The blessed darkness with the only glimmers of light coming from the stars outside of my window... That was restful... Maybe if I go back to sleep I could get that again...

Something gnawed at her, trying to poke her into wakefulness, but it looked dark out still. Time remained before she'd be required up for the day, before anyone would insist she needed to get to work on her reeducation.

Reeducation.

That word echoed in her mind.

She flew upright, eyes popping open, searching frantically all around as she finally remembered everything.

The curse. Running for my life. The corpses of my fellow witches. The vampire.

Where is he? Where am I?

Her eyes could only adjust to the darkness so much. Were those cave walls? Ruby reached through the darkness for the lump that she thought might have been her bag, tossing aside the blanket covering her.

Blanket?

She had no idea where that had come from. Had she been rescued by the witches after falling into darkness? Surely a vampire would not have brought her somewhere with a bed and tucked her in.

Unless he wants a fresh blood supply hidden away...

Ice coursed through her veins at the thought, sending her hands grasping for her bag once again.

Finding the silver dagger in her bag took a long time in the darkness. The magically expanded bag normally made itself far easier to navigate, but she felt frazzled and struggled to keep her desire for the blade in mind. Her eyes darted all along the walls, spotting the opening to a wider cavern nearby. She sat in a smaller room of some kind, part of a larger cave.

"If only I could just fucking see..." Ruby clamped her hand over her mouth as soon as she heard the words reverberate on the surrounding stone.

Silently, she cursed herself for the screw up. If she lay in the clutches of the vampire, he now knew she was awake. She would lose the element of surprise, if she ever had it at all. For all she knew, he could be watching her already.

"Oh, M'lvia's revenge, sorry about that." A deep, resonant voice called from the chamber beyond, then a soft, silvery light—like that of the stars at night—illuminated the cave.

Ruby recognized the voice instantly, but it sounded different without the mocking tone from before. She stopped, gripping the handle of the dagger with all her might, face scrunching up with confusion. Glancing at the blanket she tossed aside, she could see it constituted of surprisingly high quality wool.

Why would he give me such a fine blanket to use? Why isn't he attacking me? Why hasn't he killed me already? None of this makes sense...

The rips and stains on her clothes caught her eye, reminding her of the shadows ripping from her shortly before she lost consciousness. Her legs shook as she stood, her strength still stolen by the ordeals of the last day. Or had it been longer? She had no idea how long she had been unconscious. Ruby tried to force her steps to be strong, even, and steady. Instead, she heard each stumble echoing off the cave walls. Grimacing, she held the dagger at the ready, cautiously turning the little corner to face the rest of the cave and the vampire within.

He sat across the cave in a circular, natural depression in the center, the place oddly perfect for seating around a simple fire pit, carved into the stone floor. No fire waited in that pit, but there were strange lights attached to the walls. Ruby had never encountered magical lanterns, but she guessed that these were some form of that technology. Their unnatural light twinkled beautifully, soft despite the cool color. The presence of lighting meant that she could clearly see his face, as well as the three other apparent doorways of the cave.

One of those must lead to the exit...

She just needed to find out which one.

"Where am I? Why have you brought me here? What do you want from me?"

His sharply angled face showed no signs of the smirk he maintained during the battle with Violetta and the others. Instead, he looked relaxed, his face neutral, but without the careful control witches showed. At her questions, his lips twitched, as if he almost smiled. The slight movement infuriated her, a feeling that compounded with each passing second of silence.

"Well?!"

"This is a cave I have enchanted for hiding. I figured the corpses would draw beasts or those hunting me," he paused, looking her in the eye with a split second return of his smirk, "or even those hunting you." His face returned to the calm expression from before as he continued, "I saw how badly you wanted to live, and I wanted to respect that desire and make sure you had that opportunity. Call it curiosity more than anything."

"But why?"

He hummed, apparently considering how to respond, "Well, I'm fascinated. Why were you being hunted by other witches? And this curse of yours. It's intriguing."

My curse...

A thought bubbled up, escaping her throat before she had the chance to stop it, "How do I know you aren't the one who cursed me?"

At this, he smiled fully, the gesture incensing Ruby even more while a small part of her brain detailed the changes in his face when he seemed genuine.

"I don't know how your curse works. I certainly don't have the ability to create such a curse. The closest I could compare it to would be the curses witches used to hurl around hundreds of years ago. You can believe me or not, but I am not the one who cursed you. If anything, I think it would be funny to fuck up their curse, if possible."

Ruby scrunched her brows together, "Why?"

Some of her anger deflated slightly at the genuine amusement she saw on his face as he expressed a desire to ruin the designs of another vampire. None of this was making sense to her.

"My guess is that the only vampires in Vlideron who could have made that kind of curse are on the vampiric council. If you haven't caught on from my mention of those hunting me, I am not exactly on speaking terms with them anymore. I'd love to fuck up whatever weird plans they have with cursing a random witch, especially when going by those gnats this morning, you aren't a witch of consequence to your coven. I can't imagine why that is, when you don't seem like a fool to me, and the impression I got of those others was lackluster at best."

Ruby didn't know where to begin to evaluate his statements. He judged her curse to be so beyond the realm of normal that it had to be done by the most important vampires in society. She didn't know how much she could believe of anything he said, but the words had a ring of truth in them, and her gut told her to believe him. He apparently stood at odds with them, so he might have motive to attribute the curse to them, but he already knew she wasn't of much consequence, so what reason would he have to set her against the council without a hope of success against them? And his impressions of the others were somehow worse than his impression of her? That made the least sense of all.

I'm the failure of a witch, not them...

Shaking her head, Ruby refocused, "So you brought me here because you're curious about my curse?"

"Basically."

"Am I your prisoner then?" Ruby steeled herself for a fight, glancing at the mystery doors she could escape from.

"Nope. I don't care to keep innocents as prisoners. From what I know of you, you qualify as an innocent."

Ruby nearly argued with him, but decided to keep her mouth shut. He didn't need to know of her many failures. Being a vampire, he would probably excuse them all anyways as being inconsequential. They held attitudes at total odds with the mandates of the Great King. If he opposed the council, maybe that made him even more hedonistic. He couldn't be in line with witches, or he probably would have run rather than kill them.

While it sunk in that he'd called her an innocent, the reality she lived in made everything worse. She was a terrible witch. A good witch would have gone to the elders as soon as they found those hidden books. They wouldn't have hid them away, studied them, and searched for a loophole in being a good witch. Ruby knew deep down that she sought to find a way to excuse her pathetic nature. Even as she brought those forbidden books with her, she rationalized it as research to save herself. But that was all it was: rationalizations. She just wanted to read more. If her long history of misbehavior, even before the discovery of the forbidden texts, condemned her to this curse like Vanella suggested, then maybe she deserved to rot with it.

The curse churned slowly, calmly, as Ruby thought about how she failed at every turn to be the good witch she wanted to be. Nevertheless, it served as an excellent reminder to keep herself contained. She let far too much slip in recent days, beyond the curse riling her up ever more. Ruby had been in the library for a reason when she found the books currently in her bag. Maybe she would have been cursed anyways, even if she hadn't encountered such provocative texts, but maybe she could have resisted it better if she were a better witch.

"It's rather hilarious that you ask about being a prisoner, though."

"Why?"

"Well, you witches take so many unnecessary prisoners every day. I simply find it funny that you immediately presume someone else would take you as a prisoner without just cause."

Ruby's heart sank. She knew what he was referencing and struggled to come up with the justifications the elders always served to her for their imprisonment of so many people. She understood it with the man who punched her. While she tried to avoid participating in the most gratuitous stops, she knew that they were supposed to arrest people for all manner of absurd and exaggerated infractions. She staunchly ignored many of those occasions and redirected the others in her patrol groups during such events as much as she could.

"I don't... I don't take prisoners unless they're violent," Ruby weakly replied.

The vampire stared at her, something like amusement flashing in his red eyes, the golden tone of his skin clashing with the silvery lights, washing him out and making him look as deathly pale as she expected vampires to look.

Ruby sucked in a breath, "I will admit to you that I have never understood why we do so much with the commoners... It... I don't know if it makes sense. But I don't do that. I don't... Just take people off the streets. I try to distract the others to make sure they don't either... But I suppose at some point I just accepted that it happens."

The admission tightened the curse in her body, forcing Ruby to remind herself to breathe through the feelings. Shame crashed upon her as much as guilt. Shame greeted her for telling a vampire of those feelings and for having them in the first place; guilt stormed through her insides for how many commoners she knew had suffered from the arrests the Great King kept declaring were necessary. The elders said he was always right. Ruby didn't know how he could be, but didn't know how he couldn't be either. It all left her too confused to parse out, which made her furious with herself for failing to understand what her proper role was.

"Interesting," the vampire shook his head, "You do seem to be a good person somewhere in there. That's good."

"What do you mean by that?" Ruby's voice rose an octave; she tried to calm the swell of emotions emitting from her throat.

The vampire snapped his fingers, "There you go again. It's so strange how you have so many emotions always fluctuating around you, but try so hard to stuff them down. It creates a weird visual to see you try to grind your own emotions into nothingness like that other witch's natural state."

Ruby caught his eyes, noting the rich shade of dark red, shining like some jewel in the silvery light. Her hands started to shake as she met that gaze, wondering what in M'lvia's revenge he would know of her emotions. What would he know of her struggles to keep contained? Why should he care if she wanted to get rid of the pesky feelings? Why shouldn't she have wanted to be like Violetta? At least Violetta was a good witch.

"Do. Not. Speak. to me of my own emotions. You don't know what they have cost me..." Memory overtaking her senses, Ruby saw blinding white light reflecting off the perfect white surroundings, relentlessly baring down on her, time becoming meaningless, and contact with others nonexistent.

"I suspect I know more than you realize, Ruby," the vampire spoke, ripping her from the memory.

Ruby felt a second of gratitude for the rescue from the memory before her rage returned.

Just as she opened her mouth to retort, he continued, "I remember what witches were like before all these ridiculous rules you feel the need to follow about your emotions." He sighed heavily. "It's really such a shame."

He knew about witches from before 200 years ago. For humans, that was a long time. She hadn't thought about how insignificant that might be to a vampire.

How old is he anyway? He says he knows about witches... But how much does he really know? Can I trust anything he says? I don't even know his name... I need to put a name to the face...

"So you know my name," Ruby nodded, taking a steadying breath as she affected a sarcastic smile, "but what is yours? Or should I just call you 'bloodsucker' forever?"

CHAPTER TEN

Dorian

Suppressing a laugh at her dig, he drew in a breath before answering, "Dorian."

"Just Dorian? I thought non-witches all possessed last names."

"Yeah, we do. But just Dorian is good. I don't exactly use my last name if I can avoid it."

"Why? Are you someone of importance?"

Dorian paused for a moment, a grin spreading across his face at the sarcasm with which she delivered that question. She amused him far more than he expected, so much more like the witches of old, from when was a boy. They were so full of life and joy and personality. Full of the depth and range of living feeling. Nothing like the stunted, muted creatures haunting the streets of the poor.

"What, is something I said funny to you, Mr. Whatever-your-last-name-is?"

"It's Seagrave. Technically I guess my full name should be Lord Dorian Seagrave. But I fucking hate that, so just Dorian is best."

"I didn't know any vampires in Vlideron were nobility..." Her brow furrowed with suspicion.

"Not many are. I live in Edgefair year-round and don't maintain a portion of the militia because I am lord in name only at this point. I sold most of the lands I once held to the people actually living there. I did that before the current king, so he held no say in the matter. I doubt he's even checked into my status since he took the throne. The lands I do still hold aren't used by people anyways."

"What lands do you still hold? And what lands in Vlideron don't have a noble owning their property?"

Dorian suppressed another laugh, trying not to make her feel silly for not knowing things that weren't common knowledge in the first place, "They're in Death's Forest. Hardly desirable real estate. And the northernmost range of the forest where it meets the river coming from the mountains. There's a couple of small villages there that get ignored by the royals no matter who occupies the throne. Their lands aren't considered useful enough to even bother protecting them, so they've been self-sufficient for ages. I doubt anyone knows that no noble owns their property outside of those villages. They trade amongst themselves, and last I checked, they were flourishing. It has been a few decades though."

"And what if the Great King's men find out that they're all there? Do they not pay taxes?"

"The king has no use for them, like I said. Besides, they can throw around my name as the noble overseeing their lands if need be. I left them all with an engraved stone portrait of me and a small explanation of the role I supposedly play. I do send in reports about them continuing to be a few small villages with nothing to add in the way of tax. Small enough locations don't pay anything. That might be adjusted with me being on the run, though. But they'll discover that the people own the land, not me. So there won't be much they can do. The king can try to seize the assets of the people, but he's got much bigger concerns, what with the attempted escapes all over the place, if the rumors are to be believed."

Ruby nodded and Dorian couldn't help but notice the way the silvery light glinted off her deep, red hair, adding an extra sheen to the many thin braids, shining like wine refracting light in a crystal glass. The observation caught him off-guard. He hadn't noticed such details since Maxen occupied a spot in his life, their every motion capturing his attention and driving his brain to poetic fits of fancy.

My loneliness must be getting to me.

That would be the only explanation for taking such an interest in the woman. The feelings were his own to manage, not borne of anything to do with her innate beauty or remarkable circumstances. His drive for companionship merely reared its ugly head again, trying to trick him into becoming attached or attracted to the unique witch.

"Have I satisfied your questions on my name and title? Can you call me just Dorian? Or are you going to be a stickler for the rights of my birth and insist on calling me Lord? If that is the case, I would rather you just kept calling me bloodsucker."

Dorian watched as the corner of her mouth twitched, suppressing a smile, before her face scrunched back up, the mask of anger sliding back into place. Seeing her fighting to remain angry both frustrated and entertained him. He was filled with amusement as he watched her fight her own impulses to laugh because of her determination to hate him. He could see it in the movements of her emotions around her body. She needed to hate him, for some reason. That part frustrated him. He didn't really understand her need to hate him. Maybe it related to what those other witches screeched to and about her? Dorian couldn't be sure.

"Fine then, bloodsucker," she spat out the insulting label, the attempt at animosity made absurd by its forced nature, "where have you brought me exactly? And if I am not your prisoner, am I free to go?"

"We're a couple hundred miles north of Edgefair in Death's Forest. Still in Vlideron. Another two or so hours of travel to my real home if I run at my speed, but probably a few nights if we walk at your speed. Witches move a bit faster than regular humans, right? But yes, you are free to go at any time, though I would caution you against going by yourself."

"How... I know vampires are far faster than humans and witches... And yes, we are faster than humans, but... I didn't think vampires were *that* much faster... How long was I unconscious?"

"I ran for about four hours, and you remained out for another three or so hours after that. I was concerned that you were badly injured, but I checked and you seemed to simply be asleep."

"You traveled a couple hundred miles in four hours?!"

Dorian smiled, raising his eyebrows, "Is that really that surprising? How much do you know of vampiric speed?"

"I just... that sounds so much faster than I always assumed, is all. Wait, why would you caution me against going by myself? What does that mean? What other choice would I have if I wanted to leave here?"

"The beasts of Death's Forest grow stronger the closer to the center of the forest you are. To get to my home, I will be heading away from the center of the forest, toward the mountains. But we are currently far closer to the center than we were near Edgefair. For a witch who only knows light magic, especially one who is as weakened by a curse as you are, they would kill you in an instant."

"I am not reliant on my magic alone!"

Dorian paused, the outburst unexpected. The defensiveness seemed out of place. His eyes darted down to the blade clutched tightly in her hand, finally registering its silver coating. His lip quirked up as he met her blazing eyes once more.

"I see. That dagger would help you some against the beasts. Many are also weak to silver. But you might only manage to take the beast down with you, depending on your luck."

Ruby stiffened, her eyes still flaring, even as acceptance reluctantly took root in her. Huffing, she nodded.

"As for what I suggest, well, I want to research your curse and, if possible, help you rid yourself of it. Frankly, I cannot fathom what you could have done to deserve such an affliction, and I think it would be funny to foil the plans of whoever set it. I would bring you to my home so that we may review my centuries of texts to see if we could figure out a solution. It would occupy my time while I hide out for a while. Or, of course, I could simply house you until the pressure has cooled down from the vampiric council, and I could accompany you to another civilized location in Vlideron. Or I could accompany you to some of those villages I mentioned previously. You would be safe from the witches, as they don't have any presence out there, but you also wouldn't be able to do much about that curse."

Dorian wondered if he laid his proposition on too thick at the end. Laying it all out so directly felt a little heavy-handed. But he didn't want to be accused of tricking her or not being honest about her options. Dorian felt compelled to be as honest with her as possible about what he saw as her options; possibly staying in his home would put her in a vulnerable position, and he wanted to give her the chance to decide for herself. That he was clearly biased in favor of sating his curiosity wasn't something he thought to hide. Furthermore, that he didn't really see her surviving on her own would be too obvious for him not to mention it.

With a curse like that, she won't last long.

He hesitated to mention a theory he'd begun to develop about how he could help her survive the curse's attacks while they researched it. He needed to see a bit more closely how her curse operated before he could say with any confidence that he held the slightest clue how to manage it long enough to even get to his home.

Ruby stood, clearly frozen in thought, with a swirl of anxiety, confusion, shame, and even a hint of hope flowing around her emotional field. He admired that she weighed her options so carefully, but his impatience began to rear its ugly head. His foot threatened to begin tapping. Dorian scratched at the back of his head, trying to ignore the strange feeling welling in his chest as he watched her seriously consider his honesty and forthrightness. The scrutiny made him feel more squirrelly than he felt facing down the council.

"Or, of course, I could just take you back and hand you over to your beloved witches. I'm sure they won't blame you for the deaths of the others. Just tell them I did it. That would go over well."

Dorian regretted the words as soon as he said them. Ruby's head snapped back as if struck, her eyes flaring with renewed fire, the black-brown depths consuming his attention and burning away his reserves, his foot beginning to tap out of his control at last. He screwed up. The sarcastically delivered words may have rang true for her, but they were hardly necessary or useful. He silently cursed his nerves and the way they had decided to burst forth at the worst moment.

You'd think after 500 years I would get it through my thick skull to just shut the fuck up sometimes.

She snapped, flying across the cave faster than Dorian anticipated. If he wanted to, he could easily dodge her, but despite her rage, he didn't sense true murderous intent. She was hurt, more than anything. The betrayal she'd suffered shone as clear as the vibrancy of the night. Unwillingly, he had just rubbed salt in the wound. He let her slam into him. His seated position drove him into the ground of the cave, with her on top of him. Against his throat, she held the silver dagger. The cool bite of the blade caressed him with the barest touch.

"It was my fault they did that! You shouldn't have killed them!" Ruby screamed in his face.

Dorian reached up, gently holding her arm, impressed by the

strength behind it, considering her essentially human body. By the grip she maintained on it, he could tell she was skilled with the blade. But that all paled in comparison with the flood of annoyance he felt at her declaration. All her fault? How could it be her fault? Unless she had truly done something horrible that he didn't know about, Dorian couldn't imagine how she could have deserved the disregard they showed her life. Her desire to live.

Scanning her eyes, Dorian saw the shine of tears barely held back, and squeezed her arm as he spoke, "Why do you care about them when they didn't care about you enough to understand your desire to live? They didn't care about you at all. I saw them. I heard them. Some of them just wanted to kill you and were just glad to have a reason. Others just didn't care at all. And nothing I saw, or heard, justified their behavior."

Ruby's face crumpled as she tried to pull away, but Dorian held her in place for another moment longer. She tried more aggressively to retreat. Dorian felt the blade knick his throat, but he had more to convey despite the burning the silver caused.

"Why not allow yourself the full depth of experience? Those people who were calling you failure certainly didn't care about your life. You say I shouldn't have killed them. But then you would be dead. I thought you wanted to live. I saw that shining in the woods this morning. A person who wanted to live. So *live*."

Dorian let her go, waiting for her to finish scrambling off of him before he started to lift himself. He tried to ignore the lingering heat from where her body straddled his. He stuffed aside his thrill from her dagger at his neck. He just enjoyed getting a rise out of her, of course. That was all. It had nothing at all to do with his propensity for strong, capable, assertive partners. He enjoyed getting to provoke an emotional response, happy he broke through to her a little, and hopefully managed to rectify the damage of his earlier sarcasm. He'd driven his point home in a better way.

Glancing at the curse in her body, Dorian observed the shadows moving around more, apparently responding to her heightened emotions, but they moved sluggishly, as if still exhausted. Perhaps the curse entered a weakened state after acting up so much? He didn't know how long she had been afflicted with it, or how often it acted up, but the display from that morning must have been a lot of spent energy. If it operated like most curses, it would take some time to recharge.

While he'd never seen a curse exactly like hers, he had seen plenty that were designed to kill the victim. When they engaged in a burst of activity, they fought to kill the victim swiftly. If that burst did not work, it would take some time to strengthen itself again before acting out once more. The only difference in her curse came from the shadows occupying her. They would heal her if they didn't immediately kill her. So she would be stuck in a near endless loop of the curse strengthening and assaulting her unless she freed herself, or it finally grew powerful enough to kill her on the initial burst.

"I'm going to go change my clothes," Ruby announced suddenly.

Dorian looked at her ragged, torn robes, noting the large swaths of visible skin, coated in blood, "There's a bathroom through that alcove there if you want to clean up."

He tried not to think of why he made a semi-functional home in that cave, Leandra's face flashing across his eyelids. Dorian shook off the memory, only to find himself wishing for a distraction from the sound of Ruby marveling at the running water. What would she say about the rain baths at his estate? The magic to draw water from the various underground rivers and lakes found deep beneath the forest had been a pain to get, since such discreet work in Vlideron came at great cost even centuries past. The witches who did the work died centuries ago, making it a lost art in their kingdom.

Such enchantments had become unknown to modern witches, but were a well-appreciated specialty over 400 years ago. The look on Leandra's face when he surprised her with the upgrades to the cave they always stopped at on the way to their home had been priceless. Though the cave lacked a rain bath, the hot water in the sink was a welcome improvement. The area between Edgefair and that cave stayed too full of beasts to risk going at her pace, but Dorian relished getting to take his time from thereon with her. Leandra enjoyed the journey as well. Those memories of her were the best painful distraction Dorian could have asked for as he heard Ruby moan in delight, discovering the hot water control for the sink.

Emerging from the bathroom, she wore a new outfit, leaving Dorian speechless. Instead of drab beige robes, she wore a smooth, emerald-green top, a black laced belt, and black leather pants, which looked loose enough to be comfortable but were tight enough for him to get a far better view of her figure. Her dagger rested in a sheath at her thigh, the straps securing it creating two slight indents; Dorian could practically feel those indents in his fingertips. He felt like he might choke on air if he tried to breathe. The unexpectedness of her new outfit caught him entirely off-guard. He hadn't anticipated that she would carry anything but more of those godsawful beige robes.

Ruby's emotional field showed the dance between anxiety and hope as she spoke, "Fine. I will come with you and let you help me figure out this curse."

CHAPTER ELEVEN

Ruby

Ruby watched Dorian's reaction to her statement. He seemed stunned. She felt more than a little stunned, herself. Thinking on it while she wiped herself clean with the help of that blessed sink, Ruby had been surprised to find that she wanted his help at all. She should hate him. She just proved the others right that she was a bad, failure of a witch by going with him. Shame coiled in her belly at the thought, but she couldn't deny that she would need help navigating the forest. She needed even more help in addressing her curse. He was right that she wanted to live. No matter how selfish it made her, she wanted to keep living. She wanted the chance to experience a real life.

Maybe she could return to the coven with all the knowledge she needed to help change things for the witches. Maybe their transition to light-only magic had been a mistake. The blasphemous thought bounced around her mind, and a part of Ruby wondered if she would lose her powers because of those thoughts. They were told that witches who didn't follow their way of life were forsaking their calling and would suffer the consequences of it. Maybe the curse came as the consequences of her secrecy. She didn't really know either way. The curiosity that drove her down those stairs in the library drove her once more.

She wanted to go with Dorian. Maybe he would reveal himself

to be far more villainous and she would have to figure out how to kill him, achieving the vengeance the others would be screaming for if they could reach her. Or maybe he really could help her discover how to rid herself of the curse. Either way, she made up her mind—no matter how wrong that conclusion felt after a lifetime of hearing disparaging remarks about vampires.

Dorian appeared different from her expectations. He was far too sure of himself for her liking, verging into presumptuous and mean. But he was also strangely gentle with her. The dichotomy caught her off-guard. Did he merely pity her? That would make the most sense. The thought rankled her, but she stuffed that aside for the time being, waiting on him to say something.

He rose to his feet at an achingly slow pace, as if interacting with a frightened animal, eyes perusing her with an unexpected glean. Dorian looked at her as a starving child looked into the windows of a bakery. She took a step back, gripping the dagger at her thigh, the smoothness of her leather pants brushing against her fingertips and reminding her of the change in her outfit.

Is he reacting to my new outfit? No, that would be crazy. I have no reason to think he would be attracted to me. Stop with the wishful thinking. Wait... Wishful thinking? Why would I want a bloodsucker to be attracted to me?

Her motion snapped him out of whatever reverie had captured him. Dorian cleared his throat, nodded, and took a few steps toward one of the other openings.

"We should get going then," Dorian slung his own pack on his shoulders.

"Right, let me just get my things."

Ruby rushed through putting together her own bag, ensuring nothing looked amiss. Grabbing a ration she could eat while moving, she secured the bag over her shoulders. Rejoining Dorian, she paused, recalling where they were. She fished out the long, flowing coat she used in the winter when she wanted to go out among the humans without being noticed. The thick, black fabric warmed her without sacrificing mobility. It came down to her ankles and had a deep hood which shielded her hair from sight when she needed it. She would almost blend in with the blackened ground and trees she knew to make up Death's Forest.

"We'll go as fast as you can walk and maintain to get to my home. I have a barrier around my land that will keep us safe from anyone hunting either of us once we get there. Until we get closer though, we should just focus on the travel. It'll probably take a couple of days." Dorian stood beside what she guessed must be the exit and nodded his head in that direction, "Ready?"

Ruby processed his assertions as she followed him into the darkness, the lights of the cave going dark as they exited, leaving her almost blind. She could make out Dorian moving ahead of her, but little else was discernible in the murky world around her. After only two steps, Ruby tripped on something and fell, landing hard on her flailing hands, narrowly avoiding her face slamming into the ground.

Dorian helped her up without a word, steadying her, then disappeared back into the cave behind them. Ruby could barely see the entrance, even just a few steps away from it. The darkness, though comforting, also left her unsettled. She couldn't see enough to protect herself. Death's Forest near Edgefair had somehow been brighter, allowing greater visibility even though no sun breached the canopy above in either location. Maybe the location near the edges of the forest had made a difference, or maybe she had been too panicked to notice much and the light attacks from the others had done more for her sight than she realized.

Reemerging, Dorian paused beside her, holding something out to her, though she couldn't quite see what. When she didn't take it, she heard him mutter something under his breath. Brilliant light caused her to squint and turn away, trying to blink her way back to vision.

"Sorry, I should have warned you. I forgot you have basically human eyes," Dorian scratched at the back of his head with his free hand, holding the lantern out for her to take.

Ruby examined the lantern, noting the lack of fire within. The magic illuminating it came from some remarkable enchantments. She hadn't known such lighting devices could be portable. She reached out with a shaky hand, marveling at the invention and wondering how it worked, how it was made in the first place.

Glancing up at Dorian, Ruby realized she should probably thank him for retrieving a light for her to use. Clearly, he didn't need it. Vampires were at home in the darkness. But she didn't want to. In order to keep up with him, it would be a necessity. She doubted he provided it out of the goodness of his heart. No, the lantern served a strictly utilitarian purpose. She would slow him down way more if she were to be tripping on every root.

Instead, Ruby nodded and gestured for him to lead the way.

She couldn't bear to bring herself any closer to appreciation. She needed to hold on to some of the witch's doctrine if she were to ever return to them. To return home. She determined she would keep herself at a distance and use him for information and lodging and survival. That was all. She didn't have to be that nice to him to get that, clearly. He willingly brought her along after she held a silver dagger to his throat, after all.

No one has ever been this considerate of me... But he's a vampire... I don't understand.

Dorian led the way again. Ruby followed along, taking a moment to finally look around at the forest, the silvery light of the lantern revealing more surprises. The forest decimated her expectations. The bark of the gargantuan trees did not boast the dark brown or black of the trees near Edgefair. Instead, she spied emerald green bark, which she had only ever seen in foliage. Flowers coated most of that bark, their shapes varied but all sporting the same rich, deep purple, growing like ivy up the trunks. A few mushrooms poked through the climbing flowers, a shocking shade of bright blue, as if someone captured the blue of hot flames and molded those mushrooms from it. The ground consisted not of the black soil she expected to see, but of a squishy, vibrant teal moss spreading all over the forest floor, broken up by roots poking out of the ground near the trees.

She must have gasped as she gawked at the flora because Dorian stopped, simply watching her take in the beauty of the forest. Her face heated at her own childish wonder. Clearing her throat, she took a few steps in the direction Dorian was leading them, trying to signal that she didn't want to discuss her reaction.

"It's stunning through here. Unexpected, I know. The trees themselves began to change over time in these deeper sections of the forest, adapting to the other flora. So the trees near Edgefair look common, while the trees here are like this. The exact mechanics of it all still mystify me, though. I have some theories but it hardly dulls the intensity of it." Dorian turned away and continued walking.

Ruby nodded before realizing he wasn't looking at her anymore, "Yeah, it doesn't really make sense... It's just... shocking."

"A lot hasn't made sense to me for a while," Dorian whispered.

Ruby's head snapped in Dorian's direction. Curiosity filled her about what he meant. She debated asking about it, but enough time elapsed to create an awkward silence, killing the words in her throat. Her mind raced for something to break the quiet.

Dorian did it for her, "I really don't get how light magic became the only thing you witches use."

"It's healing and very effective against bloodsuckers."

"Ah yes, but why forsake all other magic? That's what never made sense. And that weird emotional control shtick you all do? That makes even less sense."

"I am sure we had our reasons for the shift..." Ruby's voice sounded annoyingly small to her own ears, the defense of their lifestyle weak.

"Right, and you would know so much about the reasons for the shift when I doubt you even know much of the history of your own people."

His sarcasm rankled her, but she internally admitted her curiosity about what he knew. Maybe he would know more than she did. Maybe what he knew would disprove the things she started cobbling together from the old journals about their history.

Or maybe he will prove it... And if he confirms it all... what does that mean for me?

"You know about witches of old... From over 200 years ago, right?"

"Yes," Dorian looked back at her over his shoulder, a smirk on his face once more.

Ruby wanted to slap the expression off that face. Something about it irked her, the way he lorded his knowledge over her. Gritting her teeth, she waited for him to elaborate.

"I take it you would like to hear about what I know of witches?"

"Obviously."

"Witches used to be respected and feared in equal measure. Powerful, individual, remarkable. Some villages only feared them. Some villages venerated them. The kingdom as a whole respected their individual sovereignty. They didn't used to congregate in those compounds you all occupy in Vlideron now. Witches would join covens as they saw fit and could leave at any time. Covens would meet however much the witches in them chose. Some lived together all the time in their own communities but others just saw each other every few years."

"That is... definitely different." A sinking pit formed in Ruby.

That's what the journals say.

"I respected witches back then. They would heal or harm as they saw fit. Sometimes they were wrong and might have been called wicked. Sometimes they did nothing but help the people surrounding them and might have been called virtuous. But most were just people, using their powers in understandable ways. For good or ill, they followed their own logic, not some doctrine handed down to them by a governing body of witches."

The disdain with which Dorian addressed a governing body did not escape Ruby, but she chose to ignore it. She listened, finding he described the same things she read in the grimoires. A part of her hoped that he would reveal something that explained the change for witches. Something that would say why witches had, as a whole, left their previous ways behind. Anything that would allow her to return to the coven a better witch. All he said left her feeling lied to by the elders.

We have probably all been lied to for generations now... Why? Why have we been lied to? How can I accept that we were lied to? There has to be a reason... Something that makes it understandable. Something has to have happened to explain it!

"Then, a bit more than 200 years ago, that fool who calls himself the Great King started to ascend to power. Some of the witches of the time started organizing the witches of Vlideron under them. They started gathering witches into those compounds you all stay on. Never explained it to the vampire friends they had back then, or to any of the other denizens of Vlideron."

"Vampire friends?" Ruby's brain stumbled over that detail.

"What, did you think vampires were always a witch's enemy?" Dorian laughed.

Ruby recalled reading the accounts of a witch who had been in love with a vampire, another nail driven into the coffin of her lifelong beliefs. The details were a hundred years before the shift to new practices. Ruby didn't know what happened to that witch in the end, but their journal had been completely filled, meaning they probably started a new one. Ruby was unable to get back to the library to find the next one before the curse drove her from the compound.

"I... I was told we were but..."

"But?"

"Well... never mind. You keep specifying the witches of Vlideron. Witches outside of Vlideron aren't like us?"

"HA! No. Only witches in Vlideron have adopted this

weirdness, to my understanding. That's why witches aren't allowed into the country. You never noticed that no witches from outside of Vlideron visit?"

"No one from outside of Vlideron really visits Edgefair. And I have never left Edgefair... before now, at least."

"Well, you probably were born outside of Edgefair, so you just don't remember not being there."

"What is that supposed to mean?"

"I mean, it's not like you witches are ever raised on the compounds near where you were stolen."

"Stolen? No, we were abandoned!"

Rage welled in Ruby once more as Dorian burst out laughing, the hearty sound coming from his belly. He doubled over briefly, his cackling echoing through the forest. Her free hand fisted. She debated trying to summon light magic, even though hers had always been weak, and she suspected it would hurt her to summon it with the curse. But it would serve him right for laughing at her abandonment and pain.

He looked over at her, his laughter dying in his throat as he processed the look on her face. Pity flashed over his features, making it all much worse. Ruby wondered what the M'lvia's revenge he could be thinking.

"Haven't you wondered why the people call you all kidnappers?"

Ruby tried to ignore the pit returning as she slowly responded, "Well... of course... but I just thought the people felt cheated when a child is born with our calling. They hate us."

"Some humans have always hated witches, true. I could go on and on about the things that were done in some of the smaller villages back in the day, when the only witches around them had been generous with curses. But that's not it. It's because there is a decree the witches follow from the king. When a witch is born to a human family, of any rank, they are forcibly removed from their family and placed with a coven. Nobles get extra privileges for graciously giving over their witch children, such as more lands or court privileges. Regular people have their children ripped out of their arms and are given nothing in return. Not that anything could make up for their loss. The children are taken to other compounds, away from their original homes so that the parents can't easily try to find their own children."

"But, I've seen the babies at the gate! They're left naked and wailing most of the time! They don't even leave their babies with clothes or blankets to keep them safe from the elements! We are discarded!”

That pitying gaze flared with anger for a second, leaving Ruby afraid that her own anger might soon get her in trouble with this vampire before he opened his mouth again, “Well, the manipulation goes even deeper than I thought. With a few exceptions, most witches are wanted children. Your parents very likely wanted to keep you. That’s why the public views you all as kidnappers. Because from their perspective, you take their children, then train up their children to steal others’ children. I never knew you all thought you were abandoned, so I don’t think the people know that either.”

“But... If that’s a rule from the Great King, why is everyone so much more mad at us?”

“You haven’t heard the people talking about the king, have you?”

Ruby thought back on snippets of hushed conversations disparaging the Great King, but their whispers died the instant they saw a witch. She assumed they were few and far between examples of people blowing off steam. Was she wrong on that as well? How much had she been wrong about in her life? How much did the elders know about all of this?

“They must have a reason for making us all think we’re abandoned.”

“Right. To make you dependent on the coven for all of your attachment needs.”

“No, there has to be a good reason! Elder Moss wouldn’t just do this to me and the others without a reason. She cares about the coven and us witches. She just wants better from us.”

“Does it help you to believe that?”

Even Ruby’s thoughts fell silent for a moment, the crushing weight of how close to the truth Dorian hit expelling the breath from her lungs.

“Just think of all the things you witches ignore among the nobility.”

“What do you mean?”

Despite knowing the direction he’d take his statement, Ruby needed to hear him say it. The feeling in her gut be damned, she needed to hear it all. Every last damning word. She needed to know everything she was ignorant to before, everything she stuck her head in the sand and disregarded to keep herself safe.

“Would you like to know why I am on the run?”

The shift in topic caught her off-guard. For a moment, she forgot that Dorian wasn't looking directly at her, nodding her interest. Realizing he needed a verbal agreement, she quickly stammered out a *yes*, waiting. Either he wanted to lead into something, or he didn't know how conversations worked.

"I have been slaughtering nobility for centuries. Before you feel bad for them, know that I kill the pieces of shit who use their position of privilege to harm those weaker than them. Torturers, rapists, murderers. The vampiric council found out and tried to convince me to join them."

"Why would they want you to join them? Are they killing nobles too?" confusion filled Ruby to the brim.

"No, they mistook my choice of victim as negotiable. You see, vampires gain power through consuming the blood of those we've killed."

"But I thought..."

I thought vampires were naturally stronger or weaker based on inherent talent...

"The vampiric council of Vlideron has sold a narrative that we are just naturally more or less powerful. It's a lie. They use it to control the masses of vampires they keep creating. I have only suspicions for why they want so many weak vampires under their thumb. Anyway, they work with the nobility to secure future victims to murder and drain. They wanted me to join their ranks because I am already strong and I know the truth. It would allow them to keep a lid on me. Now, I have to ask, knowing that many nobles are in on this scheme with the vampiric council to kidnap and slaughter innocent people, why do the witches only bother the peasantry?"

The question slammed into Ruby's chest like a horse running at full speed. She felt tears spring to her eyes. She wondered for years why the witches didn't investigate the nobility more. She heard the whispers. The elders, Elder Moss specifically, always reiterated the words and desires of the Great King. Could he be in on this conspiracy as well? Was that why he accepted vampires running amok in Vlideron? What did the nobility gain from that agreement? Surely they gained something. For that matter, were there people among the elders who gained something? Did the Great King gain something too? How could she believe this bloodsucker so quickly on such a wild accusation? He essentially claimed that the witches were involved in widespread corruption among the nobility! But instead of churning, why did her gut settle, as if deep down she always knew?

She had bought so many excuses Elder Moss and the others gave her about the nobility and why they were so above reproach. How could they go on believing such things when she questioned this for years? Could they somehow not know the truth?

They must not know. Surely, they wouldn't stand for such injustice! But... what if they do?

Who knows the truth among witches? Could all of Vlideron's witches be convinced to turn a blind eye to the actions of the nobility without some of them knowing the truth and redirecting those of us that don't? Could they be innocents themselves?

They have to be... Some of them... at least... Elder Moss has to be one of the fooled witches. She has to be.

Ruby needed to believe that, because her feelings about the alternative stirred the curse within her too much.

CHAPTER TWELVE

Dorian

"How did you get away from the vampiric council? What happened with that?"

Dorian tried not to grimace at the way she so obviously changed the subject. While he wasn't looking at her, he could feel the roiling emotions like waves crashing on the world around her. She looked to be feeling so much shame, confusion, and fear. He wanted to scream that she could face the truth if she tried, but he suspected that it was overwhelming to have her world view crashing down around her. She would need time to adjust to the possibilities she never considered before.

"They summoned me before the council, gave me their little proposition. I refused. They moved to kill me, and I released the shadow puppet I used to attend the meeting and took off from my Edgefair estate immediately. Now, they're hunting me."

"So you didn't really attend the meeting? Just remotely?"

"Yes."

"Smart move, bloodsucker."

Dorian glanced sharply over his shoulder at her, "Was that a compliment?"

"Don't get used to it. I just respect the choice to not actually attend a meeting that could have been a trap. Since they were so ready to attack, it sounds like a trap."

"Fair enough, I suppose. I am a pretty smart bloodsucker, huh?"

Dorian glanced behind him in time to see Ruby's mouth twitch, on the verge of smiling, before other emotions slammed in on her. Shame, guilt, disgust. She felt bad finding him amusing. Guilt tugged at Dorian for spying on her emotions like that, but the other part of him reasoned that he needed to remain fully alert in the open forest, though she was rather distracting.

"You're not as mindless as I thought you bloodsuckers were, I'll give you that. But I don't know if I'd call you smart just yet."

"But you just did," Dorian smirked, knowing exactly what she'd been saying but wanting to get under her skin.

"No, no, I said 'smart move,' as in, you seem to have done one thing right. Just one."

"Well, I guess I'll just have to work harder to earn that distinction."

He heard her blow air aggressively through her nose, and he forced himself to stifle a laugh of his own. She kept trying so hard to continue hating him.

"So how old are you? I know you creatures live a long time, so how long?"

"I've been a vampire for around 500 years. I was a human for 30 years before that."

"So you're really old."

"Well, Vlideronian vampires used to trend far older, but after the king ascended the throne, older vampires started disappearing."

"Why?"

"The council allied with the king. I don't know all the details, but I do know that they wanted strict control of power at the top. So they killed off the vampires who knew the truth and garnered too much attention, but refused to join them. I flew under the radar mostly because I ensured my victim choices were clandestine."

"So you were a conniving bloodsucker even with your own kind?"

Dorian barked a laugh, "I suppose you could say that. I didn't let anyone know how strong I got."

"Why didn't you? Didn't you have friends?"

Laughter died in his throat, "Most were mortals. Those who aren't long dead either left Vlideron, or we took different paths."

Ruby fell silent. Taking a peak at her emotional state, she was mostly contemplative, but he could see pity in there too. The thought that she pitied him was bothersome. He didn't want her pity, or anyone's. He chose to be alone. He liked it that way. It was for the best. No attachments to others meant no pain when they inevitably left or died.

The uncomfortable silence compelled his mouth to open, "So what is with you witches calling your leaders elders? I mean, they're hardly old."

Dorian turned to look over his shoulder, noting the flicker of amusement on her face once again before she tamped it down. She seemed to consider his statement heavily for a moment more, as if she never thought much about the custom. She probably never had, he realized.

Why would she question the choice of honorifics for her leaders when she was raised that way?

"I guess you do make something of a point. I'm sure to an ancient bloodsucker like you, no one is much of an elder."

"Did you just call me old, again?"

"Do I need to spell it out? I thought you were trying to prove yourself intelligent."

Dorian couldn't suppress his laugh. She possessed a sharp wit. He wondered how she could have developed it with such a stifling upbringing, but decided it best not to question her on that too much. He didn't want to spend his time poking at such glowing sore spots. While she clearly needed some prodding to examine her life, it didn't have to be constantly.

"Fair point. But I will have you know there are some elves out there that would consider me hardly more than a child."

"What would that make me? An infant?"

"Now you're getting it! So, with that in mind, how is it that your leaders are elders? It's very silly if you ask me."

Despite her best attempt, Dorian heard the giggle she couldn't stifle in time. He decided not to acknowledge it, also seeing the way her body tensed and the emotions within her swirled. The shadows were responding pretty intensely to each negative emotion. Interestingly, they didn't respond as much to her laughter or enjoyment. Just to the shame that crashed down around her after Dorian managed to provoke a positive feeling.

"I suppose they aren't in the grand scheme of things. But they are older for humans and witches, and that's what I think it's in reference to."

"Older for humans, sure. But they aren't really older for

witches. You witches used to live a couple hundred years most of the time."

"Really?!" Ruby's voice echoed along the forest, prompting Dorian to look around cautiously.

"Yes? You didn't know that? Oh, I guess you wouldn't. It changed at the same time as those weird doctrines popped up."

"How so? What happened?"

"Well, you witches used to live, oh, probably an average of 250 or so years. Some of you lived to be around 400 years old, though. It really depended, but I never knew on what. But when you witches started being weird guards for that king's policies about 200 years ago, half of you died off, and the other half started living the same lifespans as humans. Well, except the main elders who live in Mistspires with the king. They seem to be living the right lifespan of witches, for some reason."

"What? The... the elders in Mistspires... The Vlideronian witch elders are living longer than regular humans?"

Dorian stared at Ruby, noting the incredulity in her face with a growing sense of pity, "Yes, to my understanding, many of them are nearing 300 years old, actually."

"That explains so much..." Ruby's words, whispered so softly, were clearly not meant for his ears.

Dorian wondered what exactly his statement explained, but decided it would be better to leave it for when they reached his home and could really sit down and discuss their experiences.

The forest around them continued to come alive in small ways. The area near his cave repelled local wildlife because of the entrenched scent of a vampire, but the further away they got, the more of the fauna they got to see. The animals of the forest were often much the same as the ones in other forests, but with unique adaptations.

Ruby cooed and giggled as she saw a variety of furry animals stalking the forest, consuming the flowers, bark, moss, and mushrooms. Some possessed fur of shocking colors while others glowed with varied vibrancy. Deer with antlers of glowing green grazed near bunnies sporting fur that pulsed with opalescent light. Birds flitted through the trees, the trilling echoes of their songs adding to the symphony of the forest. Some came in the glowing shades of the other creatures, but the predatory birds focused on stealth, their movements blending in with the darkened surroundings, surprising Ruby a few times as they dove in and out of her field of vision.

"How do the prey animals stay safe? I thought this was a dangerous area?"

"It is. The prey animals are well-adapted, though. They can extinguish the glow that allows them to see and attract mates when they sense predators are near. They've become more adept than most of their less-unique counterparts are at hiding. The beasts this deep into the forest don't generally bother themselves with the regular fauna either. They tend to hunt each other, or any stray people they can reach, no matter the race. Many hunt the fae."

"The fae? I didn't think they were reachable?"

"They don't engage with the other races, besides sometimes the elves, because they have no interest in participating in global politics. As such, they've never established a government as we know it. All the fae live amongst each other in the deepest wilds. While they are willing to help anyone they come across, they don't go out of their way for others. They mostly avoid the other races where they can. Like I said, sometimes they will trade with the elves, but that's pretty rare and only at a whim."

"So there are fae in Death's Forest?"

"Oh, yes. Probably a lot of fae, if I had to guess."

"Do you know what they're like?"

"What do you mean?"

"I mean, what do they look like? What do they do? Since they don't participate in kingdoms and societies the way the other races do, I don't know much of anything about them. I want to."

"Well, I don't know a lot of those answers myself. They seem to wander the wilds, and they look a variety of different ways. Some look quite a lot like elves, though they often share the same glow the small faeries with wings do. Others look like moving plants. Others like regular animals, but with something just slightly strange about them. It really depends, and they avoid others so much that I don't know much else, besides what I've read and been told."

"Oh... I suppose that makes sense... So some of them don't look like humans? And the fae, they are different sizes?"

"Yes," movement caught Dorian's eye, so he pointed, "like them. Those lights out there are fae."

Dorian pointed into the distance at a trio of orange, blue, and pink lights. Their flitting about so far above the ground gave away the fact that they were fist-sized, winged faeries, going about a traipse through the forest.

"Oh!"

"Some fae serve certain functions of the land, so they fly around the forest a great deal. They help nature progress in a way that benefits themselves and the nature itself. They pay no mind to the people in the way of that, of course, but they don't go out of their way to interrupt the people, either. I expect you'll see more of them going forward."

Ruby watched the fae in the distance for a long moment. The silence stretched long enough for Dorian to wonder if she might be done speaking with him for the time being.

"And the beasts leave the regular animals alone?"

"Mostly, at least this far in," Dorian nodded, grateful for her continued conversation.

"Strange. You would think they would go for such relatively easy prey."

"That isn't the life of a beast. The life of your average predator, yes. But beasts are creatures of magic and power, like you and I. They need to grow stronger. It's a part of their very existence. Somewhat like vampires, they grow more powerful by consuming powerful creatures. That's why they prefer people and other beasts to animals."

"So the bloodsucker acknowledges he's a beast?"

Dorian laughed, "Well, I guess so. But I have the wherewithal to decide my prey much more carefully than a beast does. While beasts generally avoid vampires, many are stupid enough to try it anyway. They also wouldn't have the judgment to not try a dangerous little witch with a mysterious curse."

"I suppose you might have a point about the virtues that make you less of a beast... But you're still just a bloodsucker."

Dorian nodded in response, focusing on the subtle markers that showed the path.

"Oh!"

Turning around, Dorian saw that Ruby approached a tree, the wild blue mushrooms lighting up, its matching blue glow almost painful to behold.

"Ah, yes, the mushrooms respond to magic. They light up to alert beasts to the presence of each other, people, and vampires."

"Why would the mushrooms do that?"

"They feed on the magic that results from such battles. If the beast loses to a person, the mushrooms feed on the magic flowing from the corpses. If a beast wins, they absorb all the magic the beast can't, because their process is very wasteful. And if both die? That's their ideal outcome. But they react to vampires differently. If we kill the beasts, there is often little magic for the mushrooms to feed off of. So they tend to warn the beasts of our presence. Your magic is too enticing of a potential meal for the mushrooms to react to me at the moment, however."

"I... guess those mushrooms are perfect for this area.. But why don't the mushrooms alert to the regular animals? They clearly have some sort of magic."

"That's a bit of a long story, but I've even seen those mushrooms not even alert to some humans before."

"They alert to regular humans sometimes?"

"Most of the time, actually."

"But regular humans don't have magic... Do they?"

"In fact, they do. It's just harder for them to access and use it. How did you think druids and priests existed?"

"I guess I didn't think much about it. We were taught that witches were the only humans with magic, and that's why we look so strange."

"Strange?"

Dorian waited for Ruby to respond, but she never did. Clearly, she had some issue with the visibility of her nature, but that wasn't any of his business. Instead, he decided to drop the question and poke at her once more.

"Witches are a beast's favorite meal, of course."

"Ah, of course," Ruby rolled her eyes when Dorian turned to glance at her.

Dorian laughed, grateful for the brevity she offered so readily, despite the circumstances they found themselves in. Though she evidently wanted to hate him, he could tell that her curiosity was stronger.

He hoped that would be enough to get her thinking about what she could do with the rest of her life, after the curse. He hoped it would be enough for her to abandon the idea of rejoining the witches as they stood in the present day. He didn't think for one second—based on what he had seen and what she had told him of how the other witches viewed her and what they believed—that she would be able to reform modern witches, but taking her out of their clutches would be good enough.

"You might also like to know that they do enjoy vampires as well. We're just more dangerous prey, so most avoid us instinctively. You witches used to be terrifyingly dangerous prey. Until you cut yourselves off at the knees."

Ruby's whispered response sent Dorian choking on his own breath with amusement at her continued fight to hate him, *"You should cut yourself off at the knees..."*

CHAPTER THIRTEEN

Ruby

Ruby gazed around in wonder at how the landscape changed while they swiftly hiked through Death's Forest. This far in, the name seemed ridiculous. The depths of the forest were unexpectedly teeming with life. The plants became more frequent, bushes with flowers and leaves in vastly varied colors sprouting up from the moss-covered forest floor, which shifted color as they walked from the vibrant teal to a beautiful, soft blue, like the still waters of a particular painted lake from the center of Vlideron. She'd been told the painting looked true to life, but Ruby hadn't left Edgefair before, so she couldn't say for certain.

The forest started sloping upwards, with craggy rocks marking new hills to climb here and there. Trees became slightly further apart and, looking up, Ruby thought she could see the sky in the far distance above. They traveled for so many hours that she suspected the sun would soon rise. She couldn't tell if the wavering hints of colors high above them were a sign that she could see bits of the sky or not. Though the trees were still covered with dark purple flowers, more glimpses of the emerald green bark poked through. Normal-looking greenery, like she might have found outside of Death's Forest, started to become more common in general.

Ruby even glimpsed the glowing forms of small faeries flitting about the trees, seemingly observing them. She tried hard not to gape as she spied them, but couldn't stop watching their movements. Though they snuck behind trees as they followed her and Dorian, they weren't terribly subtle, with such wildly bright lights in the most brilliant colors. The specific trio following them were a bright fuchsia, sunset orange, and aqua blue. Against the dark purple and green covering the trees, they were painfully visible. Only the glow of the mushrooms could compete, lighting up a deeper blue than before as Ruby passed nearby.

Dorian had been annoyingly congenial throughout their trek. He responded to every quip with either infuriating sincerity or casual amusement. He didn't insult her back, though he repeatedly hit chillingly close to her heart much of the time. She found it disconcerting that he expressed such a deep conceptualization of her life with the others from such a short interaction with them. He kept reiterating that they were ridiculous in his eyes and entirely wrong for blaming her for wanting to live. He just didn't understand. They weren't wrong. Maybe they weren't right either, but they were just doing it for the good of the coven. When Ruby tried to bring this up, he scoffed and asked about what was good for her.

She kept having to switch subjects. She learned a lot about the history of Vlideron, since her lifelong lessons were apparently entirely wrong. She even learned a good deal about the world at large, though Dorian said his information would probably be outdated. That made sense, since he couldn't have left the country in the last 200 years. Only select humans were granted permission to legally leave Vlideron temporarily. Vampires were tracked by a magical barrier set around Vlideron which would alert the vampiric council to the location where a vampire exited the kingdom. All others were blocked from leaving by the patrolling witches, vampires, and human military.

"So, bloodsucker, did you travel the world to sample blood before the lock down of Vlideron?"

Dorian's laugh echoed in the forest again, cutting through the songbirds and chatter of smaller creatures and bugs, "Well, I actually haven't ever left Vlideron."

"Never?"

"No. Never wanted to. Vlideron suffered corruption long before that king took the throne, and I do so love killing corrupt nobility."

Ruby focused on climbing up the latest rocky hill after Dorian, hesitantly taking his outstretched hand to help her over the last of the rocks. As he pulled her up with one arm, lifting her completely past the rocks and setting her beside him with ease, Ruby caught his scent yet again. She steadfastly ignored it each time they came close to one another, but her eyes fluttered, threatening to close as she breathed him in. Pine trees, petrichor, nighttime in winter. The scent both comforted and infuriated her.

What right does a damn bloodsucker have to smell so... enticing? Fuck, it isn't fair... Why can't I stop noticing it?!

Shaking off the observation and stepping away from Dorian, Ruby refocused, "I hate that I believe you about that."

Despite her gut insisting on his honesty, Ruby spent the last few hours trying to poke holes in his stories about the Great King and the nobility. None landed. He had an answer for nearly every question. How he could so easily address some of her questions maddened her. What somehow made it worse, however, was the way he reacted when he didn't know an answer. Rather than come up with some bullshit, or just redirect to his previous answer and say to extrapolate from that, he would admit that he didn't know. He would just admit that he didn't have the exact answer.

Compared to the elders, Ruby couldn't help but find him impressive. The elders would tell her to look to previous answers when she asked certain questions. Ruby would always try to do exactly as they said, thinking maybe the answer really existed there. But the answers always came up short and she felt brushed off. She would sometimes get the sense that the elders were trying to portray themselves as more knowledgeable than they were. Elder Moss went further, giving half-answers, then claiming to have already answered when Ruby pushed for something more satisfying. Worse still, she would then decide that Ruby's continued questioning meant a need for reeducation.

So, I'm cursed and have to run away from the coven... Then I encounter a vampire... And despite the fact that vampires are supposed to be enemies of witches, and he killed the others, he just keeps answering my questions...

The sense of enjoyment welling up within her at his lack of attachment to being all-knowing incensed her. A quiet voice inside told the truth of it.

You're angry with yourself, not him. He's done nothing but help.

The culmination of these facts left her stuck with one conclusion: she believed that he conveyed the facts as he knew them. He might be wrong, but she somehow doubted it. He knew a lot more about the world than her, which came naturally by virtue of his advanced age, but it went deeper than that. Dorian lived a life outside of the influence of the coven. He represented the outside world in the same way as Ruby's human dalliances had, except he knew that she was a witch and he never expressed hatred toward her for it. Yes, he expressed hatred for the doctrines of the witches, and even for Violetta and Vanella, and all the others who came to kill Ruby. But he hadn't ever professed a hatred for witches in general. Just the things witches started doing. Who they became as a whole in his lifetime. He hated seeing what he perceived as a fall from grace.

Ruby didn't know what to make of that. She kept wishing she could take a long break to read through the old journals and grimoires she had brought with her on the run, but she lacked the time. With only brief stops for her human needs, they set what would have been a blistering pace for the most fit regular human. As a witch, it wasn't much better. With each step, Ruby could feel her joints aching from the long hours of exertion. Her feet felt like they were ready to fall off entirely.

Ruby refused to complain about it in front of the vampire. Knowing he had carried her to the cave, over hundreds of miles, felt like one thing. Having him carry her the rest of the way because she couldn't suck it up would be another thing entirely. Ruby wasn't sure that Dorian would actually go so far as to carry her the rest of the way to his home, but she didn't want to take the risk that he found her too slow or useless to walk herself. It would be humiliating if he needed to carry her. Worse, what if he got annoyed by her inability to go on? What if he changed his mind about continuing to guide her to the safety of his home? She would be truly hopeless in that event. They hadn't encountered any beasts yet, but that likely resulted from Dorian's presence.

If a vampire wasn't here...

She shuddered at the conjured images of how that would play out for her. She wouldn't stand a chance against some of the strongest beasts of the forest, who would surely be in the area still. The way Ruby understood Dorian's explanations on the power structure of beasts in Death's Forest earlier on in their trek, the weakest ones kept to the outskirts in hopes of greater numbers of magical beings to consume. The stronger the beast, the longer it could go without a meal, and the more they craved the challenge of powerful prey. Such beasts would then travel deeper and further through the forest, hunting for fae and particularly brave, powerful people. Vampires weren't generally on the menu, as only the strongest of the beasts could hope to stand a chance. Most instinctively avoided vampires, since few possessed the strength to legitimately challenge a vampire. But a witch like her? She would be a fortuitous meal to stumble upon for the beasts that far in, since she wouldn't pose much of a threat and would be a rich source of growth. The beasts in the area likely hadn't encountered a threatening witch in ages, so they would not maintain that fear.

"You alright?"

Ruby startled. Realizing he noticed her shuddering, she scrambled to find an explanation that didn't reveal the weakness of her body. There were so many possible explanations she could turn to, but her brain wasn't cooperating. Her chest tightened before she finally latched onto what she could say to brush off his concerns.

"Just a bit chilled... This is much farther North though, right?"

"Yes." Dorian looked at her skeptically as he resumed leading the way.

So he definitely didn't buy that... But he didn't push me on it, at least.

"We'll be arriving at the next resting spot soon. Should be able to see it after we crest this hill. It plateaus for a while, so you'll get a clearer view. And the sun is starting to rise, so it should be easier to see the distance for you."

Ruby watched as Dorian scratched at the back of his head again, wondering if he did that for a reason. Her first thought called it a nervous tic, but that didn't make sense. What would a vampire like him have to be nervous about?

"That'll be good..." Ruby tried not to grimace at the relief she heard in her own voice, knowing that Dorian would hear it too, "Not that I couldn't go on, of course... I just meant that it'll be nice to be able to see more... Because of the sun rising."

"Right. There's a bit of time left before it's fully in the sky, but we've reached a point of the forest that does get real sunlight, filtered and sporadic as it may be."

"How will that affect you?"

The question left her mouth before she could stop it. She didn't want him to think she cared about him, but she remained curious about how the sun really affected vampires. She'd been told growing up by the coven that vampires couldn't be awake in the daytime. They would suffer and die off with exposure to the light. But Dorian moved around just fine in Death's Forest during what technically counted as daytime, so it clearly wasn't based on the sun being up in general.

What is the truth?

"Ohh do you care about the bloodsucker's wellbeing now?" Dorian's hearty laugh sent heated embarrassment and annoyance through her, but he continued before she could retort, "I'll be okay. The sun isn't good for me, by any means, but the stronger you get as a vampire, the better you can handle a bit of exposure. Freshly turned vampires should avoid the sunlight entirely, because it'll cook their insides and be much too painful to function. They might combust if they can't escape the exposure soon enough, but that's rare and takes a lot longer than you might think to set in. It's rare one can't make it to shade in time to avoid that fate. As for me, while I don't find it comfortable, I can manage."

Ruby heard the way he avoided speaking about himself specifically for the most part, but decided against pursuing it, since he would just act like that meant she cared. "I don't care about a bloodsucker, for the record... I just wanted to make sure my guide to safety wouldn't get burnt to a crisp before he finished helping me."

"My, how coldly practical!" Dorian laughed again, pausing at the top of the hill for Ruby to catch up.

She scowled at him, trying to ignore the ache in her arm from holding the lantern. Keeping it up enough to see ahead, since the glow did not extend around her far enough to see her surroundings comfortably if she kept it at her side, became an exercise in perseverance. Her arms were aching as badly as her feet, ankles, and legs. Though excited for rest, she needed to keep herself going. Cresting the hill, Ruby kept her glare on Dorian for a moment longer. His dark red eyes were firmly trained on her, rather than the path ahead.

She waited for him to look away, hoping to hide any relief she experienced. He didn't look away.

Huffing her annoyance, Ruby turned away and looked ahead, gasping as she finally laid her eyes on their next resting place.

Ruby wrongly assumed they were headed to another cave, but she saw nothing so mundane as that. Ruins of what must have been a sprawling city lay before them, the details only vaguely visible in the gray light coming through the trees, marking such early dawn that no golden sun graced the sky just yet. The many buildings scattering the land were only identifiable because of the unnatural shapes she could see from so far away.

Ruby's gasp echoed as she took it in, shocked that those ruins seemed to be their destination for rest. She wondered just how broken down the city must be, if they would have somewhere truly safe to sleep. They must, or Dorian wouldn't have chosen it for his rest area, she reasoned. She wondered how long it must have sat, neglected and occupied only by the memory of the people who once lived there.

One question had her speaking before she could stop herself or control the awe in her voice, "What happened here? I mean... why is this city here in the depths of Death's Forest?"

"It's an old elven city. Death's Forest used to be an elven country, actually. Millennia ago, of course. I read some old accounts of what happened back then, which were in elvish so bear in mind that I may have missed some things. To my understanding, the king and queen of the time were deeply monogamous, and madly in love. They were both expected to keep concubines, to increase the chances of royal children, from any source. Elven fertility is naturally fairly low, so any chances increased by any source were expected to be explored, even if it meant the queen became pregnant by a concubine. The child would still be considered a legitimate heir. Neither did. Instead, they housed those in need in their palace as supposed concubines. Well, a witch apparently had his eye on the royal couple, eager to be the first true concubine.

"Anyway, he tried to gain the affections of the monarchs, but they fully rebuffed him. The king and queen supposedly saw through him and realized he was after political power and the ego boost, so they sent him away immediately. This witch stewed with indignant rage."

"What did he think would happen? One of the ruling monarchs would suddenly forsake their true love for him and he would get to climb social ranks? That's so weird..." Ruby furrowed her brow.

"Yeah, I agree," Dorian laughed, shaking his head, "But he took the rejection personally. Instead of graciously accepting it, the way other foreigners seeking true concubine status would, he traveled to the center of the country, closer to Edgefair, further southwest of here, and set to work on his plans. He spent decades cultivating the seed for a special tree. When it matured enough, he planted it in the heart of one of the largest cities of the kingdom and enacted his curse. Throughout the nation, large trees identical to the one he cultivated violently sprang up, killing by the thousands, shrouding the entirety of the land in eternal night, with no recourse or prevention. That curse spread out from that central city over the course of months, eventually overtaking the entirety of the kingdom, destroying the previous ecosystem and drastically altering the landscape. Many cities were completely destroyed. But he hadn't known one thing."

"What?"

"The curse would weaken with distance from its origination. It still extended to those ancient borders, but the closer it grew to the mountains in the North and the ocean in the South, the further apart the trees would grow. Farther from the origin, the trees tended to spring up in open areas, where it was easier to grow, and less through buildings and large natural objects. Rather than destroying the cities in horrific destruction, like it did near the heart of the country, it just destroyed the roads. It surrounded some natural features like lakes and hot springs, but didn't destroy those either. It didn't touch gardens, where in the deepest parts of the forest the new trees would rip out existing plants to take root. His curse did have a bonus effect, in that it became the perfect breeding ground for beasts, however."

"So the people who lived here...?"

"They fled when the curse neared and it became clear they possessed no way to stop it from destroying their roads out of the city. They left before it could trap them here, or attracted the beasts like it was already reported to in areas nearer the epicenter. And, as you've seen, the trees themselves began to change over time, adapting to the coloring of the other flora of the forest."

As they walked forward, there was a notable shift in the trees nearing the ruins, as even fewer of the dark purple flowers covered the trees while the bark transitioned from emerald green to a brighter, well-watered grass green, vibrant and shocking. The area featured much lighter colors and more ordinary plant life. The location of these ruins stood far enough away from the epicenter of that ancient curse for the trees to struggle taking over. There were enough openings in the canopy above that Ruby could see the sky. The light cascading down in midday would be frequently shaded by the branches swaying in the winds far above them, but it would nevertheless be open to the majesty of the sky.

The exposure to regular, if disrupted, sunlight must have allowed ordinary plants to flourish, Ruby guessed. Nearing the outskirts of the ruins, typical roses climbed a southern wall, their red flowers a stunning contrast to their deep green vines and the gray stone wall supporting them. That first note of astounding beauty overtaking the ruins proved far from the last.

Getting closer to the ruins in the growing light, Ruby's senses became enveloped in a symphony of beauty. The gray stone walls on the outskirts of the city were overtaken by ivy, roses, and other creeping plants, many blossoming with rainbow flowers. That anything still stood at all testified to the original craftsmanship, considering how intensely nature had worked to reclaim the city entirely. The multi-colored stained glass windows remaining in many of the buildings, depicted all sorts of natural scenes melded with various services and needs. Some looked like an announcement of what shop lay beyond. Others, attached to what appeared to be private residences, were of different landscapes or plants or animals.

Ruby kept turning in circles, forgetting to keep up with Dorian as they strolled through the city, her thoughts sticking on little pieces of the architecture that stood out to her. The buildings were all carefully made, and while the streets were meandering, Ruby got the sense that it served some purpose. As if the streets were built around the land, rather than clearing the way for the people. Faded signs stood vigil at every intersection, the text long gone, but Ruby assumed they must have been detailed to need to be so large. Some of the cursed trees still invaded the city, taking up former community circles or parks. But their distance left long shafts of golden light filtering down.

Captivated, Ruby almost missed when Dorian stopped at a particular door. The outside identified it as a book shop, with a large stained-glass front window depicting an open book surrounded by closed ones in all colors. The door, like many others they'd passed, was made of thick wood, tall and wide, with a curved top and a plant-based design carved into the dark surface. Ruby followed as Dorian let them in, noting with interest that he used a key for the place, rather than leaving it open. She

112

wondered why he needed a key, since this place hid so far within Death's Forest that no one would ever find it.

Inside, the place reminded her of that old section of the library back on the compound, with delicately carved designs on all of the deep bookcases, covered in old manuscripts. Ruby breathed in the smell of parchment and found herself transported back to that discovery. Shaking off the memory, Ruby scrambled to follow Dorian, who immediately strode to the back of the shop and opened a discreet door that revealed stairs up to an apartment.

Dorian paused as Ruby reached the top of the stairs, giving her an assessing gaze. His eyes glanced down to her feet, roving back up to her hands, and finally landing on her face once more. Ruby felt entirely too seen.

"There is a hot spring nearby. I think you could use the restoration it offers. You've had a long few days, and I am sure a full bathing session would be beneficial as well. I know I want a restorative bath, so I will be going whether you choose to come along or stay here and rest. This apartment has enough running water for hygiene but I never fixed the heated water enchantments. They were disrupted by the cursed tree's roots, I think, so it would be exclusively cold water here."

Ruby's bag fell heavily at her side as she considered his suggestion. She would love to fully bathe and relax, but it would be awkward with him there. Despite the ruins being in good shape, they were still ruins, not his real home. He didn't seem interested in killing her yet, at least. He didn't need to make the suggestion either, as he could have just left her there while she slept to go by himself. The offer represented a kindness; she didn't know what to feel about that.

Regardless of her reasons to be wary or reject his kindness, he was right.

That would be paradise...

CHAPTER FOURTEEN

Dorian

Dorian contemplated how Ruby grew noticeably quieter walking through the night as they made their way to the hot spring. Her pitiful attempts to hide her pain were not half as subtle as she thought. Truthfully, Dorian found it not just pitiful but grating. No good reason existed to hide one's own suffering while in the company of those there to help. While he moved through the world as a stranger to her, and would be for some time yet, he worried it went deeper. She seemed to hide her weakness as a rule. From what he'd seen of the witches hunting her, Dorian guessed at a connection to their new doctrines.

She was evasive about the details of her life with the witches throughout their trek. Dorian avoided pushing the matter, and he would continue to avoid pushing it for a while yet. Approaching the hot springs—where they would each be bathing—would likely be uncomfortable enough without Dorian making it worse by prodding at an obvious wound.

The hot springs, once the main attraction for the area, were located just outside of town in relative seclusion. The short distance allowed the trees to grow in more closely, creating full-dark over the hot springs themselves. The hedges that once bordered and marked off the springs withered away once the trees drowned out the sun. Despite this reduction of physical barriers, the springs were nevertheless shrouded by the steam curling up from them, coating the forest floor and extending up a couple dozen feet into the air.

"How is there so much steam here?" Ruby asked, her voice thick with amazement.

Turning to look at her, Dorian noticed hazy steam softening her appearance. His vampiric sight wasn't affected by the thick mist, but he could strangely see its effects because of its magical thickness. Dorian realized that Ruby could probably hardly see him already, so he slowed down to make following him easier.

"The enchantments on these hot springs were crafted and strengthened by generations of elves, so they still haven't faded. From my reading, the elves of old spent thousands of years renewing the enchantments to keep these springs in perfect condition, with varying heat levels in different parts of the spring. Every thirty or so years. I'm not sure why they did such a frequent renewal, though. The enchantments have held this long. They make the steam thicker for greater privacy, since most visitors enjoyed lower visibility."

Ruby hummed her response, her eyes wide as she held the lantern low, apparently struggling to see the ground beneath her feet, where the steamy mist was thickest. Dorian glanced down as well, noting how horribly overgrown the old cobblestone pathway looked. He'd always kept it clear with Leandra, since she boasted even worse vision than Ruby likely did. Danatel being a werewolf granted him even better vision than Dorian. Margroc, unsurprisingly, hadn't enjoyed the hot springs; she ran hot and started sweating in water Dorian thought tepid.

Maxen refused to visit the hot springs entirely, but not because they were opposed to hot springs in general. Rather, their relatives lived in Death's Forest, before it had been called that. Many died in the escape. Maxen staunchly avoided the topic. Dorian only knew that many survivors chose to leave the world early, the trauma of losing their homeland to a curse proving too much. Truly long-lived elves were rare on their continent, since so many suffered the loss caused by Death's Forest firsthand. Most of the elves who had lived in the ancient kingdom had died from the destruction caused by the curse, or fled the continent in general. To the other mortal races, the onset of Death's Forest had been so long ago that they possessed no living memories of how it came to be. It simply was.

To the elves, it marked a living trauma. A nightmare come to life. So many lost their homeland. That was a trauma in and of itself. To many, after living several lifetimes in their homeland, it became too much to handle or cope with. The losses of friends, family, and lovers, compounded the sensation for some, leaving them adrift in the world. Some wandered, searching for their futures and crafting a new life. Others succumbed to the despair and gave up. Maxen's ancestors, once assured of the continuation of their lines, were among the latter. The fact that Dorian's main residence lay within those cursed ancestral lands, let alone the history of his specific home, left Maxen feeling eternally disquieted. The hot springs themselves were too much for the relatively young elf.

As a result, the path hadn't been maintained in nearly 400 years—since Leandra. He kept it up for nearly twenty years after Leandra left, hoping one day she might return to him and he could lead her to that special spot once again. That day never came.

"Are you sure you should be taking the time to bathe in a hot springs?" Ruby asked.

"What do you mean?"

"I mean, you said vampires are hunting you."

"I'm keeping aware, but I doubt they could catch up just yet. That is why I want to get home as soon as possible, but I am not in a horrible rush, since this is hundreds of miles from Edgefair and I laid extensive false tracks."

"Ah," Ruby nodded.

Finally, they reached the springs themselves, Dorian led Ruby right to the edge of the water. From the look on her face, she could only see for a few feet in any direction, so he figured it would be best if she stood near the water to start with. Giving her a good look, Dorian hid the laugh that bubbled up with a cough. Ruby wore her dagger on her thigh, strapped over her pants. That she felt she needed her weapon, though understandable and probably wise, deeply amused him. She would realize it eventually, but she had nothing to worry about around him, so long as she didn't move to harm him first.

"You go ahead and wash up. Those enchantments also allow for visitors to use soap in the springs, unlike other places. Any grime or soap will be cleansed from the water almost immediately. I'll go around and refresh the scent markings I have to keep beasts away while you do that."

"Scent-markings?"

"Hmm? Oh, yes, I learned it from a werewolf I once knew. Vampires aren't quite as sensitive to scent as werewolves are. They taught me that vampiric scent markings are as effective as werewolf scent markings in keeping the beasts away from an area. So I like to keep the beasts away from these hot springs."

"Oh... I guess that makes sense... So I will be alone to bathe?" Her voice heightened with excitement but Dorian could also hear a strange note within that excitement.

Despite the subtlety, he saw the kernel of disappointment hiding beneath her overall delight with her forthcoming bath. Dorian tried to smother the urge to tease her about what he sensed. He tried to encourage his mind to focus on the actual question and leave the knowledge he shouldn't have out of the equation.

"Don't worry, if you want to see me naked, I'll be bathing right after you're done."

He failed.

Ruby's skin darkened with a furious flush, her mouth dropping open in shock. Quickly, her mouth snapped shut, lips pursing in annoyance. Her eyes narrowed, those large, black irises disappearing behind thick, dark red lashes. The hint of red supplied by her lashes almost tricked his brain into believing she had vampiric eyes.

Shaking away the illusion, Dorian waved off the protests before she could voice them, striding away to leave Ruby to her bathing. He only took a few steps before he heard Ruby huff and set down the lantern. Turning back, Dorian saw her already sitting at one of the large rocks lining the hot springs, undressing. She only removed one boot, but Dorian felt perverted for even looking back. Snapping his head forward again, Dorian focused on the task of refreshing his scent-markers.

Wanting to give Ruby the privacy to bathe, Dorian forced himself to meander through the process. Rubbing his head against the trees always left his hair feeling grimy, but it best ensured his scent remained strong enough to last. Thus, Dorian suffered through the discomfort over and over again to apply his scent to each and every tree circling the hot springs, forming a perfect ring of safety.

As he moved through the motions of scent marking, Dorian considered the council meeting. He realized what the vampiric council gained from ensuring so many weak vampires were employed beneath them in Vlideron. Political power. Keeping the number of vampires high ensured they could swing their weight around in the political sphere, while keeping the population they controlled weak and ignorant ensured their positions as leaders could never be challenged.

Furthermore, they could use their populace of potentially dangerous individuals as a cudgel if ever needed to threaten other actors to stand down. The leadership of Vlideron sat precariously between three major factions as a result. The human monarch with his noblemen and merchant backers, representing their own greed while oppressing the statistical majority. The vampiric council representing the second largest population, positioning themselves as a dormant army to threaten the humans. And the witches, who Dorian knew the least about, especially currently. Their roles and benefits were not yet apparent to him, but he knew they must enjoy some benefit he had simply failed to discover yet.

Unfortunately, Dorian proved incapable of moving slowly enough, even in his distracted meandering. Ruby sat near the edge of the spring, facing away from him, with her braids pulled up on her head, kept out of the water. The curve of her neck and shoulder glistened, steam caressing her as he saw the small movements of her relaxed breathing. She exhaled a relieved sigh that sent his thoughts toward what she might sound like experiencing other pleasant sensations.

Dorian shook himself. He possessed no need or reason to think about the gasping moan he could imagine her making upon being licked along her inner thigh. He didn't need to think about how she might sigh after the screams of her release abated. The last thing he should be thinking about was how her sultry voice would sound begging for a break from release after relentless release.

Turning away, Dorian kept her in his peripheral vision as he surveyed the land. Her clothes, folded neatly on the rock beside a towel and her soap, were topped with her dagger. That Ruby brought the dagger at all showed good judgment, emphasizing the reality that they were basically strangers. Ruby didn't know him and he didn't really know her. Sure, Dorian thought he had a few good hypotheses about her, but less than a full day could never be enough time to tease those out and test them.

Mushrooms lit up blue in the distance, barely visible to even Dorian's keen eye. He zeroed in on that light, evaluating the beast as best as he could without being able to see it in detail while it likely evaluated him. When it drew no closer, Dorian relaxed a little. It seemed to have decided not to test its mettle against him for the time being. It likely helped that Dorian kept the trees near the hot springs clear of the mushrooms so that beasts remained effectively blind to any presence beyond the scent of a vampire.

Movement caught his eye as Ruby started to leave the water. Dorian damned his eyesight for being too good as he caught a quick glimpse of the lean muscles in her back, the curve of her waist into her full hips, and the water sliding down her body. He turned his back to her as soon as he registered the sight, but it sent his mind careening back into those damned thoughts he sought to banish. They were entirely out of place. He did not know her. Not enough to have any such thoughts about her. For centuries, those thoughts were reserved for people he'd gotten to know. While Dorian could always appreciate physical beauty, he hadn't been one to really experience sexual desire outside of the context of knowledge. He didn't need to love someone, per se, but he did need to know them a lot more than he knew Ruby.

Breathing through the frustration coursing through his touch-starved body, Dorian felt like a pouty, petulant fool. His body desperately wanted him to turn around and take in the glorious view he knew brightened the world behind him. His mind, knowing those thoughts to be wrong and creepy, berated his body for the impulse. Feeling ridiculous, Dorian decided to give something of a show.

Dorian recalled her earlier lust, her scent flaring each time he aided her up the rocky slopes. Delicious. She smelled like his favorite wine, sweet and nutty, with a heavy dose of vanilla and caramel. He was a lifelong sweet-tooth, and the fact she smelled of confections and the absurdly sweet wine he coveted forced his mouth to water, both literally and figuratively. He tried in vain to stuff down his own imagination, laying out how much of a delicacy tasting her blood, and tasting her, would be for the both of them. Having seen her reaction to closeness with him as her eyes roved over his body, Dorian couldn't help but want to drive her wild. It only felt fair. His foolish body's response to her lust tormented him.

Maybe it isn't fair of me to tease that response from her when I'm just mad that my body is reacting like this.

"Hey, bloodsucker, your turn."

A vicious smile spread across his face. That sealed it. Dorian stalked closer to her, mentally willing his shadows to thin out some of the mist. They moved and created a slight breeze, keeping the mist in their area at bay. Ruby could see him from further away than before. In turn, Dorian realized she wasn't finished dressing. Rather, she stood with her towel wrapped tightly around her. He tried not to choke on his own breath, steeling his resolve to torment her further.

Dorian strode near her. While still keeping a respectable distance, he set down his own soap and towel near the water's edge, and began to strip. He moved slowly, ensuring ample opportunity for her to turn and walk away if she wanted. He wasn't about to force her to see him naked. But she would have as much opportunity as she wanted, especially when she stood there with just a damned towel on.

What in M'lvia's revenge is she doing not putting her damn clothes on, anyways?

"What are you doing?" Ruby's voice came out high-pitched and breathy; he could sense her desire.

"Well, you said it was my turn to bathe, so I'm undressing."

She only gasped in response, her full mouth open and eyes wide. Dorian tried not to laugh, focused on keeping his every movement slow. He didn't wear many layers, so it wasn't going to take long before he was completely naked. She needed the chance to leave for this to be any fun. Dorian made sure his shadows kept a clear path leading away from the springs for her, so she could easily leave him behind if she wanted. She stayed put. He could feel her eyes glued to his body, giving him no small measure of self-satisfaction.

A twinge of fear raised within him as he gripped the hem of his tunic, remembering his back.

How will she react? Why would it matter? It's not like her opinion of me matters. It doesn't. It's just that old insecurity again. Nothing to do about it. Nothing to worry about.

Dorian lifted the tunic off his back and bared his torso, relishing in the feeling of freedom, turning away from her as he undid his pants.

CHAPTER FIFTEEN

Ruby

Ruby's gasp, equal parts horror and sympathy, escaped before she could stop it. Thick, raised scars crisscrossed all along his back, ranging in level of healing from old and pale to new, sensitive red. They all still looked painful. She guessed he had been whipped. Repeatedly, over the course of years, and brutally. She had never seen anyone who suffered such a horrible whipping and survived. Sometimes, the witches worked with the prison to heal whipped prisoners, but none so savaged. Even accounting for the different times those events must have occurred, Ruby couldn't imagine the full toll exacted on Dorian. It looked as if no skin on his back remained untouched. Tears filled her eyes, instantly wiping away the lust that had been building inside her as she considered what in M'lvia's revenge had happened to him.

A wave of confusion rolled over her and, with a trembling voice, she asked, "Why do you have scars?"

"Any scars gained before changing into a vampire remain, though thankfully all fresh wounds are healed without scarring. My back would be so much worse, otherwise," his voice sounded tight.

Ruby hesitated to question the sensitive subject, but her mouth opened anyways, "What happened?"

Her voice noticeably softened from mere minutes before. Unless he had been a different sort of monster as a human, she could not imagine him deserving such cruelty. He could, of course, lie to her, but what would be the point when they were so isolated that she lived at his mercy anyways?

"More than 500 years ago, the human man who fathered me was a lord. He abused his power to make me and entrap my mother. She couldn't leave with me. She wouldn't leave me with him. But she hated him. He wanted her to worship him. His twisted logic had him punishing me every time she didn't do as he pleased. I was a bastard child, so no one cared how he treated me. Right before she passed, he officially claimed me as his heir. Then she died. He whipped me so badly, I needed to be turned to save my life. The whippings began at twelve years old. I nearly died and transformed at thirty."

Dorian slid his pants down, prompting Ruby to avert her eyes. Her mind whirled with the information he gave her about his past. Each word, delivered with deathly calm, allowed her to feel the weight of truth. If anything, Ruby got the sense that he left a lot out.

The last detail rattled around her mind. Dorian's own father, the pathetic excuse for a human, tortured him. A part of her wondered how the man managed to maintain such control over Dorian to be able to do it for so long, but the answer became as clear as daylight to her in an instant.

Dorian stuck around back then, taking the abuse, to protect his mother. If the man took out his frustrations with Dorian's mother on Dorian himself, then he probably feared what would happen if he wasn't around to protect her.

As he descended into the water, Ruby resumed looking at him, knowing in her bones, despite the assumptions she made, that he stayed, receiving that trauma, in hopes of protecting his mother. Maybe it worked, or maybe it hadn't. She didn't know. She didn't know much about the whole situation. But she knew enough to be thoroughly enraged.

"What happened to him? Did that fucker ever get punished?" Her voice cracked with the force of her fury, coming out louder than she'd anticipated.

"I killed him. Within weeks of becoming a vampire."

"Good."

That wasn't the first time she condoned something Dorian did. When he told her about killing monstrous nobles, Ruby understood his reasoning and choices. A part of her wanted to go back to the compound and scream at the elders for being so blind to the obvious behavior of the nobles. It had constantly raised doubts within her at the judgment of the Great King. Without the proof, however, it languished as a fruitless idea, especially as her curse would be putting all of them in danger. Despite how the others chased her, Ruby desperately wanted to keep the rest of the coven safe from her.

A uniquely bestial glee overcame her at the knowledge of Dorian's patricide, leaving her simmering in the feelings his story stirred up. While undoubtedly glad that Dorian killed the man centuries ago, frustration at being unable to do anything to also punish the man who would bring about such horrors on a child gurgled within her. Her body shook with hardly suppressed rage at the very idea of harming someone, anyone, so thoroughly, especially without damn good reason.

Even trying to think of the reasons one could come up with to justify such torture, Ruby could only think that someone capable of doing such horrible things would be the one most deserving of it. Dorian's story left her wondering what other crimes the man he had to call his father did as well, leaving Ruby sick to her stomach. Ruby helped with healing people after such horrible things were done to them. She witnessed the soul-death that could come with those experiences for the survivors. Ruby worried that had happened to Dorian's mother. Ruby hoped his father suffered the fullest extent of M'lvia's revenge.

His father... Wait...

"Is... Is that why you hate your last name and title?" Ruby regretted asking the question immediately.

She'd blurted it out as soon as she thought it. His insistence that she only call him by his first name rattled around her mind incessantly. She gathered pretty readily that he wasn't particularly proud of, or interested in, his nobility or last name. She hadn't understood why that would be. Ruby had always privately wondered what it would be like to have a last name at all. For as long as she could remember, witches identified themselves with their coven's location. Maybe their names were different in the past. But as it stood, Ruby would be identified to visiting witches as Ruby of the Edgefair Coven. She claimed no last name of her own. If she were transferred to a different coven, she would be known by that coven. Seeing small children proudly identify themselves with their parents and family by their shared names, or seeing young couples decide to take a new name together as they joined their lives in marriage, jabbed at a point of private pain for Ruby. She would never know the joy of identifying with her ancestors or experience the pleasure of creating a new legacy with her lover.

The Great King toyed with new laws for naming conventions in recent years. Though he hadn't written any decrees on the matter yet, some couples were following the proposed rules in advance. Rumors abounded that the laws would soon arrive, as the Great King would allow time for his new, sometimes unpopular, laws to stew among the populace before pushing them through. Ruby remembered fondly how things used to go, however. Couples might change their names together to craft a new one. They might take on the name of one member of the couple for their own reasons. Or they might not change their names at all. Any children they raised would be named similarly, with the new name of the couple, the name they chose, or a combined version of their names. For that reason, Dorian's story prompted her to think of his name and title issues.

From the sounds of it, his mother never married the monster in question. In such circumstances, the child normally took their mother's name. But why would he hate his mother's name? Ruby somehow doubted that he would.

"My father was named Lord Leonarch Seagrave. So yes. I hate the title and last name because of him."

Ruby took in the stilted, tight words, and the rage that rose in her body boiling her blood and riling up the shadows squirming within, sliding against her internal organs. The sensation sent a chill down her spine, even as she could do nothing to stop the empathetic fury. She tried to cool her head, turning her attention to the movement of his arms as he washed up. Despite the shame of finding him at all appealing, at least it dampened some of her fury.

"You know, you witches only serve the nobles, right?"

Ruby narrowed her eyes at him, finding she didn't appreciate the reminder that her life seemed to have been spent in the service of monsters. Only a day gone, yet Ruby found herself more and more convinced that the witches had been wrong to support the rules and regulations she'd been taught to uphold her entire life. How could she reconcile such a drastic shifting of perspective? How could she reconcile never following those thoughts through to their conclusions when she was still with the coven?

"I... I never liked that we didn't monitor the nobility."

"That's right, and you've said you didn't participate in much of the arrests either."

"No, I... Gods, I could never admit this with the others but I just tell you so easily... I don't know what's become of me... But I tried to distract the others on my patrols so commoners didn't get caught doing illicit activities that I didn't think they should be jailed for."

"Like what?"

"I... I didn't think the people deserved to be jailed for engaging in certain sexual activities, or reading certain sorts of books. I mean, the books were there for them to get, why shouldn't they read them? But we were supposed to arrest commoners for publicly reading certain books. What is that? And I didn't want people to be arrested for expressing dislike of the Great King... I didn't hear it much. Most people fell silent when they saw a witch was near... But I did sometimes hear enough that I should have arrested them..."

"Well, that's interesting. Tell me, what did your life with the witches really feel like? If this is you telling me your secrets so readily, I can only imagine you felt remarkably lonely."

Caught off-guard, ice shot through Ruby. That question did more for quelling her anger than anything else, leaving her sick to her stomach, wondering how to answer. Before the curse manifested, Ruby might have said that her life felt equally challenging and rewarding. Her many failures just meant that she needed to work harder. She would make it. She would do better, be better, and someday, the coven would finally fully accept her..

Since the hidden library and the curse, Ruby was lost for words. She didn't want to be unkind to the witches. Ruby assured herself that they didn't know the truth of the world as she started to discover it. If they only knew the truth, things would be different. Why wouldn't they? Elder Moss would be able to relax more and connect in ways she surely wanted to connect. Why else had she gone to such lengths to try to fix Ruby's behavior? It must be because she cared on some level.

She must care...

"That... is a difficult question to answer..."

"Is it?"

"Yes! It's... I was always a difficult student for my elders. I required a lot of reeducation throughout the years that the others didn't need. I... I felt lonely and I broke the rules a lot more than anyone knew. Maybe that is why I have been punished with this curse... I don't know, but I know that I always questioned too much. Always too emotional. Too difficult. They would have given up on me sooner or later. I know it... I became terrified of that... Of them giving up on me. I was scared of messing up again. I was scared of failing even more. Always an utter failure... I don't think..."

Ruby stopped herself finally, realizing what she nearly said.

I don't think I want to go back to that.

The shadows within churned faster and faster as her heart pounded, her mind racing. Ruby tried to shove away the thought. Of course she wanted to go back. What else would she do? Once she resolved the curse, she would go back! She needed to go back to the coven so that she could tell them how to fix the curse if it was ever cast on anyone else, once she fixed it herself. Then she could be useful to the coven. Maybe she would be able to change it, if the reality of witches truly matched the texts in that hidden library. If what Dorian claimed turned out to be true, she might even be able to help the general public by convincing the witches to turn their backs on corruption. That remained her goal. So why did she almost say that she didn't want to go back? Why did the idea of returning make her more nauseous than the thought of never going back?

It only took a second.

Ruby thanked her lucky stars that she hadn't dressed in her nice clothes yet, the towel around her body shredding as shadows burst forth. Dimly, Ruby recognized that they were not as wildly active as the other times they escaped the confines of her skin. Rather, the shadows rolled around her body like twisting, thorny vines, rather than shooting spikes. She screamed her pain, the sound echoing through the forest. Faintly, she heard the splashing of water a second before Dorian knelt next to her.

"Ruby!"

A strangled sound escaped her throat in response. She lay on the ground. Time became meaningless, yet it proved to be everything because each ticking millisecond dragged into an eternity of agony. Her eyes began to blur, but Dorian came closer, lifting her head slightly and looking into her eyes.

"Look at me, Ruby," he softened his voice, the deep timbre coaxing her into relaxation, "just keep looking at me."

Ruby focused, the red of his eyes reminding her of her blood on the ground in Edgefair again, but calming her. They drew her in, guiding her breathing, making her sigh, even as she still distantly felt the pinpricks of the curse rolling along her body. The rest of the world dimmed to blackness as she kept looking into Dorian's eyes, listening to his murmured words, feeling her heart rate slowing down.

CHAPTER SIXTEEN

Dorian

Dorian's throat constricted, and sweat beaded on his forehead as he concentrated. He lost track of the words spilling from his lips. The seconds passed in exhausting detail. He lacked skill with hypnotism. Other vampires were deeply effective with it, but he never found a use for it. Even when kidnapping his noble victims, he didn't bother with hypnotizing them. It always bothered him on an intellectual level, since it could be used so nefariously. Yet there he sat, trying to hypnotize a damned witch. The worst possible target.

Witches possessed natural resistance to hypnosis. Targets most connected to magic proved the hardest to successfully hypnotize. But Dorian only needed a partial success. His hypnosis just needed to calm Ruby down enough that the curse would stop acting out on its own. This wasn't the time for him to toy with the shadows themselves, since they still needed to have a thorough conversation about how her curse worked. He needed to hear how it started and about every single time it acted out, in detail. Until then, he didn't feel confident in addressing the shadows directly.

For the time being, he guessed that if he could calm her emotions, the curse would ease up on her. Earlier, Dorian had looked over his shoulder, curious why she trailed off, only to see the shadows moving alarmingly. A mere second passed before the shadows burst out of her body. He sprinted to her. After only a few seconds, and feeling otherwise helpless, he decided to try hypnotizing her.

The moment her screams subsided into pained tears had been a special relief. Dorian wryly thought how those were not the screams he imagined earlier. He never wanted to hear those screams again, but with the curse, Dorian guessed he wouldn't have a choice. He tried not to scowl at the thought. He needed to keep up his efforts to hypnotize her, no matter how much his body shook with the exertion. He couldn't turn away or change his expression or even blink. His eyes burned.

Slowly, the shadows curling around Ruby's body began to slide back through her open wounds, healing her. Though Dorian only saw this through his peripheral vision, it relieved him. The tatters of her towel would have left little to the imagination if he willingly chose to distract himself, but Dorian had a job to do still. Ruby needed to be kept calm until the wounds were completely closed. His hypothesis that the curse responded to strong emotions on her part seemed to be holding up.

Long minutes of effort dragged on until, finally, Dorian could tell that the attack had extinguished itself. He released the hypnotism, Ruby's onyx-colored eyes blessedly clearing. The glazed over look that had engulfed her face while under hypnosis disturbed him. Sitting back on his feet, Dorian looked up towards the canopy of the trees, breathing heavily and returning to his own body.

His stomach clenched with an aching need to feed. He had never performed such intensive hypnosis in his long life, and his lack of talent in the ability left him especially drained from the effort. He needed blood. Soon. The scent of Ruby's blood hung in the air around them. Dorian could feel his fangs aching to sink into her, despite what she just dealt with. He tensed painfully, refusing to give in to temptation.

A trembling hand landed on his bare thigh while she lifted herself up, reminding Dorian where he was before the curse's assault. Dorian hurriedly turned further away. It was one thing to give her a naked show when they were both capable, alert, and able to readily leave. It felt entirely different to sit so close with her and essentially force her to see him in all his glory without recourse. Despite his desire to rush back to the spring, hide himself in the water, and finish his own bathing, Dorian needed assurance on her well-being. Furthermore, he wanted to apologize.

"I'm sorry I hypnotized you there. I didn't know what else to do to help, and I just did the first thing that came to mind. I shouldn't have affected your mind, and I assure you, I will not do so again." Dorian scratched at the back of his head, looking at the canopy of the trees over his shoulder in Ruby's direction to address her without looking at her disheveled state.

"No... No, it's okay... I..." Her voice, though painfully quiet, strengthened with every word, "I don't think I would be okay if you hadn't. I... I appreciate you helping me the way you did."

Dorian nodded uncomfortably. A problem lay ahead of them. Dorian needed to finish washing up and Ruby needed to wash herself again. He hadn't thought to bring any extra towels, however. Ruby's towel was destroyed, though Dorian refused to survey the full extent of the damage.

"Why... Why did you help me?"

Dorian hesitated, unsure of the answer. He had moved to help her before he'd fully thought it through. He could have left her to ride out the curse on her own. He probably would have gained a great deal more information about her curse that way. But he couldn't. His body moved and he started hypnotizing her before thinking. Once he started, he couldn't imagine being so cruel as to stop and leave her to deal with the pain once more.

"I," Dorian took a steadying breath, "I helped you because I wanted to see if I could, and I cannot exactly learn more of your curse if you succumb to it."

That sounded like a reasonable explanation. That made sense. Unfortunately, Dorian knew it to be a lie. Even if the words were true, that he couldn't learn more of her curse if she succumbed to it, why did he really care? He never cared so much about curses. Sure, there seemed to be a connection to the council, and the possibility of fucking over their machinations remained, but that felt insufficient to explain to himself why he rushed to her aid and exhausted himself to such a degree.

Leandra's face flashed in his mind for a brief second. Her black wavy hair and honey-brown eyes were burned into his memory. Why she would come to mind while trying to figure out why he helped Ruby so readily, Dorian didn't understand. It unsettled him that his past lovers kept coming to mind in Ruby's presence. Why not think of his past friends? His past acquaintances? His past rivals? He just kept thinking of his past lovers around the witch.

"I see... Well... thank you anyways." Her voice came out hoarse, leading her to a brief coughing fit.

"Are you okay?" Dorian asked over his shoulder.

"I will be... but I need to wash myself up again."

"Did you bring another towel? I only brought the one myself, but I can run back to the shop and get another one if you need."

"No, thank you. I have more towels in my bag... This one will have to be discarded though."

Dorian suppressed a groan at the reminder that the little covering she'd had before was torn apart. That damn witch was just too physically attractive. It didn't help that Dorian was a sucker for people who were strong for their race. The way that the mushrooms throughout the forest reacted to her told him that she possessed far more magical gifts than she ever realized. The way she ran from the other witches, even in her panic, told him of her strength. From what he glimpsed of her body and her movements, he knew she possessed a physique he would find downright delectable.

Ruby naked and covered in the blood of her enemies could be fun. If she wanted me to see her.

"I... I just want to really say thank you... You didn't have to comfort me through that or check on me just now... I appreciate that you did."

The emotion choking her voice almost made him turn around to look at her. The fact that she remained practically naked while he sat entirely nude kept him facing away from her as he considered why she would be so shocked by his comfort. From what he had gathered, her time with the witches was painful and isolating. She must have grown accustomed to the insults lobbed at her by the witches Dorian killed. Not for the first time, Dorian wondered how deep her anguish went. Just how used to pain and cruelty must Ruby be to become so grateful for the barest kindness?

A part of Dorian raged at the fact that what he considered basic decency, Ruby considered going out of his way. The abuse she must have suffered to be so touched by his help and consideration made him feel powerless. He didn't have the option to slaughter the rest of the guilty parties, yet. He didn't even really know who those guilty parties were. The only comfort Dorian could cling to was that he already killed at least eight of the people who either disregarded her worth or actively mistreated her.

Since he made a sport out of killing the abusers and monsters of Vlideron who wore human faces, Dorian could easily say that he often became furious at the perpetrators. It had nothing to do with her in particular, of course. Dorian reassured himself that his rage on her behalf wasn't because Ruby in particular, had been so hurt. He would feel the same for any victim of such abuse.

In this case, however, he seethed with nothing to do about it. At least not yet. Someday, maybe he would be able to do something. For the moment, Dorian needed to breathe and accept that there were more important things to handle. He could be patient. Someday, he could enact the vengeance Ruby deserved. If she didn't want him to do it, that was a bridge he'd have to cross then. Dorian needed to focus on the present.

"I did what anyone should do in that circumstance, and I was glad to," Dorian finally replied, forcing his voice to keep as even as it could, despite his still boiling blood.

Ruby didn't reply. Instead, she sucked in a sharp breath, and Dorian felt the movement of air behind him as she stood and made her way back to the hot springs. Only a few steps away, she turned back to Dorian. He kept her in his peripheral view, considering the best way to approach finishing washing off. In that moment, she apparently processed his own disheveled state.

The squeak she made as she turned back around echoed loudly through the forest. She spluttered, apparently unable to find the words to express what she thought. If he wasn't equally embarrassed and uncomfortable, Dorian dimly thought that he would have found her reaction hilarious. Internally commiserating with her awkwardness, he debated how best to diffuse the situation. His mind continued coating a blank canvas with invisible paint.

"I'm sorry, I didn't realize! You need to finish washing up, right? Yes. You do. Of course you do. Ummm.... Maybe I could go after? Or, well..."

"I will move further away so that we might both have privacy in the water. I will say, I can easily see through the steam, but I would not dishonor myself by peeking. I say this only to comfort you that you will not be alone and without guidance back to the ruins."

"Oh... Yes... That works... So... You didn't peek before?"

"Well, I didn't intentionally observe you, no. Upon finishing the scent markings, I did catch a glimpse of your back. But I turned away immediately."

Dorian couldn't see her expression, remaining rooted in place. While he couldn't see the look on her face, the relaxing of her body language told him of her relief at his answer. He couldn't blame her. It must be unsettling to be in the presence of someone with so much stronger senses than yourself. Dorian couldn't say he spent much time in her position. Nevertheless, he could imagine the disquieting feeling of knowing someone could be watching you without you being able to see them. For that, Dorian decided to keep his shadows working to clear some of the steam between them while they bathed. Then she could see that he wasn't looking at her.

The effort to continue controlling his shadows throughout all he had already done that morning was extraordinary, but worth it. Dorian thought of Leonarch whenever he thought of the comfort of others in vulnerable contexts. Because of his monster of a father, Dorian consistently went out of his way to be considerate of others in his presence. This courteous manner naturally did not extend to his victims, but he never utilized that brand of torture when handling such vile people. Leonarch's son would be the sort to violate the vulnerable. Dorian existed proudly as Mariana's son.

"How does this sound? You can get in the water, that way you are covered. Then, you can turn your back, and I can retrieve my things from the edge and walk a ways down to enter the spring further away. Then we can both bathe in peace and I'll meet with you once we are both done, dried, and ready to head back."

"Okay... yes, that works. Alright..."

After a few moments, Ruby cleared her throat to announce her readiness for him to move. Dorian moved at top speed, the weakness in his legs prominent. He desperately needed to feed. It would be the first thing he did upon returning to the ruins. His blood packs were there, and Dorian silently regretted not bringing just one. Thirst clawed at the inside of his throat, unrelenting and distracting.

Dorian and Ruby each washed in relative silence thereafter. Dorian suspected her body felt wrung out and exhausted after so many ordeals. He kept a minimum of awareness about her, ensuring she didn't fall asleep in the water or anything, but did not look at her. He listened for her heartbeat and breathing, surprised to hear its pace. Part of him worried that she continued to suffer pain or anxiety, but if she did not want to share that with him, he didn't blame her. He wouldn't know until he looked at her.

For his part, Dorian didn't want to speak either. He hung on by a thread to control both his shadows and his urge to feed. Dorian took his time soaking in the restorative waters, sure that if Ruby saw him get out, she would feel compelled to get out too. He figured that the curse attacking her again undid whatever good the springs had done for her. She needed to relax again.

Finally, as he exited the water and began dressing, he heard Ruby announce that she finished washing as well. Seeing her face, still tight with tension, Dorian worried she needed more time to relax. There were, however, some things that time in a hot spring couldn't ease. The stress radiating off of her remained palpable. He racked his brain for some way to help, but ultimately realized that he simply didn't know her well enough.

Navigating out of the steam and into the clear forest, Dorian felt dread welling up within him. The sun had fully risen, creating golden patches of brilliant light throughout the nearby forest, which would only grow more frequent as they approached the ruins. He swallowed, knowing what lay in wait for him as they walked on. Despite the urgency to feed and the fear in his bones, Dorian did not rush Ruby, continuing to walk at her stilted pace.

That curse must take more out of her than she is willing to admit.

Admiring that she stubbornly stood on her own two feet after all her turmoil, Dorian still battled frustration. If he knew her better, he would have offered to carry her the rest of the way, so that he would spend less time exposed to the sunlight and suffering sun-sickness. As things stood between them, he didn't feel comfortable making that suggestion. He had no idea of how she would take it, but a part of him guessed that she would view it as a sign that he viewed her as incompetent or weak.

Dorian suspected Ruby of having a hidden proud-streak. Peering at her, her face set in a hard line, determination and pain warred within her as she trudged forward. Guilt tugged at him, since he knew that he would have so much easier of a time simply carrying her the rest of the way to his home. She would suffer in the nights of travel ahead. He would be just fine once he slunk back into the darkness, freshly sated on blood. Her recovery would take days at his home once they finally made it there.

A thought occurred to Dorian, which he voiced before he could think about it too hard, "I bet the fucker who cursed you never expected you to live so long. They're probably losing their minds with fury and frustration at having failed to kill you just yet."

"What?" Ruby's eyes sharpened as she snapped her head to Dorian, as if he said something outlandish, rather than simply true.

"I mean, curses on people are intricately known by the curse-wielder. So they know they haven't killed you yet. They're probably tearing their hair out by now. That curse of yours is nasty. Seems like it could have killed you several times over by now. But it hasn't. So I just imagined how pissed they must be." Dorian felt an uncomfortable laugh well up in his throat, barely escaping as he finished speaking.

Ruby's eyes lit up with amusement, which transformed as she started laughing. At first, her laughter felt contagious, prompting his own. But it kept going. And going. Her giggles rose in pitch and frequency, shifting into something hysterical. Her eyes grew wider every time she opened them to look at him as she kept cackling, despite the situation losing its humor. Her amusement morphed into something oddly grotesque, leaving Dorian uncomfortable and concerned. What started as amused laughter became the unhinged cackling of someone on the brink of full mental collapse.

Dorian wondered how he had triggered such a breakdown, cursing himself for the error as they kept walking and he waited to see what would happen with her. Would he need to use his magic to make her sleep, just so she could calm down? Or would he be able to calm her down with regular conversation?

The point proved moot as she calmed down on her own, wiping away the tears that started spilling from her eyes in the end. She didn't say anything to address the wildness of the moment, so Dorian didn't say anything about it either. What good would it do to ask when she still felt so vulnerable, afraid, stressed, and on the verge of losing her mind?

The sun spots grew too frequent to completely avoid, leaving Dorian gritting his teeth. His bones ached. His skin, though not actually burning, felt as it did when he was a human, recovering from a horrible sun burn: tight, stinging, and itchy. His throat, already distractingly dry, became molten sand on a hot summer's day. Dorian kept squinting, the stabbing light in his eyes overwhelming.

He trekked on, trying not to show the way his joints creaked with each movement in the light. As soon as they reached some shade, Dorian felt enough relief to let out a sigh. He silently hoped Ruby remained oblivious to his difficulty, but glancing at her, he saw her watching him suspiciously. Whether she noticed his suffering or something else, he could not say. Regardless, she observed him carefully. Dorian tried to keep his sighs of relief silent.

The ruins were glorious in the sunlight. The stained glass the elves used superfluously throughout their ancient town glimmered in the light, casting rainbows on the green, moss-covered stones that littered the streets, where some ancient towers had been impacted by the curse. Centuries filled the time since Dorian last saw them in the sunlight, having to avoid sun-sickness. The sight stole his breath, even more than the pain he needed to be in to see it.

Once back in the darkened safety of the old book shop, Dorian rushed up the stairs, straight to his bag, and began drinking the sweet nectar of life- and power-sustaining blood. The thirst was unbearable. As Ruby joined him in the upstairs apartment, Dorian thanked his haste in retrieving acceptable blood to drink. She smelled far too delectable.

A look of disgust crossed Ruby's face as she realized what Dorian consumed, and before she could open her mouth to speak about his blood-drinking, Dorian finished a full pouch and spoke up, "The man whose blood I am drinking was a nobleman who forced every last woman under his rule in his lands to be subjected to his depravity. That he is dead and his blood can fuel my life is something I will never apologize for or feel the least bit bad about. He deserved to die."

Ruby's mouth closed, eyes searching Dorian's until she simply nodded and entered her room.

Dorian grimaced, grabbing another blood pack.

One was far from enough.

CHAPTER SEVENTEEN

Ruby

Ruby glanced around at the forest, dark once more, as she gave voice to the question that had been plaguing her since before she'd gone to sleep that morning, "Why exactly do you bloodsuckers not just go around slaughtering everyone, if you gain so much supposed power from the blood of those you've killed?"

"Well, that's a multi-part answer. In Vlideron specifically, the council has ensured few know how to gain power. But in general, we either have the intelligence to understand that it would paint a target on our backs, or the morals to know that killing indiscriminately would be wrong."

"And which are you? Intelligent or moral?"

"Why can't I be both?"

"Because I have a hard time believing either."

Ruby felt her cheeks straining against her determination to not smile. Though still slightly uncomfortable, she had moved on from her initial, visceral disgust at his blood-drinking that morning. He was right that such people shouldn't be left to continue inflicting harm. She wasn't sure if she agreed with him just killing these evildoers, but at minimum, she understood it. It wasn't like the witches had been doing anything to patrol the nobles. Ruby itched with the need to lash out at him, a hint of guilt taunting her.

Since they arose and left the ruins that evening, Ruby poked and prodded at Dorian, only to find his answers amusing. It galled her to think, but she enjoyed trying to hit some hidden button of annoyance. She hadn't succeeded yet. Of course, she could have tried to question him about his piece of garbage father or his poor mother. She could have poked at his lack of friends and loved ones.

Those were topics she sensed were actually sensitive. After the way he helped her with her curse that morning, she couldn't bring herself to poke that hard. Instead, Ruby busied herself with these absurd conversations, the insults lacking any real bite. In turn, he responded lightly, not poking at her own obvious sore spots. She could feel him also dancing around the real pain.

Oddly, their interactions around her curse shifted things. She couldn't say she trusted him fully, but in just a little over a day, she went from fearing that he would kill her, to tacitly trusting that he would at least guide her through the forest for a while, to now trusting that he really did want to help with her curse. No matter how odd she found it, that remained the truth of the matter. She couldn't be sure that he would do much else for her, lacking the assurance that he would even help with other aspects of her survival, like food.

Regardless of her teasing, not hitting him where it hurt would be the least she could do to repay him for his astounding gentleness and consideration. No one had ever been so kind to her, or so concerned about her.

The fact that Dorian went so far out of his way to ensure that Ruby felt comfortable with him when she washed up a second time had been evident. He looked ragged, to such a degree that Ruby forgot that he sat nude the entire time he'd been helping her. She could remember the entire event with the curse, allowing her to know how carefully he behaved with her the whole time. He hadn't used his hypnotism in any untoward ways she'd been told vampires did indiscriminately. If anything, he had been far more concerned with her comfort than anyone else had ever shown.

The first time Ruby laid with Juniper, he hadn't exactly asked if she wanted to. She had, which was the only reason it happened in the first place, but the implication existed that she would have to say no, rather than expecting the both of them to say yes. The distinction hadn't become clear to her for months afterwards, and it left her feeling strangely uncomfortable with the whole memory. She had wanted to, and she would have said yes if asked, but she wasn't asked.

Juniper never asked at all.

Dorian, in such a radically different circumstance, went out of his way to respect an unspoken no. She hadn't needed to verbalize her discomfort for him to work to correct it. That degree of respect for her feelings was wholly unfamiliar and remarkable to her. She never knew that others might offer her the same consideration she gave freely.

Despite knowing how easy consideration could be, Ruby felt indebted to Dorian for his kindness. It put her in a strange position when vampires were always touted as her enemy. Repeatedly over the last days, Ruby found that her education on vampires proved, at best, inaccurate. At worst, lies. The truth of the matter would be difficult to ascertain so long as Ruby remained unsure if Dorian was simply an exception to the rule, however.

Dorian's laughter cut off suddenly as his head snapped to the side. Squinting into the darkness, far beyond the scope of her lantern, Ruby saw something strange. Blue mushrooms far in the distance were lighting up and going dark rapidly. Seconds slowed as understanding dawned. The glowing lights of the mushrooms strobing through the forest were growing closer, directly towards them.

The heavy pounding of a sprinting beast filled her ears. Dorian sensed it first, allowing him preparation time. He stepped in front of Ruby, his back illuminated by the silvery light of her lantern, revealing his shadows seeping out of his body and clinging to him, hiding their presence from the approaching beast. Ruby focused on her first glimpses of the massive creature as the mushroom lights grew close enough.

At first glance, it looked like a gigantic bull, taller than Dorian. Its width neared that of two carriages. Glowing red eyes reminded her of some vampires' eyes, though not Dorian's. The beast's eyes were a brighter red, tinged with orange. As it neared, it slowed down, seemingly evaluating them.

Dorian said only the bravest or most desperate beasts would dare to attack a vampire. Ruby wondered if this creature was foolish and brave, or smart and desperate. Its hesitation made it difficult to tell for sure. Even the most foolish creature would hesitate to attack a vampire in the darkness. The most desperate creature, if smart enough, would pause as well, to really evaluate if it needed to risk its life to such a degree. The beast before them gave no clear indication which way it leaned.

Terror froze Ruby's heart as the realization that she couldn't use her meager light magic crashed over her. It would probably hurt her more than it would hurt the beast. If Dorian hadn't stepped in front of her already, she would be dead. He stood as the only reason for it to hesitate, and if he decided that protecting her wasn't worth the trouble, she would be a sitting duck. Unable to use the only magic she really knew how to call upon, Ruby knew that her dagger would not be able to kill the beast easily.

Dorian's body intentionally relaxed in front of her, and she recognized the preparation to fight. The small adjustments allowed her to breathe, just a little. Her mind unfroze slightly, allowing her to take in more details of the beast. Aside from its monstrous size, Ruby saw that it was not strictly a bull. Though it possessed gigantic horns jutting from its head the way the largest bulls normally did, it also possessed large paws, rather than hooves, which ended in talons as long as her forearm, six on each foot. Where an herbivore like the bull would have squared teeth, the beast before her showcased razor-sharp protrusions from its mouth, which remained exposed to the elements, lacking most of the facial muscles and skin that normally covered a mouth. Its maw of countless knife-like teeth hung slightly open, revealing a strangely skeletal tongue-like thing. Only as it moved did Ruby see the point at the end of that skeletal tongue, revealing its purpose: to drain victims of something. Blood or magic, Ruby couldn't say.

The creature's size worked against it slightly as it pawed at the ground, signaling its readiness to charge. This tell gave Dorian ample time to send his shadows to the ground and spread out from him in all directions. Dorian laid his trap mere seconds before the battle commenced.

In the blink of an eye, the beast shot into the air, lifted by Dorian's shadows impaling it from all directions. Its eyes flared with fury as it writhed. Dorian's head tilted to the side, his shadows retreating from the beast a moment later. Dread welled within Ruby as she saw the wounds closing. The beast, shaking off its injuries, huffed as it refocused on Dorian, refusing to back down. Dorian grabbed two short swords from his bag, causing Ruby to notice for the first time the familiar enchantments on his bag. His shadows became frenetic just before he jumped into the fray.

Impotent fury grew within Ruby as she watched the battle. It just kept healing and healing. The wounds Dorian caused drew pained sounds and fury, but it kept going. This fight would drag on and on if something didn't change. Maybe Dorian would become too exhausted to keep its attention or stop it. Maybe she would die after all, despite his clear desire to prevent that. He fought for her life, not his own. At any moment, he could decide to leave her to the beast and he would be fine. But he was fighting for her.

And she stood there, only watching. The inability to do anything with light magic left her growling out her annoyance. Magic tingled at her fingertips, despite her fear of being burned by the light. As the fight dragged on, however, Ruby noted that the sensation of magic tingling in her hands failed to burn her. Ruby's mouth dropped open at the swirling red and black mass that gathered around her fingers. It wasn't light magic tugging at her.

Without another thought, Ruby threw the magic at the beast. The resulting howl shook the forest. Its head whipped around to look at her, allowing Dorian to jab his blades into either side of its neck. That move brought its focus back to its primary battle.

Ruby wasn't sure what she had done for several long seconds. Wounds stacked up on the beast as Dorian continued twirling around the creature, slicing and stabbing, his shadows shooting lances into the creature. Vile, black blood oozed from the wounds, sending the stench of rotting meat and death all around.

The beast isn't healing!

As if the creature realized the result of her magic at the same time as her, it turned. Ignoring Dorian, it pawed at the ground to charge at her. Dorian sent shadows along the ground to land a few feet in front of Ruby. Time slowed once more as the beast charged at full speed. Dorian's shadows suddenly lifted from the ground in a great spear. The beast impaled itself upon the shadow spear, through its chest and out its spine.

Belatedly, Ruby realized that she fell in her attempt to escape the charging beast, and that had saved her. As it thrashed through its death throes, the pointed ends of its horns slashed through the air where her head had been just moments earlier. She scrambled backwards, escaping the oozing blood and viscera as its body began breaking down even before it had fully died.

Dorian came around, eyes trained on the beast as he offered a hand to help her back up. Ruby cleared her throat as she got to her feet on her own. When Dorian looked over with confusion, she pointedly looked at him. His hands and clothes were covered with the rancid blood of the beast. The fact that the dark streaks emphasized certain muscles and bone structure didn't make up for the fact that the beast blood was unspeakably disgusting.

Seeing that she refused his help, Dorian looked down at himself in momentary confusion. Ruby watched as his nose wrinkled and he seemed to process the grime covering him. He breathed deeply, only to start gagging. Ruby struggled not to laugh, since laughing would mean breathing, and breathing would mean smelling. She stumbled a few feet away from him as she choked on her own giggles, watching in amused horror as he tried to regain control over himself. Dorian's clothes were destroyed, leaving him effectively trapped in the worst of it.

Dorian ripped the tunic he wore in half to remove it. Ruby's gleeful mockery died in her throat as she watched his muscles work beneath the streaks of grime. A part of her mind that had grown far too loud for her own good pointed out the impressive ease with which he tore the heavy woven fabric. The logical part of her brain prevailed after a few moments of unrepentant staring, driving her to turn away from his continued stripping with the knowledge that he only showed such power because of his vampiric strength.

Ruby heard Dorian grumbling for a moment about the waste of the hot springs that morning before she heard the splashing of water. Turning over her shoulder with confusion, Ruby saw Dorian standing with a canteen of water spilling out over his head, running down his bare skin. Quickly, Ruby turned away again, her face hot. She'd failed to consider how he would need to wash his own body before he could change clothes. She wondered if it would be enough to quell the stench that would surely cling to him without a full bath. Regardless, it wasn't like he could go on in those destroyed clothes, covered in the grime he earned during the battle. He needed to clean up.

Focusing on the possibility that it wouldn't be enough to remove the stench, Ruby kept her gaze trained away from him. She heard him grumbling behind her, the rustling of his bag and then more flowing water. Unsure of how effective his makeshift bath would prove, Ruby struggled not to choke on the stench growing in the area. A glance at the beast's corpse revealed the classic signs of rot already settling in. Beasts always decomposed at a remarkable rate, often showing visible fumes from the rapid breaking down of tissues and fluids. Within a week, even the bones of the creature would be nothing but dust.

Ages passed before Dorian cleared his throat. Turning, Ruby saw him looking far cleaner, dressed in a new style of shirt, the loose material an icy green-gray. Dorian even donned new boots, which were identical as well. His hair dripped onto his fresh shirt, but looked far cleaner. Only distance would allow Ruby to tell if the canteen-bath proved enough to disperse the stench on his skin.

Dorian's old clothes were heaped into a haphazard pile a few feet away from him. Ruby glared at the soiled materials, certain she could see the stench flowing from them. They needed to get the M'lvia's revenge away from the creature, if only so that she could breathe more fully again. Unfortunately, Dorian paused, earning a glare from Ruby at his hesitance to move.

He licked his finger and stuck it in the air. Ruby cocked her head at him, wondering why he would be testing the wind here. Surely, the direction of the wind mattered little underneath the dense canopy of Death's Forest. Pausing, Ruby felt the subtle breeze. Awe stirred within her just like that morning, when she'd gazed upon the elven ruins bathed in gold.

The forest she had known all her life now left her speechless with wonder time and time again. Rebelliously, it left her imagining what else existed in the world she didn't know she didn't know. What else could there be to discover? To experience?

Dorian swiftly drew a flint and striker from his bag and set the soiled clothes on fire, backing away just as thick smoke began to rise from the pile. Ruby backed up in alarm. When the smoke began to slowly drift away from them, she realized why he'd checked the wind. They took off in hurried silence.

Once far enough away to breathe again, Ruby found that Dorian's bathing methods at least made the stink far less noticeable, though he still needed a more thorough bath. He certainly didn't smell as good as he had before the attack. Still, she could breathe normally, and that would have to be good enough for the moment.

"So how do you bloodsuckers decide who to turn, anyways? Is it like a lottery of misfortune, or do you just pick someone you don't like to curse with your existence for eternity?"

She expressed the question, borne of genuine curiosity, lightheartedly. She wanted to make him laugh, and she figured that her question would do the trick. His expected laughter soon rewarded her, making her feel better. Dorian risked fighting a dangerous beast that wasn't going down easily to protect her. She had helped ensure the outcome in the end, but he kept up the fight for far longer than she would have ever expected. The witches enforced a policy to retrieve whatever remained of the fallen later in those same circumstances. None of them would have stayed to keep fighting on her behalf. Dorian did. At every turn, Dorian seemed as invested in keeping her alive as she was.

"Generally, we like to get the consent of someone to be turned. Some violate that guideline, of course. But I have always thought the process rather intimate."

"Intimate?" Ruby's voice caught in her throat strangely.

"Yes. The act itself requires a closeness that feels far too intimate to do on a whim. For that reason, I've never changed anyone. That, and the consent factor. I reveled in being changed, myself, but I couldn't have really given my consent to it either. I was dying. I understood why Sigrid did it. In other circumstances, some have not wanted to become vampires. They were changed anyways, whether through the malice of the vampire who changed them, or ignorance to their wishes. In either case, it rarely turns out well."

"How so?" Ruby tilted to her head, listening intently as he spoke of things she hadn't really considered.

"Well, if someone didn't want to become a vampire but is changed anyways, they tend to fall into a horrible depression. As you know, considering your nickname for me, we survive on blood. Not everyone is up for a life involving that form of sustenance, even when there are options to ensure no one need die to obtain it. Most vampires in Vlideron operate without ever killing anyone. I would guess many vampires around the world operate that way, to some degree. I can't be sure about places like Plarishak, where they apparently function on merit. I can only imagine that vampires in that nation would need to kill to survive the political and social landscape. But in the rest of the world, I don't think vampires would be so welcome if they were murderous on principle."

"That... makes sense..."

"With that being the case, those who don't want to drink blood tend to live unfortunately short lives for vampires. Sometimes even short lives for their base race. Few make it past the first deaths of their mortal friends, if they make it that far at all. That's why few choose to change those who did not want to be changed. Granted, some change their minds, adapt, and come to enjoy their new lives, but that's a real gamble."

"Well, I asked a question to be snarky, only for you to give me a real answer... And now I am sad for people who were turned against their will... How dare you make me sad for bloodsuckers?" Ruby laughed at the end of her question, trying to lighten the mood.

Dorian laughed, though his eyes looked tired, as if he had seen too much in that facet of vampiric life.

He probably has seen too much...

Deciding not to focus on that for the time, she shifted to another snarky question, earning a more lighthearted answer.

The hours of hard travel passed with Ruby calling Dorian a bloodsucker and Dorian poking lightly at her in return. While never insulting her for being a witch, he fully insulted modern witch behavior.

Dorian briefly interrupted a soliloquy on the merits of the witches as they used to be to point out the cottage they would be spending one last night in before they reached his home. Explaining that he needed to wash and rest before they could go on, Ruby silently rejoiced, aches and exhaustion threatening to overtake her at any minute. It would be good to at least spend some time sitting and eating, rather than jerkily eating while speed-walking.

"Well, like I said, the witches of old used to be masters of themselves and their own lives. Regular monarchs could do little to limit their individual power and freedom, and they largely left them alone. Witches back then forged their own paths, lived their own lives, free of foolish restrictions. They didn't limit themselves to one role in the world around them. They lived fully, with the strength of their personal convictions. Some were awful and hurt people needlessly, like any other group of people. But others were amazingly selfless, running one-person hospitals out of their homes. Some saved others from oppressive environments and relieved abusers of their lives. They spread equity and justice. Most were somewhere in the middle, but they were so admirable for the way they moved through the world as a force of nature."

"That's why you despise witches today?"

"EXACTLY!"

Ruby jumped at Dorian's sudden shout of excited agreement, stifling an amused smile at his strange enthusiasm for the topic, while a small part of her felt inadequate against the metric he held for witches. So long ago, they were so many things. Dorian surely found her lacking, since she hardly resembled those witches of old. She spent nearly thirty years under the restrictive doctrines of witches in their modern Vlideron. That left little room for her to establish herself as anything but a present-day witch.

Near the cottage, the landscape shifted again. Though still surrounded by the grassy greens that dominated the land near the ruins, the deep purple flowers grew to cover more of the trees once again, and the colors were joined by teal and blue once more. The glowing mushrooms even began growing in patches on old human or elven skeletons poking out of the ground.

The sight made her shudder. She forced her attention to other new details. Colorful rocks peaked through the moss covering the forest floor that turned teal once more not long after leaving the area near the elven ruins. More and more, Death's Forest revealed color and variety within its depths, shocking her. As they reached the cottage, Ruby noted with surprise the crispness to the air.

"How far is this cottage from the cave where I first woke up?"

"Somewhere around a hundred miles, I would say," Dorian answered, opening the door for them and ushering her inside.

Ruby couldn't move for a second, shocked by the answer. As a witch, she moved faster than the average human, but walking so far in just two nights astounded her.

No wonder I'm so tired... But I can't rest yet.

Thoughts about what she wanted to accomplish silenced before she even finished thinking them. Standing inside the doorway, taking in the delicate details of the cottage, her mind quieted.

CHAPTER EIGHTEEN

Dorian

Dorian couldn't breathe. For the first time in centuries, someone occupied the cottage besides himself. While Dorian sometimes spent the day and always kept up on the repairs the old place needed, no one else had stayed there since Leandra had been in his life, about 400 years ago. It still served as the marker for the path through the enchantments concealing his real home, so it remained important to keep it in good condition. Dorian's attachment to the little cottage, however, went far deeper.

From the carefully carved flowers in the woodwork on the mantle of the fireplace and in the cabinetry of the kitchen, to the murals painted on the walls, to the plush furnishings in each room, it all screamed of Leandra. She painted the murals, but Dorian handled the rest of it, catering to her tastes, needs, and desires. He never changed it after she left. At first, his grief made him refuse to believe she'd left for good. Fondness for its memories eventually took over.

As Ruby gazed around at his first home with Leandra—just while they fixed up the palace—Dorian felt a pang of fear. He didn't want to deal with any negative opinions about the space, even if it might be outdated. Plus, the colors were the opposite of what she'd grown up with: deep and rich. Whether or not she liked it was ultimately irrelevant, but Dorian dreaded hearing anything negative about the place where he fostered love for the first time.

"I doubt you have taste this good, so who decorated?" Ruby finally asked, her breathless voice conveying both enjoyment and deep exhaustion.

Dorian couldn't stop his relieved chuckle. "I should have figured you'd like it. I decorated it to the tastes of a human. The murals on the walls are hers. The rest, I actually did, but all to her liking. Don't get me wrong, I do have taste enough to like it as well. But I concede your point that it wasn't my choices that created this home."

Ruby's brows were furrowed when she turned to look at him, her gaze turning contemplative. She stared at him that way a lot throughout their trek that night. Over and over, she would try to hide the curiosity and confusion apparently plaguing her. Dorian hadn't addressed it. If she wanted to know something, she would have to ask. He only offered unrequested information when necessary.

While he cherished the memories with his former lovers, he didn't really want to spend time discussing them. With the way Ruby swayed on her feet, Dorian guessed that she wouldn't be able to stay awake long enough to listen to his ramblings anyway. She needed to wash up and get to sleep as soon as possible.

"Come on, I'll show you to the washroom and your bedroom. Then you can get the sleep you clearly need."

"I am fine..." Ruby yawned as she tried to finish her sentence.

"Right. And I'm mortal." Dorian's sarcastic reply earned him a glare.

Dorian merely led her to the small hall and started pointing, "Through that door is the bathroom, and that door will be your bedroom. I will be in this one," he patted the door nearest to him, "And I will wait for you to finish washing up before I sit down on anything I own, because I still stink, but you will pass out if you wait too long to wash."

"I'm fine, really..."

"I insist."

"Fine." Ruby stomped past him into the bathroom.

Dorian shook his head, not understanding why she became so upset by his insistence that she needed to get some sleep. He turned and entered his kitchen, his mind wandering to thoughts of logistics. Ruby would be at his home the following evening. The journey to the estate would take an hour at most. They really only needed to stop because Ruby looked dead on her feet and Dorian desperately needed to fully bathe.

Once there, Ruby would have to rely on his stores of regular food for her sustenance. He had fresh water access through the same enchantments that allowed full plumbing. The biggest concerns would be warmth and food, as a result. Dorian hadn't bothered with fires in centuries, since he didn't need to worry about things like hypothermia. Ruby, on the other hand, would require the heat offered from his fireplaces. He needed to find how much firewood he actually had once they arrived. He also needed to check how long his stores would last, so that they would know how long she could stay uninterrupted.

While he hadn't entertained visitors in centuries and he refused to share his home with a mortal in that time either, Dorian knew he still had food. The pantries in the basement of the main building were enchanted for preservation.

The food pantry split into two sprawling rooms featuring shelves lined with anything his mortal friends and lovers could have wanted. He kept it well stocked a few hundred years earlier, and he hadn't bothered with it since he stopped engaging mortals. One room kept goods at room temperature. That one benefited from enchantments to keep pests away from the food and to preserve it perfectly, ensuring it remained in top condition and would only be affected by the passage of time once removed from the room. The other food storage pantry, a cold one, ensured the same preservation and pest-repelling, while adding in a mechanism to keep any consumables brought into the room cold, leaving the air relatively comfortable for the mortal entering.

Leandra loved the surprise of the cold pantry that didn't freeze her when she went into it. Dorian was thrilled to see the look on her face as she gripped her arms, preparing to be frozen, only to enter and become confused. At first, she thought the enchantments weren't working, only to touch a bottle of some sweet drink she loved and discover just how cold it was. Her face lit up. Dorian loved watching her pad down to the cold pantry with bare feet, yawning and shivering only when she grabbed the cream for her morning coffee, the luxury uncommon to most in Vlideron. Her comfort meant everything to him back then.

Separately, the blood pantry practically overflowed with pouches and canteens of blood, ready in single-serve amounts for him to consume as needed. The wine cellar even boasted an enchantment to keep each wine preserved at its own optimal temperature.

Ruby exited the bathroom, calling out to Dorian as she threw the door open, "Go wash up, you filthy bloodsucker."

Despite the harshness of her words, Dorian could hear the laugh in them, bringing a smile to his own lips. As soon as he heard the door to her bedroom close, Dorian turned the corner from the kitchen into the little hall and rushed to bathe as well. He could hear Ruby rummaging around in her room as he washed up. Then he heard her door open and footsteps walking out to the living room. Dorian waited to hear what else she would do.

Belatedly, Dorian realized that she might already be cold. The air became chillier as they traveled further North. It would only become worse once they reached his estate that evening, but even there, the air could almost bite his own vampiric flesh. Maybe she hoped to ask him to start a fire for her in the fireplace out there. Wondering if he had the firewood for that, Dorian hurried to finish up his own bath. Drying off and redressing in comfier clothes for his own meditative rest, he rushed out to the living room. Ruby sat with the lantern to illuminate her surroundings.

Cursing himself silently, Dorian realized he also forgot that she would need light. Before he could make a move to correct the issues and figure out solutions if he didn't have any firewood at the cottage, Dorian realized what Ruby kept trying to do. Despite the nodding of her head as she fought to stay awake, Ruby attempted to read from what looked like a grimoire.

Maybe that fight affected her more than I realized.

As she slowly closed her eyes only to snap her head up and shake it once more, Dorian finally cleared his throat, giving Ruby a pointed look.

"What?" she snapped at him.

"You clearly need to get some rest. Go to bed."

"I'm fine."

"You're not. You're falling asleep on my couch and, while I am willing to carry you to your bed if need be, I think you would much rather I didn't need to do that. Am I right?"

"Why not just leave me on the couch if I fall asleep? ... Which I'm not going to do until I've done what I wanted!"

"You need a good bed to sleep on. That couch may be comfortable, but not enough to sleep on. I would be a bad host if

I let you hurt your back on that."

Ruby glared at him. He stared back at her. They stayed like that for several long seconds, Dorian crossing his arms, feeling like he was arguing with one of his drunk friends back in the day, trying to get them to go to sleep on the bed rather than continuing to drink on the couch. Though, that wasn't the best comparison he could connect to, when he thought about it some more.

Danatel had been similarly obstinate about going to sleep when the full moon approached and he needed to get ready for the monthly rituals with his pack, those cultural festivals too exciting to sleep near. Ruby acted a bit like that. Like she needed to prepare for something approaching.

Dorian sighed with sudden understanding, "I see why you want to expand your magical strengths, but you will have plenty of time to do so at my estate. I will also give you full access to my library, which includes a great many grimoires that you might study. Should you so choose, I will help you practice your magic, within reason. But none of that can happen unless you get adequate rest now. You do yourself no good when you're dead on your feet."

Finally, Ruby nodded, snapping the grimoire shut aggressively but offering him a small smile of acknowledgment as she trudged past him, into the guest room, and closed the door.

Dorian stared at the closed door, feeling more than a little surprised that his educated guess was spot on. How long had it been since he made such a guess about someone else and been right about it?

When had he started second-guessing his evaluations of others?

Dorian knew the answer to that, but pushed the painful memory aside in favor of getting his own rest. After downing a whole six packs of blood, shocking himself with how much he still needed, Dorian sat on his bed to meditate. In the room across the hall, he heard Ruby whimpering from her nightmares. He heard them the day before as she rested. Knowing they weren't tied to her curse, Dorian felt powerless to help her with them. What right would he have to enter her room unless some true emergency popped up?

No, he concluded he ought to leave it be, at least until he knew her better and could discuss with her what she might want him to do in that circumstance. Still, the sounds of her fear and devastation were difficult to bear. Dorian drove himself deeper into his own meditation to try to escape the sounds, struggling to find a balance that allowed him to still maintain awareness of the world around him to some degree.

The likelihood of the vampires hunting him making it to the cottage any time soon seemed slim, but that didn't make it impossible. Dorian knew he needed to be prepared in case the worst happened and they found him before he stepped within the barriers of his estate. Those barriers, extending for a hundred miles in every direction and creating an inescapable maze if guests were not personally granted guidance by him, provided the best protection he could imagine. But until they were behind those barriers, Dorian wasn't safe. By extension, Ruby wasn't safe either. If the vampires hunting him came upon a witch, they would kill her too, or worse. If the council was involved in her curse, as Dorian suspected, they might be incentivized to torture her with the curse first.

The hours ended up restless as Dorian struggled with maintaining the right balance of meditative seclusion and awareness, eventually giving up. Feeling the many hours until sunset, he stayed in his room, not wanting to disturb Ruby from her own restless sleep. Pulling out a book from his nightstand, Dorian began rereading the old, familiar tale within. The mundane love described between characters within the book remained a refreshing change of pace from his own life, where his immortality kept getting in the way of happiness.

The sunset on their third and final night of travel began before he heard Ruby stirring and getting ready for the day. The perfect time to get going. Dorian sighed, putting the book back in the nightstand where Leandra first left it for him. A part of him wondered if he would always be haunted by the what-ifs of his former loves. Shaking off the melancholy thoughts, Dorian dressed for the day in fresh clothes and exited his room, and ready to finish the journey to his real home. He waited in the living room, noting once again that he forgot to light any candles for Ruby's benefit. As she exited her room with the lantern, Dorian silently chided himself for his forgetfulness. The cottage didn't have the same magic lighting system his home did, so remembering that she would need light felt more inconvenient.

Leaving the cottage, Dorian took a moment to find the easiest path. Beyond the cottage, the land rose sharply for a few hundred feet. At the top of the ridge, they would encounter the barrier. It took him a while, since he hadn't needed to consider a mortal's capabilities in so long. The old steps that he built into the ridge were still there and in decent shape, but they suffered from far more neglect than anywhere else in his route home.

"I'll have to help you up in some spots," Dorian scratched at the back of his head, "The rocks have shifted a bit since I last came out and maintained this path."

"Oh... okay then..."

Nearly halfway up, Dorian spotted it. Ruby was stretching to reach up to him, accepting his aid in climbing the steep steps, when her shirt lifted. Low on her belly, just peaking out from her pants, were even, defined, clean scars in a line. Unnatural in origin. His eyes snagged on those scars and stayed there. Even as her shirt shifted back into place when she stood next to him, covering her skin once more, he kept staring. Impolite, he knew, but his mind froze once he saw those scars.

Those are too small to have come from whips. What caused them? Why are there scars there on her body? Are there more scars? What happened? Who did that to her?

His heartbeat pounded in his ears. Vampires were accused of lacking hearts because of their strange connection with death, shadows, and blood, but his heart furiously raced as fast as the questions flying through his mind.

"You can ask whatever questions you want..." Ruby's voice came out unusually quiet, eyes downcast as Dorian snapped up to look at her face.

"What happened? Why are those there? Where did they come from? Who did that to you?!" His voice crescendoed uncontrollably.

Dorian tried to breathe through the alarm that rose within him, hoping to force himself to slow down and simply listen.

"I did those... It's... It's a long story."

"I have time." Dorian ground out, some of his anger bleeding out to be replaced by pure concern.

How old are those scars? Does she still hurt herself? How do I stop her if she does?

CHAPTER NINETEEN

Ruby

Ruby inhaled deeply, cursing herself for giving him permission to pry into those painfully glaring memories. She didn't want to think of that time. It made the curse inside of her swirl around uncomfortably. She needed to keep calm, stick to the facts and avoid her own feelings. That was her task as a witch. A lifetime of failure didn't inspire confidence, but it may help.

"As we have established, I've always been a failure of a witch."

"That remains to be seen from my perspective, but go on," Dorian interjected, his normally smooth, deep voice instead sounding like the warning growl of a caged predator.

"A failure," Ruby reiterated stubbornly, "who has always needed a lot of reeducation. We are meant to stick to many rules as witches. I don't expect you to know all of them... But one of them is to avoid matters of the heart."

"Matters of the heart?"

"Love. Romance. Sex. Even in books. We're encouraged to read, in theory. You see, the genres and topics are contained and controlled. Our books are supposed to be approved by the elders before we read them. Most focus on reading the old grimoires and journals of the witches before us. A curated library in the compound that only extends back less than 200 years. Few read for pleasure or to learn anything of subjects outside of our calling."

"Absurd, but what does this have to do with those scars?"

"I'm getting there... I started reading... unapproved books. Juniper, one of the men you killed, knew of my books... They were romances... And Juniper... He had a change of heart and told Elder Moss about my books. Violetta, the one you kept saying felt nothing, assisted with the search of my room, the seizure of the books, and the final decision on my reeducation... Ultimately, they decided that I would need to undergo a solitary retreat to appropriately learn from my weakness."

"A solitary retreat," Dorian ground out.

"Yes... For ten days, I sat, with nothing to do, in an all white room, alone, with bright white light shining down on me the entire time. I didn't see another soul for the entirety of my stay there... All to encourage me to focus on the calling I had been given when born as a witch! I could focus only on the doctrines we lived by and the reasons for them... I would be required to embrace the solitude of my emotions and learn to control them better so that I would not give in to such temptations for connection in the future. The constant light served to remind me of the constancy of the light we embrace with our magic..."

"By the gods..." Dorian whispered.

Ruby breathed deeply, trying to ignore her underlying discomfort, "Suffice to say, this method failed with me as well. I... Well I did these to myself to try to keep my head... But upon my release from the retreat, I knew that these were another failure all on their own, so I hid them. That's all there is to it. I needed reeducation and the method failed... Fate chose the wrong one to make a modern witch..."

"That was torture. What you went through was torture. It is, some think, a worse punishment than death. One thing all the races of this world seem to share is a social element. We are all social beings, to one degree or another. I could tell you glossed over much of your suffering, but I need to say outright, no matter how much you don't want to believe me right now, that they tortured you."

Ruby's breath hitched, a lance running through her chest. She looked down to make sure the curse hadn't just done that to her, but there were no signs of it acting out too much. It still moved, slithering around her internal organs, giving warning squeezes, but it remained inactive for the moment. Compressed as she felt by the overwhelming sensations, Ruby forced herself to breathe, in and out. She couldn't afford for the curse to attack her in earnest there. They still needed to make it to his actual home, and they had barely left his cottage.

"Surely, that's an exaggeration…" she finally managed to say.

Dorian moved closer, ensuring eye contact as he spoke, "Ruby, I am not exaggerating. What they put you through is an example of at least two known torture methods. Isolation and sleep deprivation, because I would bet my last pack of blood that you could barely sleep in those conditions. I will not let you downplay this in my presence, because I don't even do that to people who would deserve it in my view."

Ruby tried to shake her head, but one look at Dorian's stony face told her to stop. She recognized his staunch refusal to allow her denial. Not knowing what to do with that, Ruby gestured for Dorian to keep leading the way. They still needed to reach the top of the ridge, and they weren't doing it by standing around discussing her history and their interpretations of events.

His words stuck with her the way dirt stuck to sweat when she trained with her dagger in the summer. They ascended to the top of the ridge in renewed silence, Dorian's jaw still clenched, apparently frustrated with her. It just wasn't that simple for her. If she accepted that it was torture, what did that mean? Was any of her reeducation acceptable or normal? Was all of it wrong? And if it was all wrong, what did that mean for her after she rid herself of the curse?

It all tied back to her fears and feelings about the grimoires and journals. What did it mean that the witches had forsaken their past in favor of this new way? What did it mean that it seemed connected to the Great King, who cozied up with the corrupt vampiric council and nobles? What did it say about how they lived? What did it say about how she had been forced to spend her life so far?

More and more questions flooded her as she wandered behind Dorian, ramming into the wall of his back. Ahead of him looked to be uninterrupted forest, but after only a second of observation, Ruby saw the tell-tale shifting of magic in the air.

The barrier…

Ruby took a step back to get a better look at it. The barrier seamlessly blended into the surrounding forest. If Dorian's back had not stopped her, she would have continued walking right into it, becoming ensnared by whatever trap it possessed before she even recognized the taste of magic in the air. Transcending subtlety, the masterfully crafted barrier ensured the minimum amount of notice to trespassers. One needed to know of its presence to see it at all. She still could not see it clearly, despite actively looking at it with the knowledge of its presence.

"Remarkable..."

"When we walk through the barrier, you will need to be touching me at all times."

"What trap does it spring if I am not?" Ruby couldn't tamp down her curiosity.

"Those not connected to me, who have not passed the barrier with me before and have my continued blessing to enter, find themselves in an endless, shifting maze of plants, rife with the beasts that have crossed into the barrier over time as well. Regular animals are unaffected, since their bodies merely process magic. Sentience and magic cannot be hidden from the enchantments, however. A creature needs only one or the other to be affected. Some fae are also granted access by virtue of their nature. They have a duty to the land, regardless of the ancient curse on it, and any barriers cannot prevent them from carrying out that deal. They also enjoy playing in the barrier."

"Playing in the barrier...?"

"The barrier spans about a hundred miles in a circle. Because of the enchantments, it takes around an hour of vigorous walking to traverse it with me or my permission once granted on the other side. Mind you, such permissions only grant the individual access. Guests cannot guide others through the barrier. But in reality, it is expansive. When we cross the threshold, it will look entirely different as well. I designed the path through while working with the witch who did the barrier."

"A witch did this?!"

"Yes. Who else could have?"

Dorian's bemused smile grated on Ruby, making her feel mocked and foolish, but she hadn't heard of such intensive workings done by witches. Then again, she never knew who created the enchantments she saw. While she'd assumed the lanterns came from the elves, she'd thought little of other enchantments. With the variety of magic discussed in the forbidden texts, her shame grew. Witches possessed so many forms of magic she had never dreamed of being capable of; it only made sense that a witch could have created such barriers at one point in time.

"So if I don't keep contact with you, I will be stuck in a maze that spans a hundred miles that loops around in a circle, never to be seen or heard from again?" Ruby nervously chuckled.

"Well, I can find you pretty easily if I want to in that case, but it would probably be pretty freaky for you. Best not to test the barrier's ability to let me find you, right?"

"Yeah... So whatever I'll see past the barrier is... an illusion?"

"Well, it's more complicated than that. Magic makes the maze and the path through the barrier as real as these trees are out here, and essentially ignores the real trees that exist in there. It's a separate dimension anchored to the land. The land is still there and continues existing, just as it does on either side of the barrier. But those affected by the barrier aren't able to connect with that land. Those metrics push someone directly into this alternate land, meaning their bodies disappear from the real land and only reappear when on the other side of the barrier. Which extends into the sky and ground, completely surrounding my property from all angles."

"So if someone tried to fly onto your estate on the back of a dragon..."

"The dragon would be granted safe passage, as a result of another deal the barrier required, but their rider would disappear from their back. They would still be subject to gravity, however. So they wouldn't be trapped in the alternate dimensional space for long. Bodies are ejected from the barrier's dimension."

"That sounds messy."

"I wouldn't know. No one has tried to ride in on a dragon before." Dorian grinned.

Ruby schooled her face to stop a smile, nodding to the barrier, "So, how should we do this? I don't want to risk getting lost in that maze you're describing."

Dorian's eyebrows raised as he looked at her silently.

"What?" she finally asked.

"I'm just surprised you believe me without seeing it for yourself."

"I mean... I don't see a reason you would lie about it. It's not like you're some pathetic puppy needing to make up excuses to touch me. You're a bloodsucker. If you wanted to harm me, you've had a few thousand chances to do so by now, yes? So I see no need to doubt you, but," Ruby rolled her eyes, her voice beginning to drip with sarcasm, "if you want me to be more suspicious, I guess I could work on it."

Dorian's hearty laugh echoed through the forest behind them but sounded muffled through the forest in front of them. The phenomena felt hardly noticeable, but Ruby listened carefully to the differences. Unsettled energy rolled through her as her proximity to the barrier began to send prickling tendrils of magic along her skin.

"There are a few options, so I'll have you decide. Least contact, you put a hand on me wherever you feel most comfortable and we pass through the entire route that way. Keep in mind, it will still take an hour of walking. Any moment you drop your hand, you would be disconnected from me and sent into the maze. Option two, we each have a hand on each other, holding hands or hands on shoulders or something. Potentially more uncomfortable depending on where hands would need to go, but twice the security of option one. Option three, I carry you on my back, where we have a lot of secure contact, but you are required to hang onto me to maintain secure contact. And option four."

Ruby waited through Dorian's pregnant pause. She couldn't imagine what option four would even be when the others covered the gambit of physical touch she could think of while moving. Patience running out, Ruby gestured for him to spit it out.

Dorian scratched at the back of his head, avoiding her gaze as he spoke up, "A little less contact than option three but the most secure one in my view because I would just run through the barrier. I could carry you through in my arms the way that I did when I carried you to the cave."

Her face heated as she thought about that option. Somehow, it felt so much more intimate than option three, despite realistically being less physical touch. It would make sense to get the trip through the barrier done as soon as possible. If it took an hour of walking to get through it, how much less time would it be if the vampire ran? But then why...

"Why not run with option three?"

"If something happens to jostle you off of me in option three, I would be much further away from you when you landed and you would have a much harder landing. Option three requires you to hold onto me as well. I'm sorry to say this, but I trust vampiric physical strength more than I trust yours. If I knew you could use enhancement magic, I might feel differently. But to my understanding, you don't know how to use that yet."

"Right... makes sense..." Ruby pursed her lips as she considered the options given.

Option one left too much to chance, and she immediately eliminated it. Option two would potentially be good enough, since they would each need to let go for her to be stuck in the maze at any moment. Option three was the best for her control over the situation and ensuring she wasn't stuck in the maze, however. Option four seemed oddly embarrassing for the both of them, to that point that she couldn't seriously consider it. Ruby noticed the way Dorian scratched at the back of his head when something made him uncomfortable or nervous. After another night around him, she recognized the tell. He radiated nervous energy just mentioning option four.

With all of that in mind, Ruby made her choice and directed Dorian to continue forward, with her wrapping her arms around his shoulders, his arms tucking beneath her legs. Dorian shifted his pack to his front and entered the barrier.

Glowing, aqua blue mist clouded her vision for a brief moment. Ruby gasped as it cleared. With the flood of sensations, her grip around Dorian's neck and shoulders loosened. He squeezed one of her thighs, bringing her back to the moment. Renewing her grip, Ruby gazed in wonder, breathing deeply the scent of the brand new forest around her.

A copse of pine trees created a perfect mirror image on either side of the path for the distant parts of the forest, while the path ahead was lined with arching oaks and willows, branching out to create a breathtaking visual. The archway that covered the entirety of the path that she could see ahead and even behind them allowed the branches to weave together in the sky above. The hints of a sky at dusk filtering through the vibrant green leaves of the trees were glowing with purple and pink lines caressing the fluffy clouds, coalescing for coming rain. Ruby could smell the rain, though she always could on Dorian's skin. The strength of the scent in the air told her that the path imitated Dorian's scent, or Dorian based his soap on the path.

The deep, purple flowers covering the real forest trees were growing in large bushes on either side of the path. But the most awe-inspiring part was not the sky above, the remarkable archway the trees formed, the bushes of those flowers, or the scent infusing the land. Ruby's eyes grew wide as she saw sparkling butterflies flitting through the landscape, glowing with silver light as they touched on the various plants that filled the forest floor on either side of the path. Each glowing butterfly of silvery moonlight captured her eye, distracting her from the path itself for several long moments. They danced in the air around her and Dorian as he moved along steadily, almost slowly.

With a glance down at Dorian, Ruby finally noticed the path itself, glittering with a line of radiance Ruby could only liken to the crushed quartz she once saw sparkling in the sun at a stall in Edgefair. As she gawked with wonder, she realized that they were walking on a path of those glittering rocks rising from a shallow creek. They shimmered from within, as if producing their own illumination, the water reflecting that light in tiny rainbows all along the bottom of the path.

"You walk this path every time you go home...?"

"Yes," Dorian sighed, his voice low with blissful relaxation.

Dorian really loves this place...

He had offered to rush through the path for her sake, but he sounded grateful to be able to meander his way through.

That would explain why he's walking so slowly. This path means something special to him.

Ruby could understand why. She had never seen anywhere quite like it. Not that she could profess to have seen much of the world at all. But, in the moments she snuck away from the compound to engage in banned activities with regular humans, Ruby spent some time observing the paintings of other landscapes that some enjoyed as reminders of places they, or their ancestors, visited. There were places in their world far more grand and impressive than she had glimpsed through their small journey, but the simple beauty of the path to Dorian's home was unparalleled in the peace it brought her.

Ruby fell silent for a time, enjoying the sounds filling the forest. The trees rustled with a slight breeze, bringing more of the petrichor that Ruby so loved to smell. Small birds flitted around. An owl hooted in the distance. The insects sang their nighttime chorus. Frogs joined in, though Ruby couldn't see any along the path. The sounds were all clearly a part of the illusion. The fact that none of it was strictly real didn't matter. It felt real enough to settle something in her that she hadn't realized needed it.

"That reeducation I dealt with... that you called torture... I'd call that the worst one, but I experienced a lot of other things for reeducation..."

Dorian stiffened slightly beneath her. For the first time, Ruby noted his heartbeat, pounding fast. She hadn't thought of vampires as having heartbeats. She was determined to ask him about that later. For now, there were other things to think about.

"I thought I might... ask your opinion on some of them..."

"If you're sure you want a bloodsucker's thoughts, be my guest." His light tone came with an undercurrent of strain.

She was touched by how affected he was on her behalf. Enough to make him seem almost afraid to hear the rest. She smiled slightly, despite a welling sense of fear. Ruby breathed deeply, steadying herself with the sights, sounds, and smells of the pathway. It calmed her nerves, allowing her to speak.

"One time, I had an angry outburst at the treatment another witch endured while in town. As a result, Elder Moss tasked me with reciting the lines from our main book of doctrine whilst kneeling on a bed of small grains..."

"Torture."

"Another time," Ruby continued on, listing more of the reeducation methods used on her.

Over and over again, he called what she went through torture. Sometimes, he used less harsh words for her experiences. When she just had to write lines, for example, he called it ridiculous and unneeded, but not torture. When she discussed having to handle her entire dorm's laundry alone, he emphatically referred to it as excessive, unreasonable, and even abusive, but he didn't go so far as to call it torture because she had not been required to skip sleep that time.

"Sleep deprivation is torture, Ruby. You should be aware of that. I have used it on those who truly deserve to suffer. But it's a longer-term torture that can mess with the quality of blood I get, so I don't do it often."

Ruby nodded on his back, growing quiet. She could sense that they were getting close to the end of the path, though she wasn't sure how she knew that. Something about the magic in the air shifted. She didn't want to discuss too much more of her reeducation outside of the comfort the path provided her, and she certainly didn't want to talk about it while forced to actually look Dorian in the eye.

Already, Ruby found herself more than a little embarrassed by the depths of information she shared with him. It just poured out of her, unbidden, as Dorian continued to walk them forward at a leisurely pace.

With only a second of warning, the path disappeared around them, and Dorian stepped through to the other side of the barrier into a noticeably colder land. Ruby saw her own breath puffing out in the chilled air as Dorian set her securely on her own feet once more. Her legs felt like jelly, perhaps because she had not used them in what she guessed to be far longer than an hour.

"I thought we only went around a hundred miles?" Ruby asked, confused as to the sudden difference in the temperature.

"We did. We're deep in the foothills, though. There's a large rise in elevation between here and where we were before. That was another excellent reason for the path, actually. It prevents the need to climb a few sheer rock faces that were there when I first discovered my humble abode." Dorian's smile grew mischievous.

Ruby looked at him with suspicion before turning her attention to the land around them. Pulling out the lantern once more, Ruby found the trees were much further apart in this new portion of the forest. She could see through the canopy above regularly, revealing the glittering light of stars intermittently, though the trees were still overwhelmingly large and concealed most of the sky. The sloped landscape around them emphasized that they indeed emerged nearly in the mountains.

Looming amongst the trees in the murky distance stood a large structure, imposing itself upon the land with unexpected intensity. Dorian began to head in that direction, prompting Ruby to follow along in awe. As they got closer, the light from her lantern began to illuminate the details. Solid, iron gates stood tall against large stone walls spreading out in either direction as far as she could see. Walls were erected on the far side of deep, empty ditches, while the gate seemed to guard the bridge across. As she got even closer, Ruby noted the filigree detailing the front of the solid metal, creating a delicately beautiful pattern in the imposing work.

Beyond this, Ruby could only imagine what she would see. Dorian had discussed his home briefly, but nothing he said or alluded to truly prepared her for this.

The knowledge that this represented only the beginning of what he would consider truly his home rendered her entirely speechless as the gate creaked open at Dorian's touch.

CHAPTER TWENTY

Dorian

Dorian's nerves kicked up with each step towards home. He couldn't help but notice Ruby's silence since spotting the gate. They passed through the first bailey, which featured the derelict buildings of the ancient elven empire's administrative quarters. Dorian hadn't gotten around to fixing any of them up; he knew no one to occupy them. Why would it matter if they were in working condition? At the second gate, he heard her sharp intake of breath, apparently surprised by its presence. After a moment of confusion, Dorian remembered that she could not see very well in the dark and her lantern only did so much. Glancing ahead, Dorian realized how much of his home's layout would surprise her, since she probably could not see the main keep looming over everything below.

He kept his mouth closed as they passed through the second bailey, the same shame enveloping him at the sight of the broken down guard towers, barracks, and shrine. Only as they passed through the third gate did his embarrassment begin to abate. The third bailey housed the two fixed up guard towers, pristine armory, and perfected consort housing. His friends in centuries past would stay in those consort houses when they wanted some space from him and his lover. Dorian felt a small measure of pride looking over the fully restored buildings and how he'd kept them in good condition.

The fourth and final gate came into view for Ruby, earning her first commentary, "How many gates are there?"

Her voice sounded as if she hadn't realized she spoke aloud. Dorian stifled a laugh at her disbelieving tone.

"This is the last one. The palace used to be the primary residence for the elves that once ruled this land. So it's extensive, but the main keep and gardens are beyond this gate."

"Gardens?"

"Yes, there are gardens on this level of the palace, as well, but the ones attached to the uppermost bailey are my favorite, personally."

Ruby only nodded, her attention focused on the gate ahead, as if holding her breath. So close to the gate, she probably couldn't see the keep beyond. Dorian would have killed to get her first thoughts as she took in his estate, but he would settle for carefully watching her reactions if she didn't want to share. Pushing open the final gate, Dorian held it open for her and rushed in after, eager not to miss what she looked like as she came out on the other side of the covered bridge beyond the gate.

A sliver of moonlight fell through the trees above as Ruby stepped off of the bridge, the light finding her just right as she lowered the lantern to gaze in wonder at the main keep. Her mouth dropped open on a gasp even Dorian could barely hear. The silvery light glinting off her dark red hair was breathtaking on its own. Her eyes, widened as she gazed up at the keep, were lit from the moonlight as well, revealing the warmth of rich, earthy brown that hid in their onyx reflection.

Imagining seeing his home through Ruby's eyes, Dorian looked up. The wood and stone building stood five stories above ground, presenting a grand and imposing view of the land. He refreshed the paint on the outside, renewing the colorful exteriors the elves had been so fond of. Though he painted the trim black, the majority of the keep sported a brilliant shade of indigo. The unique shape of the roof lent the whole manor a mystical quality, since elves in other countries didn't use the same shapes in their architecture. It practically became a lost design after the elves who escaped the cursed country refused to relive their losses.

Ready for Ruby to see the inside, he cleared his throat, "Right, so there are two paths up to the main keep. We could take the stairs, which are direct and would put us inside in no time, or we could take the smooth path through the gardens. It's a gentle, sloping way up to the main keep."

"There's a sloping path through the gardens? What do you mean?"

"Well, a few centuries ago, I—" Dorian's throat constricted from the memories, forcing him to clear it before he continued, "I had someone special to me that we expected would not be able to walk easily forever. So I made sure to install a path through the entire grounds that would not require the use of their legs. They could use a wheelchair if they needed. I had plans for retrofitting the house to be more accessible."

"I bet that came in handy..."

"They never used it, but it never hurts to maintain such features. They're worthwhile in the event that one needs it. So, which path would you prefer to use?"

"Stairs, for today. I will want to look around this garden path you have some other time, though, if that's alright..."

"Of course."

Trying not to rush ahead too far, Dorian led the way up the stairs to the main entrance. Throwing open the double doors, Dorian looked around for the light controls, belatedly realizing that he would need to refresh the system in the basement before he could grant ready light to the rooms of the house and give the tour she needed.

"Sorry, if you could wait right there, I need to fix something."

Dorian ran to the basement before she could answer, using vampiric speed to accomplish the task in a matter of seconds. The magic lighting system took a lot of energy to feed. Dorian stood there for several seconds, feeding magic into it while bouncing on his feet. It felt wrong to leave a new guest in the foyer, waiting on him to be able to look around or set down her bag, standing in cold darkness. Finally, the hum of the system whirring to life told Dorian that he could stop, but he felt weak from the drain.

Dropping his own bag off near the blood cellar, Dorian hurried back up the stairs and greeted Ruby once more, apologizing for taking so long.

"The system is rather greedy with magic," he said by way of explanation, waiting only long enough to see her eyebrows begin to knit together before he touched the light control on the wall.

All throughout the foyer, low, warm lights like those of candles began to illuminate the space, creating comfortable lighting and showcasing the details that filled the home. Dorian displayed his sculptures on thin console tables lining the foyer. The dark cherry-wood floors shined beautifully under long, ornamental rugs. The same wood made up the railing for the grand staircase, curling up either side of the wide foyer to the second floor. Silver and gold filigree with flowers and vines stood out against the burgundy walls they were painted on.

Ruby's eyes sparkled in the light, a small smile gracing her lips as she admired the space. In an instant, Dorian's earlier anxiety about showing her his home melted into excitement. What other expressions might she show in relation to his home? He needed to know.

"Come on, let me show you around so you can navigate the place. Just touch these runes on the wall for light control. You can even command the brightness and tone of the light with a thought. I heard the warmer lights were nice on the eyes, but the cooler, brighter light is good when I have to clean in here."

Dorian felt himself on the verge of rambling and cut himself off, hurrying to the room to the left and sliding the pocket doors open. The sitting room had been carefully decorated with plush furniture and rugs, thick curtains, and beautiful artwork. Dorian could still recall Leandra's reaction to seeing her favorite pieces on display in the room, despite never telling Dorian what art at that gallery in Mistspires she'd loved. Glancing at Ruby looking over the art, his throat constricted again, heart pounding in his ears. The soft expression of admiration on her face, peace radiating from her, resembled Leandra's gaze in that gallery so much that Dorian felt sick.

Am I just projecting Leandra on this woman because I have been lonely too long?

If that was the case, Dorian knew he needed to emotionally distance himself from Ruby as soon as possible. She deserved better than to be the stand-in for a vampire's mortal lover. Furthermore, Ruby deserved privacy. Dorian hadn't given her much since interrupting her hunters and bringing her along with him. Now that they were in his private home, it would be impossible to justify keeping his senses fully engaged all the time. During the trek to his home, he needed to listen out for vampiric hunters and beasts. Safe in his home, there were no such threats.

Dorian intentionally dulled his hearing and withdrew emotional view. Those two measures would afford her a great deal more control over how much she could hide from him and do on her own. Considering his goal accomplished with those changes, Dorian directed her through the rest of the tour, forcibly shaking off the thoughts of Leandra that kept threatening to overtake him. Intentionally focusing on Ruby throughout the tour wasn't helping him fight the memories of the woman who shattered him once upon a time, but the look on her face as she admired each room of the luxurious keep transcended the cost on his heart.

She hummed with delight in the grand dining hall. Mouth agape, she wandered the sprawling kitchen with joy. She loved his enchanted pantries, but wrinkled her nose at the door to his blood cellar. The sprawling library really sold her on the keep when she realized that it took up the entirety of the second and third floors of the manor.

"Why is the library so massive in the main house?" Ruby asked in awe.

Dorian watched her face, her glowing skin reflecting amber in the warmer light, admiring the way her cheeks rounded with her broad smile, almost forgetting to answer her question, "The elven monarchs loved books. In all genres they could get their hands on. I heard that they were even accused of hoarding texts. Looking through the library over the years, I doubt they were simply hoarders. More like avid collectors. Most genres of their collection are refined, excellent quality works of literary art. The nonfiction pieces are similarly impressive. Well-researched or first-hand accounts by experts."

Looking around the third floor of the keep, the second floor of the library, Ruby nodded her understanding, a smile still gracing her face, her eyes dancing in light.

Dorian cleared his throat again, scratching at the back of his head as he gestured to a section of the library, "Over there is the section on witchcraft and magical practices. I have added to that section over the years, so there are many more recent texts than the elven leaders had possessed. You're free to read any of the books in the library, of course, but I figured you would want to know about that section first."

"Oh! Thank you! That will be great..." Ruby cast her eyes down, her voice trailing off oddly.

Cursing himself for not continuing to monitor her emotional field, Dorian silently wondered what her reaction indicated. Was she actually excited? Had he only served to remind her of the curse and why she stood there in the first place? Or perhaps something else lurked beneath the surface that he knew nothing of? It frustrated Dorian to have to rely on her expressions and statements alone.

Moving along, Dorian walked her through the fourth floor's numerous luxurious rooms. Finally ascending the stairs to the fifth floor, Dorian directed her to one of the two doors. Ruby looked at him curiously as she passed him to open the door for herself. She released a strangled cry of delight as she slowly stepped into the opulent room beyond.

"The former monarchs kept separate bedrooms for appearance-sake, but I read that they simply traded whose bed they slept in," Dorian scratched at his head once more, eyes darting around the room as he avoided looking at Ruby, "The last monarchs, as I mentioned before, were not inclined to keeping consorts. Regardless, they kept their separate rooms as a cover for the nosy nobility that visited sometimes. This would have been the queen's chambers."

"I can see that... But these furnishings and details... They couldn't have survived thousands of years until you came along, right?"

"No, I refurnished and stocked the place myself—though many of the books in the library were here to start with—but I kept to the styles that were here originally. It felt wrong to move into this abandoned palace and treat it as if its history didn't matter. I adjusted the colors to fit the taste of—" Dorian cut himself off abruptly, shaking his head.

Ruby doesn't need to know all the details.

"Well to fit. Anyways, you are welcome to this room. My bedroom is across the hall. If you'd prefer some more distance, you are welcome to any of the other rooms on the fourth floor, but I would imagine we should keep your chambers in the same building as me, for when the curse attacks."

"That makes sense... This room is... It's probably too much for me but I'll take it... thank you... Dorian."

Dorian turned to leave, nearly smacking into the wall instead upon hearing her say his name. She'd called him bloodsucker since their introductions. Sobering to the knowledge that she was sharing genuine appreciation for the room, Dorian fought for composure.

"Think nothing of it, Ruby. You need a room and this is the best one besides mine, so it only makes sense that the only other person here would get it. I'd have to be some weird, self-obsessed fool to try and stick you in a lesser room when you're my guest here."

Dorian turned to watch Ruby as his words sank in, wanting to find himself on better footing before he tried to leave the room again. While she had dropped the antagonism for him quickly, she hadn't been particularly warm with him either. The way she used his name told him that things had shifted further for them. Maybe they could actually become friends.

Friendship presented a risk. He would be opening himself up to grief once more; she would die someday, like most of his friends did. However, refusing to allow friendship to grow would make things between them unbearably awkward.

Her eyes welled with sudden tears as the muscles around her jaw tightened so much Dorian worried it would snap. He watched with alarm as she forcibly steadied her breathing, unsure what he said to trigger that concerning response. His own face tightened into an apologetic grimace. Dorian opened his mouth to apologize to her, only to be silenced as she held up a hand to stop him. He waited, watching as she turned away from him, apparently steadying herself.

"That wasn't about anything you said..." Ruby whispered just loud enough to hear.

Dorian nodded, eyes darting around the room to find an excuse to leave and return in a few minutes. Ruby clearly needed a little bit of time to herself, but he wanted to speak with her more. Originally leaving to change out of his travel clothes, he needed to check in on her once he was done as a result of her reaction. Searching for an excuse, Dorian realized that Ruby hadn't been looking at him to see his nodding.

Feeling foolish, Dorian shook his head at himself before speaking, "Okay, I am going to get some firewood for you so your room can warm up. I can imagine the manor is very cold for you right now."

Dorian fled the room before she could respond. He hadn't watched anyone decent cry in centuries. Flying down the stairs, Dorian eagerly sought to rid himself of the discomfort drowning him at her distress.

CHAPTER TWENTY-ONE

Ruby

Spending the rest of the previous night in her brand new bedroom proved restorative, giving her the opportunity to enjoy time alone, but that restoration disappeared after a day of fitful sleep. Dorian kindly started a fire in the room's grand fireplace shortly after the abrupt appearance of her tears. She'd thanked him quietly, but when asked, she refused his offer of company while she started reviewing grimoires in the library below. Dorian nodded as she explained that she would prefer to stay in her room. He offered to come if she called for him and left without another word. Ruby then spent most of the night dwelling on her thoughts, pondering the turns her life had taken in recent days, and wondering why it all turned out the way it did. Above all else, she stewed on her transforming opinions of Dorian.

Having proven so different from everything she had been told about vampires, Dorian began also proving himself different from many of the men she encountered in her life at large. Juniper and other men she spent one-on-one time with would argue with her to stick around when she didn't want them. They would regard her tears as a nuisance to manage or a problem to solve. Dorian hadn't done any of that. He accepted her wishes and moved along without argument or being pushy. In fact, he'd gone out of his way to make her more comfortable with no expectations.

The interaction proved nearly as restorative as the blessed rain bath in her grandiose bathroom. That had been the only time she saw Dorian after he'd gotten her fire going. He explained the contraption, calling it a rain bath and detailing its function.

Once he finished demonstrating it to her, Ruby found herself positively giddy for the experience, ushering him out of her room so that she could experience it sooner. Standing in the hot water had been a revelation. She had heard of such magical plumbing in the homes of the wealthiest nobles. Ruby hadn't been sure what to make of those rumors, however, since she saw no explanation for why such an efficient way of washing would be overlooked by the witches. They valued cleanliness highly while resenting the time it took.

As she languidly soaked up the hot water pounding on her aching muscles in a chaotic staccato, Ruby felt a smile forming through the sigh that escaped her lips. If nothing else, Ruby was glad to have outlived the others if for no other reason than to experience that blessed rain bath. She possessed no idea how long she took to cleanse herself of the last few days.

She devolved into tears at some point. Cathartically sobbing into the loud, running water settled something in her that she hadn't realized was coiled up. The curse threatened her as she cried, but never strengthened enough to act. The squeezing shadows within her faded as her emotions finally wound down, granting her the ability to breathe once more.

Ruby finally slipped into bed at dawn, not daring to glimpse the outside for a moment before she snuggled under the covers, too afraid to see the glorious surroundings and become overly energized. She needed to stay on the same schedule as Dorian, since he offered to help her. Seeing the sun shining through the trees on the gardens she knew lay outside the keep would be too stimulating. So, she forced herself to sleep. The bed provided the perfect lulling factor, coaxing her to sleep with silky sheets that surprisingly maintained just the right temperature for her and the perfect balance of soft and firm to support her as she drifted off.

Waking that evening, despite her new exhaustion after another series of nightmares where the other witches continued berating her, she knew it had been for the best. Shoving aside her guilt at being glad for how things went for her, she stood, yawning and stretching away another a fruitless attempt at going back to sleep, since all of her tiredness did not grant her sleep. An ache had settled into her bones from the days of hard travel, making Ruby wince.

Glancing around the sumptuous room, Ruby cracked her neck and pulled back on the clothes she had traveled in, not having any other outfits available. She would have to wear the pajamas that she had brought from the coven at some point, if only to thoroughly wash her clothes, but she would wait for that as long as possible. Those coven-provided pajamas were too damn scratchy to tolerate if she didn't absolutely have to.

Ruby exited her room, noticing the door to Dorian's room lay wide open. Inside, she spotted a mirror image of her own suite, though decorated in red, rather than the blue found in her room. Both suites featured the same dark cherry wood as the rest of the house, with silver accents painted onto the walls and inlaid in the chandeliers. Otherwise, the rooms were exactly the same, down to the fact that both rooms were now empty.

Rushing down the stairs, Ruby noted that she would be getting a workout every day in the keep. She hurried through the kitchen, into the basement pantries, only processing that she'd seen the light on in the living room once she made it to the storage. Realizing Dorian waited there for her, Ruby made herself a quick breakfast and a cup of tea, downing the food while standing in the spacious kitchen and washing up before joining Dorian with her tea.

"Have you been up long?" Ruby asked.

"No, not long. Don't worry about it. How did you sleep?"

"Oh..." Ruby hadn't expected the question, stopping to set her tea on a low table situated between two couches before sitting on the couch opposite Dorian, "I slept well. Thank you... How about you? Or do you sleep?"

"I slept well," Dorian smiled.

The movement drew her attention to the sharp lines of his cheeks and jaw, emphasizing his fuller bottom lip and closing his eyes slightly. Were it not for the hint of fang against that bottom lip, Ruby would have thought herself observing a remarkable human man, rather than a dangerous vampire who could kill her with minimal effort. The knowledge that he had no interest in killing her calmed the momentary flare of nerves that had overtaken her.

"Good... Good. That's good. I didn't know vampires slept."

"We can. I don't always have to, though. Most of the time, I spend a few hours in meditation and am fine. But I decided to sleep today."

"I see... Well, it's good to know that bloodsuckers need rest." Ruby smiled as she reached for her tea, hoping that her joking tone came across plainly.

Dorian's laugh relaxed her for a moment before his eyes traversed her body, stilling his laughter and ramping up her anxiety once more, "Do you not have other clothes?"

"I... didn't have many clothes, no. Outside of some pajamas from the coven which are... awful in so many ways, I have nothing besides this outfit anymore. The attack of the curse in my previous robes took away my only other outfit."

Dorian stared for a moment, his eyes rapidly moving back and forth as he thought about something, before he abruptly stood, "Come with me."

Before she could respond, Dorian was out the door. Ruby hurried to keep up with him, following as he led her outside, through the fourth gate and up to one of the smaller houses located in the third walled off area. Her eyebrows drew together. Inside the house, Ruby waited in the dark for Dorian, who had disappeared upon entry.

Suddenly, the lights came on, revealing the building's elegant details. Soon, he reappeared, only to dash up the stairs. Ruby scurried up the stairs after him, panting to catch her breath when he finally stopped.

"Wait, Dorian, what are we doing here?"

"I had a friend a long time ago. She had me store her old clothes here. Her eldest son had taken over her finances and kept trying to bleed her dry. She didn't want me to do anything about him, but wanted me to keep her things safe so that he couldn't squander them. In the end, she never came back to retrieve them. Before she passed, I asked if she wanted me to pass her belongings on to her grandchildren, but she said I should hold onto them. I never understood why, but you're a similar size as she was," Dorian threw open the door he had stopped in front of, "If you find anything you like among her things, you are welcome to wear them. They're all a few centuries out of date, but if you don't mind, then they're yours."

Turning on the light to the room as she entered, she gasped at the rows and rows of gorgeous gowns, tops, pants, skirts, undergarments, and shoes. The room, once a rather large suite, became transformed beneath the weight of the garments consuming its space.

"Your friend kept all of these clothes?" Ruby asked incredulously.

She couldn't imagine being able to wear everything in there even once. Perhaps with an immortal life like a vampire, or a nearly immortal life like an elf, one would have the time to experience wearing every item of clothing there. But for a mortal to have owned all of those clothes sounded simply preposterous to her. Ruby couldn't help the giggle that escaped her lips as she spun in a circle, taking in the wall-to-wall racks of elegant clothes.

"She was something of a collector when it came to popular designers of the era. I didn't get it; I just played storage."

"Thank you... I don't know how I can use this as a good closet, but I'm sure I can move things over a little at a time."

Her mind whirred with the logistics of transporting the clothes she wanted to wear, thinking of the climb to the house and the climb up the stairs. It would be arduous and her back screamed at her before she even began, but Ruby refused to put Dorian's gesture of generosity to waste.

"Nonsense. We'll empty a rack and have you fill it up with the clothes you want. I'll take that to your room and deposit the clothes in your closet, then return and repeat until you have all the clothes you want."

Ruby stopped to stare at Dorian, dumbfounded. Clearly the task would be easy for him, with his vampiric strength and stamina, but that didn't change that she would be imposing on his time greatly for a frivolous task that most other people she'd known would refuse. For him to offer at all shocked her.

Ruby almost refused his generosity, realizing before she could even utter a single syllable that she didn't need to be that stubborn. She'd gleaned in the short time she'd known him that Dorian wouldn't have offered if he wasn't willing to do it. Despite all of the kindness he had shown her, Dorian also showed himself to be a capable killer and formidable fighter, willing to end the lives of those he barely classed as enemies. By offering, he exemplified to her once more that she did not exist in that category.

Instead, Ruby nodded and turned her attention to the nearest clothing rack, perusing the pieces carefully. Before she knew it, she had directed Dorian to take so many clothes back to the main keep that she saw no way she would be able to wear them all in her time at his estate before she was killed by the curse, cured, or needed to leave. Regardless, she reveled in her choices, thanking Dorian profusely for his aid and her access to the quality garments. She sent him off with the last rack of clothes, which consisted of undergarments and shoes.

As he hurried off with the clothes with reassurance that she could handle putting those away herself, Ruby fought against the flush creeping up her chest and heating her cheeks, even as she smiled to herself. He'd scratched at the back of his head again as he said that he would leave her to put away the undergarments herself. His apparent nerves on the subject mirrored her own. It served to put her oddly at ease. If he felt uncomfortable, then it couldn't be weird or bad that she felt uncomfortable.

He now knows what undergarments I have and will be wearing...

Ruby tried to shake off the absurdity of the thought, following in his wake and turning out the lights in the former consort house. She rationalized that Dorian seeing her undergarments didn't matter. He had surely seen undergarments thousands of times in his long life and he would hardly be the first person to have seen hers. Flashes of time spent secretly in Edgefair, hiding her hair and darkening her eyebrows to look strictly human, whirred through Ruby's mind, reminding her of each moment stolen with humans who didn't recognize her later.

It was one thing to secretly engage in a sexual relationship with Juniper, another witch. Besmirching the reputation of the Edgefair coven by laying with one commoner human, let alone as many as she did, would have been another entirely. Ruby couldn't have afforded to be caught by being careless. A pregnancy or a disease she couldn't heal on her own would surely have gotten her exiled. Her abilities as a witch ensured that she never needed to worry about the issues of diseases and pregnancy, since those fell under the purview of light magic. Even as incompetent as Ruby often proved herself to be with light magic, she was more than capable of those spells. Protecting herself from such afflictions was easy and invisible to the naked eye. Ruby took full advantage of that ability.

Dorian probably doesn't need to worry about those problems either...

Ruby stopped dead in her tracks on the bridge to the main keep, feeling her body heat as she rapidly shook her head once more. Her braids smacked against her arms, slightly stinging despite the layer of clothing between. The sensation snapped her out of her embarrassed reverie. The intrusive thought continued to rattle through her head, despite her attempts to shake it out, distracting her as she ascended the steps and reentered through the open doors of the manor.

"Oof," Ruby exhaled sharply as she collided with Dorian.

"Sorry, are you okay? I wasn't paying attention, just hurrying to get back and make sure you didn't want to grab anything else. I didn't even look where I was going."

"Yes, no, I'm fine... I'm the one who should be sorry. I wasn't watching where I was going. I'm all good on clothes..." Ruby pondered that for a second, jokingly adding, "For probably the rest of my life."

"You've got a few decades left, at least. I'm sure you'll need more eventually," Dorian said congenially, "Well, I'll get the consort house all shut down, then."

"I turned out all the lights in there before I left."

"Oh," Dorian looked between her and the door, "then I find myself with nothing to do while you sort your clothes. I will get started looking through my collection of books for information on curses from sources other than witches." He scratched at the back of his head again. "I'll be on the first floor of the library, near a fireplace, if you want to join me when you're done?"

Ruby cocked her head as he asked for her company. Naturally, she would sit near him while they worked on finding any information about her curse, but once more she spied that same nervous tic of his.

Why is he nervous about asking me to join him so that we can do what he brought me here to do? I don't get it...

"Yes, that sounds good... I probably won't be long..."

Upstairs, her closet was brimming with clothes, leaving Ruby a little embarrassed by her greediness. She quickly discarded such feelings as she changed into a comfortable ensemble. The soft, cobalt blue top caressed her skin with a gentle halo formed of the woolly fibers, enveloping her in comfort. She put on a similarly woolly black skirt. The clothes fit remarkably well. Staring into the full-length mirror in the closet, Ruby thought that she looked more alive, surprisingly, despite the curse having ravaged her body in recent days.

Had her skin always glowed so much? What had changed? Maybe the colors of her clothes? Or was she just... happier? Ruby shook her head, grabbing one of the grimoires she had brought with her and rushing from the room. She needed to rid herself of such silly notions. It wasn't possible that she could be happier living in a secluded palace in the middle of the most dangerous forest she knew of while afflicted by a curse that had indirectly led to the deaths of eight of her fellow witches.

Joining Dorian in the library, Ruby started reading when Dorian held out his hand, gesturing for her to stop. Confused, she stared at him, waiting for him to explain himself. She had to hurry to get to the bottom of this curse. She wasted too much time already on silly emotions, fanciful and foolish endeavors for clothes, and overall avoidance. The time had already passed for her to get serious about resolving this problem, and Dorian seemingly stopped her for no good reason.

Dorian, getting the message, explained himself, "I think it would be helpful if you told me everything that happened to lead up to the manifestation of the curse. Where it all started until you ended up running into me. If I hear the details, I may be able to better focus my own research attempts."

Ruby slowly nodded, finding the patience in his gaze oddly comforting.

"So, tell me everything," Dorian gently directed.

CHAPTER TWENTY-TWO

Dorian

"That's incredibly strange." Dorian shook his head as Ruby finished explaining.

She hadn't appeared to hold anything back. He respected the way that she faced the events clearly, despite her obviously mixed feelings.

"What do you mean?" Ruby looked at him suspiciously.

"Well, that isn't how vampiric curses work. We don't curse without receiving and giving something. Generally, when hired to perform curses, we receive a piece of the would-be victim from the person hiring us, then we give them something to give to the victim, having attuned the curse to the victim's energy. Without that exchange, I cannot see how a vampire could have cursed you," Dorian held up a hand to make Ruby wait a moment so that he could continue, "But I also cannot see how a vampire was not involved, since the shadows are so strictly vampiric. It's puzzling," he trailed off.

"What is it?"

"It is similar to how curses manifested when a witch cast it."

"That's impossible. Witches today don't even know how to curse others!" Ruby stood abruptly, her chest heaving.

"I'm sorry, but it's what it sounds like to me. I cannot think of another plausible explanation. But maybe we can find something out," Dorian hoped to placate her.

Despite his words, Dorian did not believe for one second that a witch wasn't involved in cursing her. Why, or how for that matter, he did not know. Regardless of the specifics, the situation screamed to him that, while a vampire had been involved in some capacity, a vampire did not place the actual curse. Given the lack of druids and priests, of darker orders or not, in Vlideron, he found it only natural to assume a witch directed and controlled the curse. Being the most diverse magic-users in the Known World, witches made the most sense.

He quietly hoped that Ruby would be able to see that on her own as well. She settled back into her seat silently, casting a long look at Dorian, as if waiting for him to say something else. When he didn't, she opened the tome she had brought with her and began to read. Dorian turned his attention back to the books laid out on the table beside him. Stifling a sigh, he reopened his own book, in spite of knowing there would be no clues within.

A few hours later, Dorian decided to break their stilted silence, "So this Elder Moss you mentioned. You have a lot of respect for her, I take it?"

He didn't know why he'd chosen to ask about her elder, but she was so frequently mentioned.

"Oh... Yes. I do. I mean, of course I do. She is... such an impressive witch. She ascended to the rank of elder at only thirty years old!" Ruby's eyes widened for emphasis, "I mean, she was always there. Elder Moss basically raised me. When she ascended the rank of elder, many expected that she would take a step back from guiding us. Vanella, Violetta, Juniper, and me. But she kept up with us, and the others from our age. The rest started to drift out and fill into the coven on their own, but I was always... such trouble. So Elder Moss decided to be the one who took charge of helping me and managing me for the rest of the coven."

"She set those punishments you told me about?" Dorian couldn't control the edge of ice that entered his voice as he realized who this Elder Moss woman had been to her.

"Well... Yes... But she was just doing what she thought was best for me. I swear. She was. She must have been... Maybe she was wrong in her methods, but that isn't her fault."

Dorian bit back his arguments, knowing they would pass through her as if she were a ghost, refusing to let anything he said stick to her. He recognized that defensiveness on behalf of the woman Ruby considered a parental figure. She didn't seem prepared to address it. Instead, he simply waited for her to continue, trying to loosen his grip on the book.

"Elder Moss even made it to the grand position of leading the elders of Edgefair. She might ascend to the Vlideronian Elders! If my disappearance and curse doesn't cast a pall on her, that is..."

"That's not your fault if it did."

"Right..." Ruby's voice dripped with sarcasm, "Anyway, I think that if I can rid myself of this curse, I can go back and help Elder Moss see the truth of our history. Then maybe she can lead the charge to reform the modern witches. She would be the best suited for that... Everyone respects her. She's a strong witch and has always lived to the best of our ideals. I disappointed her so much... But maybe if I can show her that I might represent another way of life for witches at large... Maybe she won't regret guiding me all those years."

Dorian felt his stomach sinking with every word. He couldn't bear being the one to shatter that illusion for her. Despite the hope brimming in her eyes, Dorian spotted the telltale shadow of sadness that told him that Ruby knew she was deluding herself. This Elder Moss willingly tortured a young woman in her charge just for falling short of absurd and overly oppressive rules. After such a short while, he couldn't be entirely sure of Ruby's character, but he knew her enough to eliminate the possibility of her being a monster lying in wait to harm people for her own pleasure.

Rather than commenting on Elder Moss, Dorian chose to pivot to a new subject, finding something less fraught with danger to discuss. "What other nonsense did those witches teach you about the history of Vlideron?"

He relished the small smile that flashed over her lips before she readjusted her expression and fixed him with a hard glare. "If you must know, we were taught that the Great King attained his position through divine choice. Am I to believe that is not true?"

Dorian snorted with derision, "Not even a little bit. He had a lot of help ascending to the throne, to be sure. But divinely chosen? Not in the least. Many gods directed their orders to leave Vlideron when he successfully wrested the throne once more, not trusting the sanctity of their religions to be left intact. They were correct for that move. The ones who remained were relegated to the fringes of society at best, and completely overtaken by his lackeys at worst."

"How did... I mean... If he wasn't divinely chosen, then how did he gain the throne? For that matter, how did he have the throne and lose it? No one ever answered those questions clearly for me..."

Dorian took a deep breath, launching into the sordid tale at length. He described the original ascension, during which the previous royal family's line ended with no heirs. The "Great King" presented himself as a candidate for the throne, rallying supporters behind him by virtue of his long life as a merchant. Already considered something of an old man, there had been many who had discounted the possibility of him attaining the throne. His fringe ideals were all the more reason to brush him off entirely. However, he had many connections among the corrupt nobility. No matter how hard he worked, Dorian had never been prepared to incinerate the corrupt in one fell swoop.

So the "Great King" worked to rally others behind him, drawing to him radicals from many groups and building a veritable army of swindled commoners behind him. The nobility in charge of deciding upon the new royal line decided that he had the most support behind him. The first time he ascended the throne had been a nightmare blasted out over the people of Vlideron, until the regular people could not take it anymore. The nobility in charge of overseeing the throne heard the pleas of the people and removed him from authority, selecting a new family to rise to the monarchy.

With the help of the vampiric council, and nearly half of the witches in Vlideron, the man who insisted on being called the Great King violently retook the throne from the new family, silently ousting the nobility that had opposed him and staging a takeover the likes of which the known world had never seen before. Then he stayed in power, far beyond his natural life. Despite having been an old man by human standards when he attained the throne the first time, his life had continued. There were no signs he had been transformed into a vampire, so one could only assume he garnered some help in extending his life into unnatural proportions.

"I still don't know how he's doing it... But he's made his continued life everyone else's problem."

"You really hate him, don't you?"

"To my understanding, he is even more corrupt than the nobles I normally occupy myself with killing. I simply have never had the chance to get my hands on him. I don't think it would be worth it to die in an attempt to kill him that I am unconvinced would succeed."

Dorian saw the moment that Ruby accepted his answer and his version of events, the shift in her eyes visible. It seemingly did something for her soul. The sadness in her eyes decreased, replaced by a small, glimmering spark of anger. Her shoulders rolled back as she nodded her understanding.

"That answered my questions far better than they have ever been answered before. Thank you..." Ruby glanced at him before training her gaze back on the page in front of her.

"Any time at all."

The hours passed in back and forth discussions of the history of Vlideron, each of them clearly tiptoeing around sore subjects. Dorian could see the moments that Ruby started to ask something about Dorian's personal life, only to pivot with a follow-up question that actually changed the subject. Dorian focused on correcting the propaganda-driven education she had been given about Vlideron and the world at large.

Ruby took a few breaks for meals and managing her human needs, but returned promptly to her studies and their discussions. He enjoyed seeing her as a diligent worker when it came to her curse. Curiosity poured from her presence. He respected curiosity in others. Sooner than he would have, a familiar unease tingled in the back of his mind.

"I should get to bed. The sun will be rising soon."

"Already?"

Dorian nodded solemnly, not wanting to retreat to rest, but deciding it best to stick to a steady schedule. He hadn't missed her yawning nearly every other sentence. She needed to rest and he somehow doubted that she would unless he did as well.

Despite her obvious reluctance, Ruby set down the grimoire and waved goodnight to him. Dorian waited, giving her plenty of time to settle into her room without his presence nearby, reminding her that he rested so close, before he ascended the stairs after her.

I'm being excessive with giving her space. She knows this is my house, so why do I keep going out of my way to keep away from her when she might feel vulnerable?

His own behavior aside, Dorian decided he would actually sleep once more. The refreshing feeling of having slept the day before had lingered, leaving him glad for the experience. After bathing and throwing on a pair of trunks to sleep in, in case Ruby needed him in the day, Dorian crawled into his own bed. The cold sheets paired with the cold, dark room, settled into his bones in a way that had not affected him in two centuries. Dorian stubbornly shut his eyes to the connections that threatened his mind, lulling himself to sleep with his own shadows before he could spend too much time contemplating the coldness of his large, empty bed.

Waking that evening, Dorian felt eager to face the night of reading and conversation. She arose shortly after he left his room, joining him in the library after dressing and eating. They sat in silence for a time, each reading carefully. Dorian wasn't having any luck finding information on curses cast by vampires that didn't necessitate that she be given something prior to the curse taking hold.

"How is magic different for non witches?" Ruby broke the silence.

"That depends on the race and circumstances. Elves and orcs both use nature and light based magics, though their methods are different. Orcs utilize extensive rituals, frequently involving entire clans to strengthen the results. Elves often specialize in more specific magic. One might become so adept with plants that they can command their growth and movement with a gesture. Another might learn the magic of the animals and focus on those connections. Yet another might specialize in healing light magic or control over the weather to aid the land. So on and so forth."

"So nature magic is just magic involving the natural world directly?"

"Yes?" Dorian found the question temporarily unexpected, "Right, you weren't taught much about the types of magic."

Ruby just stared at him, not bothering to read from the grimoire.

How hasn't she picked that up from those grimoires? Is she trying to verify knowledge via an outside source? Clever, if she is.

"Vampires, as you know, use shadow magic, as well as darkness and blood magic."

"I think I understand something of shadow magic, but I thought that was darkness magic. And blood magic?"

"No, darkness magic and shadow magic are not the same thing. Hmm," Dorian pondered how to explain the difference, but gave up after a moment, "Well, I don't really know how to explain the differences right now, but I have a book somewhere that discusses the many forms of magic. Elemental and all of its subtypes, dark, light, shadow, nature, blood, the list goes on."

"Oh, okay..."

"Then there are the dwarves, who utilize a variety of disciplines depending on their familial lineage, inheriting what type of magic they are capable of. Finally, there are the humans who train to use magic. To my understanding, the options are limited and involve great deals of hard work, but it can be done. Priests, druids, and shamans all work to connect with various patron spirits to access magic. Priests connected with gods. Druids and shamans both connect with the land, but I'm given to understand it is in different ways. Regardless, witches take the top spot in flexibility with magic."

"How is that?"

"Witches are the only magic users in the world not limited by discipline beyond innate talents and drive to pursue skill. Some witches are better in some disciplines than others. But none of you are barred from any type of magic completely."

He watched as Ruby considered that, nodding her head slowly before smirking, "You're quite the useful encyclopedia for a bloodsucker."

"Happy to be of service, madam."

"Madam?"

"What? Would you rather some other honorific?"

Ruby stared at him, her smirk sliding into a full smile as she shook her head, "I guess madam will do."

Their next few days passed in a steady routine, with Dorian answering Ruby's questions about magic and the workings of other magic users. He found her that book on types of magic and spied her setting aside the grimoire of the moment to look something up in the provided reference material. She had already finished the grimoires she'd brought with her. Her eyes lit up as she understood new concepts of magic, delving deeper into it, despite finding nothing that could help her with her curse thus far. Dorian wasn't having any luck either in that pursuit. He went on calling her madam, while she continued to call him bloodsucker most of the time. Their interactions were light and congenial.

It took nearly a week into her stay at his home before Ruby started to tiptoe back into questioning Dorian's personal life. She cleared her throat, sitting in the same chair in the library where she always sat, but Dorian spotted the way she squirmed in her seat, shifting between positions as if wildly uncomfortable.

"So... I noticed some bath oils and soaps in my bathroom... Who... Who did they belong to?"

Dorian froze, setting the latest tome of magical knowledge down immediately to stare at her. Whatever he thought she would say, that had not been it. The memories he kept holding back in her presence flooded him, making him dizzy.

"Those... those were Leandra's." His voice cracked.

He wasn't sure why he answered, but he had to.

"Leandra? I'm sorry, I shouldn't pry..."

"It's okay. She-" Dorian took a steadying breath, "She was someone very important to me a very long time ago. I guess she left those behind... If they are still good, which I expect they would be because they were of elven make, then you are free to use them."

"What if Leandra wants them back someday?"

Dorian almost laughed at the absurdity of her question until he saw the earnest concern written over Ruby's face. "Leandra was a human. She last lived here nearly 400 years ago. She, well, she won't be coming back for them."

Water invaded Ruby's eyes, sympathy crafting an unfamiliar expression on her face, "I'm so sorry..."

"Don't worry about it." Dorian tried to be nonchalant.

Inside, his heart ached, reminded of its festering wound, transforming into a fetid infection beneath the surface of his soul.

CHAPTER TWENTY-THREE

Ruby

A week after Ruby's horrific choice to question Dorian on Leandra, she was still contemplating how to feel more comfortable with him again. While she knew that there were a lot of details missing about Leandra, Ruby could tell that Leandra had been his lover. That left her feeling horrendously guilty for dredging up those emotions and shoving her foot in her mouth over the woman's centuries-ago death. Since then, Ruby had dealt with unrelenting awkwardness in Dorian's presence. They worked side by side and continued to discuss a variety of topics pertaining to magic and history, but Ruby steadfastly avoided any more personal topics.

The awkwardness she'd first suffered after pouring out the details of so many punishments had been minuscule compared to how she felt about jabbing such a tender topic with indelicate hands. However, after days of tiptoeing around him, she found herself more and more disquieted by maintaining such emotional distance from someone she spent so much of her time with. To a degree, Ruby knew that she needed to trust him. She would be living with him for likely the next few months. Furthermore, he wanted to help her with the curse.

For Ruby, that left her with only one real option: she needed to get to know him better on a personal level. If she held on to any hope for a friendly co-existence continuing throughout her time with him, she needed to get over the shame of making him relive something sad. She needed to face her own discomfort with her history to let him in, too.

On that note, she debated what she wanted to reveal to him. For some reason, it felt only fair that she reveal some painful details to him in return for the trouble she had caused him when she had dredged up obviously unwelcome memories. Acknowledging to herself that her upbringing may have been leading her to that conclusion of sacrifice, Ruby still felt that it was the right thing to do. She teetered on the edge, unable to decide what to share. It didn't seem enough that she had shared the specifics of so many punishments she had endured.

Plodding down the stairs to the pantries, Ruby continued to consider what she would tell Dorian about herself while she prepared a quick breakfast. Despite her initial awe at the marvels of magic, the pantries had become commonplace in the nearly two weeks since she had arrived at Dorian's home.

How did his home become so familiar so quickly?

Much had changed in the time she had spent with Dorian, though seemingly little had happened since they made it to the estate. They hadn't made any progress in understanding her curse, but it hadn't attacked her again either. She could feel it, tight around her organs for the moment, but nothing significant had happened with it. What changed for Ruby, more than anything, were her own views pertaining to her history. The longer she spent away from Elder Moss and the other witches, the more she read of the grimoires, and the more she spoke with Dorian, the less she could think of them as authority figures.

Elder Moss kept proving more misguided in her enforcement of such new principles, since it finally sank in for Ruby that their principles were truly new in the grand scheme of their long history. Everything in the outside world had discounted the history she'd been taught. The fact that the elder witches had not questioned their status quo spoke to their inflexibility in a way that told Ruby she needed to reexamine them as a whole and as individuals.

As she numbly ate her breakfast, Ruby couldn't stop thinking about how her opinions had changed. Naturally, by learning new information, she adjusted. But how much more adjusting would she do over the coming weeks or months? When she returned to the coven to encourage reform, would she even be able to entrust the changes to the very same elders who had so discouraged her questioning mind? Those same elders who would be willing to punish her or cast her out if they knew the true extent of her apparent fall from grace and how long that fall had been going on? The fall that began when Juniper started messing around with her.

Maybe that's what I should talk about with Dorian?

Ruby considered it for only a moment before deciding that she had landed on the right thing to talk about in greater detail. She rushed through cleaning up, hurrying to meet with Dorian. He sat in his usual spot, perusing yet another text. Ruby had finished the tomes she had brought with her, so she picked a text from Dorian's collection of witches' grimoires before settling in her usual seat.

Her heart pounded in her ears, eyes darting between the book in her hands and Dorian beside her. The warm, comfortable light cast shadows that perfectly emphasized his sharp bone structure. His eyes, shining like some sort of gemstone, sped down the pages before him, drinking it all in with ease. Ruby tried to read from the grimoire, the witch who wrote it having specialized in curses, but she couldn't keep her eyes trained on the pages.

"Dorian..." her voice croaked.

"Yes?" He lifted his head, eyebrows furrowing together as the corners of his mouth slightly tugged upward.

"I think... I want to... I mean..." Ruby sighed heavily, trying to organize her thoughts in a semi-coherent fashion, "I am going to share some of the specifics of my time in the solitary retreat."

"Why? Don't mistake me, I am here to listen, but this feels out of the blue," Dorian cocked his head to a side, the slight smile he'd sported shifting into a frown.

"I... think we ought to get to know one another a bit, since it's clear I will be staying here for some time... It would be better if we were more friendly, right?"

"I see. I agree, but if you would rather do this another way, we can. You don't need to feel compelled to share the personal details of your traumas with me if you don't want to."

Ruby's breath rushed out of her lungs in exasperation, "I don't want you to be the only one who is dealing with intense emotions while I am here. I could tell that how I responded about Leandra last week threw you, and it isn't fair for you to deal with that more than I do. So just let me tell you my story, okay?"

Dorian winced, but ultimately nodded and waited in silence.

Ruby started in, "I told you the broad strokes of my solitary retreat and what led to it, but I avoided a lot of it as well. You see, I engaged in a sort of... sexual relationship with Juniper. This was about five years ago, but he and I participated in elicit activities for years prior to my solitary retreat. Something changed for him shortly before he turned me in for the romance novels. He... declared me a temptress leading him astray from the correct path he was meant to take as a witch. He broke things off with me, calling me all sorts of names as he did so. He demanded that I stay away from him as best I could without telling a soul what we had been doing."

"You keep giving me reasons to be glad I killed him," Dorian muttered so quietly that Ruby almost didn't hear him.

Continuing without acknowledging his statement, Ruby's voice quavered, "I think that he turned me in for the romance novels because he hoped it would be enough to get me kicked out of the coven, or sent to a new one. I don't know for sure... In any case, Violetta and Elder Moss were the ones who approached me in my room, searched for and seized my books, and discussed what should be done about me while I sat there on my knees in the middle of my bedroom, disarray surrounding me. When they finally told me, I thought I had gotten off pretty easy..."

"Because torture is easy for doing nothing wrong," Dorian snorted, though Ruby could tell his derision came not from his views on her but the situation she described.

"Right, well, they took me to the solitary retreat rooms in the compound immediately. I wasn't able to do anything else. They immediately locked me in the room, alone, and... well they didn't tell me how long I would be there at first. I started to feel my mind slipping from my grasp. It was... I just didn't want to be alive anymore. I didn't think I deserved to be. But I couldn't besmirch the witches by ending my own life. So I started hurting myself while trapped in there. It was the only thing that seemed to keep me present in my own body. The seconds became hours in that relentless light."

Dorian shifted in his seat, staring at her with gentle eyes.

Ruby shifted in her own seat, hoping for the shadows in her belly to stop squeezing her organs so tightly, and continued, "I couldn't stand sunny days for months after that. I still hate to be under the open sun in midday, with no shade trees available. I need the shade, or else it's just too familiar."

"I can only imagine, Ruby. I'm sorry you ever had to go

through that. I hope you can forgive me for this, but if I ever get the chance, I will be killing Elder Moss."

"What? No, why?"

"Well, I already killed Juniper and Violetta. They clearly deserved it more than I thought. But nothing you have ever said about Elder Moss has given me reason to believe that she deserves a different fate. If anything, the more I hear about her, the less I can forgive."

"But she was my mentor. She taught me and guided me through life until just recently. I couldn't... I couldn't condone you killing her outright just because she did what she thought best to help me! She was just... misguided. It's not like she enjoyed harming me..."

Dorian gave her a long, skeptical look.

Ruby felt the twisting shadows moving faster and faster inside of her as she breathed deeply, stuffing down the doubt that she felt about Elder Moss's experience of punishing her. It wasn't worth it for her to become so overwhelmed by her doubts when she could do nothing to resolve them for the foreseeable future. Maybe one day she could take a deeper look at how she felt about Elder Moss in particular.

When the curse continued threatening her, Ruby couldn't take that chance. She calmed herself, but something was wrong. The curse refused to slow down the way that it normally did when she got her emotions under control. It had been so clear that the curse attacked when she let her emotions get out of hand in a negative way. She had been so good about keeping control over it all, but something hadn't worked this time.

Shoving aside the book she had been working on, Ruby stood and took a few steps towards the fireplace, afraid of being in range of anything should something happen. She turned to look at Dorian for a brief moment, opening her mouth to tell him that something was horribly wrong.

She didn't get the chance.

In a split second, the curse went from uncomfortably churning faster within, to bursting forth from her body in all directions. Ruby's flesh ripped as tendrils of shadow tore through her skin and began to lash out around her. Her voice tore into a raw scream, the shadows exiting her body, ravaging her flesh, only to bore back into her in another spot.

Worse, Ruby realized, the shadows began to heal parts of her as they decimated her body. On the floor, writhing around in agony, Ruby felt everything too acutely to ignore anything. Her nerves felt as though they were being held on the licking edge of a flame. She could vaguely hear Dorian's shouts of alarm and concern, but nothing made sense. All she could hear were his screams; something to her about her clothes?

My clothes!

The remaining scraps of tightly woven fabric were catching in her wounds as the curse destroyed her body and attempted to heal it in one go. As a result, her skin wasn't healing up correctly, leaving her raw and bleeding profusely. Her head spun as she tried to move her arms to help herself. No response came, her body lost to the flailing experience of the curse as it tossed her around, each impaling shadow accompanied by an exiting tendril.

The attack sought to prove itself worse than anything she had suffered before. She couldn't imagine what she could do to help herself, let alone how she would even survive the ongoing pain and blood loss. That Dorian's hypnosis couldn't help her this time left her despondent.

"GET THEM OFF ME!!!" Ruby finally managed to scream coherently, though she had no idea where the strength came from.

Dorian, for his part, seemed to understand quickly, the excruciating pain of clothing scraps that had fused to her skin being ripped away following immediately. She thrashed uncontrollably, forced to endure the agony as the curse continued to act while Dorian helped alleviate her overall suffering by causing swift moments of devastation. Each lifted scrap represented a minuscule measure of relief in the grand view of her predicament. It helped, nonetheless.

Finally, rid of the last scrap of cloth from her skin, Ruby felt the shadows slowing. As the last tendrils slithered back within the confines of her skin, the last bits of her injuries healing of their own accord, Ruby opened her eyes and looked around. They were clouded with her own blood, which she tried in vain to wipe away. Suddenly, Dorian handed her a piece of dry cloth to help. Wiping away the blood in her eyes and on her hands, she saw that he had handed her the shirt off his back.

"Tha..." a coughing fit cut her off, her throat too dry to speak.

"Stay there for a moment. I will get you a few towels and we can get you to your rain bath. Just don't move. You must be exhausted and weak. Oh, but we also need to get you food. Rain bath first, though. Rain bath first for sure. I don't think you want to eat while covered like that. No. That—Right, I'll be right back."

Ruby blinked as Dorian disappeared in a blur of movement. He returned before she could even think to stand. Not that she thought she could. Her head spun just from the effort of sitting up.

"Careful now, here you go," Dorian unfurled a large towel, wrapping it gingerly around Ruby's bare shoulders.

Only as she hugged the towel closer to herself did she realize what that meant. Her eyes darted down to her body. Her own blood coated every inch of her. A large pool had formed on the hardwood around her. To the side lay a pile of what had been her clothes. Every last scrap of fabric she wore prior to the curse attacking her. Beyond the fact that her clothes were utterly destroyed, loomed the realization that she sat naked. Her eyes widened as she gripped tighter to both Dorian's shirt and the towel he had so gently wrapped around her.

He unfurled another towel, offering both the towel and his hand to her, "When you're ready, I will help you stand. Then you can secure those towels around yourself better and I can get you to your rain bath. I—" He scratched at the back of his head, clearing his throat the way he always did when nervous, "figure you would rather be more covered when I assist you in getting there."

Ruby's eyes drifted along his own body, her brain belatedly realizing that he handing her his shirt made him bare from the hips up. The lines of his muscles were cast in the same sharp detail as the angles of his face that she'd been observing earlier. She finally nodded, knowing she didn't have the power to speak yet.

As Dorian helped her up and she secured the towels around her better, she wondered how she would be able to bathe in her current state. She couldn't even stand properly on her own yet. From the weight of her arms, she lacked the strength to even reach for her things in the rain bath. Ruby silently cursed herself for placing her things on the higher shelves within the rain bath's tiled walls. Those would prove problematic for her. The whole prospect of the rain bath would be problematic. But a simpler bath would also be worthless. She would end up stewing in a tub of her own blood as she waited for the bath to empty and refill over and over again. The rain bath would prove more effective. But how could she do it alone?

Dorian gently lifted her into his arms, carrying her upstairs. In an instant, they were on the top floor, passing through her bedroom, and landing, at last, in her bathroom. Dorian carefully settled her on the long seat in the rain bath.

She glanced around, wondering if she had the emotional strength to ask for help.

I need help...

CHAPTER TWENTY-FOUR

Dorian

His skin crawled as he steadfastly avoided looking at her. In precisely none of the intrusive and unwelcome fantasies Dorian had suffered that involved Ruby naked and covered in blood was she covered in her own blood. The sight of her writhing in agony, going in and out of consciousness as he was forced to hurriedly remove every last strip of fabric that remained after that blasted curse had torn her apart seared itself upon his very soul. Dorian hurried to ensure she could be comfortable, but his mind raced with all the things she would need to recover from such a taxing experience.

He held no doubt that she felt weak beyond measure. He surmised she might also feel lightheaded. The hot water would help any lingering pain, but it could affect her head more. Should he set it to merely warm then? He wasn't sure. She needed to drink some water to replenish her fluids and she would need a filling meal. Dorian started to mentally peruse his own catalogue of memorized recipes, deciphering which would be the best for her stomach and recovery.

"Dorian?"

Just speaking sounded painful for her. After the screaming she had done, Dorian could only imagine that her vocal cords were completely fried.

Certainly not the way I ever wanted her screaming.

Why did that thought keep haunting him? Dorian had been pushing aside any notice of her appearance for a couple of weeks already. Though he kept having intrusive thoughts about her and what he might enjoy seeing from her, or doing with her, he had been fastidious in denying his mind the chance to follow through with such untoward thoughts. If anything, it was wrong of him to have such thoughts at all. It wouldn't be fair for him to show even strictly sexual interest in the woman. She was dealing with a horrific curse and staying in his house. If he expressed anything of the sort to her, she might feel compelled to go along with him. Dorian would never put someone in that position.

Feeling like a monster for the thought having crossed his mind at all, Dorian finally replied, "Yes, what can I do, what do you need?"

"Help."

"Help?"

Ruby weakly gestured with a hand towards the wall behind him, then looked down at herself.

Dorian turned to see the rain spout and all of her bathing products on the shelves built into the dark tile of the wall. Turning back to her, he started to understand what she asked of him, feeling a growing sense of unease.

"You want me to help you bathe?"

Ruby nodded.

Dorian gulped, knowing that once he saw that, he would be unable to scrub the images from his mind. He would have to behave with excessive care to ensure she didn't feel unduly uncomfortable with the whole situation, and would have to strictly keep a lid on his own thoughts, lest the wrong connections be made. He needed to keep in mind that her own immense suffering resulted in her own blood covering her.

The image of Ruby screaming in pain cooled any thoughts besides how badly she needed his help in that moment. Beyond any of the myriad reasons Dorian had for ignoring her physical attractiveness or the way she intrigued him with her personal perspectives and abilities, there lay the fact that she needed his aid in a clinical fashion. No room existed for his own urges or obscene thoughts. They were not only inappropriate and wholly unwelcome; they were a disservice to her.

Finally, he nodded, "Well, okay. I'll grab a chair we can use and be right back. I'll help get you into place and help you however you need. We can have you facing away from me, so you'll be more comfortable. I'll get some more towels, too," Dorian started to walk away, but had another thought, "Oh, and I shall bring you water, Madam."

Ruby nodded slightly, having apparently decided not to push her voice too much further.

Dorian hurried as fast as he could through the tasks he had set himself. The chair he found was actually a well-made chair of high-quality wood, but after a rain bath with Ruby's blood drenching it, it would have to be burned. Even if the chair could be salvaged, he wouldn't want the memories to taint his home. Dorian grabbed that and a tall glass of water for Ruby.

In the bathroom, Ruby had begun to shiver. Dorian cursed himself for not starting the hot water before he left.

The blood loss would make her cold, of course.

He set the glass of water down beside her, turning the water on. He put the chair down partially in the water in a way that would allow her to lean out of the water as she so chose. Before helping her to move to the chair, Dorian paused to lift the glass to her lips.

Her own blood clung to every inch of her, having soaked through the once white towels. Despite the color matching her hair, he could tell that her blood had also soaked into the numerous braids. He grimaced at that detail. It seemed impossible that she had bled so much and remained among the living. Yet there she was.

Despite witches normally having a longer life than regular humans, they were still basically humans. Humans were mortal. Ruby would one day die. That represented the biggest and best reason Dorian held fiercely for trying not to get too close to her. He wasn't ready to suffer another loss. But he could admit to himself his relief that she would not die yet.

After Ruby had finished half the glass, she indicated she was ready to wash off. Dorian carefully helped her to the chair. The position allowed him to take the soiled towels from her and deposit them in her bathtub before rejoining her, without too much becoming visible to him. The steamy water hit her legs, running over the blood that had cooled slightly, throwing the scent of her blood into the air around them.

Dorian felt thirst raking its vicious claws down his throat as her scent strengthened. He had managed to ignore it for the most part during the active danger. It clung to his clothes and even his skin, since the pooling blood around her had soaked through his pants as he knelt beside her, and carrying her had put his skin in contact with the soaked towels, smearing some of her blood on his chest and abdomen. That scent of hers, vanilla and caramel baked goods paired with sweet, nutty elven wine, warmed in the air by the steamy rain bath, left his mouth watering for a taste.

Refusing his impulses, Dorian swallowed on his dry throat. Handing Ruby some of her own soap, Dorian reached for the shampoo she would need, deciding to focus on clearing her braids as best he could. Using his shadows, Dorian directed some of the water from the raining bath to Ruby's head, noting that his shadows cooled the water down slightly. It would have to do. He carefully wet her hair, applying thin lines of shampoo at her scalp, around her braids, and delicately massaging it through. The braids themselves were just thin enough to allow him to get the shampoo through, though he worried he wasn't being thorough enough.

As Ruby washed up the front of her body, Dorian continued focusing on her hair. He carefully inspected each braid for signs of blood. The color of her hair wasn't making that task easy, but Dorian felt he could hardly call himself a vampire if he couldn't find all of the blood in her hair. Finally finishing with cleansing her hair of blood, he realized she had fallen still.

"Ruby?"

"I can't... reach..."

He paused, unsure what she meant until he realized that, while his endeavors in clearing her hair had helped with the blood on her back to some degree, she still needed a great deal more of her body washed. Furthermore, her lower legs weren't within easy reach. Flushing with shame, Dorian hurriedly grabbed the soap from her and set to work lathering up the exfoliating net she utilized to wash, before running it along her back.

The intimacy of the moment suddenly pressed itself upon him as he watched the soap break up the blood, causing it to run down in rivulets, revealing the soft, smooth, brown skin that kept reminding him of smoky quartz. The sloping of her shoulders and the subtle movements of her softened back muscles threatened to captivate him before he remembered what he was doing and why. Though her skin always shined with a silver undertone, the blood loss added a grayness to it that snapped him back to reality with a jolt of shame.

He should focus on nothing more than helping her as she

needed him to. He directed the water with his shadows more, allowing her back to rinse freely. Dorian carefully applied conditioner to her hair, taking care to ensure each braid was thoroughly coated, knowing that such long, braided hair required a lot after being so stripped by the washing she had just required. Pulling her hair up and placing a waiting cap over her head, Dorian breathed, deciding how best to go about washing her legs without looking at her more than necessary.

"You're very good with my hair," Ruby croaked out so quietly that Dorian almost didn't hear her.

He hadn't allowed his senses to expand to normal, leaving everything somewhat muted, but he felt glad to have heard her.

"Why, of course, Madam."

"You don't have curly hair or braids, so how?"

"Well," Dorian saw Danatel flash before his eyes, a stab of grief hitting him once more, "A few hundred years ago, I loved a werewolf. His hair was a lot like yours, so I learned how to care for it when he was exhausted after a forced transformation."

"Forced?"

Dorian winced at his own terminology, "Well, forced is probably not the best word for it. Werewolves can choose not to transform at the usual times when the moons are calling them, but it's often psychologically distressing. So the call essentially forces the issue. And when a werewolf isn't prepared to transform but the moons are calling for it, they can find the experience physically draining. Danatel often forgot when the moons were getting ready to call for him, so I decided to start helping him afterwards in any way I could."

"That makes sense."

Dorian darted from the bathroom and returned with another towel, offering it to Ruby, "Here, you can cover yourself with this and I can wash up your legs for you. Then, when you're ready, use me to lean on so that you can stand up and finish rinsing up your body."

He felt like an inexperienced young man again, fumbling through his early 20's with the embarrassment he had felt at the time being around those he found attractive. This felt far worse, however, because he didn't want to notice her attractiveness. Dorian didn't want to be thinking of the line of her spine, showing the combination of delicacy and strength intrinsic to her character. The whole situation left him trying to stare a hole into the tile floor as he knelt in the water and washed the last remnants of her blood off. Absurdly, Dorian could hardly stand to look at her, the glistening of her wet skin highlighting the fullness of her lips proving too much for his mind to ignore.

Once he finished, he did as he promised and stood, his hands hovering on either side to catch her if she lost balance, acting as a sturdy wall for her to lean against so that she could reach the last remaining areas. Only the towel he had retrieved for her stood between her body and his. It hadn't been worth it to take time away from her to go get a shirt, but he started wishing he had. She steadied herself against him with her shoulder, that arm working to keep the towel against her front. He stared into the ceiling, trying to count the tiles there, but losing track with each slight adjustment she made. Each moment that her silken, slick skin slid along his body sent shock waves through his veins.

When Ruby finally finished up, Dorian breathed a sigh of relief, glad to finally be able to get a little distance from the woman. He removed the cap and helped her rinse her hair of the conditioner he'd placed earlier, then stopped the water and rushed to gather towels for her to dry off. Once she stood snuggly fitted with two towels around her body and one around her hair, Dorian guided her to her bed and retrieved the glass of water for her to finish. He had to do far less to help her drink as she sat comfortably on the bed.

"Thank you..." Ruby's downcast eyes glistened for a moment before she abruptly sniffed and looked back up at him, blinking away the wetness he had just spied there, "I appreciate all your help. I am sure I can manage from here."

"No," Dorian snarled before he could stop himself.

"No? What... what do you mean, no?" Ruby shook her head, eyebrows furrowing.

Dorian took a deep breath, "I mean, you still need to get dressed and you need to eat. You need warmth and sustenance and then rest. So, until I can be sure you've gotten all of those things, I cannot, in good conscience, leave you to deal with this alone. Plus, you need to wait for your hair to dry before you can sleep. I won't have you ruining the work I just put in, Madam," Dorian added with a smile, hoping to add some brevity.

Ruby shook her head again, the ghost of a smile crossing her lips as she did so, before finally shrugging, "Okay sir bloodsucking caretaker."

Dorian barked out a laugh as he turned away from her, setting his sights on her closet. Perusing the options, Dorian picked out a cozy set of sweater and pants that looked like they would work as pajamas if she didn't have the energy to change from them later.

Setting the clothes on the bed beside her, Dorian paused, "Will you be able to get these on yourself? I want to go start some food for you but I want to make sure you can get dressed the moment you're ready, and I don't want to risk you falling and hurting yourself if I leave. Be honest with me."

"I can manage just fine, but can you?"

"What do you mean?"

"*HA*, when is the last time *you* even stepped foot in a kitchen?" Ruby asked with eyebrows raised.

Dorian, relieved to see her humor had returned in full force, set aside the still hoarse quality to her voice and laughed heartily, "Yes, I know how to cook. Some even told me I am rather good at it, once upon a time."

"If you say so..."

Dorian rushed to start the mild curry he had decided on for her, starting with the rice. Thanking his vampiric speed, Dorian flew through the rest of the prep work. He washed his utensils and dishes as he went, making the hearty meal with care. It would go a long way towards helping her feel better, if she liked it. If she didn't like it, he would just have to figure something else out. His hands shook as he realized that he should have asked her what she would like to eat. The realization that she might not like curry at all hadn't occurred to him until it became too late for him to stop. If she didn't like curry, he would just have to have it himself. Regular food might not fuel his body anymore, but he still enjoyed it.

A few minutes before everything would be done, Dorian hurried back to Ruby's room, knocking on the door and waiting for her to say something before he entered. She sat on the plush bed, surrounded by sapphire blue bedding, dressed once more and squeezing her braids to dry them. She smiled wearily at him, leading him to note yet another change in her. That first night of their journey together, she had only allowed the barest of changes to her facial expression. Every day since then, and sometimes by the hour, her expressions grew more varied and intense.

"I made curry. It's almost ready, but I realized that you might not like that so if you would rather have anything else, I will see what I can do, just let me know."

"Curry sounds good," Ruby slowly rose from the bed, her movements slow and stiff.

"Allow me to carry you down, please. It's painful to watch you try to move right now," Dorian blurted out.

Ruby scowled at him, tossing the towel she had been using at him with annoyance before her face crumpled slightly and she nodded her head.

Dorian set his lips in a hard line, struggling against the urge to apologize. He hadn't done anything to apologize for. Not really. He had just spoken the truth and offered to help more. So what if he'd not delivered the way he wanted to? He carefully picked her up again, carrying her from the room and down the stairs.

She devoured three bowls of curry, reminding Dorian of how much blood he would soon need himself. Once she was satisfied, Dorian brought Ruby back to her room, carefully situating her in her bed with more water on her nightstand. Her hair was not yet dry, but when he pointed that out, she pointed to a grimoire, asking him to bring it over. Flipping through the book, Ruby located a specific spell and closed her eyes to focus. The caress of a hot breeze floated over his face shortly thereafter. With a glance, he confirmed that her hair looked fully dry.

A wide grin spread over his face as he looked at her, "So you're learning how to do more magic than just light, I see!"

Ruby only nodded, her eyes racing back and forth, though not looking at anything on the page before her but rather deep in thought.

"Okay, well, in that case, whenever you're ready, get some rest. Just don't forget to drink some more water. You're a witch, so you'll recover faster and should be okay within just a few hours, but if you need anything at all, I am at your service, Madam."

Before he left the room, Dorian allowed his hearing to expand just a little, just in case, as he retrieved both the chair and the blood-soaked towels. He had a lot to accomplish back in the library. That pool of Ruby's blood had been allowed to set in the same spot for well over an hour and it would be arduous to clean. No matter how long it took, Dorian would not be able to rest until every last trace of that horrible event vanished, erased from his home. The towels would be burned, along with the chair, and anything else he needed to use to clear away her blood. He wouldn't allow any stain to be visible from where her body had lain.

Overcome by the scent of her blood as he approached that

section of the library, Dorian felt a growing sense of dread, the thirst in his throat catching. Somehow, he would have to figure out how to clean up that delicious smelling blood without tasting it either.

I don't need to become some beast licking the fucking floor for blood. I have more than enough to satisfy me in the cellar.

But wouldn't hers taste so much better?

CHAPTER TWENTY-FIVE

Ruby

Ruby stared up at the ceiling of the four-poster bed she woke up in, lost and confused for the briefest moment before her brain caught up to the present. Despite being away from the compound for weeks, she still found herself confused when she woke up in the lavish bedroom rather than the sparse one she knew all her life. The hint of light peaking in from behind the curtains told her it remained daytime, though the light would soon fade. She'd fallen asleep not long after Dorian left her the previous night, and Ruby thought she'd been asleep for over sixteen hours— though it proved far from restful, after all the nightmares. Further, the fire had died down considerably, leaving her room a little chilly.

Groaning with the effort and the cold, Ruby hurried over to stoke the fire and add wood to it, grateful that Dorian kept her so well stocked on the stuff. She didn't know where he got it from, but she gratefully accepted it. She winced as the cooled hardwood floor made contact with her bare feet. After fixing the fire, she hastily recovered a pair of thick, woolly socks to add to her ensemble. She still wore the pants and sweater Dorian grabbed for her the night before. Though he failed to retrieve any undergarments for her, which she had been grateful for at the time, the fact that she hadn't gotten them herself made her grumble as she looked around the room.

She would need to remove clothes to be able to add any undergarments she wanted. But she could always go without. She doubted Dorian would care either way. Thinking back on his behavior every time she had been naked and vulnerable around him, she could only conclude that he didn't see her that way. No matter how she might feel about the hard lines of his muscles that were still comfortable to lean on, she knew that nothing would ever come of it. The idea that he didn't see her that way in the least but was rather uncomfortable with being forced to interact with her felt disappointingly comforting. It would be fun to mess around with him, but not getting the chance would save her in the end.

One thought kept growing in the back of her mind as she gained more distance from the witches: how could she ever trust anyone again after the way they betrayed her? It just didn't seem possible. Was it truly a betrayal? Maybe not. The heartbreak that crushed Ruby as she sat in that meeting chamber with the elders and the rest of their coven had planted a seed within her, however. That seed kept growing the more she saw how wrong they were all along. The first blooms of that seed told her that she had been a fool to trust that the others cared about her at all.

I would have to trust someone to care about me to let them close ever again.

Ruby couldn't handle giving herself to another Juniper, who didn't care for her. Who she couldn't trust.

Dorian not finding her sexually appealing was a boon in ensuring she didn't end up acting a fool for his attention and affection. She could better make sure she didn't end up in the same position, falsely believing someone cared for her as much as she cared for them. While Dorian proved time and time again that he cared for her life and safety, she didn't need to take that further and delude herself into thinking that he felt anything more for her. The fact that he'd so carefully avoided taking advantage, the way that Juniper or the other humans she'd lain with surely would have, only served to prove that point. His respectful actions and demeanor towards her could mean nothing other than friendship.

Friendship is more than I ever expected.

Ruby smiled, knowing they weren't quite friends yet, but she believed they might be, soon. Evidence backed that connection better than any connection she thought to have with the coven.

Dorian listened to the punishments she endured with horror on her behalf. He told her some of his own pains, though admittedly less than she previously told him. While she felt compelled to deepen their possible friendship by expressing her own history, she wondered if she needed to encourage him to do the same, or if he would share more on his own.

Those thoughts drove Ruby's mind to the reason for her lengthy sleep: the curse. She'd been so sure she had a handle on when it acted out, but it proved her horrifically wrong. How could she know when it would assault her next? What had she missed? Had she been too loose with her emotions? She only just started thinking the curse might not be some divine retribution for forsaking her duty as a witch to reject emotionality. Perhaps she was too hasty in that assumption. Or maybe she missed something else.

Ruby's fingers fidgeted as she paced the room, wondering what she would do about the curse. The books available to her were dwindling fast. She became more adept at parsing through the tomes to determine which ones might begin to help her, since some did not discuss curses at all. Focusing on only the texts that included knowledge on casting and/or curing curses, Ruby found herself with far fewer books to review.

Deciding to forgo waiting for the sun to set, Ruby hurried from her room and flew down the stairs to the area of the library where she normally sat. The fire burned low there as well, but it offered just enough light to see the new rug positioned over where she must have fallen the night before. Her steps slowed as she approached it. Her heart thumped in her ears as she knelt down to lift the edge of the rug. For no discernible reason, Ruby needed to see what Dorian chose to hide underneath.

The wood beneath the rug had been sanded clear of any finishing or wax to protect it. Dorian worked excessively to clear away her blood. The rug simply hid the remaining evidence of the incident. Ruby felt her lungs constrict, burning for a moment until she inhaled at last.

I have to figure this damn curse out…

Ruby dropped the edge of the rug and rushed to stoke the fire before resuming her perusal of the tome she had set aside the night before. Lighting a few candles by which to read until Dorian awoke, she set to work. Too much was at stake if she couldn't even reliably guess when the curse would hurt her again. She needed to get it figured out before anything else could happen. A part of her, growing louder by the moment, didn't believe she would survive another attack like that.

Time passed in a slow-motion blur until Dorian joined her, giving her a long look before sitting down and opening his own book. Ruby left to eat breakfast, speeding through the necessity before hurriedly returning to her studies. The night passed with only the occasional moment of magical inquiries. By the morning, Ruby's every hope plummeted, along with her heart.

As if sensing her distress, Dorian spoke, "I think I know why your curse acted out as it did."

"You do?" Ruby straightened.

"I think so. Well, it is just a hunch, but I think that your curse showcases a design to act out in regular intervals so as to ensure your eventual death. Obviously, we have realized that it reacts to strong emotions on your part, but you seem adept at managing that. If whoever cursed you suspected that you could control your experience of your emotions to some degree, it only makes sense that they would design it to act anyways. I noticed it grows weaker after acting, so it is following a common curse pattern for—" Dorian cut himself off, shifting in his seat, "Well, these curses tend to spend time gathering up energy before they attack, attacking, then growing nearly dormant as they continue gathering the energy they need."

"Common curse pattern for who?"

Dorian winced before he answered, turning to look away from her, "Witches."

"Witches?!" Ruby shouted, her voice cracking as her own volume irritated her still healing vocal cords.

Dorian nodded solemnly, his gaze flicking over to her with something like pity in his eyes, "I'm serious, Ruby."

"No, no, no. That's ridiculous. I know you said it sounded like the curses of witches from before the king, but no! No witch in Vlideron nowadays knows how to curse anyone! What reason would a witch have to work with a vampire to curse me, of all people, anyways?! No. Absolutely not. Someone else must have figured it out. Some vampire must have figured out how to do this."

Dorian looked at her for a long moment before slowly nodding, clearly unconvinced.

Ruby ground her teeth together, biting back insults to the bloodsucker for even suggesting such a thing. There was no reason to think it was a witch. A witch couldn't have obtained the shadows of a vampire to create the curse. Some vampire must have just figured out a way to curse the way witches used to.

Rushing to bed that morning, Ruby didn't bother to say anything to Dorian to wish him good sleep. The insinuation that a fellow witch cursed her rankled her more than it had any right to. Deep down, she could see where he might have gotten the connection. Many of the curses she read involved that mechanism he discussed. She hadn't thought about it connecting to her curse, since she already felt so rattled by its attack. While a sensible conclusion, Ruby couldn't stand the thought that one of her own would not only know about curses, but would use one against her. For what purpose? The fact that Dorian brought it to her attention, reminding her that she saw the very same mechanism written about by witches of old, left her even more unsettled.

A few days later, muffled noise roused her from sleep.

Ruby glanced around the expansive bedroom, finding no discernible source for the disturbance. Her sleep-addled brain crawled to the realization that the noise came from outside her room. Staring at her bedroom door, she contemplated ignoring it and forcing herself back to sleep.

Her conscience refused to let her. Groaning, Ruby dragged herself from her comfortable bed, wincing at the chilled floors beneath her bare feet, and, with great trepidation, eased open the door. The small hallway between her and Dorian's rooms greeted her, empty. The noise grew notably louder and Ruby figured out it originated inside Dorian's room.

Before she could think to stop herself, Ruby flew across the hall and threw open his door. In the room beyond, the anguished cries of Dorian reverberated off the walls, filling her ears. Dorian thrashed on the bed, the sheets clinging to his sweat-covered skin.

He looks like I probably do during my nightmares...

Ruby shook her head, dismissing that thought, only to have it replaced by a far more salacious one.

Who am I kidding? He looks far tastier than I ever could right now...

Instantly, Ruby smacked the side of her face as punishment for thinking about the way his muscles bulged with the effort of thrashing about the way he did. She had no business examining the long lines of his legs through his bunched-up sheets or noting the way they clung to him so tightly that they might reveal enough details about his anatomy to make her private fantasies more vivid and enjoyable.

Glimpsing the scars marring his back reminded Ruby why she stood in his doorway at all. Carefully, she inched her way into the room, repeating his name with increasing volume in hopes of waking him before actually reaching him.

"Margroc," Dorian wheezed.

Ruby's ears perked up, curiosity temporarily overshadowing her desire to help and silencing her.

"Danatel," Dorian choked out a sob.

Ruby waited, confusion growing.

"Maxen?" his questioning tone flooded with anguish.

Ruby felt tears pricking at her eyes, though she didn't know why.

"LEANDRA!" He screamed so loud that Ruby swore she felt the world rattle beneath her feet.

"Dorian!"

Rushing the rest of the way to his bedside, Ruby hoped to finally wake him from whatever devastating nightmare held him in its clutches. She reached out to touch his shoulder, her fingertips barely grazing his skin before his upper body lifted from the bed. The room spun around her as his arms wrapped around her, dragging her into the bed with him.

Ruby froze, terror momentarily overcoming her, an instinctive fear that Dorian meant to feast on her squashing her thoughts. The room fell silent. Her mind caught up to reality. Dorian's soft breathing brushed the top of her head. He encased her body in a vice grip made of his thick arms. Yet his hold on her felt careful, gentle somehow. As if, unconsciously, he recalled his own strength and tempered the force of his hold for her safety. She couldn't leave his arms, but she wouldn't struggle breathing either.

More details filtered in. His scent. The feeling of his hard body plastered against her. His heart beat pounding in her ear. In his sleep, Dorian positioned her so that his head rested at the top of hers, her head nestled against his chest. One of his arms snaked beneath her neck, wrapping around to grip her shoulder, while his other hand held her hip in place. He'd even thrown one of his legs between hers, making them entirely intertwined.

Dorian's heartbeat slowed in her ear as his breathing calmed. Comfort with a hefty shot of lust coated Ruby's nerves. The feeling of his hands on her body, his legs entangled with hers, his strength pinning her in place, would haunt her wildest fantasies for years to come, if she had that long. But the sensation of safety laying in his arms, in his bed, provided her was unparalleled.

I should try to wake him now...

She repeated that more times than she could count as she drifted off to sleep. Her dreams vacillated between the orgasmic delights she would never dare pursue with Dorian in her waking hours, and a peaceful night spent reading with Dorian at her side. They were the most enjoyable dreams she'd had in years. Long before the curse became a problem, Ruby suffered from horrendous, paralyzing nightmares nearly every night. In Dorian's bed, Ruby enjoyed a shocking respite from horror to enjoy dreams that would embarrass her upon waking.

"Ruby?"

Her eyes snapped open, greeted by garnet red staring back at her. Dorian's jet-black, straight hair fell over his face gently, and Ruby felt his body pressed against her, their positions unchanged. Her heart beat faster, face heating.

"What are you doing in my bed? Are you okay?"

"Are you? I came in here today because you were having some sort of nightmare. Practically screamed the doors off their hinges. When I got close to wake you, you kind of snatched me and dragged me into your bed with you."

Dorian's face paled; Ruby wondered how that worked for vampires, because of the whole blood situation.

"I am so sorry Ruby. I didn't hurt you did I?!"

"No, it's fine Dorian. Honestly... I think maybe we both needed that," Ruby softly admitted.

"Because you've been having nightmares too?"

"You knew about those, huh?"

"Yeah, I heard you the first day, when you were sleeping."

Ruby nodded, trying to shove away her discomfort at the realization. The seconds dragged on; Ruby grew increasingly aware of the heat pulsing within her as she recalled the lewd part of her dreams, finding herself able to compare dream to reality the longer she remained plastered against his body.

"Dorian?"

"Yes?"

"Did you want to let me go, now?"

"Oh! Sorry, yes. Of course, I'm sorry."

Ruby scooted away from Dorian, remembering only as she made to the edge of his bed what she wore to sleep that morning. She had begun avoiding wearing any excess clothing to ensure the curse could not destroy too many more fine garments, and would be easier to strip away if necessary. Her face heated as she stood and ran from Dorian's room, mortified to be wearing only a thin, black nightgown that hardly covered anything. Slamming the door to her own room, she groaned with the knowledge that he likely saw her hardened nipples and may have glimpsed a flash of her missing undergarments.

Dorian didn't ask any more about her nightmares as they continued making steady progress through the remaining texts. Both of their remaining piles quickly disappeared, until Ruby found herself despondently reviewing the last of the texts available to her. Already reaching a week after the last attack of the curse, Ruby marked about three weeks spent with Dorian. Nearing the end of the last grimoire involving curses, finding nothing particularly useful, tears poured from Ruby's eyes.

Setting down the last of his books, Dorian looked around, landing on her face as his own shoulders slumped, "I'm sorry, Ruby. I haven't found anything in the other forms of curses or the books about them. Beyond the vampiric shadows, I can't find any other connections to vampiric curses."

"I figured as much..." Ruby breathed deeply, steeling herself for her next words, "While I can admit there is a connection to witch curses in the mechanics of it, it's otherwise unlike other curses. The utilization of vampiric shadows in this way hasn't been recorded in any of these texts... Which leaves me with no clues about how to resolve it."

"I thought my library was more expansive and detailed than this," Dorian sighed, his voice low with regret.

"It is expansive... I'm just unique, I guess..."

Ruby's heart plummeted as she spoke, suddenly certain of her own death. The thought chilled her to the core, but what hope did she have if she lacked leads on how to resolve it?

"I suppose now would be a good time to discuss what to do the next time the curse acts out," Dorian stated.

"What do you mean? I don't think there's anything we can do."

"About that, I had some ideas," Dorian launched into his thoughts.

Ruby listened, answering his few questions, a sliver of hope returning to her as she took in what he suggested "So you think that could really work? It could help?"

"It's worth a shot."

Ruby soon set aside that last book involving curses within Dorian's estate. There were a few hundred grimoires she could go through for information on other forms of magic and the details for each of those witch's lives, but none of them would help her in getting rid of the shadows twisting inside her.

On the other hand, Ruby beheld a golden opportunity present in her time away from the coven, surrounded by the accumulated knowledge of generations in how to be a skilled witch, adept in a variety of magical disciplines. If she just put in the effort and practice, what could she accomplish? Was she truly as hopeless as her lifetime of exclusively light-magic led her to believe? Or had her talents lain elsewhere all this time? Fear of continued failure warred with her driving curiosity.

Ruby straightened her shoulders, looking Dorian in the eye as she asked, "Is there a large, clear area of land you have around here that I could practice some spells?"

CHAPTER TWENTY-SIX

Dorian

Lightning flew past his head as he sprinted. The narrow miss elicited a giggle from the devious witch who tossed the spell at him with a disturbing spike in accuracy. Dorian ducked to avoid an ice spike that sucked the warmth from the air around it to the point that his vampiric skin, normally nearly immune to temperature changes, felt the sharp sting of cold. He broke into a wide grin.

As soon as Ruby asked for somewhere to practice magic, Dorian thought of the old training grounds near the decrepit barracks. Though not spared from the trees' incursion, the land remained an excellent area for the practice she sought. Offering his services as moving target practice, Dorian noticed her improvement over the last few days with a growing sense of awe and delight. Ruby started out unsure of herself, bringing along some of the grimoires to study as she worked through how to move the magic within her to create new effects.

She was a quick study. Within the first two nights, Ruby figured out how to play with her own magic enough that she left the tomes inside. She'd begun experimenting with envisioning effects and calling upon her magic to make them without reference material. Thus far, she succeeded with nearly every other discipline of magic she tried. Shadow magic lay beyond her reach, a result of not being a vampire, and light magic remained off-limits as a result of her curse, but anything she could call upon instantaneously flowed freely from her fingertips.

After four nights of diligent practice, she grew closer to actually hitting him with one of her spells for the first time. He moved with slowly increasing speed throughout their practices, ensuring she could still see him but keeping to a pace that challenged her. She started leading her aim based on where he was headed, rather than directly at him, showing cleverness he respected. He hadn't given her any feedback, yet she kept improving based on her own intuition.

The more time he spent as her target practice, the more she reminded him of the witch family he admired as a boy. They reached beyond the skilled use of their magic, delving into revelry, delighting themselves and those around them with the remarkable things they could do. Nostalgia gripped his throat as he watched Ruby gleefully weaving magic in the air around her.

Deciding to throw her for a loop, Dorian pivoted and sprinted towards her directly. As he hoped, the move caught her off-guard. She sent a wave of thorns she'd been in the middle of conjuring towards him. Dorian jumped to avoid the edge of the attack, landing strangely as he slowed down considerably, his fumbling steps sending him crashing into her. Before they hit the hard ground, Dorian pivoted so Ruby would at least land on him, rather than the ground.

Wincing, Dorian looked up at her, laughter lighting up her face in the darkness of the forest. Ruby refused any lanterns to aid her as she practiced, seeking to improve her non-visual sight. With greater control over magic, she could use it to allow her to see the magical wavelengths of others. Eventually, she might even be able to track spells to users based on the essence of their magic. In the darkness of the forest around them, Dorian enjoyed that she hadn't mastered that ability yet. He dreaded answering why he kept staring at her, far beyond was necessary for him to engage in their practice battles. He nearly missed environmental dangers because he was paying so much attention to Ruby herself. The nest of thorns Ruby threw in his direction paled in comparison to the one that lived in his own mind about why he couldn't keep his eyes off of her.

"I think I might need a break," Ruby panted, her laughter starting to subside.

Her chest pressed against his with her every heaving breath.

As she shifted her legs to find purchase beneath her, her hips ground against his own. While he'd dodged her magic earlier, there was no escape from the electric jolt that shot up his spine as she moved against him. Dorian bit his tongue, hard, to avoid making any sound. One thigh nestled between his legs, both soft and firm, as she settled her hands against his chest and used him to lift herself up.

Sitting back on her feet, Ruby looked down at him, hints of starlight through the trees above and behind her casting the slightest glow on her sanguine hair. The urgent need to stop looking at her at that angle overtaking his good sense, Dorian sat up as well. Her face was mere centimeters from his own once again. Her eyes widened, dropping momentarily to his lips. Dorian glanced, involuntarily, at her full, open lips, noting how her heavy breathing hitched.

He forced his eyes closed before he could follow the urges that sprang up unbidden, reminding himself of the myriad reasons he held for ignoring any physical attraction towards the woman. He needed to remember, above all else, that nothing could happen between them. Even if he wanted to, Dorian realized long ago that he could not stick to just sex with the people who genuinely attracted him. His heart would get mixed up in it, and the shattering losses he previously experienced left him incapable of allowing that for himself ever again. All of that held weight without even mentioning the possibly-temporary power imbalance between them and the issue of genuine desire.

Dorian guessed that if she did show any interest in him, it would only ever be strictly sexual, and it would probably be borne of curiosity, innate physical drive, or proximity and the weird situation they found themselves in, rather than genuine interest.

If I took advantage of that right now, I would be a monster.

With that firmly in mind once more, Dorian murmured an apology and shifted away from her. Ruby shot to her feet, also apologizing, and stalked back to the main keep.

After a moment, Dorian followed her. Their days fell into an easy rhythm for the most part. These awkward moments of closeness passed too frequently, however. Dorian reached for the same book as her more times than he could count, brushing hands as they did so. Every single touch set his skin ablaze. He just wanted to read over some of the books she studied on her breaks, but he seemed destined to grab for the same book as her at the same time. He readjusted his tack, waiting for her to grab a book and step away before he reached for one at all.

They also kept bumping into each other in the halls and doorways of the keep, exiting rooms and preparing to leave at exactly the same time. Without seeing the surprise on her face in those moments, he might have begun to wonder if she might be messing with him. Still, a part of him wondered if she somehow knew of the absurd thoughts, of the haunting dreams he kept having about her, but dismissed that thought as quickly as it came. Ruby wasn't the sort to play around with him so indirectly. She could be teasing and direct when she wanted to be, but she never expressed any actual interest in him. If she knew of his physical interest in her, surely she would be visibly uncomfortable or outspokenly furious.

Watching Ruby walk ahead of him towards the keep, the sway to her hips forced his eyes to the ground in front of him. Worse than the accidental touches and watching her night after night were the dreams that plagued him. Dorian, used to sleeping once more, debated giving up the practice because of the recurring dreams of her. Every night, his mind conjured visions of her from the night of the curse's last attack, in the rain bath. Only, in his dreams, it went entirely differently.

In his dreams, Ruby wasn't weak from blood loss, or anxious over a curse. The blood in his dreams was not her own. The sight of her came not from an awkward accident of circumstance. She stood, statuesque and covered in the blood of her enemies. She transformed into a goddess before his eyes, radiating power and confidence, washing off the sacrificial blood to her beauty and power, beckoning him to join her in reverie as proof of his worship. The dream version of him would sink to his knees and prove his devotion as many times as she wanted and more.

Then Dorian would wake up, furious and uncomfortably hard. He would spend several long minutes trying in vain to banish the images burned into his mind. He didn't like that he knew exactly what she looked like while naked and covered in blood during his waking hours. His unconscious state might take full advantage of that knowledge, but he preferred to forget the sight. She hadn't invited him to see her in that capacity, which left him raging at his own imagination. It had all gotten so much worse after his nightmare incident, when he'd woken holding her in his bed as if he'd been holding a lover. Watching her leave his room in nothing but a thin, short negligee drove him wild. That she wore nothing beneath it sent him into a fit of lust unlike anything he had experienced in centuries.

Ruby fell into her usual activities when she took a break. She ate and drank water, read some of the grimoires, and relaxed as her energy returned. The time she needed after eating to recover her magic decreased with each night, Dorian noticed. He guessed that meant she was improving upon her magical efficiency. The first night of practice, she nearly lost consciousness from overusing magic. Dorian silently rejoiced that she stopped herself before that happened. He really didn't need any reminders of how perfect her body felt in his arms again to fuel his damned dreams.

Dorian flowed through the rest of the night with her, following their usual routines, waiting for her to head to bed before he walked down to his blood cellar. Ruby's disgust from their time traveling to his estate told him that he should feed when she didn't have to watch. After their journey, Dorian settled back to once a week feeding for the first two weeks. The curse's attack drained him considerably, however. He needed six servings of blood to regain his strength that night. Though he figured he was able to return to one serving a week, he suspected that the curse would seek to act out again soon, so Dorian consumed two servings a week once he started playing target practice.

Normally, Dorian strictly controlled how much blood he consumed over time, to ensure he never risked running out. His collection consisting of hundreds of years of blood accumulated in his cellar allowed him some leeway in ensuring he remained in top condition to help Ruby. It was an easy decision, especially since the increased consumption also allowed him to grow stronger.

Two nights later, Ruby knocked on his door, informing him of the curse's increased activity, following the plan they had developed for when she felt the curse stirring. Dorian sprung into action, hurrying from his room in only the pants he slept in to retrieve everything they'd need. Ruby returned to her room, making her own preparations. Dorian moved as fast as he could without destroying his house, returning to her room and entering the bathroom where he found her sitting in her bathtub wearing only a towel. Dorian swiftly placed a door from one of the extra bedrooms' closets over the tub to hide her body more thoroughly. Ruby moved the towel to cover herself where she wanted, without risking showing anything she did not want to, or risking the destruction of any garments, if the curse didn't act the way they thought it would.

Dorian ran through retrieving food and water for her to have after. Setting it aside, he considered her demeanor. Her lips were set in a line, jaw tense with the nerves he could see writhing behind her eyes. Her chest, covered by the towel, rapidly moved with her breaths. Dorian rested a hand in front of her on the covering door, grabbing her attention.

"Breathe with me for a moment," Dorian directed, hoping to convince her he felt any calmer than she did, "I will do everything in my power to help and I won't let anything like last time happen to you, okay Madam? We're prepared. We can do this."

"Right... Okay," Ruby swallowed hard, her eyes sharpening as she nodded for Dorian to begin.

Dorian reached out with his own shadows, feeling for the spot on her side they had settled on to make the incision. The moment his shadows made the cut, the curse shot out. Ruby's sharp inhale teetered on the edge of a whimper as Dorian grabbed her shadows with his own. Pulling them from her body slowly, Dorian allowed the shadows to dance in the air away from Ruby, forcing their energy to be used upon harmless air rather than ravaging her body.

The shadows sought to retreat back into her body directly, but Dorian directed them with his own shadows to reenter her from the incision they exited from, creating a loop in which they could minimize the harm the curse caused. Sweat broke out on Ruby's forehead, breathing through the pain. Sweat dripped into Dorian's eyes as well, his world narrowing to keep control over the shadows.

Seconds passed like hours, the smell of her blood filling the air and threatening to distract him, before an idea finally came to him. The curse's energy seemed to be running low, so Dorian cut off some of her shadows before they could re-enter her body.

Setting to work, Dorian focused his own shadows on the task of absorbing them. The process happened quickly, but not without a great deal of effort on his part. The curse that bound the shadows to Ruby's body made it clear that Dorian would not be able to absorb all of her shadows at once, their tight connection to her body making such a sudden attempt potentially fatal. Nor did he believe he would be able to absorb them all for years to come.

As the last shadows of the curse finished their route back into her body, Dorian gave them a push to heal her swiftly. More thoughts about the experience came to him as he sat back, panting. Ruby dropped her head to the edge of the tub, relief pouring from her skin. Dorian could feel the curse in her body still, though he knew without her saying anything that it was sluggish and quiet. The shadows he'd taken into his own body were still touched by the curse, though they would not seek to reenter her. He felt no pull of the shadows he had successfully siphoned off seeking to escape his body and return to her. The ability to siphon away any of the shadows presented an opportunity.

"That worked better than I dared to hope," Ruby whispered.

"I thought of something else while doing that, I hope you don't mind. I took some of the shadows for myself," Dorian went on to explain what he accomplished, why he attempted it, and began to touch on what he thought he could do, "I think that if I can take some of the shadows every time we do this, we can extend the time between your curse acting out. And I think I will know when it's ready to act out as well, since I can feel it a bit now."

"That... is very helpful... Thank you... you've gone so far out of your way for me," Ruby looked at Dorian with an unreadable expression.

"This is fascinating for me," Dorian waved her off, "you should eat though, here."

Handing her the food and water, Dorian waited as she regained her strength to some degree. When she was ready, Dorian lifted away the door, waiting for a moment to hear that she made it out of the tub okay, before he backed out of the bathroom and left her to clean herself up. Despite minimizing the injury caused by the curse, Ruby was still left with some bleeding. Depositing the door back where he'd found it, Dorian breathed a sigh of relief that he had time to rush down to the blood cellar and sate his appetite before the temptation of Ruby's blood became too enticing.

As Ruby joined him downstairs, a realization hit him. "Humans are supposed to see the sun."

Ruby stopped a few feet away from him in the kitchen, her face scrunching with confusion, "Where did that come from?"

"Well, I just thought of it. The first snow should be coming soon, but I thought you might enjoy seeing the gardens before that happens. The flowers in this garden were borne of seeds first cultivated and enchanted by the elves. They created varieties that bloom year round, in different colors depending on the season and weather."

"That sounds incredible... So you're, what, encouraging me to walk around your gardens after the sun rises?"

"There's a spot with a gazebo in the gardens, so I could accompany you, if you wanted," Dorian watched Ruby's face for her reaction, "But ultimately, yes, I think you should enjoy the gardens in the light."

CHAPTER TWENTY-SEVEN

Ruby

Dorian's garden was truly something to behold in the glowing, golden radiance flowing between the long shadows, subtly warming her skin against the biting chill of near-winter. Despite having spent so much time outside in recent nights, Ruby failed to notice how cold the season turned until she felt how little warmth the sun offered. Sitting under the boughs of the gazebo he previously mentioned, Dorian stiffly watched her, the expression on his face a poor attempt at hiding his pain. Ruby cringed internally, debating whether to put him out of his misery by acknowledging his suffering, or to soak up the light he sacrificed his comfort for her to have.

Truthfully, he didn't need to be there at all for her to enjoy the sun. He joined her outside just in case the curse unexpectedly decided to act out. Ruby knew that it wouldn't, and based on his assessment with taking some of the shadows into himself, he would know as soon as it did. Nevertheless, she didn't want to squander his kindness, leaving her stuck on what to do.

For his part, Dorian worked valiantly to put on a brave face. He wasn't even bad at it, necessarily. After a month in his presence where nearly all of her waking hours were around him, Ruby liked to think she gained a degree of insight into his facial expressions. The strained one he currently wore in a macabre attempt to smile at her was hardly convincing.

The other problem with her excursion into the sun settled in with time. Ruby sat with the reality that attempting to bask in the light pushed memories of the solitary retreat into her thoughts. Staring at the myriad, warm, autumnal flowers to calm herself, she knew the light itself was terrifying her.

Directly confronting that fact would have sent her spiraling into self-loathing a month earlier, but sitting with herself, she greeted the thought calmly.

Why wouldn't the light scare me?

Not only could it burn her through the curse lazily rolling through her body at that very moment, but the light persisted as the only true constant in her solitude when left alone for ages. Ceaseless. Maddening.

The golden light of the sun wasn't as bad as that pale light landing on the pure white surroundings of the solitary retreat room, but her confinement there nevertheless created the connection. Light hurt her, in more ways than one. Comforted now by the darkness of the night, Ruby relished the softer lights of fire or the silvery lights of the moon and magic lanterns. Even in the garden, the greatest calming factors for her were the long shadows of the trees, the vibrant colors of the flowers, and the chill in the air.

"When they locked me in the solitary retreat, the room was sweltering... I didn't think much of that at the time, but I think I was pretty dehydrated in there too..."

Ruby looked to Dorian, watching as his expression changed from one of false pleasantness to one of fury and outrage. That vampire was terrible at hiding his emotions if he wasn't plastering on his sarcastic smirk. In the month since they'd met, when he'd murdered the others, Ruby noticed that his face only stuck in a convincing facade when he smirked. Every other attempt at a fake emotion failed miserably. Without his prescribed mask, Dorian was an open book.

It's almost... endearing how poorly he hides his responses without that mask.

"I'm afraid that I can't promise to leave any of them alive if I ever encounter them." Dorian's voice dropped so low that Ruby envisioned it scraping the bedrock of the land beneath their feet.

"Dorian... I... I appreciate the sentiment but you can't..."

"Why the fuck not?" Growling, Dorian got to his feet, glaring at the sky, then pacing under the gazebo's protective shade.

"Dorian," Ruby plaintively sighed, "I want to change things. When I get rid of the curse, I want to go back and reform us to maybe approach the former glory of the witches. So that we might be free and powerful again, out from under the thumb of the king... I can't do that if you've gone and killed all of them for something they did when we all believed it to be the right thing to do."

Dorian gawked at her. Ruby held her ground, staring him down. She'd been thinking a lot about her own stance and feelings on the king, deciding after everything that Dorian was right on one thing: the king did not deserve the title he bestowed upon himself. He lacked greatness. He couldn't even claim goodness, or being good-enough. That selfish man exploited the witches somehow. Ruby wanted to figure out how he controlled the witches and break his hold over them. But first she needed to resolve this curse.

"Fine," Dorian finally ground out.

Ruby decided to have mercy on him, and herself, by leaving the garden after only another half an hour. Dorian remained silent since their exchange and Ruby quickly declared herself ready to head back inside.

Dorian held back as she started to walk up the stairs to her bedroom. A thought struck her, forcing her to turn and look down at the vampire.

"I haven't seen you drink blood once since we arrived here."

"Is there a question in that?"

"Yes, there is. Why is that?"

Dorian looked away from her, scratching at the back of his head as he always did, "You were disgusted by it when we were on the way here. I figured it would be polite to keep my consumption practices out of your view. It would make you more comfortable."

"So you've just been hiding away to drink blood when I'm not looking... In your own home?"

"Well, yes, you could put it like that."

Ruby burst out laughing. She couldn't help it. It was absurd that the vampire who slaughtered eight witches while hardly breaking a sweat would go so far out of his way to make her feel better about staying with him. At the same time, a hint of concern wormed its way into her mind. Still, she laughed for a long minute before forcing herself to stop. Her cheeks and abdomen were starting to hurt.

Dorian stared slack jawed at her as she laughed. Beyond the obvious shock, Ruby spied an emotion crossing his face she hadn't seen before, leaving her a little perplexed.

Was that... embarrassment?

Finally, she slowed her breathing down enough to give voice to the concern that showed up in the midst of her amusement, "Stop that. This is your home. I... I was wrong to be so uncomfortable in the first place. That's your real sustenance and you should be able to relax in your own home."

Ruby turned away and hurried up the stairs before Dorian could reply, though she saw the way his eyes bulged in a split second before she scurried away. Despite her statements being entirely true and how she really felt, she struggled with speaking up at all. It left her oddly embarrassed. The laughter she fought died in an instant as she considered how he may have taken being told what he should do in his own home. She almost rushed back down the stairs to apologize.

Instead, Ruby returned to her bedroom, enjoyed a rain bath, and settled in for bed for the day. Surprised at her own exhaustion, she reminded herself that the night *had* been exhausting. Before her time in the sun, Dorian gave her a detailed tour of his library's other genres. Before that, the curse acted out. She hadn't needed to sleep immediately after the curse's attack because of Dorian's aid, but it was catching up to her at last.

Their new method of handling it felt almost too perfect, since it allowed her to forget for a moment why she would be so bone tired. A part of her kept waiting for the other shoe to drop. It would eventually. Nothing in her life went so smoothly for long. Something was bound to get in the way of her comfort and happiness at some point. But those thoughts weren't ones she could sleep to. Ruby needed rest. Drifting her hands below the sheets, Ruby explored herself lazily. She focused for a time on the fantasy of Dorian finding her appealing. While determined to stick to friendship, and appreciative of his lack of interest in her, she still kept touching herself while imagining his hands on her body, his touch sending her into the depths of the night sky to dance among the stars. Her pleasant release lulled her to sleep.

Fast-paced nightmares hurried through her mind, the same images that always occupied her disturbed sleep. Her eyes snapped open, but the lack of light peaking from behind the curtains told her that she'd slept for a long time. Now that they possessed an effective strategy for dealing with the curse, Ruby felt free to enjoy her routine again and try branching out with her outfit selections. After the violent attack of the curse shredded her clothes and bloodied her body, she'd avoided the clothes she liked best, fearing for their safety in the event of an unexpected attack.

Dorian's method for handling it and the reassurance that he could now feel the curse as well gave her the confidence to revel in her options. Ruby swirled in the spacious closet as she donned the new outfit: a deep teal skirt paired with a fluffy white sweater, brought together with a black waist belt. The skirt hid deep pockets within its folds, but without the belt, Ruby wouldn't have been able to make full use of the storage opportunity. Through adding the belt, she found herself able to keep the skirt up while stuffing books into the pockets. Vitally, the outfit would keep her warm while she traipsed through the forest with Dorian, practicing her magic.

While Ruby could see the improvements in her magic, she was merely playing around with what her powers could do. There were many things she'd never dreamed possible for herself before, when her life had been so limited. Though she was lifting away those limits in her own mind, a long road still spread into the distance ahead of her before she could measure up to the witches that once lived in Vlideron, let alone the witches who lived in the rest of the known world.

They would surely look on her endeavors as child's play.

That precisely described the feelings Ruby got during practice with Dorian. Running through the forest, casting spells to throw at him, only to miss, gave her the giddy feeling she'd spied on patrol watching children playing back in Edgefair. Nothing granted her so much joy as trying, failing, and trying again, laughing all the while.

Ruby paused before leaving her bedroom, sitting with the feeling that practicing her magic in newfound ways with Dorian felt like being a child at play with their dearest friends.

How sad is that? Is Dorian already my dearest friend? Have I held so little in my life until now that this man I met only a month ago carries such weight in my life?

Ruby shook her head, opening the door to her bedroom and getting on with her night. She couldn't keep uselessly focusing so much on those thoughts when there were better things for her to think about. How could she return to the other witches and change things if she didn't keep up the practice with all new forms of magic? What if discovering her magic more fully somehow helped her discover the way to rid herself of the curse because her intimate knowledge of magic gave her some inspiration? She would never know if she didn't keep going.

A few nights later, Ruby sat at the kitchen counter to eat her dinner when Dorian ascended the basement stairs and joined her in the kitchen, already holding an abnormally large wine glass and a pouch she recognized as one of his blood containers. His eyes darted to her repeatedly as she continued eating her pasta. Realizing he was still evaluating her comfort, Ruby leaned back, deciding it was the perfect time to sate her curiosity.

"How does the blood change you over time? I mean... How are you different from how you were when you were first changed? You said it strengthens you and talked a bit about that, but I wondered what the specifics were... if that's alright?"

The slight furrow between Dorian's shoulders visibly relaxed and he began pouring blood into the glass, "That is a bit of a long answer. If I were to shorten it, I'd say it has made me faster, stronger, more sensitive, my shadows more responsive, my shadow magic stronger and more expansive, and reduced my vampiric weaknesses."

"I'd love to hear more," Ruby leaned forward and resumed eating.

"Well," a small smile hit Dorian's face before he lifted the blood-filled glass to his lips and took a sip. "The shadow magic thing. I can do a lot more with shadow magic than I could when first turned. I wasn't always capable of creating the shadow puppet I used to attend the vampiric council meeting. Then there is the management of sun sickness. I still get it, but not as bad. I can go longer without blood, too. Normally, I only need one of these," Dorian held up the pouch, "per week. I've been having more lately, but that's just what it is when you use powers you don't normally utilize."

"Powers you don't utilize?"

"I needed a lot more after hypnotizing you back at the hot springs. I have never been very good at that. But I also need more after controlling the shadows of your curse. I'm not accustomed to controlling another's shadows. It normally isn't even possible. But because you aren't a vampire, they aren't bound to you in the normal way," Dorian lifted the glass, drawing her attention to his lips as they parted, a hint of his fangs peaking out as he sipped delicately from the glass, blood staining the inside of his mouth.

"I see," Ruby squirmed in her seat, uncomfortable with realization that her curse caused him an inconvenience, and with the way her attention caught on his mouth, "so you're stronger and faster, too? And your shadows are better?"

"Yes, I—well, I guess I don't know how much more I could really say about the physical strength and speed. I noticed it over time as the decades passed. I would have probably gained a great deal more if I over-consumed blood and didn't store it the way that I have, but I wanted to always ensure that I had a supply available for the day I needed to go into hiding. That day came and I've been glad I have a stockpile."

Ruby nodded as she finished up her own dinner, "Thank you for explaining that... I almost wish I could ensure my own safety and security like that, being able to stockpile sustenance for decades to come. To not have to worry about it and, in fact, be able to get stronger just by feeding. That's... almost enviable."

Ruby washed her plates in silence as Dorian continued sipping blood. She didn't explain her thoughts any further. Dorian didn't ask her to. The wistfulness in her own voice echoed in her ears as she walked away from him. She knew he heard it too. Though she obviously didn't want to be a vampire, Ruby wished she possessed the freedom to pursue her life the way Dorian did. He became a vampire, started killing the nobles he deemed deserved it, and moved through the world with the guarantee of unlimited time to accomplish the things he wanted if he just prepared for the times that he would be restricted.

She never knew those luxuries. Even in Dorian's keep, she couldn't profess to be half so free. She remained tied to her bodily demands, needed practice to improve her control over her magic, and remained limited on time. The rest of her life cowered beneath a series of big questions, starting with how long it would last and ending with what she could actually do with it. Dorian didn't have any of those worries. Eternity stretched before him, during which he could make his life into whatever he wanted, and wasn't facing down a curse that could kill him. His body's limitations lessened with time as he just sustained himself the way he wanted.

The fluttering sensation in her stomach as she'd listened to Dorian's description of his growing power, yet another reminder of the physical attraction she'd felt for him from the start, further unsettled her. In spite of his incredible attractiveness, she couldn't fool herself into thinking there would ever be anything between them. He clearly didn't see her that way. Besides, she didn't have time for that. He was kind to her, that was it. She couldn't go obsessing over a man just because he was kind to her, physically attractive, powerful, capable, and they were both locked up in a hidden palace together.

That conviction wavered more with each passing night. Ruby improved at targeting Dorian during practice, prompting him to try new things to catch her off-guard. More and more, these incidents led to collisions and unexpected touches and odd landings together. Every time one of them misjudged as they were hurtling through the forest at each other, Dorian maneuvered so he hit the ground rather than her, and her heart would race upon landing on top of him. The consideration in that gesture always floored her.

Their time in the main keep became more intertwined as well. Ruby and Dorian began to spend more time together in the kitchen each morning, discussing their lives while she ate her dinner and he sat with her or drank blood. She learned of the details around Leandra, the woman he loved 400 years earlier. Ruby felt for him as he detailed her refusal to become a vampire, respecting her choice but hurting for it all the same. Eventually, Leandra left him after twenty years together, deciding that she didn't want to grow old with him there while he remained eternally young. She'd left Dorian a letter, which he still kept, explaining that she wouldn't want to be an old, gray woman, with others assuming that she was his mother. Worst of all, Leandra didn't want Dorian to have to watch her die.

While Ruby could understand Leandra's perspective, it rankled her that the woman hadn't given him the chance to make his own decision on the matter. Dorian obviously would have given anything to have more time with Leandra, regardless of her aging and eventual death. He had loved her dearly.

Ruby listened again as Dorian described his time with Danatel, the werewolf. They split up because werewolves were bound to their chosen mate in ways Dorian could not stomach: werewolves could not leave their chosen mate, ever. The breakup nearly killed him after fifty years spent together, but there was little else he could do.

"I wanted someone who would spend eternity with me because they wanted to be with me. I couldn't handle the thought of someone being with me for eternity because they were compelled to," Dorian explained.

Speechless, she understood why, ultimately, Dorian and Danatel could never have worked out. Since werewolves suffered from a strange affliction inherent to their life-force, once they formally chose a mate, that would be their mate for the rest of their lives, no matter what. It left them deeply vulnerable, resulting in long courtships to take great care in their selection. They had the benefit of living nearly 800 years, so time was of little consequence. If a werewolf chose in haste despite their abundance of life, especially with a non-werewolf, there could be no undoing their decision, resulting in far too many horror stories that illustrated the need for abundant caution. Sometimes, that still wasn't enough.

Margroc, the orcish woman Dorian loved next, stayed in his life for only five years before she decided that she never wanted to become a vampire. For Dorian, Leandra had warned him off engaging in relationships with people who would die in decades, not centuries. In the grand scheme of Dorian's life and relationships, their early breakup allowed him to move on with relative ease.

What hadn't been easy for the poor man was his relationship with Maxen. Ruby listened as Dorian described his longest relationship yet, with the relatively young elven person who spent eighty years with him. They built a life with Dorian, allowing him to believe that he finally found someone he could be with forever who would be there because they chose to be. They had told him countless times that they were in it for life.

"Then, I came home early to find them packing up their things, telling me they had a lot more exploring the world to do before they could possibly think of settling down. They were leaving, and while they had fun with me, we'd only spent eighty years together after all. I shouldn't take it so hard," Dorian rolled his eyes, taking another sip of blood, "They weren't even going to tell me they were leaving. They said they figured it wouldn't be a problem since it was all just good fun."

"By the gods, how selfish! I mean, I get that they wanted to go explore more, fair enough, whatever. But they spent so long reassuring you that they were in it for life and working with you to build something real. To so callously dismiss you like that... I'm sorry you had to go through that."

Dorian only shrugged it off, as he always tried to do when she sympathized with him, but she could see the appreciative smile he hid behind his goblet of blood.

The curse stirred again two weeks and a day after the last incident. She still needed to keep a lid on her feelings, but that lid grew easier to keep as time went on. After she and Dorian ran through their new routine to manage it, controlling the attack successfully, Ruby took stock of how her mentality shifted around the curse.

At first, she feared she would never recover from her own out-of-control emotionality. Ironically, it seemed that her time with Dorian, who encouraged her to know what her feelings were and where the hurt came from, made it all easier for her to deal with. As the days passed, she became less and less concerned that she would have an unexpected outburst as a result of emotions. With the knowledge that she had time between its organic outbursts, she could breathe a little easier.

The bigger problem in her life was food. The stores in Dorian's pantries were starting to dwindle noticeably, and they needed to talk about what to do. She might need to leave the palace, and all of the safety it provided.

"We should talk about your food situation. How about over dinner in the morning?" Dorian asked.

Her heartbeat kicked up, only nodding her agreement.

"I look forward to it, Madam."

Worry suffused her bones, concern about what she might do if Dorian decided she wasn't worth the trouble filling her mind.

What will become of me after this?

CHAPTER TWENTY-EIGHT

Dorian

Dorian struggled not to fidget in his seat as he waited for Ruby to join him in the formal dining room. He knew that they needed to discuss what to do about her food situation and come up with a plan, but there were a few million things he thought could go wrong. Not the least of which was the dinner itself.

He offered to make their dinner, excusing himself from her training a few hours earlier so he could go all out. The bread and roast he'd made took time to complete. The many sides along with dessert also took time, despite his vampiric speed making it easier to breeze through and clean up. Certain things with cooking required time that Dorian couldn't simply make faster. With that being the case, Dorian worried that his palate may have changed too much since he last regularly ate human food, leaving him insecure in his prowess as a chef. She enjoyed the curry he'd made her, but that had been a dish his dear mother made him a million times as a child. He didn't have to think about it the same way.

His anxiety about the food paled in comparison to a topic he desperately wanted to bring up with her. The more Dorian thought about needing to leave his estate to gather supplies for Ruby, the more he realized that she would be at greater risk from whoever had cursed her. They may see her in Edgefair, where they would most likely be going. Edgefair was the nearest larger city. The nearer villages would raise alarms at encountering a random witch and vampire together, leaving them too exposed. Edgefair, for all its risks, would be the safest option to start with, at least. It would be easier to move through Edgefair into the rest of Vlideron if they so chose.

Leaving Vlideron would be possible for Ruby, in theory, but Dorian knew of the tracking barrier placed around the borders of the kingdom to alert the vampiric council of escaping vampires. Until Dorian knew how to circumvent such tracking, or could deal with the vampiric council himself, he couldn't risk crossing the border. Ruby might be strong enough to go it on her own, however, if she did not have to worry about the curse assaulting her.

Hearing Ruby approaching, Dorian straightened, forcing his hand to drop the fork he'd been playing with unconsciously. Glancing around the table, Dorian ensured that everything remained appropriately covered with the enchanted iron domes that maintained the temperatures of the food within. Dorian rose from his seat just as Ruby entered the room.

His mind stopped. Wearing one of the elven gowns from the old collection, Ruby glowed in emerald green. Delicate details were sewn into the gown in silver thread. The silken piece clung to her body, with a draping shoulder that hugged her upper arms, baring her shoulders, back, and much of her chest. The sleeves ended with a loop that wrapped around her middle fingers, the v-shape leading up to the end of her sleeves embroidered with silver vines. The tight chest of the gown emphasized her every curve, while the skirt loosened, flowing into a long train behind her.

Ruby gazed around at the lit up formal dining, reminding Dorian that she hadn't seen it since the tour. She marveled at the dark wood furnishings and the glory of the three crystal chandeliers running through the center of the room. Her eyes sparkled with wonder.

The gods must have crafted the perfect onyxes to put in her eyes.

Those onyxes landed on him, catching for a long moment.

Gaze sliding down to herself, Ruby spoke, "I saw this dress and I hadn't had an opportunity to wear it and I thought... well I might not get a chance to wear it if I didn't just put it on now..."

Dorian swallowed despite the protests of his dry throat, "It's a stunning dress."

The croaked out statement brought a smile to Ruby's face.

Dorian rushed to the other side of the dining table, pulling out her chair for her, "Madam."

Hurrying back to his own seat, Dorian used his shadows to lift some of the iron domes, revealing the first course to Ruby and releasing the scent into the air.

Ruby moaned, "Ohhhh that smells so good."

Dorian only smiled as he served her the light soup and bread he'd prepared to start the meal off, adding some to his own bowl and plate after.

Ruby raised her eyebrows at him.

"I occasionally like to eat mortal food as well."

"I see... You are quite the surprising bloodsucker," Ruby laughed, "In more ways than one. I would have thought you'd put yourself at the head of the table, oh great Lord Bloodsucker."

Dorian broke into a full grin at her jab, grateful at the way she refrained from using his last name, "It's so much easier to talk like this though, don't you think?"

"I wasn't saying I thought you'd put me at the clear other end of the table," Ruby shook her head, "I meant that I'm surprised you didn't put yourself at the head and me at the side."

"My point stands. It's easier like this," Dorian grew more serious.

Ruby nodded, a glimmer of understanding crossing her eyes as she dropped it.

He hadn't been raised as a noble, living his childhood in the slums with his mother, trying desperately to avoid the wrath of the man whom he'd inherited his title from. Emulating that man in any way would be an insult to his mother's memory.

Dorian struggled through consuming his soup, his ears pricking with each moan of delight from Ruby. He didn't have the heart to discuss the need to leave the estate when she only just started enjoying the meal he made. He numbly finished his own portion, waiting for Ruby to finish hers.

When she finally finished, Dorian cleared the bowls to a nearby cart and set about serving the main dish. Revealing the roast, potatoes, and assorted vegetable sides, Dorian couldn't help but smile at Ruby's delighted gasp. Her eyes fluttered closed as she inhaled the steaming scents.

"Did you get to really enjoy your food while with the witches?"

Ruby's face fell for a fraction of a second before she recovered, her smile tighter, "I suppose not... We were encouraged to get enough food, of course, but truly enjoying your meals was considered a bit... uncouth."

Dorian rolled his eyes, listening as he plated her up.

"This is... so much better. Being able to whole-heartedly enjoy things..."

"Did you get to drink wine ever?"

"No, we weren't allowed intoxicants."

"Would you like to try some? I—" Dorian debated following through with explaining, but a glance at her curious smile forced his mouth to move once more, "I have one that I think would be interesting to get your thoughts on."

"Why is that?"

"This is a bit odd, but you smell like it."

"I do? Interesting... I guess I have to try it now."

Dorian retrieved the bottle from the cart, pouring her a small glass to taste. He poured himself a much larger glass and drank deeply as he waited. She lifted the glass to her nose, smelling it curiously, then took a small sip. Her eyes lit up as she tasted the sweet, elven wine.

"I smell like this?!" she asked incredulously.

"Yes."

"How do you resist drinking me dry every day?!" Ruby giggled.

Dorian returned her laughter, shaking his head, "I have excellent willpower."

"I guess you must!"

Dorian waited as Ruby cooed over the food, complimenting his skills as a chef and talking about how greatly she was enjoying herself. He listened appreciatively, though he struggled to eat his own meal. His eyes kept landing on her, noting the many changes she'd undergone in a month and a half.

At some point, Ruby stopped calling herself a bad witch, or a failure. She'd stopped calling the king by the bullshit title he had granted himself. She ceased doubting her powers the way she did before. She no longer disparaged herself to justify the elders, though she still did too much to excuse that Elder Moss. She feared her curse, of course, but she moved forward in spite of that. There she was, trying wine with a vampire, going against everything expected of her for the last thirty-ish years, and doing it with joy.

"When is your birthday?" Dorian asked, interrupting her effusive compliments to another side dish.

"Umm... I'm not totally sure, actually... the whole thing with supposedly being left at the gates means that I never knew when I was born. I was apparently still an infant, however... I guess my birthday could be whenever I want it to be. I was always just given an age based on the time of year the coven took me in."

"I'm so sorry, Ruby."

"Don't be... It just... is. I guess today could be my birthday. I'm dressed up and enjoying a great meal, after all!"

Dorian's stomach churned as he tried to smile in agreement. Loss lay in her lack of a birthday, whether she wanted to acknowledge that or not. He could tell by looking at the sadness in her eyes, however, that she felt that loss too.

"We should discuss what we'll do about my food situation, though..." Ruby sighed into her wine glass.

"Right," Dorian lifted his own glass, drinking deeply before continuing, "That would be wise. You'll run out of food in the next month or so. I've been putting a lot of thought into it, and I think we need to return to Edgefair to get you supplies."

"You aren't just going to leave me there?" Ruby asked, head tilting to the side as her face scrunched in confusion.

"No, why would I?"

"I just thought that it would be so much trouble for you to come with me to get food, only to bring me back here afterwards..."

"I agreed to help you with your curse. We still have work to do to figure it out. Maybe we can find out more by visiting Edgefair, but I am also prepared to simply go there and return. I am likely still being hunted, so I doubt I can afford to linger, but we can definitely pass through there if nothing else."

"Thank you, Dorian... that means a lot to me," Ruby's eyes welled with unshed tears she tried to blink away, presumably before he noticed them.

"I am happy to do it. So the timing will be important."

"Right, I think if you were willing to help me, it would be best to go right after the next attack of the curse. That will give us the most time to work with."

"That's the conclusion I reached, as well," Dorian smiled, reaching to add some more roast to his plate.

Ruby's hand brushed his, apparently reaching for seconds as well. She snatched her hand away as soon as their fingers brushed, glancing aside. Dorian added more roast to her plate before adding to his own.

Her scent began to shift in the air, surprising Dorian for a moment before he realized that the wine started hitting her already. Elven wine was known to be particularly strong, coming in mostly fortified varieties, but Dorian had forgotten that she would be struck particularly hard by this. Those new to drinking often experienced the greatest effects of it.

"Your eyes are like garnets," Ruby said suddenly, resting her cheek on her hand as she lazily finished her glass.

"Yours are like onyx," Dorian responded before he could stop himself.

Flashes passed through his mind of pursuing her, of seducing her, but he quickly shoved all such thoughts aside. She was far too drunk already for him to take anything she said as genuine interest in him. It would be best to move along with their discussion.

"We'll need to make a list of supplies to gather, but rest assured, I will handle everything I can. We could theoretically walk to Edgefair from here at your pace, but that would take about six nights of travel. There and back, we'd barely have the time to properly gather supplies in Edgefair and poke around about who cursed you."

Ruby straightened, shaking her head as if trying to clear it from the buzzing of drunkenness, "Right... That makes sense... So... what do we do then?"

"I could carry you, running at my pace if you can handle it. That would allow us to arrive in Edgefair in one night of travel. Then we would have nearly the whole two weeks to work with."

"That... would be embarrassing... You already smell too good, and having to be carried by you the whole way would mean I couldn't escape that... and it would emphasize how damn strong you are and it's bad enough that I have to feel the power in your physique when you practice with me. It's just not fair that you're so attractive... and you aren't even attracted to me..." Ruby rambled, her voice gently slurring.

Dorian sat up straighter, looking at her incredulously for a moment until he burst out laughing, "Where in the gods' names did you get the idea that I'm not attracted to you?"

"I mean... It's not like you've ever tried something with me. How many times have I been naked around you and you hardly even peek at me. If anything, you seem to avoid looking at me naked like I'll infect you with some plague if you do."

"Ruby, I don't look at you when you're naked because none of the times you've been nude around me have been entirely your choice. I don't make any moves because you're in my home under my protection while we work on your curse. That is an uncomfortable power imbalance to me. None of that to mention the fact that you are still a human, who is going to die someday. Hopefully of old age. But I mean... I can't engage with you for any of those reasons," Dorian cleared his throat, scratching at his head and shifting in his seat before continuing, "If you were a vampire who could readily leave me whenever you wanted, but decided that you wanted me?"

"Yes?" Ruby leaned forward, her already dangerously low-cut dress becoming even more revealing.

Dorian finished his wine in one gulp, "I would place you at the head of this table, worshiping every last detail of you, physically and emotionally, until you'd screamed in pleasure so many times that you lost your voice, and only then would I dare pursue my own. I'd reassure you of your every positive, deliciously attractive quality until you could do nothing but agree with every fiber of your being, viewing yourself as the goddess I'd eagerly worship. Every. Single. Day."

Ruby stared at him, breathing heavily, for a long moment.

Dorian broke the moment intentionally, unsettled by the tension his unfiltered honesty produced, by moving them along to dessert. The statements were so unnecessary; she was a witch. Why would she ever willingly become a vampire? She would lose any chance at reforming the witches she still felt she had. All of it was moot in the face of that. She would hopefully one day be free of the curse, therefore able to leave him if she so chose. She would be able to choose to express sexual interest in him freely, in that case. But she would still die someday.

Dorian couldn't get past that. He could barely envision getting past his fear of abandonment in general, but first he would need someone who could live forever with him to even approach that problem.

"Why do you need someone who can leave you so badly?" Ruby suddenly asked between bites of pie.

Dorian felt a pit in his stomach, knowing the answer already, "My mother. She couldn't leave Leonarch the way she wanted to. He used his position as the lord over her to manipulate things so that she couldn't leave him. Because she couldn't leave him, she was subjected to a lifetime of torture at his hands. She could still refuse to marry him, and she never bore another of his damned children, but she couldn't escape him either. I won't do that to anyone. Ever."

Tears welled in Ruby's eyes once more, "I'm so sorry that happened, Dorian. I'm always so glad you killed that son of a bitch."

Dorian only nodded, his earlier lust quelled, replaced by a deeper appreciation for the empathy she showed him so consistently. Ruby could have closed herself off to his lived experiences and focused on the murderous rampage that brought them together. She could have clung to the propaganda she grew up with. Instead, she spent time exploring who he was and why, relating to him and even crying on his behalf. Though the action seemed unconscious on her part, as if it was only natural, Dorian saw the rarity of her ability to connect with him. He observed throughout the course of his long life how few people took the time to examine their thought processes, or a person beyond their first impression. He admired that about her.

For that reason, Dorian took a chance, "I think some witches must have helped the vampiric council to curse you. Why, I don't know, but, well, I think it's the only thing that makes sense. Obviously a vampire participated for the shadows, but the rest of it reeks of witchcraft and I just can't imagine who else could have done it. I don't know what to do with that right now, but I want you to at least think about it."

Ruby's face stiffened as she leaned back, her last bite of pie still sitting on the fork she set down. She looked at him for a long moment, eyes searching.

Without another word or acknowledgment, she stood and swept out of the room, nearly knocking over her chair. A few moments later, Dorian heard her bedroom door slam shut.

He'd hinted at that before, but still failed to reveal his worst suspicions.

It could have been her elders.

CHAPTER TWENTY-NINE

Ruby

"Where is that attitude coming from, Ruby? I think you are in need of reeducation." Elder Moss repeated the phrase over and over and over again.

The sound filled her ears.

"Failure!" Vanella's voice echoed in the background.

The repetition of their voices elevated the overall volume.

"No, you need to do better!" Elder Marigold added to the growing cacophony. The shrill tone filled out the highest registers of sound.

"Be better." Violetta's monotone voice overwhelmed Ruby's senses.

"Temptress!" Juniper's shrieking accusation sent Ruby running.

They surrounded her. Blinding light filled her vision so that she couldn't even see where she ran. Ruby slammed into the white walls of the solitary retreat room. She looked all around, seeing no signs of the people screaming in her ears, their echoing statements and accusations taunting her. Screaming, Ruby beat on the walls, begging for release from the room, for release from the awful repetition of her failures.

Ruby shot up in bed at last. Disorientation left her scrambling for understanding. Her head pounded. Blessed darkness greeted her for the most part, but even the dying firelight felt excessive in that moment. Nausea roiled in her belly, barely contained. Lambasting herself for getting so drunk that morning, Ruby tore herself out of bed, simultaneously cursing the fact that the shadows wouldn't heal her of this affliction. They healed all her external wounds, and Dorian implied that they would heal the internal ones as well, but evidently they did not spare her the suffering brought on by too much wine.

Shuffling to her bathroom, Ruby groaned over the events of that morning. She could remember it all clearly enough, though everything looked fuzzy around the edges. She recalled becoming entirely too forward with Dorian, only to be shocked in return. Ruby never imagined that he would express such fervent attention to her in any capacity. He'd rendered her speechless with his proclamation and explanation.

Looking back, it made perfect sense. Of course he wouldn't be so disrespectful as to ogle her in her vulnerability. He wasn't that sort of person. Of course he would continue keeping his distance because of the power dynamics at play in their current situation. Most of all, of course he would avoid any deeper connection when, from his perspective, she would die too soon. None of that changed the thrill Ruby got at the image he painted in her mind, as vague as he was.

Ruby stared into the mirror, thoughts about Dorian's words the night before sending her hands drifting lower along her body, her vivid imagination running away with all self-control. She could see his words playing out in her mind's eye. Propping her up on the edge of the head of the table, placing her in the position of power, and kneeling before her. Ruby frequently read about men who delighted in tasting every inch of the woman they adored, but Dorian stood out as the first one she thought would actually do so. The women she'd lain with eagerly went above and beyond in the name of pleasure and touch. But the men pursued their own ecstasy, putting hers on a back burner.

Ruby's pleasant, if lackluster, experiences with them granted her the opportunity to explore more of what she did and didn't like. But if she wanted an orgasm, she sought a woman for a companion most of the time. With Dorian she knew things would play out differently. He clearly would value her ecstasy in the event they ever did cross that line. The thought of his fangs scraping along her inner thigh before he tasted her, licking rather than biting. She could see the way he would derive pleasure from hers, garnet eyes rolling into the back of his head as he delighted in her taste.

Ruby imagined the waves of pleasure now coursing along her nerves, rolling from deep within, came from Dorian's careful ministrations. These quiet moments to herself, broken only by the running water and her own gasping moans echoing his name off the bathroom tiles, grew more accurate after Dorian had held her for a whole day's sleep. His words that morning made them more vivid.

Coming apart with an uncontrollable scream, *Dorian* slipping from her lips, Ruby prayed he could not hear her. But a rebellious part of her didn't care if he had. It would serve him right.

Splashing her face, cold water doused her absurd thoughts, simultaneously reminding her of how the morning ended—Dorian's statements on the likelihood of witches somehow being involved in her curse. Ruby knew it would make sense in most circumstances. She even knew that Dorian probably thought that to be the most likely explanation. She could even acknowledge that the witches she had known her whole life didn't care about her the way she always cared for them. But they wouldn't curse her. And they couldn't, even if they wanted to. Witches in Vlideron didn't know how to curse anymore. Witches possessed no knowledge of any magic beyond light magic, except for Ruby.

How any of them could have cursed her just didn't make sense in light of that information. Furthermore, Ruby never invited retaliation from her fellow witch. Why would any of them seek to curse her? She saw through his implications, knowing that he meant that witches in her coven must have been involved somehow. But that simply didn't make sense.

Beyond that, the betrayal of Juniper, Violetta, and Vanella would pale in comparison to the betrayal of her fellow witches being behind this curse in any capacity. It would represent a conspiracy among the upper echelons of witches, creating categories of those in-the-know and those not. Ruby couldn't believe that might be the case. Witches were a misguided group of brainwashed individuals. That was all. If in-group existed among the witches in her coven, Elder Moss would surely be in such a group, being the Grand Elder of the Edgefair coven. She would be the one to know the most. If such an in-group existed, she would be a part of it. If this theoretical in-group cooperated with vampires to craft her curse, then Elder Moss would have been involved in cursing Ruby personally.

No, Ruby couldn't fathom that. Elder Moss raised her. She taught Ruby everything she knew about the world and life and being a witch until Ruby reached adulthood and started experimenting behind the elder's back with other facets of existence. Nothing Elder Moss did or said implied that she was anything but a pious, upstanding witch, adhering to their doctrine perfectly. Ruby spent her life admiring the woman as much as she feared her. Regardless of anything else that Ruby learned to accept as true in her time away from the coven, she could not accept the thought that Elder Moss participated in cursing her.

There has to be another explanation. There has to be.

No one knew about her finding the grimoires in the hidden library, either. Elder Moss surely would have confronted her. Ruby wouldn't have stood a chance in a direct confrontation with her elder. Moss would have known that. Finding those tomes was the only thing Ruby ever did with her life that could provide motive to get rid of her beyond simply being a failure by the terms and definitions of the present day Vlideronian witch.

Her time practicing with all other sorts of magic demonstrated to her that she could hardly be called a true failure of a witch. She didn't know if she was powerful or not, but she could feel her improvements. She could use pretty much any other magic she wanted, besides shadow and light. Shadow existed exclusively in the purview of vampires, and the light hardly responded to her even before the curse manifested. But she'd found no other non-ritual magical disciplines to be a struggle. Maybe she wouldn't be good at potions, but she would need ingredients before she could play around with that, so she hadn't gotten a chance.

Ruby dressed in a cozy sweater and matching wool skirt, prioritizing comfort as she plodded through the still-dark bedroom to the door. Upon arriving in the kitchen, she carefully guzzled water, glaring at the door to the basement, knowing she needed to descend the stairs and get herself something to eat, but dreading the thought of food with every fiber of her being. She'd never known how strong wine could be. She wondered how in the Known World the commoners seemed to drink so much.

Ruby's stomach churned again, reminding her of the curse for a split second before she felt it separately, still mostly dormant despite her elevated emotional state. Its energy remained too spent to respond just yet. Relief warred with concern at the worry of when the curse would act out again. Mitigating factors shielded her from the curse in new ways, but she nevertheless feared any changes pertaining to it.

Even still, Ruby felt a small burst of smug satisfaction at the thought that whatever vampire actually cursed her, with whoever helped them, were failing so far. She remained alive, despite the best efforts of the curse. Without Dorian by her side, she surely would have died already. But she still lived, safe and almost thriving. Their plans were failing, even if she wasn't yet cured. The only thing holding back her joy at continued survival was her confusion over who could have created such a curse.

She wondered if that vampire employed the help of an elf, a dwarf, or even a werewolf in creating the curse, but none of those concepts made sense for Ruby. Maybe a werewolf turned from a witch? That might explain the use of methods involved in tying the curse to her person. But that wouldn't make sense. The king decreed more than a century ago that werewolves were henceforth banned from Vlideron. Surely, any werewolves who remained in Vlideron prior to that fled before the present day, and since they were also turned away at the borders, it was even more unlikely.

How could a vampire, who couldn't leave the kingdom because of the stringent controls of the Vlideronian vampiric council, have gained access to a werewolf who happened to have been a witch prior to turning? And why would they use such an elaborate and valuable curse on her, for that matter? Ruby thought that would be too absurd.

Eventually, Ruby managed to stuff some eggs and toast into her mouth, finding her headache calming rapidly as she did so. She assumed her witch healing was coming in handy with the hangover, at least. Ruby filed that knowledge away for another day, hopefully some day soon when she could celebrate freedom from the curse. Finished with her breakfast, Ruby headed out into the night to begin her practice.

The night air greeted her differently as she exited the main keep. Fluffy, soft flakes of snow drifted down from the gaps in the trees. Ruby's breath looked like steam as she exhaled in wonder. The flitting lights of fae danced through the glittering snow coating whatever land it could reach. Their shimmering motions sent swirls of snow flying all around, spreading it out to coat the entire forest floor and all of the plants that grew beneath the towering trees. Hundreds of them filled the lands around

Dorian's palace, dancing in flight through the magic of the first snowfall of winter.

"I suppose I won't be practicing my spells today..." Ruby whispered aloud, deciding not to ruin the fun the fae were having by potentially harming one.

"You could practice your hand-to-hand if you'd like," Dorian nearly whispered in response, startling her.

"I didn't realize you were already out here..."

"I came out a few minutes before you to inspect the keep for any problems with handling the weather. It looks good. I figured I would come ask you if you wanted my help with your practice or, well, if you would rather I leave you alone tonight."

Ruby took a moment to stare at him, noting the way his eyes shifted guiltily, "I would appreciate your help with my hand-to-hand. It has been a while since I practiced."

Dorian only nodded, gesturing for her to lead the way.

Ruby decided to put aside her frustration with his insistence that she think about the idea that a witch could have cursed her. It made sense for him to think along those lines, and she couldn't really blame him when he only wanted to look out for her. She just deemed it misguided. Was that really any different than her own recently misguided beliefs about the world in general?

Making it to the training grounds, Ruby and Dorian began properly sparring. Dorian threw a punch. Ruby redirected it and threw her own. Dorian dodged her, moving to sweep her legs. Ruby grabbed him as she lost her balance and brought him down with her. Then, things became less serious. Dorian tossed some snow at Ruby from his position beneath her.

"Ahh!" Ruby yelled in mock outrage, grabbing a handful of snow as well and covering Dorian's face with it.

Roaring with laughter, Dorian grabbed her around the waist, lifting her up as he shot to his feet. Ruby saw Dorian's face light up as he located an undisturbed pile of snow.

"No, no, no!" Ruby giggled as she saw what he planned to do.

Dorian only grinned in response as he brought her back down to the ground, the impact cushioned by Dorian falling with her.

They continued to fight their way through the snow, separating to chase one another around, lobbing snowballs at each other, only to come back together in playful battle where the fae had not yet danced through the snow, allowing a thicker cushion for the fall. The fae danced around their battlegrounds sporadically. Ruby could barely make out their songs over the sound of her and Dorian's laughter. Her face ached. The sweater and skirt she'd worn were not quite enough for such cold temperatures, but her witch blood kept her safer from hypothermia than a regular human, and their activity kept her blood pumping.

By the time she needed to call for a break, she lay panting in another snowdrift, laughing and sweating from the exertion, "Oh this was fun... I don't think I've ever gotten to enjoy the snow this much!"

"I don't know if I have either," Dorian whispered.

The weight of that landed heavily between them. His years numbered more than 500, if they included his years as a human. Ruby's laughter softened into silence as she considered that.

Three familiar colors stood out amongst the singing and dancing fae. The trio apparently only traveled together. The sunset orange, aqua blue, and fuchsia pink lights twirled around one another in the distance, growing closer, the circles their lights made becoming tighter, spinning faster. Their song grew louder as they danced nearer. Ruby and Dorian remained silent, continuing to lay in the snow side by side for a moment that spread into eternity. Listening, Ruby realized that she could understand them.

"Young, though they are,
> *Long may they live*
Confusion with rest,
> *Horror so sweet*
Love may yet blossom,
> *But not yet thrive*
For a lover May Yet still die
But the lovers will be,
For it is clear,
> *The moment they meet*
They are so different,
> *They are the same*
Here, they will be,
> *For here they came*
The lovers will be
> *Only once the lovers can see"*

CHAPTER THIRTY

Dorian

Nearly two months had elapsed since Dorian first met Ruby. While he'd admired the strength and resolve she'd shown at the time, Dorian couldn't help but think that her past self seemed small compared to who she was becoming now. Time flew by in his estate. Based on their estimates, they were in their last week in the palace before they needed to embark on a quick journey to restock supplies for her. In the brief time they'd shared thus far, Dorian noticed a marked shift in her.

She stood straighter. Her eyes sparkled brighter than ever. Ruby was certainly stronger. She no longer argued against him when he complimented her magic during their practices. After the first snow, the fae sporadically and haphazardly kept up with moving the snow around the forest floor. There were solid banks of snow built up beneath the gaps in the trees, allowing Dorian to tackle Ruby during practice with less fear of hurting her in the process.

Her laughter rang out, echoing through the forest in a wondrous melody. He couldn't stop the smile that broadened his face. She now delighted in her surroundings without hesitation.

"Madam, are you holding back on me?!"

"Holding back on a bloodsucker? Why would I do that? I mean... Yes. Yes I am," Ruby laughed heartily.

"Why *would* you do that?" Dorian shifted to his side to look at Ruby beside him in the snow.

Ruby closed her eyes, smiling up at the tree tops, snow gently falling on her face once more, "I could do much more powerful spells now. I can feel it... But I don't think I ought to hurt you. Or these trees. Or the buildings nearby. I figure it's best to hold back a bit for now..."

"Well, that makes sense. I appreciate the concern," Dorian chuckled as he flung himself back into the snow. Looking up at the flakes falling above them, he squinted because some hit his eyes.

"I should head inside and get something to eat," Ruby sighed regretfully.

"I'll come with you. I have nothing better to do out here, anyways."

"Oh, don't want to get lonely out here, bloodsucker?"

Dorian laughed in response, but the jokingly tossed out question caught him unexpectedly as he followed her inside. In the last two months, he had grown accustomed to her presence in his home, in his life. His previous bouts of loneliness always went away eventually. He normally felt fine with being alone. It allowed him so much time to relax, not worrying about another person to engage with or maintain any understanding of. When alone, he never worried about anyone leaving him.

Ruby shook up his existence when she waltzed into his life. He'd come to his fortress of a home to hide away from the vampiric council while he gained strength, so that he could face them in a more empowered position in the distant future. Now, he prepared to head back into the world, risking running into one of their lackeys hunting him, or worse, the council members themselves, and he was doing it for her. Granted, he'd become stronger than he'd been before. The challenges with Ruby's curse provided him ample opportunity for growth in skill as well through blood consumption. He needed less blood to restore himself after each time he aided her with the curse, even becoming able to scale his consumption back so that only four pouches restored him after handling the curse with her the last time.

Still, he knew he wasn't ready to face them alone. With Ruby's help, it might be possible, but that stood as a big question mark in his mind. She remained afflicted by the curse, and if someone in the council directly aided in crafting it, they may be able to force it to act up in order to take her out of the picture for the fight. Then they would both die.

Yet he risked exactly that scenario because the alternative would be Ruby starving or her leaving alone to find food for herself. Neither of those options sat well in his soul. He needed to accompany her. She needed him, for the time being. The idea of the day Ruby didn't need him made Dorian shudder with delighted horror. She was a force to be reckoned with, merely held back by a pesky little curse.

The more she practiced with her magic, the more self-assured she became.

The more she examined her history, the more she grew into a secure person.

The more she reevaluated the witches she grew up with, the less she disparaged herself. She still couldn't fathom anything being truly bad about the witches she'd once admired, but she stayed on the path for personal growth.

Dorian respected that, even if she kept stubbornly clinging to some idealized versions of people, she showed the ability to move past their imposed perceptions of her. With each passing day, she became more like the witches that flashed through his mind when he first spotted her running through the forest, only two months earlier.

In the last week, Ruby expanded her reading horizons. Instead of exclusively reading grimoires, Dorian noticed her devouring his romance section. Though she showed no signs of sleep deprivation, the rate at which she plowed through books worried him that she wasn't sleeping. He already thought her examination of the old grimoires impressively speedy; her ability to read romance novels so quickly set that speed to shame.

Looking through the books she'd read, Dorian found he was able to tell which ones she'd enjoyed the most. The spines were more cracked and her scent clung to the pages stronger. Quietly, Dorian started to read the ones she enjoyed the most when she finished with them. The night would start with Ruby waking and making herself breakfast. Upon completing that, they would go outside for Dorian to play target practice. After anywhere from one to four hours, Ruby would need to head back inside. Sometimes the night would be too cold for her to keep going. Other times, she simply needed to eat. In any case, they ceased going out for more training after a recovery period once the snow had settled in.

Instead, they spent the rest of the night in the library or living room, reading and talking. When Ruby departed to eat and handle being a human, Dorian would speed through reading whatever romance he'd noticed she adored, tucking away the book for later when she returned. In her presence, Dorian would pick up some horror or mystery novel, though his mind remained stuck on her and the romance she'd read. He blankly turned the pages of his own books while wondering what parts of that particular novel were her favorites.

With observation, Dorian had figured out roughly how far into the book she was when her reactions came. He couldn't be entirely sure what parts impacted her the most, however. This led to some guessing on his part. Which only fueled his frustrating dreams that grew more troublesome as time with her progressed. Further, he could still sometimes hear her moaning, screaming orgasms in her suite. He could swear, despite his intentionally muffled hearing, that he overheard her screaming out his name. The smell clinging to her as she exited her rooms would tell him she had brought herself to orgasm. Those sounds invaded his dreams as well.

This made the realization that he didn't want to be alone in the forest without her all the more unsettling. Their night progressed as the previous nights had, with Dorian still secretly reading through the romances Ruby enjoyed. She paused her reading to occasionally ask his thoughts on something she'd experienced before she met him. He would talk with her about it, sometimes detailing similar events in his own life. She would smile at him with amusement dancing in the depths of her eyes, despite the sadness that often accompanied their personal histories.

The night was pleasant and simple and terrifying. Dorian recognized something irrefutable and irreversible in himself as he'd contemplated his potential loneliness and examined his recent life critically. Ruby had, without trying to, and despite his own efforts, become important to him. His physical attraction for her aside, she'd become his friend. He enjoyed her company and preferred to have her around. He replaced her presence in his sphere with books she enjoyed when she wasn't around. He sought her company all the time. Dorian turned downright social when it came to her.

Ruby was funny and intelligent and strong. She was a powerful witch, to be sure, but he saw in her a deeper strength that allowed her to go on despite the hardships. She faced the betrayals of her past head-on, for the most part. She stubbornly couldn't let go of the absurd thought that the witches could simply be approached with facts and logic, and that they'd realize the need for reform as she had. She remained ignorant to what a rare gift she possessed in her ability to examine the facts of history to reach conclusions that contradicted her previously held beliefs.

For all his frustration with her naiveté, he admired her the way he'd only ever admired his greatest friends and lovers. Among his many distant acquaintances of the last few centuries since his self-imposed isolation, there were none he held in such high regard. There were none he felt half as close to. Perhaps spending a few months constantly in the presence of another person you could get along with created some of that.

Were it not for her human needs and the curse driving urgency, Dorian would have been happy to spend the entire winter in his home with her. But they would need to depart. As Dorian said his well-wishes for her sleep that morning, he thought of the dangers that would face Ruby in particular once they did head out. How would the witches truly react to her? Would she even be safe near them at all? What about the vampires hunting Dorian? Would they possibly leave her be? Would she be killed by a vampire because they were hunting him? What about the beasts of Death's Forest? They often grew hungrier and more desperate in the winter because fewer travelers dared to traverse the woods in the cold.

Dorian heard his own voice growling in his head, declaring that he would kill anyone and anything that raised a finger to Ruby. He would slaughter the witches who looked at her wrong. He would tear the entire vampiric council to shreds if a hair on her head was touched by one of their ilk. He would decimate the population of beasts in Death's Forest, even if it destroyed some of the ecosystem, if it meant keeping her safe.

His fears drove him for the remaining days before her curse readied to act once again. He prepared his own bag ahead of time, with far more blood than he would have ever carried on his person before Ruby. He needed to be ready to help her with the curse, and it proved easiest to do that on a full stomach. He also ensured his own pack held supplies for Ruby, in case she ran out of anything. Retrieving the old pack he'd used centuries earlier when he regularly stocked up his estate, Dorian dusted it off, recalling that despite its relatively small size, it would hold enough to fill both pantries to brimming. He set that with his personal bag, which seemed much larger but held far less, ready to go as soon as Ruby was ready.

Everything would be so much easier if she were a vampire.

The thought had occurred to him a few times, despite the selfishness of it. Dorian thought about how she wouldn't need mortal food to survive. She wouldn't need to leave the palace protections until enough time passed for Dorian to feel safe with her. She wouldn't even need to worry about the curse, in all likelihood. Her own shadows would either drive it out or subsume it. But he saw no way she would willingly become a vampire, and Dorian would never force vampirism on someone. It occurred to him as a possible permanent resolution for her curse weeks earlier, but she was a witch. Her disgust the first time she watched him drink blood remained palpable in his memory. Why would he ever believe she would want to be a vampire? He couldn't push that on her, so he never brought it up.

The curse finally decided to act a full two days after they'd initially expected it. Dorian hoped that was because of his efforts in siphoning away some of the shadows. His fears and questions plagued him as he followed the routine they laid out for the curse that evening. They would leave as soon as she'd eaten and gotten cleaned up. The nearness of their excursion left Dorian on edge in a way he couldn't have dreamed of before he met Ruby.

Leaving her in her bathroom after they successfully managed the curse once more, assured that she was alright, Dorian realized that he hoped she would return with him no matter what. A part of him wanted her to return with him, to stay with him, whether or not the curse remained a factor. He'd thought as much when he imagined getting to spend the whole winter with her.

If only she was a vampire.

That thought wouldn't leave him alone.

Dorian wanted Ruby in his home with him. A word echoed in his mind, taunting him with its meaning in more ways than one. If he truly felt that way about her, that would mean he had opened himself up for another great heartache when she inevitably left him or died. Dorian didn't do that to himself anymore.

It can't be that. I won't let it!

But it was. He knew it, despite his refusal to say it. Despite his refusal to finish the thought in his own mind, Dorian knew that his feelings for Ruby transcended casual, existing far beyond the bounds of friendship.

After finishing the blood he needed to restore his own strength, noting with happiness that he needed only three pouches of blood this time, Dorian waited for Ruby in the foyer. Glancing around at the details of his home, Dorian felt sickened by dread. Dorian thought of his willingness to become a monster if it meant keeping Ruby safe and happy, but he could never risk becoming a monster in her eyes. The difficulty there lay in a single question: could he protect her and her happiness without being monstrous? If, like he suspected, she wouldn't be safe around the witches, what could he do? He wanted to obliterate anyone who dared harm her, be that physically or emotionally, but he couldn't slaughter all the witches that did so without her ire. He could respect her need to try with them, but how would he stand by and allow anyone to mistreat her? Could he handle not ripping into them with the enchanted dagger he used to torture nobles, not to collect their blood but to make them suffer for hurting her?

Ruby descended the stairs, the nerves she'd arrived with on full display once more. He noticed that she wore nearly the same outfit she'd worn on their journey to his estate. The emerald green top, black pants, and dagger at her thigh were all the same, leaving the only difference the heavier cloak she wore with it, from the clothes he had given her. The impact of seeing her like that hit him in the chest, knocking that one thought into his mind in a way he couldn't deflect or deny. Dorian could do nothing but bask in the glory of her presence and the fear of their future as he scrambled to banish the thought rattling around in his head.

I love her.

"Don't worry. The trip to Edgefair will be a lot faster this time."

"I know..."

"I'll be on the lookout as I run. It'll be okay."

I'll make it okay, no matter what.

"I appreciate that, Dorian... I guess I'm just... processing. We should go."

Dorian flung open the front door to the keep, following her onto the front steps, barely remembering to close the door behind him before he lifted her into his arms and sprinted off. He released his senses to full-strength, noting her emotional field for the first time since they'd arrived at his home. Unfamiliar colors danced within her. Fearing the dangers of distraction, Dorian ignored it.

Nothing else matters except getting Ruby to Edgefair and back safely.

CHAPTER THIRTY-ONE

Ruby

Ruby struggled to ignore her aching back. The position he held her in was mostly well-supported, but after an hour or two, it started to hurt. The scenery of the forest flew by in a blue of dark masses. She was getting thirsty and hungry again, despite it only being a couple of hours since she'd eaten last. While Ruby could reason it was normal to be more hungry after the curse attacked, she couldn't shake her annoyance with it all.

Annoyed with her aching back, her thirst, hunger, and the damned inability to see very well in the dark, Ruby lamented the limitations of the human body. Even being a witch, she functionally remained a human, and that came with so many frustrations. Dorian didn't have half as many restrictions on his life. Sure, he couldn't really handle going in the sun and he needed blood to survive. But he held eternity in his hands. He didn't necessarily have to sleep. He could spend all day inside his home and enjoy all of the things he liked. He didn't have to worry about mundane things like eating multiple meals a day or drinking enough water.

He certainly didn't need to worry about his back aching like hers did. Dorian didn't need to be carried around because he was too slow to make their trip to Edgefair efficiently. Ruby struggled not to grumble about the many issues she found with being human, staying silent in his arms. Above all else, from her view, Dorian was the free one between them. In his presence, she almost tasted freedom, but in her bones, Ruby knew that she had never truly drank from freedom's cup. She may never experience it in full the way Dorian could at any time.

Sure, he couldn't actually leave Vlideron without the council being alerted. But he could go anywhere in Vlideron he wanted. If he ran fast enough, he could probably get far away from Vlideron before any of the hunting vampires caught up to where he crossed the border. He seemed determined not to, for whatever reason, but the point stood that he could. He lived his life exactly how he wanted, making no apologies for it.

Edgefair loomed large in her mind, despite the relatively short buildings that made up the majority of the town. She and Dorian briefly contemplated cutting straight through the countryside away from Edgefair to get to another larger town, but ultimately decided against it. The villages that dotted the border of Death's Forest always kept at least two night-time guards. In the poorest villages, they were volunteers from the town itself. Regardless, they risked being spotted far more easily if they were skulking around outside of small villages, where no one ventured into the forest and everyone talked. They couldn't risk that much attention on themselves.

Edgefair marked the only large town near the border of Death's Forest, making it the only place in Vlideron where one could exit Death's Forest without drawing too much attention. The pair of them exiting the forest would only raise lascivious eyebrows that would turn away for propriety's sake. The edges of the forest were well-enough patrolled that sometimes couples hid away in the trees for quick fun. It provided the perfect cover for the pair of them.

Dorian skidded to a complete stop, his eyes narrowed on the distance, jaw muscles flexing.

Ruby looked in that direction, alarm rising in her as she did. Lights were flashing red, something racing towards them. On the journey to Dorian's estate, the mushrooms responded to her magic and that of the beast by glowing blue. Understanding sent her heart pounding in her chest as the mushrooms flashing red grew closer and closer. They only flashed counter to their natural coloring for one reason: a vampire. Vampires warranted warning.

Dorian carefully set her down, ensuring her feet were firmly beneath her before he stepped in front of her, rolling his shoulders and cracking his neck in preparation.

Ruby wracked her brain for the right spell to use. Something that would end the fight as soon as possible so that they could keep moving without too much exhaustion or drawing any attention.

The nearest mushrooms glowed blue from her presence, casting shadows all around them, which Dorian took advantage of before the other vampire reached them, his shadows melding into the long shadows cast by the glowing light.

"My, my, my, what have we here? Dorian Seagrave. I've been looking for you. And who is this? Oh I think I see. You're that witch we had to help deal with. I see your curse hasn't claimed you just yet. Is that what you're doing, Lord Seagrave?"

She froze. 'Help deal with' implied that the vampiric council were not the instigators, but the assistants. But for who? Why? What had she ever done? Why was she always so singled out for suffering?

"Just Dorian is fine, you know," Dorian's voice almost sounded calm, but Ruby could hear the edge to it, born of his resentment for the title and last name.

"Oh but it's so much more proper to call you Lord Seagrave," the other vampire viciously smiled.

A haunting similarity to Dorian when he'd confronted Vanella and the others just a few months earlier struck Ruby. The moment of familiarity passed as soon as it came, however, as she thought about the inherent differences between Dorian and the vampire before her. Dorian donned that face as a mask to hide behind. Without it, he revealed himself to be the nervous, respectful, playful man she'd gotten to know over the last two months. The one who slaughtered monstrous nobility because he held empathy for those they subjugated. He held the same power as those nobles, if not a great deal more. But he used his entirely differently, in service of the regular folk who couldn't stand up for themselves.

He did so for his own selfish reasons, of course. He did it to continue avenging himself and his late mother. But he wasn't cruel for cruelty's sake. He didn't do it just for fun. He'd been quick to kill the other witches, but it became obvious that he could have just slipped away if he'd really wanted to. The more she'd thought about it, the clearer it became that he'd really killed them for her benefit. He saw her being hunted down unfairly, and rather than making a discreet run for it, escaping the notice of the witches before they could think to attack him, he'd saved her from them. Even standing between her and the stranger, Dorian positioned himself to protect rather than seeking a fight.

The vampire stranger, on the other hand, exemplified the opposite mentality. His suit, despite being so far into Death's Forest, was made of fine silk and velvet. He looked absurd, hunting another vampire in such attire. His blond hair smoothly swooped over the top of his head, perfectly controlled with not a strand out of place. Perfectly clean-shaven, the man was immaculately groomed. An unnatural sight so deep in the forest. His fingers were adorned with several gaudy gold rings, adding to the obscene display of wealth created by the suit he apparently valued so little, he willingly hunted another vampire through the forest in it.

The whole ensemble added to the excitement radiating off him at the prospect of the coming fight. He bounced in place, looking forward to the bloodshed and death that may happen. His vermilion eyes flared with anticipation, darting between Ruby and Dorian. The vicious smile that momentarily reminded her of Dorian's morphed before her eyes, despite not changing at all, chilling her to her core. This man, Ruby realized, relished in causing pain and suffering, and hoped to do so with her and Dorian. Hence his insistence on calling Dorian by that godsawful title and name. Further, it explained why he tossed that hint in her face.

"Do you want to know the people you work for? What they really want from you?" Dorian taunted.

"Why should I care?" the hunter vampire sneered.

"They're using you and every other vampire in Vlideron to secure themselves as the real power at the top. Don't you understand? You're just an enforcer for people who are tightly controlling your growth."

Instead of responding to Dorian, he turned his attention to her, "Ruby, isn't it? I do wonder what you must have done to get the vampiric council working with your own elders to off you. Alas, I was not privy to the details. They'll be fascinated to hear you were spending your time with Dorian here. That might ease their minds on how you've managed to survive this long," The vampire's twisted laugh mirrored the dagger he'd planted in her heart with his claims.

It can't be... But isn't that what Dorian's been suspecting?

In an instant, the vampire wormed his way into her head, shutting her down just long enough to make a move. He lunged at Dorian, slower than Dorian himself, but no less strong. As Dorian implied, different vampires grew in different ways sometimes. He never excelled at hypnotism. His strengths lay elsewhere. The fact that Dorian lived longer and worked harder than the hunter to gain power on his own terms became evident in seconds.

Despite their speed, the fight played out in slow motion ahead of her, the vampires lunging at one another, blocking and deflecting blows. As they moved through the forest, the hits that missed one another to land on a tree sent the tough bark flying in splintered showers. Their impressive power lacked the strength to slow her mind's racing. Could it be true? Could her own elders have conspired with the vampiric council to place the curse on her? Would Elder Moss have done something so horrible? Ruby needed to believe that couldn't be true, but the stranger saying it without provocation left her uncertain. Frightened. The curse in her belly began to wind around her organs unexpectedly, but Ruby couldn't stop watching the fight blankly, scrambling to find any way to believe it wasn't true. Any way to believe it wasn't Elder Moss who condemned her.

Watching Dorian take a punch to the face, Ruby finally reeled her mind back in. Deciding in a snap which hex to employ, Ruby reached out, tendrils of her magic latching on to the vampire and sinking into him with pulsing red and black lines forming beneath his skin. Despite never practicing the spell, Ruby had studied it thoroughly, finding the usefulness limited but important. The magic woven into the tendrils spreading through the body of the stranger was designed to deplete a vampire's blood supply, driving them to swift exhaustion and total body shut down in a matter of minutes. Ruby learned the spell early on in her time with Dorian, deciding to be safe just in case something shifted with him later on.

The sigh of relief she nearly exhaled as she saw her hex take hold never came; the vampire shifted to look at her, hunger overtaking his expression. Only then did Ruby remember what else would happen with that hex. The vampire would go into a blood frenzy before they gave in to the exhaustion. Ruby practically glowed as the only human nearby. The hex was best used in more controlled circumstances, or at a greater distance.

She felt her blood drain from her face, realizing her mistake too late.

The sudden shift in attention made Dorian hesitate as well, "Ruby, what was that spell?"

"The hex drains his blood, to weaken him... He's going into blood frenzy..." she whispered, already stepping backwards, away from the dueling vampires.

Dorian cursed as he wrestled to gain full bodily control over the other vampire. The fight shifted from the hunter trying to kill Dorian, to Dorian simply trying to keep a hold of the hunter. Each passing moment caused the vampire to weaken slightly, the hex designed to work in minutes, but each second lasted an eternity. Soon, Dorian was holding the vampire by the throat against a tree, his arms fully extended to ensure a firm grip. Sweat dripped down Dorian's brow in the glowing red light of the mushrooms nearest the pair of vampires.

The breath of motion behind her was the only warning Ruby got. Claws raked down her back as something stabbed clean through her, ripping through lower ribs and her stomach before coming out the other side. The scent of her blood filled the forest as an airless scream tore from her throat.

"RUBY!!" Dorian cried helplessly. The blood-frenzied vampire in his arms struggled even harder, her blood in the air ramping up his fight to get to her. Dorian needed to hold him back until the hex weakened him enough, or the vampire would kill her in an attempt to recoup blood.

As whatever stabbed her exited her body, Ruby rushed forward and turned around to face her attacker. Searing pain clouded her vision, but Ruby thought she saw what looked like some sort of cross between a large cat and a strange arachnid with a tail. The smooth black fur covering its lithe, muscular body seemed out of place with the segmented tail covered in her blood, but the multiple sets of cat-like eyes on its head, with eight legs ending in classic cat paws, cut a horrifying figure.

A barbed, cat-like tongue licked her blood from its paw as it sauntered over to her. Ruby's eyes focused on the bulbous tail swinging in the air behind it, noting the vicious needle at the end. It paused, standing directly over her, waiting.

It's waiting for me to die.

The thought sent the curse into overdrive once more, but it wasn't strong enough to act out much. The shadows shot out of her in a single spike, impaling the beast and sending it flying into a nearby tree. The sickening crunch of its spine breaking filled her ears as the curse retreated back into her body, spent from its lucky release.

Ruby keenly felt her life force draining away, flowing from her body too fast. She could feel the shadows trying to heal her, but they wouldn't be able to keep her alive. A witch's body was just too human for that. The beauty of the curse for those who cast it lay in the fact that it would cause her unspeakable suffering before she got to die. It would let her feel the shadows trying to heal her, only to die anyway.

If the elders were involved... if Elder Moss was involved in cursing me... I need to personally thank her in kind.

Ruby's vicious thoughts lit enough anger in her to fight her fate. She couldn't let those who'd cursed her win. She couldn't let them take her future from her. She couldn't let them steal from her the life she had only begun to glimpse.

The other vampire had apparently weakened enough, and Dorian rushed to Ruby's side at last. His frantic eyes roved over her body, hardening with realization at what she already concluded. Without intervention, she would die.

"Please, Ruby, please let me help you! You—" Dorian's voice cracked, "You don't have to—" he shook his head, choking on his words, "Please."

Dorian... Thank you!

He uttered the magic words to go on and live the life she wanted. The lifeline she needed to allow her to exact her revenge on those who put her in that position.

Her vision started to go black; knowing she was running out of time, Ruby whispered only, "Don't let me die, Dorian."

CHAPTER THIRTY-TWO

Dorian

Dorian watched as Ruby lost consciousness before he could ask any clarifying questions, a cold spike driving down his spine. Was she saying yes to becoming a vampire? Was she deliriously begging him to figure something else out to save her? What did she mean? Did she even know? Maybe the blood loss was too much. He didn't know. He couldn't know. She would die in minutes—despite the fervent efforts of the curse that ravaged her body and her own witch blood—if he didn't do something.

He had never changed anyone before. The process was easy enough. A simple exchange of blood with intent on the vampire's part. Dorian needed only take a sip of her blood, then allow her to drink her fill as he intended for her to be changed. The blood magic would begin to work on her body instantly. Becoming a vampire was one of only two ways to cheat death in the Known World, and as far as Dorian knew, there were no werewolves in all of Vlideron to provide her another option. It would be a couple of hours before the whole process completed itself, but she would live if he moved swiftly.

Taking a deep breath, Dorian leaned down to Ruby, locating a spot on her throat. The magic for vampirism required a bite, which, for reasons beyond Dorian's knowledge, needed to be near the head, the heart, or the sexual organs. The throat was a common choice. Lovers sometimes chose the chest or the inner thigh for another sort of intimacy, but any location represented a deeply intimate act. The throat seemed the least intrusive of his options. Quickly biting down, Dorian heard a faint moan escape as Ruby unconsciously exhaled. He took one small pull of her blood, lapping the wounds with his tongue to encourage them to seal up before his mind could process the taste.

He wasn't fast enough.

The first taste of the divine nectar that was her blood set his every nerve ablaze with rapturous ecstasy. In all his centuries, Dorian never tasted anything so heavenly. She was a revelation to his senses, ruining him for his favorite wine. How could he partake of his once-favorite wine when he now knew it to be a pale comparison to the real delicacy? In tasting Ruby, he glimpsed true divinity for the first time in his life.

Hurrying through the process, even as he ruminated on how badly he wished he could taste her again, Dorian grabbed her silver dagger from her thigh, slicing open his wrist with the burning silver to ensure the wound stayed open long enough. Dorian gently opened her mouth, allowing his blood to pour down her throat before lowering his wrist to her mouth. Without warning, her hands snapped up and gripped his arm, holding him tightly against her mouth as she drank deeply. He focused on his intent. She needed to become a vampire to live.

He wondered how long it would take for him to know if he accomplished his role in turning her. His answer came almost immediately, as he watched with amazement while the shadows that previously writhed within the confines of her body stilled, taking in the burgeoning transformation. To his amazement, Dorian saw as her obliterated organs and bones began to reform, suspended appropriately in her body, before the muscles returned, and skin finally covered where moments earlier lay a gaping wound. Only the tattered remains of her top and cloak, along with the blood soaking into everything around them, provided evidence of her near-death.

Eventually, as Dorian became lightheaded, Ruby dropped her arms from his wrist, letting him go. He replaced her dagger back in her sheath, despite knowing soon she wouldn't be able to use it without a glove. Watching her for a moment longer, Dorian felt conflicted. She would live, but would she be happy with him, or furious? He would have to take full responsibility for his failure to understand if he'd guessed wrong. Dorian would dedicate the rest of his life to making her vampiric life acceptable if she wasn't happy about it. By choosing to change her, he accepted a commitment to her. If she expressed happiness about it, he could let that feeling go and they could move on as equals. But if he had failed in understanding her and chosen this life for her, he would have to atone for it somehow.

The hunter who interrupted their journey crawled on the ground towards Ruby, his movements pathetically small. The spell she'd cast left Dorian helpless to aid her, too busy preventing the hunter from killing her, but had likely ended the fight faster. The other vampire was clearly younger than him, but showed a talent for physical strength. Dorian could only fight him off so well because of his overall greater power. It still would have taken him some time to defeat the man if he hadn't been cursed. Then, would Dorian have been able to save her at all? Would she have been dead by the time the fight concluded?

The fear of losing her stirred rage within him. Standing tall, Dorian walked over to where the other vampire began losing steam in his attempts to reach Ruby's blood. Dorian stared down at him in disgust. His fancy suit was covered with dirt and soiled beyond repair, likely wearing such fine clothes in such an inappropriate environment to accomplish something for his own ego. Dorian would never know what that was. He didn't care. The vampire who nearly cost Dorian his Ruby existed far beneath him, a pathetic and worthless mite, but Dorian needed to get out his fear and rage somehow. A memory of the cruel, weak nobleman who started Dorian on his path to fleeing the vampiric council and meeting Ruby flashed through his head at the blond vampire waiting for his boot.

Dorian lifted his leg and stomped on the head of the other vampire. Over and over and over again, Dorian pounded his foot onto the body of the other vampire, crushing his skull and moving on to his ribs and spine before he finally exacted enough of his fury. The gory mess that greeted him as a result of his excessive brutality made Dorian wrinkle his nose in disgust. Discarding his own clothes and changing into fresh ones from his bag, Dorian piled the soiled materials on the body of the other vampire. If given blood, he still might come back. Dorian refused to allow that to happen. He set the discarded clothes and vampire on fire, watching to ensure it caught before gingerly lifting Ruby into his arms once more.

Dorian took stock of where they were once more. A small sliver of amusement crossed his mind as he recognized the area more clearly, taking off for his cave. The first place they'd enjoyed a real conversation would be where she woke from her transformation. Sprinting through the forest, Dorian arrived at the cave and set her down in the center of the main room before beginning to pace. The hours dragged on as Dorian waited, watching over Ruby's body, observing both physically and magically as the transformation overtook her, a lead weight gathering in his stomach.

Not knowing how her curse would react to the transformation, Dorian felt compelled to keep careful watch, determined that even if it killed him, he would keep her from suffering if he had made the wrong move. When the shadows crept through the cavern to reach Ruby's body, an inherent part of the process, Dorian stood ready to wrest the cursed shadows away from her body if that was what it took to keep her safe. He worried the shadows would reject one another somehow, or start going haywire. Quickly, his fears were assuaged.

The shadows from Ruby's curse slid from her body cleanly, causing no wounds as they did so, greeting the shadows coming to bind to her in a slithering dance. Tendrils of shadow raised from the ground, swirling around the tendrils of shadow reaching up from Ruby's body, pausing for just a moment before they began to wind around one another, like snakes embracing. Soon, Dorian saw the shadows from the curse melt into the shadows that would be Ruby's, becoming one before sliding back into her body. The shadows Dorian shaved off during her stay in his estate ceased moving, fully melding into his own shadows completely, at last.

A hint of power flooded him as that happened, giving Dorian his first real clue where the council got the shadows. Looking sharply at Ruby, a grin spread across his face. If his conjecture proved correct, she would be far stronger than a newly turned vampire had any right to be. Assured that the curse would never harm her again, Dorian felt a droplet of relief trickle over his nerves. He just needed to wait for her to wake to see if he had decimated her life or had done as she wished.

Sitting against the wall of the cave to give her space when she woke, Dorian hoped he hadn't been hasty in his selfish desire to save her life. To keep her in the living world. She would be facing a whole new life, in a way. Many vampires only quantified their age to others based on how many years passed since becoming a vampire, the existence a complete departure from everything they knew before. Would she be comfortable with this transition? Even if she did mean for him to turn her, would she regret that impulse upon waking?

The worst part of the transformation occurred just before the new vampire woke. Dorian couldn't remember what Sigrid said of the process. Since he never personally turned anyone, the details had become useless information. He searched his mind for the explanation she gave on the process, but came up blank as he watched Ruby's form writhing in silent agony, her body twisting and turning from within. His heart raced with terror and concern as her transformation finished.

A hint of movement on Ruby's face alerted him to her approaching consciousness. He stood, unsure whether he should hurry to her side and begin explaining, or prostrate himself in apology before she even fully processed the change in her reality. He didn't have the time to decide as Ruby shot upright, looking around. Her eyes locked on his, stealing the thoughts from his mind.

Those black eyes developed the most unique sheen of blood red he ever beheld on a vampire. The layered appearance of her new eye color gave the impression of blood smeared on onyx, shining in the sunlight. Strangely, it made her look complete, as though her face missed that one little piece of her appearance her whole life, destined to have those eyes the whole time. Dorian couldn't speak, staring into her eyes for several long seconds.

Faster than he'd expected her to, Ruby stood up and rushed across the cave to him, slamming him against the wall in a move similar to their first conversation, where she'd held a dagger to his throat. Her hand wrapped around his throat as she leaned back to look him in the eye, her face serious. Dorian felt the lead in his stomach settle further down, shoving his thoughts of her beauty into the distance as he considered the years ahead he'd spend trying to convince her it could be worth going on despite being in a vampire's body.

"You saved my life again," Ruby's voice came out strangled, "thank you."

Her hand slid away from the front of his throat, snaking around to the back of his neck, her other hand sliding around his body to wrap him in a tight hug, pulling his head and body closer to her.

Dorian stood stock still for a second, processing that she was actually hugging him in gratitude, before his own hands slid around her shoulders to hug her in return. This embrace, a first, left Dorian inhaling her scent from her hair. Morphing a little, her scent now carried the edge of vampirism. He loved it. Dorian held her harder, arms wrapped tightly around her shoulders as she squeezed him around the waist, burying her face in his neck for several long moments.

Leaning away again to look at him, Ruby searched his eyes, "Are you okay?"

"I should be asking you that! I mean, I wasn't sure you meant for me to turn you into a vampire, but I couldn't think of what else to do. There were no werewolves on hand to offer an alternative, but you were dying and you said you didn't want to die. I just acted and I've been freaked out that you would hate me for it this whole time. To have you hug me after that, it's relieving in ways you can't know. I couldn't lose you and I was so scared and I thought maybe I just twisted your words into permission to turn you because I'm so irredeemably selfish. But you're alive and you don't seem angry with me yet—"

"Dorian," Ruby smiled, new fangs peeking out from her lips.

"Ruby."

"I did want you to turn me when I said that. I knew what I was asking for."

Relief fully washed over Dorian as he listened, his arms still holding her shoulders, hers still wrapped around his waist and clutching his back. Dorian took the chance to bring her in tighter again, continuing the hug to steady his own nerves. He felt grateful for the cave wall at his back, keeping him upright as his knees began to sag with shed anxiety.

Ruby pushed herself away, Dorian letting her with a sheepish grin. He'd been holding on too long, and he figured it would probably get weird soon. His feelings were making him act out, but they were overwhelming. The thought that she wasn't angry with him for being a vampire brought with it the realization that she wouldn't leave him by dying of old age or sickness. That barrier to connection crumbled against the edges of his soul. The worry remained that she would simply leave in general, but Dorian realized that if she truly reciprocated, maybe, just maybe, he would become the luckiest bastard in the Known World.

Her eyes dropped to his lips as he released her, her own hands still gripping him for a moment. To his shock, she began to slide her hands from his back to the sides of his waist, and up his chest. As Ruby wrapped her hands around his throat, gripping his jaw and sliding into the hair at the back of his head, Dorian felt his own hands fly to her hips, pulling her in tighter in an instant. Her lips hovered just over his own, her breath caressing him. They hung there, suspended at the threshold of no return. His fingers tightened with each passing second, waiting for her to make the final move. It needed to be her choice. Dorian couldn't live with himself if he pushed that onto her. So he waited, feeling his own heart pounding in his ears even as he felt hers pounding against him.

His pants grew tighter with each passing second as well, feeling Ruby's hips against his own, their closeness broken only by the clothes between them. Her breaths grew faster. Dorian felt his head growing lighter, finding himself unable to breathe as he imagined he could feel static electricity between their lips. His eyes searched hers, wondering if she would make that move or if she was having second thoughts. In an unconscious reflex, Dorian's tongue darted out to wet his lips.

The slightest brush against her lips broke the dam.

Ruby's eyes closed and she leaned the rest of the way in. The second her soft, full lips met his, Dorian's own eyes closed in consuming ecstasy. Her lips tasted of the vanilla and caramel he always smelled on her. Her blood put wine to shame, but her skin put the baked goods he'd once loved to the grave. All Dorian's vivid imagination ever conjured about kissing her and tasting her skin vanished from his mind, permanently banished. Nothing could stack up to the real thing in any capacity. Ruby unwittingly ruined Dorian for kissing anyone else, ever again.

His hands gripping her hip slid down her ass and gripped her thighs on their own, lifting her in the air as she moaned into his mouth. Dorian turned them around, pinning her against the cave wall while she wrapped her legs tightly around his hips. He released one hand from around her thigh, dragging it up her body, noting the smooth, silky skin bared by the tattered top, to wrap around her throat. His thumb caressed her jaw line as she'd gripped his. His mind blanked as her hands left his neck to roam his body, lifting his shirt up to caress the bare skin beneath it, sending shivers through him as she brushed against his old scars.

He was starving, claiming her kiss, feeling his hips grind against her in unconscious rhythm, each gasp and moan of delight from her as they embraced fueling him to go on. Her hands lifted to grip his shoulders, nails digging into his skin in delicious pinpricks of pain he hadn't felt in centuries. Only another vampire could dig their nails in so intensely. Securing her against the wall, Dorian dropped his remaining hand from her thigh, gliding it along the bared skin of her torso, sliding up tortuously slow.

Even in his hazy delight at their entwined state, Dorian remembered himself, breaking their kiss to ask, "Is it okay if I keep going?"

"Don't you dare stop."

Feral delight took over.

CHAPTER THIRTY-THREE

Ruby

This is what I was meant for.

Ruby gasped as Dorian's hand finished its aching ascent beneath her top, the heat hovering just over her breast sending a shiver of pure delight down her spine. She arched her back, forcing his hand to finally touch her. The thin band of fabric covering and supporting her breast beneath the top offered the only separation from his skin actually meeting hers.

Dorian snarled in response, his hand snatching the fabric and pulling it down, landing directly on her breast before she processed the vicious removal.

His rough hand ran along her skin, gliding across her chest, running down her ribs, then back up to tease her oversensitive nipples, sending quaking pleasure between her legs. Dorian's length ground against her, driving her wild with the need to remove all barriers between them. Ruby broke their kiss, crying out as he teased her ever closer to the precipice of release.

If he gets me so ready for him from only this, will being a vampire now even save me from death by orgasm at his hand?

Dorian shifted, running kisses down her neck. As his fangs scraped along the skin, Ruby's eyes rolled into the back of her head. Raking her nails against the scarred skin of his back, she relished the feeling of him. The cold cave wall at her back would have marred her skin prior to the transformation, but as a vampire, she savored the opportunity to be pinned there. Suspended in the air, her legs wrapped tightly around Dorian's hips, pinning him against her in turn.

A whisper of memory caressed Ruby's mind, of Dorian's teeth sinking into her neck, only to leave too soon. Her own moan, equal parts pleasure and pain, rang in her ears before the darkness consumed her once more. She dreamt of somehow drinking down the very essence of the rain, soothing her soul so that all of her senses narrowed in on the joyful experience. She wanted both his bite and to return to that dream, all at once.

"Dorian..."

Her stomach growling interrupted her from begging Dorian to bite her again. Stopped her from biting him in return.

"Fuck..."

"Gods damn it," Dorian groaned simultaneously.

Ruby looked around, sipping on another pack of blood, noting how different everything was from the first time they'd been in the cave. She could see every detail without the magic lanterns lit, for one. For two, she recently spent several, long minutes embroiled in passionate kissing with a vampire. Most importantly, she was now a vampire as well. The turn her life had taken in just a little over two months proved wildly unexpected, but not unwelcome. One last thought tugged at her mind, but she felt too high on the feelings of connection and consumption to care.

Finishing the third pack, she waited for a moment to decide if she needed anymore to sate her thirst. Her mind began to clear from the intense desire that overcame her as she realized how much Dorian wanted to save her and thought about what it meant for her to be saved by becoming a vampire. The degree of care and concern he showed her set off bursts of throbbing joy deep within her. She'd found him physically attractive the first time she really saw him, but something changed for her in the previous months. For as much as she found him physically appealing, she found him safe to be around. He kept showing that he would show up for her and care about her.

Wasn't that what she always craved for someone else to do for her?

Kissing him so passionately left her itching for more. She could tell by the way each touch, each thrust, each caress of his tongue left her panting that she would thoroughly enjoy herself when they finally resumed what they started. The desire she glimpsed within him curled her toes without even a whisper of touch. He sat across from her, only staring at her. They avoided touching as soon as they broke apart to allow her to feed, as if knowing that the slightest caress would send them careening toward the pursuit of ecstasy.

Ruby's thoughts finally cleared, catching up to the thoughts she felt tugging at the back of her mind. The curse. Her near death. That vampire hunting Dorian. What that vampire claimed. It all came rushing back to her as she glanced down at her bared belly. She still wore her destroyed top.

Her mind focused on the curse first. Ruby could feel the shadows within her, but they were entirely different from before. Rather than a mass swirling among her organs, separate from her, she could feel the connection to them as if intrinsic to her being. They were not some thing sitting inside her, but one with her. No pain accompanied her as she moved them around intentionally, pulling them from her body instinctively and letting them return to her just as naturally. Ruby's eyes narrowed as she looked up at Dorian.

"I saw as the curse was negated while you were transforming, yes. The bit of shadows that I siphoned from the curse melted into my own as the ones that remained in your body melted into the shadows that came to join you. Ruby, I think the council took a vampire and ripped their shadows from them somehow, and used those to curse you. You now effectively have twice the vampiric shadows a newly turned vampire would normally have."

"So I am cured because I became a vampire? At the loss of another vampire?"

"Yes."

Ruby's mind flashed to the vampire claiming the council worked with her elders to curse her. Denial battled with logic as she considered the facts. If one perfect method existed to get rid of a witch in Vlideron, the end result of her curse would be it.

Either she died from the curse, which was likely. Or she somehow convinced a vampire to turn her, with no guarantees of the outcome, which would be exceedingly unlikely. But even in the event that she did manage to become a vampire, that would only serve to make her an enemy of the witches of Vlideron. Her being a witch, even as a vampire, would make her suspicious to the vampires of Vlideron. No matter what happened with her, she would be out of the way. If the elders did this, they selected the perfect method to rid themselves of her.

It was either that or someone brilliantly framed the elders to get rid of her. It made less logical sense, Ruby knew, but she wanted to believe that option. The only reason anyone would have for getting rid of her would be the knowledge she gained from finding that hidden library in the compound. If anyone wanted to get rid of her for that, it would be someone involved in the cover-up of the real history of Vlideron and witches. Maybe someone connected to the king would know of that sort of thing, Ruby tried to reason. Her mind flashed to Elder Moss lording over the assembly of the coven the night the curse infected her. She enjoyed herself as she wielded her power over the room, as she always did, but could she be so sadistic as to curse Ruby and then play judge over her life?

Fury rose in Ruby's veins, beyond anything her formerly human body could have handled. Black and red power crackled at her finger tips as she stood, eyes glazing over. Regardless of who had done it, someone had devised a curse nearly guaranteed to kill her or ruin her chances of ever helping the other witches see the truth. She would be targeted for slaughter by the vampiric council and witches alike. If that vampire told the truth, she had been betrayed in ways she could not have fathomed only a few months earlier. Shadows seeped from her body, curling around her in a protective shell as Ruby ruminated on recent events.

Coming out on the other side simply wasn't enough.

Maybe those behind my curse didn't think this through as carefully as they should have... Did they not realize I would still be a witch as a vampire? Or did they just underestimate me that much?

"Whoever did this to me... Whoever ruined my chances of helping the other witches by backing me into a corner... they may have helped to free me from my prior life... but that wasn't why they did it, and they are going to fucking regret daring to cross me. I am going to make them pay in blood."

Dorian smiled up at her, nodding, "I will do everything in my power to make that happen for you and stand at your side while you get your vengeance. For the rest of my life, I will do whatever you need. I have another estate outside of Edgefair. It's rundown and basically abandoned, but as a result, I doubt the vampiric council remembers I have it. We can go there to get started on your revenge."

"Do you have any friends who can help us find information?"

"I think so. Sigrid, the vampire who turned me, is more of an acquaintance these days, but she left a standing invitation to me. If I agree to help her with assisting the human resistance, she'll give you anything you want."

"Human resistance?"

"Most commoners hate the king. Some have been working for decades to get the right people in place to take him down once and for all. Sigrid got involved with that immediately. I just wanted to go on killing the nobility, so we parted ways. She said I could always come help, though. I will do anything if it means you can get the vengeance you rightly deserve to claim."

With Dorian's unwavering support, Ruby finally let out all of the emotions she forcibly bottled up her whole life, the emotions she'd kept under smooth control while with Dorian at his estate. She ranted about the pains and difficulties. She raved about the foolishness of those she used to admire. Ruby sobbed as she detailed the heartaches and loneliness she experienced. She raged at herself for her participation in the harm of so many others and how much of a fool she had been to defend them so ardently when they may have been the ones to not only harm her, but knowingly perpetuate harm against others.

Her magic flowed out from her finger tips in a haze along the ground, crackling like red lightning in a black cloud before dissipating. Her power sent sparks along the rocky floor of the cave, thankfully avoiding a fire by virtue of their cold. The magic spreading along the ground, crackling as it was, seeped the heat from the air all around, until Ruby could see her breath despite the temperature controls the cave evidently possessed.

On and on she continued, not knowing how long had passed before she was finally spent, her magic calming. Collapsing back into a seated position, Ruby took another blood pack from Dorian, drinking it down swiftly. Throughout her rant, Dorian listened attentively, staring at her with gentle eyes that transformed into pride as she finished her blood. She looked at him curiously.

Tilting her head, Ruby asked, "What? Why are you looking at me like that?"

"Getting to see you fully yourself is the most glorious thing I have ever seen."

Ruby breathed through her desire, barely holding herself back from launching across the room to straddle him. Feeling the day disappearing and the approach of sunset, Ruby squared her shoulders. She needed to clean up. She needed to change. Then she needed to get to work. She didn't have the time to mount him just yet. Vengeance needed to be her first priority.

First, she needed to get back to Edgefair. She needed to meet this Sigrid woman. She needed to be able to get more appropriate clothes for the fights to come. She needed to gather information. If that vampire had been lying to her, and she ended up wrongly killing innocent people, she'd never forgive herself. She needed proof before she could exact her revenge on the fools who sought her death. Who sought her suffering. Those who sought to subjugate her and everyone else in Vlideron. They would all suffer the consequences. She could taste Dorian's lips again when she had at least gotten started on sating her fury.

"Don't you go trying to seduce me just yet, bloodsucker. You promised to help me with my vengeance. I intend to take you up on that offer."

"Anything you want, my beloved Madam."

I want my vengeance.

Thank you so much for reading Cursed Desire!

If you are interested, please join my newsletter, reachable from my website www.trortego.com
I would love to have you there. If you sign up, you will receive a free novella following the love story between a witch and a vampire Ruby found in one of the forbidden grimoires, as well as first access to all news coming from me!

Look out for Nightfallen Duet Book Two!

About the Author

T.R. Ortego enjoys living in the Pacific Northwest with her husband and two cats. She got into writing as a child, starting with fantasy and horror. She incorporated romance into her writing as she grew older, still retaining her love of the genres that got her into writing. She enjoys incorporating her experiences as a bi woman with chronic illness into her writing.